The Woolworths Saturday Girls

Also by Elaine Everest

The Woolworths Girls series
The Woolworths Girls
Carols at Woolworths (ebook novella)
Christmas at Woolworths
Wartime at Woolworths
A Gift from Woolworths
Wedding Bells for Woolworths
A Mother Forever

The Teashop Girls series
The Teashop Girls
Christmas with the Teashop Girls

Standalone novels
Gracie's War
The Butlins Girls
The Patchwork Girls

Elaine Everest

The Woolworths Saturday Girls

MACMILLAN

First published 2022 by Macmillan
an imprint of Pan Macmillan
The Smithson, 6 Briset Street, London EC1M 5NR
EU representative: Macmillan Publishers Ireland Ltd, 1st Floor,
The Liffey Trust Centre, 117–126 Sheriff Street Upper,
Dublin 1, D01 YC43
Associated companies throughout the world
www.panmacmillan.com

ISBN 978-1-5290-7802-2

1 3 5 7 9 8 6 4 2

A CIP catalogue record for this book is available from the British Library.

Typeset by Palimpsest Book Production Ltd, Falkirk, Stirlingshire
Printed and bound by CPI Group (UK) Ltd, Croydon, CR0 4YY

MIX
Paper from
responsible sources
FSC® C116313

Visit **www.panmacmillan.com** to read more about all our books
and to buy them. You will also find features, author interviews and
news of any author events, and you can sign up for e-newsletters
so that you're always first to hear about our new releases.

To all the Woolworths Saturday girls and boys who remember Woolies with fondness.

1

'That woman could talk the hind legs off a donkey,' Alan Gilbert said as he helped his wife, Sarah, into her coat. 'I'm not sure I can be doing with women getting involved in politics. And I don't need to sit and listen to a load of boring speeches just to decide who I will vote for.'

Sarah gave his arm a squeeze. 'Good grief, Alan, you are becoming such an old fuddy-duddy. Dad says everyone thinks highly of Margaret Roberts. Look, here comes Dad now. Why don't we see if he wants a quick drink in the Prince of Wales before we head for home?'

'That sounds more like it,' Alan said, loosening his tie. 'You know I'm not one for dressing up and going to meetings like this. The only time I've ever been in this building is for wedding receptions and parties. They have the best sprung dance floor in town.'

Sarah smiled to herself. Electricity House was certainly Erith's best venue for parties and official occasions, but she much preferred the informal hall behind the Prince of

Wales pub. She only ever visited the building in Pier Road to go into its ground-floor showroom when not at work and look at all the shiny new appliances, daydreaming of what she would buy for her lovely new home when their ship came in. It might take time, but she had faith in her husband and his business. She hugged his arm. 'There was a time, Alan Gilbert, when you enjoyed dressing up. And you looked so smart in your RAF uniform,' she said, gazing up into his sparkling blue eyes.

'Those days are long gone, and thank goodness they are,' he said as he took her hand and held it tight. 'I feel in my bones that our family will prosper. We have a bright future ahead of us, my love, and our children will want for nothing.'

'I'm happy with our lot. I don't need big dreams. I just want you and the children safe; is that too much to ask?'

'What about that cottage with the roses round the door you've hankered after since we married?'

Sarah chuckled. 'Youthful dreams, my love. I'm no longer that innocent bride who celebrated her twenty-first birthday on the day war broke out. Although I'd not say no to a cottage if it was going begging.'

'You don't look a day older than when you walked down the aisle towards me,' he said, giving her an appreciative look. Her glossy dark hair was curled away from her face, showing her English rose complexion to perfection. 'I'd give you the world, if that's what you want.'

Sarah blushed, looking round to make sure no one was listening. 'I'll leave the big dreams and plans to others.'

'Like our Maisie, do you mean?'

'I'm pleased for her. She's not doing badly at all, especially considering she never really planned to turn her sewing into a business. That little shop of hers in the High Street is always busy. And I have a feeling she's up to something – I've not seen much of her lately. She wasn't there when I popped in to collect my coat. She did a lovely job of the alterations, though,' Sarah added with a glance down at her forest green woollen coat. It was nipped in at her slender waist, flaring out around her calves.

'Not getting too posh for her friends, is she?' Alan joked.

'Who's getting too posh?' George asked as he joined them, kissing Sarah's cheek and shaking Alan's hand.

'We were talking about Maisie and wondering what she's up to lately,' Sarah said, giving her dad a sideways look. Perhaps he would be able to fill them in? Ever since he'd become a town councillor, George always seemed to know everything that went on in their small town.

'What, our Maisie getting too posh for the likes of us? Never!' he said, raising his hand to wave goodbye to some of the other people leaving the hall. 'She's the salt of the earth. Nothing will change her – even if she does have big plans for the future.'

'So you do know what she's up to!' Sarah said, looking triumphant.

'I'm sure she will tell you when she's ready. It's not for me to say,' George said, giving Alan a wink.

'But we've never had secrets from each other,' Sarah said, a little sadly.

Alan put his arm round her shoulders and gave her a squeeze. 'Don't go getting yourself upset. You've been friends with Maisie far too long for that. She will tell you in her own good time, I'm sure. She might not drop her aitches as much now that she dresses the important women of Erith, but she's still the Maisie we know and love. Now – how about we take a brisk walk round to the Prince of Wales and have that drink? What do you say to that, George?'

'I say it's a good idea. I just need to say goodbye to somebody, then I'll be with you. By the way, did you spot Betty and Douglas over there? Looks as though they're making their way towards the door.'

Sarah stood on tiptoe, scanning the crowd until she spotted the Woolworths manageress, Betty Billington. Catching her eye, she waved energetically.

Betty was dressed in a pillar-box-red coat with black accessories, her salt-and-pepper hair pinned back in a French pleat. She waved back, working her way across the crowded hall towards them with her husband, Douglas, not far behind.

'That was a good evening, Norman,' George said, turning towards a man in a black overcoat and trilby hat who was escorting the speaker and her small entourage towards the exit.

'George! I thought I spotted you in the front row. Let me introduce you to our prospective member of parliament,' Norman Dodds said, turning to the smartly dressed young woman beside him. 'Margaret, this is one of our local councillors, George Caselton; and his daughter and son-in-law. Alan runs a business in the town. And,' he added, as Betty and Douglas joined them, 'here are Mr and Mrs Billington – Douglas is a funeral director, and Betty runs a branch of Woolworths as well as looking after their young family.'

Margaret Roberts shook hands with everyone. 'You have

an enterprising group of friends, Norman,' she smiled. 'I congratulate you all for helping to rebuild productivity in this town.'

'It's you we ought to be thanking,' Betty Billington said to the prospective member of parliament. 'You are showing the way forward for young women to be able to further their education and speak for all of us in the Houses of Parliament.'

Margaret Roberts gave her thanks before Norman led the little group towards the exit.

'Come on, let's go get that drink,' Alan said. He turned to the Billingtons. 'You will join us, won't you?'

'Do you need to ask?' Douglas Billington said. 'That's the joy of having a housekeeper who lives in – it doesn't matter if we're a little late home.'

They left Electricity House, shivering as they stepped out into the cold night air. Betty took a deep breath. 'Ah – that's much better. I must say, it was a little fuggy in there, with so much cigarette smoke.'

'And so many smelly bodies,' Alan chuckled.

Sarah tutted. 'You shouldn't say such things, my love – many of those people must have come straight from work. I'm just pleased we had a good turnout and were able to listen to the people who will represent Dartford and Erith in the elections. I know who will be receiving my cross on the ballot paper . . . Alan?'

Alan had stopped to gaze into the showroom windows that looked out over Pier Road. 'That's the business to be in,' he said, nodding to the display of wireless sets arranged around a television with a polished wood cabinet. 'That's the future, right there in that display . . .'

Sarah tugged his arm. 'Hurry up, dreamer. The future is in our children, not a shop window full of electrical nonsense.'

'Look, there are some empty seats over by the fire,' Sarah said as they stepped into the crowded public bar of the Prince of Wales. She and Betty made their way quickly over to claim the spot while their husbands headed towards the bar.

'That was handy,' Betty said, unbuttoning her coat and pulling off the scarf she'd tied over her hair for the short walk. 'I pray spring isn't far away – I'm sick to death of these cold, drizzly days.'

'I know what you mean. I'm having a devil of a job keeping the children's clothes clean; I'm forever scrubbing mud out of Buster's shorts. Goodness knows where he finds it all, when he's usually playing with Georgina. Somehow she seems to keep twice as clean as her little brother.'

Betty flinched. Still, after all these years, she couldn't quite believe her friend called her youngest child 'Buster' when his Christian name was Alan, just like his dad. 'Thank goodness mine are too young to play outside,' she said. 'But I still have mucky clothes to launder, as Charlie seems to end up wearing most of the food I put in front of him. At least Clemmie and Dorothy are almost adults now and appreciate the clothes we buy for them.'

Sarah pulled off her gloves and tucked them into the top of her open handbag. 'They are such pretty girls – quite the perfect young ladies. You must be so proud of them. Remind me, how old are they now?'

'Dorothy is fourteen and Clementine is almost eighteen.'

'Why, before you know it Clemmie will be married and off your hands,' Sarah smiled.

'Good grief, I hope not!' Betty looked shocked. 'We both have high hopes for her. Listening to Margaret Roberts this evening and seeing what a success she's made of her life – well, I'm going to have a word with Douglas. I think our Clemmie might have a chance at getting into university. After all, Margaret Roberts's father is in trade – a grocer, I believe – and look at her now.'

'I understand he too is involved in politics, from what Dad told me, so not just a grocer; but that's certainly something to aim for. Your Clemmie is extremely intelligent and that private school you sent her to sounds very good. But do you really think she's got it in her for all those years of studying? And what would she do at the end of it?'

Betty had a faraway look in her eyes. 'Well, as our Maisie would say, the world is her lobster.' She smiled at Sarah. 'So much has changed for working women since the wars. When you think what was available for me all those years ago, when I suddenly found myself without a fiancé and facing a life alone . . . there was very little for me to do. Why, even during the last war, women who succeeded in business had to give up their jobs for the men when they came back. I know one thing: I do not want to see Clemmie working behind the counter at Woolworths for much longer. Saturdays and the odd holiday cover are fine, as she's earning some pocket money and learning to grow up. But I feel I would be letting her late mother down if I didn't encourage her to aim a little higher.'

'What about Dorothy? Many girls are working at her age.'

Betty sighed. 'I have no idea, but there is time to decide. And at least she too has her Saturday job at Woolworths, where I can keep an eye on her while she continues with her education.'

'Hello, you two! I'm glad I spotted you.' Maisie appeared through the crowd, tall and leggy with an elegant little hat perched on her blonde head, and flopped into a spare armchair next to the roaring fire. Leaning down, she rubbed her legs. 'I haven't been warm all day.'

'I thought your shop was warm and snug?' Sarah said.

'Yes, it's very cosy in the shop, but it's perishing cold at the . . .' She caught herself and paused for a moment, weighing up her next words. 'There's something I need to tell you both. It's been a bit of a secret – mainly because if it failed, I didn't want to look a fool. But now everything is signed on the dotted line, I want to share it with my friends,' she said, her eyes sparkling. Just then, the men arrived with a round of drinks.

'Whatever have you been up to?' Betty said to Maisie once they were all settled. 'I hope it's all above board,' she chuckled.

Maisie snorted. 'You know me well, don't you, Betty? But I can assure you, this is all kosher. I've not got hold of a load of dodgy perfume, or cans of fruit from my mates who work on the docks.' She grinned, giving them a crafty wink. 'I'm expanding my business – and that's all I'm going to say for now. If you're both free tomorrow morning, I'll collect you and drive you over to have a look.'

'I'm afraid it's my day in the store, although I'd love to play truant and come with you,' Betty said. 'And I know Freda is working, too, as I was looking at the rota just this afternoon.'

'Not to worry. I can do another tour one evening for the rest of the gang. What about you, Sarah, are you up for it? Now I can talk about what I've been up to, I'd like to share the news with all my chums. It's only right after we've been through so much together in the past.'

'Wild horses wouldn't keep me away. But there is one thing I'm concerned about . . .' The women laughed. Sarah was known for her cautious ways.

'What's worrying you?' Maisie asked.

'Well, you mentioned driving. Since when have you been able to drive a vehicle?'

'Ah, that's something else I meant to tell yer – I've been having lessons. George has been teaching me in my van.'

Sarah frowned. 'You kept that quiet, Dad.'

George ran a finger round his collar as if it suddenly felt tight. He'd known that when the news broke, he might get it in the neck from his daughter. 'It was only a few times, and it slipped my mind,' he said, looking uncomfortable. 'Your Alan took her out as well.'

Sarah raised her eyebrows at her husband, who avoided her gaze. 'Er, it slipped my mind as well,' he muttered.

'Oh, forget all that,' Maisie said, waving her hand. 'If you want to learn to drive, Sarah, I can teach you in the van. It's a doddle really. You just have to toot the horn a lot in case anyone steps out in front of you, and remember to use the brakes. Be ready at half past eight tomorrow morning and we can be on our way, if that's all right with you?'

Sarah couldn't stay miffed at her friends or family for long. 'It sounds intriguing and I'm eager to know what you've been up to. I'll be ready and waiting on the doorstep.

I can drop the children off round Nan's, as she's having them after school. In fact, why don't you pick me up there to save me walking back home again, when you live just up the road?'

'That sounds perfect. Don't forget to dress warm. Where I'm taking you, it's bloody cold. I think I've developed chilblains.' Maisie pulled up the leg of her siren suit and poked a finger at her calves, still purple with cold. 'You'd not think these legs once attracted wolf whistles.'

'I haven't seen you wear that outfit in a long time. Not since our days of spending time down in the air-raid shelters,' Betty said as she sipped from her small glass of port.

'Needs must, ducks. I don't want to get my decent clobber dirty.'

Sarah raised her eyebrows. 'Wherever are you taking me?'

She was rewarded with a wink and a grin from her friend.

2

'Are you sure you'll be all right with the children, Nan? Buster can be a right little handful at times. Be strict and don't give him too many biscuits; I know what you and Bob are like. He's taken to refusing to go into school, so if you have any problems when you get to the gates, call out to his teacher. I've put clean clothes in the bag for later, as he's bound to get mucky – I don't want his school clothes spoilt. He can get messy just standing still.'

As her granddaughter paused for breath Ruby Jackson chuckled, shaking her head. 'Honestly, Sarah, I can cope with the pair of them. As for little boys getting mucky, your dad was a right one for that, so perhaps that's where Buster has got it from. I'll have Bob drop them off at Crescent Road School; he can handle the lad. Buster idolizes him, I have no idea why.'

'Oh Nan, so do you! Bob's the apple of your eye,' Sarah said. She sighed. 'You should see Alan when he's been tinkering with that motorbike – there's more oil and grease on him than on the bike. I wouldn't mind, but it's hell trying to get things dry in this weather. Roll on the spring and some sunshine, that's all I'm hoping for. I seem to be running out of clothes, the pair of them are growing so quickly. I'm forever letting down hems and adding longer cuffs onto jumpers. Who'd be a mum, eh?'

'Don't you worry about messing with things like that. I've got some wool put by from unpicking one of your dad's pullovers. It had worn at the elbows, so I had it off him and unpicked before he asked me to patch it,' Ruby chuckled. 'I can get the kiddies a couple of jumpers out of it. I bet our Freda will help me, she's quite a dab hand with the knitting needles these days. Mind you, by now I'd have thought she might have a little one of her own to knit for.'

'The babies will come; she should stop counting the days. One day Freda will have a brood of her own running round her legs,' Sarah said, thinking of her youngest friend, who lived just across the road with Tony, her husband.

She smiled to herself at the thought of the young couple. They suited each other so well, and Tony adored Freda. He was not a tall man, but with his slim frame he suited his sport of cycle racing, which kept him busy when he wasn't working at Woolworths as a manager. 'They've only been married fifteen months,' she added, turning to look as a vehicle pulled up and the driver honked the horn noisily.

'Crikey – Maisie can't really be driving that van, can she?' she said, hardly able to believe it despite their conversation the evening before.

'She certainly is.' Ruby shook her head, looking worried. 'I've seen her go up and down this road a dozen times at least, and she's got the biggest smile on her face. You must tell me what she's up to when you come to collect the kiddies after you finish work this afternoon. Don't worry how long it takes. We've got a busy time planned once they're out of school. Bob said he'll take them down the allotment. As for me, I intend to sit down in front of the wireless with them and listen to that new radio programme for children. It's called *Listen with Mother*, have you heard about it?'

'Oh yes. Our Georgina adores it, although I'm not sure Buster will sit still long enough to listen. He's partial to a bit of music and might jump up and down and dance; he's got a bit of a singing voice as well, just like his dad and his nanny Maureen.' She smiled, leaning over to kiss Ruby's cheek. 'I'll see you later.'

She hurried over to the van as Maisie hopped out and opened the passenger door for her daughters, Bessie and Claudette. 'You'll have to climb into the back, girls, your Auntie Sarah needs a comfy seat.'

'I don't mind—' Sarah started to say, but Maisie shushed her.

'No, it's a rule of mine that adults get the seats and kids climb in the back. So you can stop looking at me like that, young madam,' she added, wagging a finger at her older girl.

Bessie pouted and tossed her dark hair. 'I hope none of my friends see me, that's all. I'm not a child, you know.'

'And yer not an old woman, either. You might be sixteen and old enough to go to work, but yer still a kid in my eyes, so shut up. That's if you want to live long enough to see your seventeenth birthday.'

'Maisie, that's a bit harsh,' Sarah whispered as she climbed into the vehicle. Pulling the door closed, she turned to the two girls, who were sitting on boxes in the rear of the small van. 'How are you both? It's an age since I've seen you.'

'I'm very well, thank you, Auntie Sarah,' said Claudette.

Sarah thought how different the two girls were. Claudette, with her fancy film-star name, was the slightly tubby, mousey-headed younger sister, the more affable of the two; Bessie was the glamorous one, just entering adulthood. Sarah hoped Maisie wouldn't have problems with her later. The girls were actually Maisie's nieces – she had adopted them after her brother's death – but she had taken naturally to parenting them and seemed able to read them like a book, keeping them strictly in hand even though she adored them both.

'Are you enjoying working at Woolworths?' Sarah asked, twisting in her seat to speak to the girls. 'I don't work Saturdays, so I haven't seen you in action in your Woolies overalls.'

'I love working there,' Claudette grinned.

'She likes the dinners in the canteen more,' her sister sniffed, giving Claudette a dig in the ribs with her elbow.

'Ouch! That hurt. I do like working on the haberdashery counter. And Mrs Caselton makes nice cakes for afternoon tea breaks.'

Sarah smiled. When she'd first started work at the store in 1938, along with Maisie and Freda, they too had enjoyed the cakes – until rationing started. Even now, with things so tight, she could produce something from nothing. Maureen, who still ran the staff canteen with a rod of iron, had eventually become Sarah's mother-in-law; and in a strange turn of fate she was now also married to Sarah's dad, George.

'Just like me,' Maisie guffawed as she honked her horn at a cyclist riding in the middle of the road. 'Me and Freda worked that counter. I was in my element amongst the sewing thread and ribbons, and always had first dibs on anything new. I swear it's not so much fun now I get it all from a warehouse up the East End.'

'What about you, Bessie? Will you stay working at Woolworths, now you're old enough for a full-time job? Or will you work with your mum?'

Maisie didn't give the girl time to answer. 'They'll both be working for me. They need to learn the ropes. It's all part of my plan.'

As Sarah turned back to face front, she caught a glimpse of the grimace that crossed Bessie's face. 'Where are we off to?' she asked, changing the subject.

'You wait and see,' Maisie grinned. 'I'm taking you to see the next stage of my business empire. You never thought you'd hear me say that, did you?'

'Is it another shop? That would be wonderful. I know how busy you are at Maisie's Modes.'

'Nah, this is something else.' Maisie turned to give Sarah a broad wink. Then she had to swerve to straighten the van as it veered dangerously to the right, causing Claudette and Bessie to scream as they slid across the floor.

'I've told you before, hold onto the rope,' Maisie called over her shoulder. 'You kids never listen to me!'

'We wouldn't have to if you could drive properly,' Bessie snapped back as she righted herself. 'We told you to buy a car, or borrow David's car.'

'I wish you'd call him Dad rather than David,' Maisie said. 'It's not respectful. I haven't dragged you up to be rude. Next time I'll borrow one of his hearses and you can travel in the back of that,' she added, giving the steering wheel another jerk that sent the girls grabbing the rope anchored to the side of the van. 'That'll shut them up,' she laughed out loud.

Sarah, who had been gripping the sides of her seat, took a deep breath. She felt quite queasy. 'Perhaps you could drive a little slower, Maisie, the girls will be covered in bruises.'

'Don't worry about us, Auntie Sarah, it's fun,' Claudette called back.

'Speak for yourself,' Bessie muttered, leaning sideways to rub her backside.

Sarah burst out laughing. Maisie might not have given birth to the two girls, but in many ways they were just like her. It made her wonder about their real dad, Maisie's late brother, and what life would have been like for his daughters if he'd not been killed in a brawl on the night the country celebrated Victory in Europe. Would he have taken them away? If he had, it would have broken Maisie's heart; by that time, she'd already been caring for the girls for several years.

'We will never know,' she sighed, before clapping a hand over her mouth. 'Sorry. I was just thinking aloud . . . things might have been so different for them.'

This time Maisie kept her eyes on the road. 'If you mean what I think you mean, the girls would have stayed with me regardless. I'd fight to my dying breath to keep them with me. David feels the same. You know he was going to pay my brother off before . . . well, before he was killed,' she said, lowering her voice for once.

Sarah glanced over her shoulder. Bessie and Claudette were busy looking out the small rear window, and the rumble of the van would keep them from overhearing. 'Do they know?'

'Yes, we've no secrets from them. They know we love 'em just as much as little Ruby and the twins. I would almost say I love 'em even more, after me and Freda had to fight to get them out from that crush of bodies at Bethnal Green. They've had charmed lives, that's for sure.' Maisie cuffed a tear from her eyes and kept driving.

Sarah patted Maisie's knee. 'They are lucky to have you, and you them. It was meant to be.'

'Yer could say that. That's why I want to build my business, so they've got something for their future. And they can look after me when I'm in my dotage,' she added with a grin, sounding more like the Maisie Sarah knew so well. Nothing much kept her down for long. 'Do you know where we are?'

'Of course – this is Slades Green,' Sarah said as they came to a stop at the crossing gates. They waited for a steam train pulling an array of goods wagons to pass before the man in the signal box turned a large wheel and the gates slowly opened.

The van jumped and lurched as Maisie drove forward.

'Oh, we're heading towards the Thames,' Sarah said, wondering why Maisie had driven in such a wide loop from Erith, through North End towards 'the Green', as they called it. 'My Aunt Pat's farm is over this way. I have to confess to not having been here for years. I usually see her when she pops in to visit Nan with a basket of veg; she's always been so generous. Of course, for much of the war she was down in Cornwall with my young cousins . . . I'm not sure the farming life would be for me, but they seem to love it.'

'Me neither,' Maisie said, as they left the road to join a dirt track.

17

'Nan once told me Aunt Pat wanted to be a farmer when she was a kid. Even Dad knew he wanted to work for Vickers when he was a little lad. I've never been like them.'

'Thank goodness you decided on working for Woolies, or me and Freda would never have met you,' Maisie commented thoughtfully. 'I've never asked, but why Woolies?'

Sarah shrugged her shoulders. 'It seems a lifetime since I moved up from Devon to live with Nan after Granddad Eddie died. I'd not been living at number thirteen for more than a day when the *Erith Observer* dropped through the letter box. Betty had placed an advertisement for Christmas staff, so I jumped at the opportunity and wrote a letter straight away. It saved queuing down the Labour Exchange.'

'Just as I did. And who'd've thought that staff supervisor was our Betty? She scared the daylights out of me.'

'Me too,' Sarah agreed. 'At least you never showed how fearful you were. Me and Freda thought you were so glamorous and self-assured.' She heard a movement behind her and turned to see the two girls had moved closer, just behind their seats.

'We like hearing about the old days,' Claudette said, making Maisie and Sarah laugh. 'Why are you laughing? It was over eleven years ago!'

'My love, that's a mere hop in time. Wait until you're our age, then you'll be talking about the old days. When your old mum drove like a demon and made you work your fingers to the bone in her business empire.'

The girls groaned good-naturedly while Sarah frowned. What was Maisie up to?

'Are we there yet?' she asked, sounding just like her own children when they were taken to the coast by train.

'Almost. You know, I've been thinking of moving down here, away from the busy town. It would be good for the little ones to grow up in the countryside. David's keen, too, but then his family are country people.'

'No, you can't!' Bessie howled in horror. 'I'd hate it in the country. I'd need to catch a bus just to get into Erith to see my friends. Besides, you'd not have anyone to come out here and look after little Ruby and the twins while you're working.'

'It won't be long before you're too busy working to gallivant about with your mates. Besides, aren't they working as well? I'm sure I spotted one of them in the Co-op shop standing behind the cheese counter. Just be thankful you'll have a decent job to go to before too long.'

Bessie stuck her tongue out at her mother's back.

'And don't think I didn't see what you just did. You should know by now I have eyes in the back of my head, young lady.'

'I wouldn't mind moving, if it meant I had my own bedroom,' Claudette piped up.

'By the time we move, you two will be married and out of my hair. Let's forget I even mentioned it,' Maisie said. The van slowed down, and she pulled on the handbrake so fast that it juddered to a halt. 'Everybody out. Let's go look at the future of Maisie's Modes.'

Sarah climbed from the van and rubbed her back as she looked around her. Maisie had driven further down a dirt track, stopping in the middle of a group of old factory buildings set around a courtyard. A few of them were no more than walls, without windows or roofs.

'Why on earth are we out here? Surely you can't have a shop in the back of beyond? Your nearest customers would be from the ships on the river, and I doubt many sailors would want to buy a frock.'

Maisie looked at Sarah as though she were mad. 'Why would you think I was going to set up a shop close to the banks of the Thames? No, follow me, there's so much for you to see.'

She strode off towards one of the buildings, then stopped in front of a peeling blue-painted wooden door and fumbled with a large set of keys before finding one that opened it. 'Mind the step,' she called behind her as she made her way into what, as far as Sarah could see through the gloom, appeared to be a small warehouse. Clouds of dust were stirred up by the breeze as they entered.

'There's a light switch here somewhere . . . That's it.' Maisie turned to them in triumph as the room was flooded by the glare of a row of lightbulbs. 'What do you think?'

Sarah blinked as the light cut through the gloom. 'It's a workshop – rather like the one my Alan had for his motorbikes. This one looks a little larger,' she replied, gazing around at the space. It must have been all of a hundred feet in length, and just as wide. 'I'm still none the wiser as to why you've brought me here, or what it has to do with Maisie's Modes?'

Maisie grinned at her friend. 'I know it don't look like much at the moment. But once the sewing machines are delivered and the place has had a good clean, this will be the hub of my business, and where much of my stock will be made for the shops.'

Claudette took Sarah's hand. 'Let me show you around. This is going to be where Mum has all the clothes made,' she said proudly as she led Sarah to the far end of the room. 'We are going to have a cutting table and sewing machines – big ones, not like the one we use at home. Through here . . .' she opened one of three doors, '. . . we will keep the material and stock, and the room off that will be where the completed frocks are hung before they're taken out to the shops.'

Sarah shook her head in amazement. 'You have been busy. And you, young lady, seem very involved. I take it as you left school at Christmas, you will be working here for your mum – and you too?' she said, looking at Bessie, who was staring at her feet and didn't seem interested.

'I'm sorry not to have told you sooner,' Maisie said as she joined them. 'I really wanted to, but it all depended on whether David's inheritance came through. Otherwise we might not have got this place.'

'Inheritance? Oh Maisie, I'm sorry; I didn't know he'd lost one of his parents? The couple of times I met them, I thought they were pretty decent people, considering how rich and posh they were.'

'They're very much alive, thank goodness! It was his godfather who passed away, in America. That's what made it all a bit tricky. David wanted to invest in both our businesses and perhaps have a family holiday. I felt that if I shared the news too soon, it might jinx our plans; you know how superstitious I am,' Maisie explained, leaning over to touch a wooden window frame. 'It still doesn't feel real; that's why I keep touching wood all the time. To think I didn't even want a shop in the High Street, and had to be convinced by all of you that it was a good idea. Now I want much more – if only to give my children a good start to their working life. Come and see the rest of the place,' she said, opening another door that took them to an office and what would become a small canteen for staff.

As Sarah followed Maisie, feeling excited for her friend, she looked back to see Bessie turning away and wiping tears from her eyes. Why was the girl so upset?

3

'You're back earlier than I expected.' Ruby looked up from where she was sweeping the front path of her bay-fronted terraced house in Alexandra Road.

'I've not been into work yet. I thought with Maisie bringing me home, I'd stop off for a cuppa with you. She said I could tell you her good news.'

Ruby stopped sweeping and rubbed her back, wincing. 'I must get Bob to put a longer handle on this broom so I don't have to bend over as much,' she said as they walked back indoors.

'I'll finish the sweeping for you, after that cuppa – I'm parched after wandering around a dusty building. There's an hour before I need to be at my desk in Woolies. Sit yourself down, Nan,' she instructed, going into the kitchen to fill the kettle and put it on the hob before joining Ruby and sitting opposite her at the table.

'So, what's Maisie been up to? Don't tell me there's another baby in the offing – I'd have thought five was enough? I know she gets some help from Sadie, looking after the little ones and doing a bit of house cleaning, but it's still a lot to take on.'

'Maisie is a wonderful mother, but no, it's nothing to do with babies or children. She's expanding her business,' Sarah said, watching Ruby's reaction. Her nan was looking tired these days, but in her seventieth year she was still insisting on doing all her own housework. Today she was as smartly turned out as ever in one of her favourite flower-patterned crossover pinnies.

'What do you mean? How can she make that shop any bigger than what it is already? She'll end up spreading into the undertaker's next door,' Ruby cackled.

'No, Nan, it's nothing like that. It seems she's got all sorts of plans. David's godfather died and left him some money, and he is generously investing not only in his own business but also Maisie's. They see it as securing the children's futures by providing them with jobs. She's renting a small factory down near the Thames. You have to travel out by Slades Green, then back down the lane to get there. No wonder she's got that van – she couldn't rely on a bus as it's still too much of a walk at the other end.'

Ruby was interested. 'What's she going to make in this factory? I thought she liked her sewing and making something out of nothing for her shop?'

'What she plans to do is make as much of the stock as possible for the High Street shop, as well as another that she's planning to rent in Bexleyheath Broadway. There was even mention of a special shop just for brides.'

'Well, fancy that.'

'Indeed. But that's not all: in time she wants to be able to sell her clothing to other shops. My head was spinning with everything she told me. I'm quite excited for them, in a way, but it'll be hard work.'

'What do you mean, "in a way"? The eldest two are of working age. They already work at Woolworths part time. I should think they'll be glad of being able to work with their mum.'

'That's true,' Sarah said as she went back to the small kitchen to warm the pot. She spooned in tea leaves, added water from the boiling kettle and put on a colourful knitted cosy. 'I do feel Maisie's got a problem on her hands, though,' she called back through the open door to the living room, where Ruby sat at the large square utility table. Although number thirteen had a comfortable front room that looked out through a bay window onto the busy road, it was kept for best. Many in the street only used the front room for Christmas, or for laying out loved ones.

'Why? Do you think she's running before she can walk? It must cost a fair bit to set up a business like that. I wouldn't be able to sleep if it were me.'

'You're right there, although she has got David's business head to rely on. And you know Maisie's always had a knack for making something out of nothing and making money. It's more young Bessie I'm thinking about,' Sarah said thoughtfully. 'Maisie told me her plans and Claudette kept chiming in with her own ideas, but Bessie had nothing to say. She looked so sad. And sometimes bitter, as if she was unhappy about the whole venture.'

'How can a sixteen-year-old be bitter, when they don't know the meaning of the word?' Ruby snorted. 'I'd think it more her not fancying having to work every day. That girl can be a bit airy-fairy at times. Working Saturdays at Woolworths and helping out at her mum's shop when she's busy hasn't stretched her enough. I've often spotted her leaning on the counter, chatting or gazing away into the distance while the queue got longer. Why, Vera from up the road told me she had to have a short word with the girl just to get her to take her hands out of her pockets and serve someone. Would you believe Bessie turned round and poked her tongue out at her? Honestly, I don't know what's become of the staff at that store.'

Sarah held her stomach as she laughed. 'I've wanted to do that plenty of times over the years. I know it's naughty of Bessie, but I'd have liked to see it. Vera must've been outraged.'

'I'll say she was. She was like a terrier with a bone. Every time I see her lately, I get it in the ear about my grandchildren being rude and how I should have a word with them.'

'But Maisie's kids aren't really your grandchildren. It was unfair of Vera to say such a thing. I know you've always looked on Maisie, as well as Freda, as your own; but in times like this it's best to keep your nose out. Well, that's what I think, anyway,' Sarah said, putting cups and saucers on a tray along with a small milk jug and carrying them through to the table.

'All the same, perhaps we ought to keep an eye on the girl. I'll make some excuse to have her down here for a cup of tea and a chat. She's a nice enough kid and is bound to listen to a word of advice.'

'I'll do the same, even if it's just to keep an eye on her. I don't usually work on Saturdays, but Betty Billington has been asking me if I can fit in another day. She's putting in more time as well while her Tony is away on Woolworths business.'

'Hmm,' Ruby muttered, thinking of Freda's young husband, who had started out as a trainee manager but was now promoted to temporary manager, which meant being at the beck and call of head office. 'What with him going off doing all this bike training, then the Woolworths bosses having him off with their team inspecting other stores and whatnot – not only does it keep our Betty away from her own family, but it makes me wonder how the goodness Freda's ever going to have a baby? It needs a husband at home for that to happen.'

'You've got a point there, Nan, but I can assure you Betty has her home life well organized. It helps having a live-in housekeeper. The Erith store wouldn't be the same without our Betty being in charge, even if Tony is sometimes around to assist her.'

Ruby considered her granddaughter's words. 'Now, tell me more about this factory of Maisie's, will you? Exactly where is it, as I'm a bit confused? I do know Slades Green, but you lost me talking about the side roads and her driving.'

Sarah poured the tea and explained how they'd headed towards the river, up no more than a dirt track, before driving past derelict buildings and arriving at the small factory on the marshes not far from the river. 'It will need some doing up,' she started to say, before noticing her nan's face turning pale. 'Why, whatever is wrong? You look as though someone has walked over your grave.'

'In a way they did, love. I've never told you about when I was younger, have I? I was injured in an explosion down at Gilbert's munitions factory. It was your Granddad Eddie that saved me – otherwise I could've died alongside the others. There were twelve women who perished.' The pain of the memory was clear on Ruby's face.

'Oh Nan! I had no idea you were caught up in all of that,' Sarah said, horrified. 'No one ever mentioned it, not even Dad. I remember reading about it in the paper on the twenty-fifth anniversary last year.' She spooned sugar into Ruby's cup and slid it across the table towards her.

'You know I don't have that stuff in my tea. I gave it up in the war and I can't stand it now.'

'It's for the shock – you look as though you need it. You never know, perhaps when you go down to have a look round, it won't be the same as you remember? After all, it's not the same factory.'

'I'm not sure I want to go anywhere near there,' Ruby said, biting her lip. 'It took all my strength to go back to visiting . . . well, to go to Brook Street cemetery, knowing I had to walk past the memorial to those who died.'

Sarah was confused. 'Why would you even want to go up to Brook Street, when all our family are buried at Saint Paulinus? Mum, Granddad Eddie . . .'

'There is someone. My daughter, Sarah, was laid to rest at the Brook Street cemetery.' Ruby paused to let Sarah take that in, then added, 'I should've told you about her years ago, but it never seemed to be the right time. And then, as the years passed, I thought it best just to let it rest. But now . . . well, I would hate to go to my grave thinking that no one knows about my Sarah. You're named after her, you know.'

Sarah put down her cup. 'If I may, I would like to use your telephone to let Betty know I'm going to be a little late. And then you and I are going to have a fresh cup of tea and a good chat. Is that all right, Nan?'

'I'd like that,' Ruby said, giving her granddaughter a weak smile. 'It's time I told you all about the past.'

Sarah placed her hands on the heavy double doors that led into the Erith branch of Woolworths and pushed them open. It was just after eight o'clock in the morning and already Pier Road was looking busy, with shop owners opening up for the day.

She raised her hand and waved across to where the manager of Missons' Ironmongers was putting out an array of brooms, buckets and dustbins while chatting to a customer who'd just left the shop. They always opened earlier than any other shop in the street; she wasn't sure why, but it was handy at times. Just around the corner she knew that her husband, Alan, would be setting up for the day in his bicycle repair shop. In the couple of years since his motorbike workshop had caught fire and his consequent move to the High Street shop, he'd all but given up repairing motorbikes. Instead he concentrated on bicycles in the small back workshop, while the front of the shop displayed gleaming new bikes along with an array of puncture repair kits, bells, lamps and all kinds of other things that cyclists seemed to require. He had good staff working with him these days, and seemed much happier.

'Hello, girls,' she said as four chattering young women came in, taking the weight of the door from her. 'You all seem rather excited this morning.'

'I really like working here, Mrs Gilbert. I want to learn all about Woolworths. Betty – I mean my stepmother – I mean,

Mrs Billington . . .' Dorothy Billington blushed. 'She has told me so many exciting stories about what's happened here in the past. I must admit, it's going to be hard remembering to call her "Mrs Billington",' she added, turning even pinker. 'I'm sorry, I'm so excited. I know I'm talking too much.'

Sarah smiled at the young girl. At fourteen years old, she stood shorter than her sister Clementine but both had similar blonde hair, although Dorothy's was longer and hung in a plait down her back.

'You'll get used to it, Dorothy. How about you, Clementine, do you enjoy working here as a Saturday girl?' Clementine smiled politely without saying a word. 'This is the first time I've worked a Saturday in ages, so I've never seen you all at work before.' Sarah turned to the other two girls, Maisie's daughters Bessie and Claudette. 'I suppose you'll both be leaving before too long, once your mother's factory is up and running and she's opened her second shop?'

Bessie muttered something Sarah didn't quite catch and pushed past them, running up the staff staircase without looking back.

'Oh dear. I seem to have put my foot in it,' Sarah said to the younger sister.

'Don't worry about her. She doesn't know what she wants to do,' Claudette said. 'I do like working here and look forward to my Saturdays helping customers and learning how a big store runs. I've told Mum that for now I want to remain a Saturday girl at Woolworths, even though I'll be working at her factory during the week. Do you think that's the right thing to do, Auntie Sarah?'

Although they weren't blood relatives, Sarah was touched that Maisie's children all called her their auntie. They also referred to Ruby as their nan, and always treated her with respect. She was sure that when the time came and Freda had little ones, her children would do the same. They were all one big family.

She smiled at the young girl. 'It's an exciting time in your life, Claudette, but don't overdo things, will you? You've got to go out and enjoy yourself sometimes. Why, it may not be too long before you have a boyfriend – and no lad wants a girlfriend who can never go out because she's too tired for a social life.'

Dorothy and Clementine giggled at Sarah's words, but Claudette considered them and thanked her.

Sarah didn't know why, but she didn't seem to get on as well with Betty's two stepdaughters. Dorothy wasn't so bad, but the older one, Clementine, was a right little snob and not as friendly as the other girls. Sarah couldn't put her finger on it, but the girl just didn't seem happy.

As they reached the top of the staircase leading to the long corridor on the upper floor of the building, Sarah bade them goodbye, wishing them a nice day on the shop floor. Her own small office was next door to where Betty Billington worked as store manager. These days she shared the workload with Tony Forsythe, Freda's husband. When Betty had her own babies she had given up working for Woolworths, but the lure of the store where she'd had such happy times had kept calling her back to help out during busy periods. When the opportunity to share shifts as manager with Tony had been offered to her, she'd jumped at it. Fortunately Douglas approved, and they'd both agreed it was time to hire a live-in housekeeper to take care of the family.

Sarah nodded to herself. Betty was lucky to have an understanding husband and the wherewithal to enjoy a lovely home and hire staff, making it possible for her to go out to work. Not many women had that privilege – even after the war, when their lives should have changed so much for the better. Instead, many had given up their jobs to the returning men.

'Thank goodness I've caught you,' Freda said as Sarah was going into her office. 'There's something I need to talk to you about. If I promise to bring tea and a bun, can I join you during my morning tea break? I can't stop now, as I have to check which counters need Saturday girls assisting – and try to find someone who will keep an eye on . . .' She nodded discreetly over her shoulder to where Clemmie Billington was propping up a wall, chatting to another Saturday girl.

Sarah couldn't help smiling at her friend. Freda was like a live wire, dashing about. If it wasn't her job as a supervisor for Woolies, it was helping out with the Girl Guides and Brownies. She was so different to the small, shy girl in ragged clothes Sarah had first met in 1938, when they'd both interviewed to become shop assistants.

'By all means. You only have to mention sticky buns and I'm all yours,' Sarah giggled as her youngest friend hurried away down the passage, still fastening the belt of her supervisor's uniform. 'I too have something to talk to you about,' she called after her.

Sarah's plan had been to clear her desk of filing and set to work on a pile of queries that had mounted up during the week. Half an hour later, there was a tap on her door and Betty Billington walked in.

'I'm sorry to interrupt,' she apologized, looking at the neat piles of order sheets and invoices scattered over Sarah's desk. 'I need to discuss something with you.'

'Oh dear; that sounds ominous.' Sarah removed a leather-bound ledger from a wooden chair so that Betty could sit down.

'It's not meant to be,' Betty reassured her. 'If I'm not smiling much, it's only because I'm concentrating on keeping my eyes open. The youngest apple of my eye kept us awake most of the night – why, Douglas went to work this morning looking as deathly pale as his clients.'

Sarah couldn't help but chuckle; Douglas owned the local undertaker's business, along with Maisie's husband David. 'Oh Betty, you have my sympathy. I thank God my two are past that stage.'

Betty had the good grace to laugh. 'If we couldn't chuckle together about such things, Sarah, I don't know how I would cope at times. I love my family dearly, but there are moments when I look back to before I was married, when I had my own little house and could do as I pleased . . . Well, you know what it's like.'

'I certainly do. Living in what was once Maureen's house is lovely, but it's still a two-up, two-down with a scullery on the back. With the children getting older, I'm wondering how much longer it will hold us all. Having a daughter and a son can be a problem in a smaller home – but then I think of people who only have one room to live and sleep in, and I feel guilty for my thoughts.'

'We need to chat about this more often and remind each other that we are indeed very lucky women. We have good husbands and lovely families.'

'Even if they do keep us awake at night?'

'Yes indeed, and even if the older one can be a right little madam.'

'I thought she had settled into her Saturday job. What's happened?'

Betty sighed. 'She's a clever girl – extremely bright – and as you know, since that night we went to hear Margaret Roberts speak, I've hankered after getting her into university at some point. She could have such a bright future. Did you know that Miss Roberts is some kind of scientist?'

Sarah shrugged her shoulders. Like most people, she'd followed Margaret Roberts's speeches in the *Erith Observer*. She wasn't generally one for politics, but she did admire the woman, even if it was partly for her stylish clothing. She thought it would do the area good to have a woman MP, and could see it would put a few men's noses out of joint. Her dad had said as much, too. 'Does Douglas not wish to put Clemmie through university, is that your problem?'

'No, it's Clemmie herself; there is no talking to the girl these days. She won't say what she wants to do with her future. We've kept her in school long after the leaving age and the only work she does is here on Saturdays – and that's very half-hearted at the moment. I don't know what to do. Perhaps I should spend more time with her. Being a stepmother can be so hard at times. If I put my foot down too much, she reminds me I'm not her mother, and that can be painful. Douglas is a wonderful father and it's been a few years now since our marriage, and many years since their mother's untimely death; but at times I still feel like an outsider and have to watch my step. That's why I wanted to have a word with you.'

Sarah was alarmed. 'Do you mean you want me to take Clemmie under my wing? I've got enough with my pair . . .'

'God forbid, no. I just thought that if I could distance myself from her here at Woolworths – so that I'm not her mother at home and her boss at work – we might get on slightly better. Also, I won't have supervisors coming to me complaining that my daughter isn't pulling her weight.'

I take it Freda's not the only one to have commented about Clemmie, even if it was only to me, Sarah thought to herself. 'What is it you'd like me to do?' she asked, still confused.

'I've had a word with head office – no, not about Clemmie,' Betty said as Sarah raised her eyebrows. 'I've told them it's time we had a manager to look after our Saturday and part-time staff, as neither Tony nor myself has time, with our heavy workloads. After all, these young people are the future of the country, and if we look after them well, they may decide to stay with Woolworths throughout their careers. That's why I'd like to offer you the promotion.'

Sarah was surprised to hear she'd been discussed as a possible candidate for promotion. 'Of course, I'm honoured to be offered the job – although I'll have to talk to Alan, as I'm assuming it would mean longer hours? I only work mornings at the moment, and I'd have to work on Saturdays. But I'd be delighted,' she beamed.

'I hoped you would be,' Betty smiled in return.

'But what about Tony? He shares the management of this store with you; what is his opinion? I'd have thought he might want his own wife to be promoted to manager;

Freda would do a super job. And she is a full-time employee.'

'Now you're going to think badly of me, because I had the same thought, and I did discuss it with Tony. However, you've always had some seniority to Freda, even though she's currently a full-time supervisor. I didn't say this to Tony, but my other thought was that Freda could very soon be expecting a baby – and then, of course, she might well leave our employ. Why, they may even move away from the area if Tony is given a store to manage elsewhere by head office. He's a bright lad and at the moment, with all this extra work he's been doing, I feel he could quite easily be given a much larger store. So you see, I have thought it through; and even if you weren't exactly my first choice, I'd still like to offer you the promotion.'

'But if it wasn't for Freda possibly having a baby or moving away, she would have been offered the job first,' Sarah said with a serious expression.

'I'm so sorry if I've offended you . . .' Betty looked concerned.

Sarah couldn't keep a straight face any longer, and laughed. 'Oh Betty, if I can agree with Alan, and we are able to sort out who will have the children while I'm working, then I'd be more than happy to take on the challenge. Although it is a shame Freda has to be ruled out because of a possible pregnancy. That's something men don't have to worry about.'

'We can only hope that in years to come, there will be more opportunities for women who want families and a job in management too. Until then, we can only do our best to show the world that women are just as capable.'

'I'd say we are more than capable. But then, we have a forward-thinking manager who happens to be a woman.'

Betty got up from her seat and hugged Sarah. 'I was worried there for a moment; you girls always tease me. I should know by now what you're like. I'll leave you for now, as I can see you're busy. Perhaps, when you've had a word with Alan and chewed things over, we can talk about money and hours and such like. You know this will move you up into junior management? In fact, you could become a potential manager eventually, if this works out.'

'I didn't realize . . .' Sarah faltered as she wondered how Alan would take the news. Men could be so funny about wives who had a more senior position than they did, or indeed brought in more money. A couple of years ago, when his motorbike repair workshop hadn't been doing so well, this would really have hurt Alan's pride. However, he'd all but turned his business round and was now doing quite well. He'd even intimated Sarah should give up work and they should think about having another child. Would her news be welcome?

'I can't think of anyone I'd rather have doing the job,' Betty said. 'I've never told you this, but the day you came for your interview, way back in December 1938, it was my first day as a staff supervisor. I was petrified I'd make the wrong choices when hiring you girls. Thankfully I was right in my decisions,' she smiled, turning to leave Sarah to her work. Her own slightly larger office, in the room next door, was shared by visiting people from head office, furnished with a mish-mash of old furniture and piles of stationery that had not yet found a home.

'You came across as a formidable person who knew her job,' Sarah smiled.

But as she watched Betty go, her thoughts returned to what her husband might have to say about her new promotion, and how it would change their lives.

4

'That was delicious,' Freda said, brushing crumbs from her sticky bun off the front of her overall. Both girls were savouring the break from work as they sat in Sarah's office. 'Although I really shouldn't have eaten it – I swear I'm putting on weight around my middle. Tony commented on it just the other day.'

Sarah raised her eyebrows and gave her young friend a knowing look.

'And there's no need to look at me like that; my friend made her monthly visit last week, so I've no news for you on that front,' Freda admonished her, looking a little sad.

'It'll happen. I know it's no comfort at the moment, but babies arrive when you least expect them. I was only saying as much to Maisie the other day.'

'I didn't know my lack of a baby was being discussed amongst my friends.'

'Oh no, it wasn't about you,' Sarah said hastily. 'We were talking about babies in general, and I asked Maisie if she planned to have any more. She was adamant she didn't want another, what with her business plans, but as I said, just look at our Betty and how late in life she had them – and they were just as welcome as if she'd been a slip of a girl. You have much to look forward to, Freda, so don't be too unhappy. Enjoy your time with Tony; believe me, once the children come along you'll never be alone with your husband again.'

'I suppose you're right. But what's this about Maisie?' Freda asked, brightening up at once. 'Whatever is she up to now? I was thrilled when she started selling wedding dresses in her shop, especially the ones that came from old fabric so brides would be able to walk down the aisle in white – that's if they wish to. I know my wedding day wasn't so lucky, with what happened, but it is still a good thing she is doing.'

'That had nothing to do with you or the dress,' Sarah sympathized with her. 'It's like this . . .' She started to explain Maisie's plans, describing the rather run-down building that would soon be her factory. 'If you hadn't been working the other day, you could have come along with us when she showed me around. She's promised to take us all again, that's if I can talk Nan into joining us.'

'Why – is there something wrong with Ruby? She's always interested in everything we do. She was over the road like a shot when I said I'd made new curtains for the bedroom.'

Sarah sighed. 'Maisie told me to share her news as she was too busy to meet up with us all, but Nan didn't give me permission to say . . . Oh, I'm sure it will be all right. It's all in the past, but Nan was upset when she told me.'

'Oh dear; now I'm upset. I hate to think that something in the past is weighing on Ruby's mind at this time in her life.' Freda crossed her hand over her heart. 'I promise it'll go no further.'

'Nan told me something, and it was awful to think she'd kept it to herself all these years. When she was a young woman, she almost died in an ammunition explosion down on the riverbank. I didn't even know she'd worked in a factory; I just assumed she stayed at home, looking after Dad and Auntie Pat when they were kiddies.'

Freda's eyes grew wider as she listened. 'Blow me down, to use one of Ruby's favourite sayings. You know, I've never given a thought to what life was like for Ruby before I came to Erith, although that was . . . eleven years ago now,' she said as she stopped to count on her fingers. 'So much has happened to us in that time. It stands to reason that her earlier life would be filled to the brim with all sorts of incidents. When was she born?'

It was Sarah's turn to stop and count on her fingers. 'Well, Dad will be fifty very soon . . . and I can recall her saying she was twenty-five when they moved to Erith in 1905. Auntie Pat hadn't been born at that time, so that makes her . . . blimey, that makes Nan seventy on her next birthday. We really ought to do something to celebrate. That's quite an age, considering she's had the war to contend with.'

'Don't you mean two wars, as she lived through the First World War, just as your dad did.' Freda became thoughtful. 'You know, if we don't ask older people what their lives were like, we will never know — and then when we lose them, their stories will be gone forever. I have an idea. I'm going to have the Brownies and Girl Guides start a project to ask their parents and grandparents about their childhood years and the early years of when they lived in Erith. The girls can paint pictures, and perhaps some people may even have photographs they can lend to us. I'll ask at the library for information. And the Baptist Church, I'm sure, would let us put on an exhibition of the work,' she beamed.

'Maisie's Claudette will help you. She's always asking questions and likes to get involved with things. I know she's very helpful with the Brownies; and even though my Georgie is young, I feel she'd be interested in her granddad and her great-nanny's younger days.'

'Don't forget Gwyneth and Mike's Myfi. She is a keen member of my Girl Guide pack and can explain about her dad and granddad being policemen in Erith. I'm going to look forward to this.' Freda saw that Sarah suddenly looked rather sad. 'Whatever is wrong?'

'It's just knowing how old Nan is, and thinking she may not be around forever; it doesn't bear thinking about. Even my dad's getting old. He will be fifty the week after next.'

'And look at what he's done in life. All his work during the war at Vickers, and now he's a local town councillor and doesn't stop helping anyone that needs it. You have a lovely family. Just be grateful, as some of us haven't been so lucky.'

'But you and Tony are all part of our family. When you think of Maisie as well, we've got quite an extended family around us, even though some of us aren't blood relatives.'

Freda's eyes lit up. 'I'm lucky in that respect.'

'We should have the children draw an extended family tree. It can be part of the project.' Sarah smiled and became thoughtful. 'I wonder if Maureen has anything planned for Dad's birthday? I've been rather remiss in not asking her. Dad is always here for us, but what have we done for him?' She sipped her tea and grimaced; it had turned cold. 'It'll be nice to have a party. Yes, let's put our heads together with Maureen and see what we can come up with.'

'Did I hear my name mentioned?' Maureen said as she stepped through the slightly open door with a tray in her hands. Sarah never stopped being surprised by how much her mother-in-law looked like Alan, even though his hair was sandy in colour and Maureen's had been dark as night until it became speckled with white in recent years. 'I hope you don't mind, but I brought a cup for myself as well. I'm relieved to escape for a while as it's like bedlam in that canteen today. I want a quiet word with you; that's if you can spare me a few minutes? And I know you'd like a fresh cup,' she said, looking between the two girls.

'I'll need to go and wash my hands before I go back onto the shop floor,' Freda said. 'That bun was delicious, but I do make a mess when I'm eating my food.'

The other two chuckled, as Freda was known for making a mess.

'Please, do stay,' Maureen pleaded. 'It's just that I know as soon as I start talking in the canteen someone will want serving, and then I won't get round to saying what I've got to say.'

Freda stood up. 'Sit yourself down here, Maureen, you need to rest your feet. I can perch myself here.' She sat on the edge of Sarah's desk.

Maureen cleared her throat. 'The thing is . . . well, the thing is, I've decided to cut my hours at Woolworths. Your dad says I don't really need to work as much as I do, what with my leg still playing up since my injury.'

Sarah's heart skipped a beat. She wondered if this meant Maureen wouldn't be able to look after the children as much as she had been; and then she felt guilty for even thinking of asking her to take on more grandparent duties. Here she was thinking she'd be able to do longer hours herself, but expecting Maureen to be there to help her, when she really should be taking things easy. Maureen's health had not been the same since she was caught up in the New Cross bombing during the later end of the war – the same incident in which Sarah's mother, Irene, had been killed.

'You need to do what you think is best,' Sarah said, looking a little glum.

'We'll miss your delicious lunches and cakes,' Freda added.

'I haven't told Betty or Tony yet,' Maureen said. 'I just thought I'd let you know first, Sarah, what with you being family. Of course, that includes you too, Freda.'

'When do you think this will be?'

'Not for a few weeks, as Betty will need time to find someone else who can work in the staff canteen. When I discussed this with your dad he suggested I start a couple of hours later in the morning and finish after the lunchtime rush, and work one day less. Do you feel it's too much of a cheek to suggest such a thing to Betty? It could make a difference to you as well,' she said, looking at the worried expression on Sarah's face.

Here it comes, Sarah thought to herself. Perhaps Alan's wish for me to give up work and be a full-time mum is about to come to fruition. 'You have to do what you think is best. No one wants you to tire yourself out, and being on your feet in the canteen must really take it out of you. I know that the few times I've helped you in there, I've been exhausted by the time I got home. I don't know how you've done it all these years,' she said, trying to keep her tone upbeat.

'Yes, and it means I can spend more time with the children. I'd dearly love that, and I might even have a bit of puff left in me at the end of the day to help you at the Brownie pack meetings, Freda.'

'I'd not say no to that, Maureen,' Freda grinned.

'I'm a little confused,' Sarah said. 'How will you see more of the children? Of course, I love them being with you, but if you're cutting back on what you're doing . . . ?'

'Oh dear, I've not made myself very clear, have I? It was your dad's idea. We thought it would help you and Alan out if we were able to care for the children a little more. Perhaps take them to school in the mornings and collect them afterwards, and keep them until you finish work? Your nan is getting on a bit now, and although she dearly loves having them, I know the stroll up to the school isn't easy for her – especially when the weather is bad. Your dad suggested I take over, that's if you agree? He said he would help out too, as he can now use the car more with petrol rationing finally easing up. Of course, we would need to put all this to Ruby in such a way that she doesn't think we're saying she's over the hill.'

Sarah clapped a hand to her mouth. Thank goodness she hadn't said anything. She'd completely got the wrong end of the stick. Here she was assuming that Maureen wanted to give up work and caring for Georgina and Buster – when in fact, all along she'd been thinking of the family and how much more help she could give. Getting up from her seat, she gave a surprised Maureen a big hug.

'You've got no idea how helpful that would be. But perhaps I ought to say – and of course you've not heard this either, Freda – I've been asked to put in extra hours. Betty has offered me a job managing the part-time staff and the Saturday girls.' She looked sideways at Freda, hoping that her friend wouldn't be disappointed. She needn't have worried.

'That's a marvellous idea. Tony had hinted to me that a vacancy would be opening. I got the feeling he was sounding me out, but to be honest, I love being a supervisor on the shop floor. Sitting behind a desk and having to tell all those Saturday girls what to do and what not to do would scare me rigid. You will be perfect for the job, Sarah.'

It was Maureen's turn to hug Sarah. 'I love having the children, and the extra hours don't matter to me. If ever I do have something on, I'm sure your nan will take them for a few hours. But don't you worry about that. Fancy me having a daughter-in-law who works in management. Wouldn't your mum have been proud of you,' she said, pulling a handkerchief from her sleeve and blowing her nose loudly. 'It's silly of me, considering I'm now married to your dad, but Irene was a friend of mine for many years. I do miss her, even with her funny ways.'

The three women fell silent for a moment, thinking of Irene Caselton.

'I don't thank you enough, Maureen, for keeping Mum's memory alive and telling the children all about their nanny who died. It means a lot to me. Thank you,' Sarah said, leaning over to give her another hug before wiping her eyes. 'Just before you came in we were talking about Nan being seventy later in the year, and how it's Dad's fiftieth birthday soon. It's very remiss of me not to have thought of this before now. We wondered if you'd thought of anything we could do to celebrate the event?'

Maureen beamed. 'Well, it goes without saying I'm going to bake a cake. I thought perhaps we could have everybody over to our house for a bit of a party. But you know what that would mean, don't you?'

The younger women chuckled. 'I do indeed,' Sarah said. 'The men would be in the garden with the beer barrel while the women sat in the front room with tea and cakes, and perhaps a glass of sherry.'

'That's why I've decided we ought to have a good old-fashioned knees-up. So I popped into the Prince of Wales and the landlord said the hall's available for Saturday week. Do you think we can organize a party by then? And should we tell your dad?'

Sarah clapped her hands in glee. 'Oh, that would be wonderful; it seems such an age since we had a party. We've had some lovely celebrations in that hall, haven't we?'

'We've had some sad events too, but let's forget about them for now,' Freda said. 'Tony should be home from his travels as well, so I'll have a husband to dance with.'

'There is one small thing,' Maureen said. 'We should start the party nice and early, with so many children in the family now. That will mean they can join in and be part of the celebration.'

'With us just living across the road, the youngsters could kip at our house. I'll have my next-door neighbour and her daughter keep an eye on them,' Sarah suggested. 'I'll fit them all in somehow.'

'Then that's a plan,' Maureen said, getting to her feet

slowly. 'I must get back, but just before I go – was that Maisie I saw driving a van? Whatever is going on there? I knew George was giving her lessons, but . . .'

'Maisie did say that I could let you all know,' Sarah said before explaining about the factory as quickly as she could, knowing Maureen needed to be back behind her counter. 'The only problem is, as I've just told Freda, the thought of that location down on the marshes seems to have upset Nan. She told me about how she used to work in the munitions factory down there – until the explosion.'

Maureen's face clouded over for a moment. 'It was a dark time for the town. You know there were twelve young women killed, along with their foreman? It was awful, the whole area was in mourning. I've a newspaper tucked away at home – I'll dig it out to show you. It was even in the national papers. Someone said they saw it on the Pathé News, that's how tragic it was. Your nan was hurt, but not too badly, and of course your Granddad Eddie rescued her. I always thought that was quite a love story, after everything that had happened to them before that. You'll need to sit down with your dad, he will tell you all about it. I'd not bring it up with your nan, as there was too much heartache at the time. And now Eddie has passed on and she's married to Bob . . . it's not good to rake over old coals.'

Both girls nodded.

'No one would think to look at her and Bob that they've not been together much longer than five years,' Maureen went on. 'She's truly a lucky woman to have fallen in love twice in her lifetime. Some of us have had to wait many years to marry the man of our dreams.'

Freda cuffed a tear away from her eyes. 'That's so moving,

I've come over all unnecessary. You'd never think older people would fall in love, would you?'

Maureen roared with laughter. 'Not so much of the old, young lady. There's a lot of life in the old dog yet, as they say,' she grinned before waving goodbye to them.

Alone in the office, the two women looked at each other, amazed at what Maureen had just told them.

'You do know, Freda, that we can't put all of this in the children's projects. But it would be lovely to know what happened in Nan's life. I'm going to ask Dad before it's too late . . . Now what's going on?' she said, as somebody hammered on her office door. 'Come in, please, before you knock the door off its hinges.'

The door flew open and one of the younger employees rushed in. 'Please, miss, I didn't want to bother Mrs Billington,' she gasped, looking fearfully towards the wall that separated the two offices. 'Something's going on downstairs with one of the Saturday girls and a customer. There's such a ruction. Do you think you could come and help?' She looked between Sarah and Freda, trying to catch her breath.

'Lead the way,' Sarah said, looking longingly towards their half-drunk tea. All that talking had made her dry. No doubt this cup would be cold too by the time they got back.

'Don't worry,' Freda whispered as they followed the young girl down the corridor, 'let's have a fresh one when we get back. I wonder which of the girls is causing the problem? I have a feeling it may be Betty's eldest, and that's why we've been summoned rather than Betty.'

'You may just be right,' Sarah grimaced.

5

'Oh my goodness, whatever is all this noise?' Sarah said as she came onto the shop floor from the staff entrance. All the customers appeared to be watching a kerfuffle by the haberdashery counter. 'Betty will be livid if she finds out what's been happening down here. Where are all the supervisors?'

'Well, I'm one of them, so that leaves three working today. Two are taking their tea breaks, as by now I should have been back from mine – not that I'm making excuses for anyone,' Freda said, hurrying to keep up with Sarah, who, hands on hips and an indignant expression on her face, was heading for the scene of the altercation.

Tapping the shoulder of a shop assistant who was standing watching, she gave a sharp instruction: 'Joan, please serve these customers.' Then she turned to the audience, smiling politely. 'Ladies, if you'd like to go to the other end of this counter, you will be served immediately.' She ushered them towards the opposite end of the long mahogany counter, calling on two other assistants to help clear the crowd.

Freda hurried over to where a Saturday girl was arguing with a young woman, who had her by the hair and was berating her loudly.

'You think you're so posh, and look at you there, in your scruffy shop girl uniform. You'll never amount to anything, Clementine Billington, as long as that woman your father married works here in this cheap store. I'm surprised you've got the nerve to even attend our school.'

Clemmie Billington cried out in pain as a handful of her hair came away in the girl's fist. 'Get off me,' she spat back. 'How dare you talk to me like that? I'm better than you any day of the week. My proper mother came from a respected family – it's not my fault I'm made to work here. I shall have my father report you to your parents.'

Sarah joined Freda, noticing that Clemmie's younger sister was crying. 'Go upstairs and wash your face, Dorothy, and then return to your counter. Freda, I'll deal with this – would you make sure we don't have any other customers watching? Perhaps ask the other assistants what happened?'

'Consider it done,' Freda replied, hurrying off to rally the staff and get the store back to some kind of normality.

Sarah tapped the shoulder of the girl who was still spitting words at Clemmie. 'You can let go of her hair now. This is not very ladylike, is it?' she said, looking stern.

The girl glanced at Sarah, noticed that she was dressed in a suit rather than the burgundy-coloured uniform of the other Woolworths workers, and immediately let go. 'You're not her mother, are you?' she asked, looking worried.

'No, I'm not,' Sarah said through pursed lips.

'Well, she started it. She was rude to me, so she got what she deserved. Clementine and Dorothy Billington act far too superior considering they work in Woolworths.'

A red-faced Clemmie shook her head, cuffing away angry tears from her face. She made to step forward, but Sarah held her at arm's length with one hand. 'Oh no you don't, madam. You are to go to my office. But first wash your face, and then wait there until I join you. Do you understand?'

'Yes, Mrs Gilbert,' Clemmie replied in a sulky voice.

'Young lady, you are a customer in this store. If it were not so, I'd be telling you how I feel about your actions. I know the school you both attend, and I will be writing a letter to the headmistress as well as Mr and Mrs Billington. We will not have this kind of behaviour in our store, do you understand? May I help you complete your purchases before I escort you outside?'

'Don't bother,' the girl snapped back. She stomped away to join a group of her friends who were waiting, giggling, by the main doors.

Sarah took a deep breath. That was an initiation of fire, she thought to herself. As she turned towards a line of women being served further along the counter, they burst into a spontaneous round of applause.

'Well done, love,' one of them called out. 'I know we was all young girls once, but blimey, that was a right catfight.'

Sarah gave them a demure smile and beckoned Freda to her side. 'I'm going to have a few words with Clemmie up in my office. When, or if, she comes back downstairs, would you move her to another section? That way she won't end up chatting with the girls on her counter about what happened, and hopefully it will all blow over.'

'Of course; I can put her on the bread counter. She'll be busy there and not have time to chat. What do you intend to tell Betty?'

'I'm not sure. First I'm going to see what that young madam has to say for herself.'

'Good luck with that – she's a right little snob. I've always felt sorry for Betty having to bring up that girl. Her sister Dorothy is a delightful child.'

Sarah had always thought there was more to Clemmie than Freda was suggesting, and now she felt a pang of sympathy for the child. 'I promise I'll catch up later; perhaps we can have lunch together? I fancy stepping over the road to Mitchell's cafe, or we could collect a sandwich from our canteen and take a walk. I know it's chilly out there but it's not raining, and if we wander down to the riverside, at least it will blow the cobwebs away. You can tell me what it was you came to my office to talk about?'

'Let's do that,' Freda said before she headed off to check that all was in order on the shop floor.

Sarah climbed the stairs to her office, full of trepidation. As a rule she had no qualms about interviewing staff who had problems; it was something she did often when Betty wasn't available, as Tony never wanted to deal with staff. He was always busy and left that kind of thing to Sarah. She regularly came into work to find a note on her desk asking her to talk to a member of the female staff.

Standing outside her office door, she ran her fingers through her hair and straightened her jacket. At least she was wearing a suit today, and although she said it herself, the dark green tweed looked very smart as work clothing. She liked to follow Betty Billington's style of dress, as she believed it commanded respect.

Pushing the door open, she could see Clemmie standing by the window looking out over the busy shopping street. From that window could be seen and heard the hub of the busy town, with shops that stretched the length of Pier

Road. Even from behind, Sarah could see the girl was extremely tense. Her shoulders were stiff and her hands were clenched at her sides, the knuckles showing white.

'Sit down, Clementine,' Sarah instructed, taking her own seat on the opposite side of the desk. Leaning her elbows on the tabletop, she threaded her fingers together and tried to project what she hoped was an air of authority, while still appearing friendly.

'Can you tell me what that was all about?' she asked, hoping that the girl would explain and make things easier for both of them.

Clemmie looked towards the door. 'You won't call my stepmother, will you? She will be so angry with me. And please, can you call me Clemmie?'

Sarah nodded. 'Of course I can. Clemmie, I am staff supervisor here, and as long as we can sort out any problems, they won't have to go further than this room. However, if I do have any concerns, they will be placed on your employee record. You understand, don't you? To be honest, if there are complaints from customers over this, I may have to consider giving you your cards. That wouldn't make a very good start to your career, would it?'

'It's only a Saturday job – it's not as if it's proper work. Besides, she started it.'

Sarah sighed. This wasn't going to be as easy as she'd hoped. 'As far as I'm concerned, anyone who clocks on here, whether full time or part time, works for F. W. Woolworth and carries out a valid job. Even if you only planned to be here for a few months, you are an employee and as such you will obey our rules. Do you understand, Clemmie? When you do move on to full-time employment, whatever that may be, you'll take with you a reference from your time here. How would any future employer react to hearing that you had a record of fighting with customers? Now, why don't you tell me exactly what happened?'

The penny seemed to drop as Clemmie Billington looked down into her lap and gave a shuddering sigh. 'She hates me; that's why I don't like working here.'

Sarah was confused. Was she talking about Betty – were things that bad at home? 'Who hates you?' she coaxed, as the girl fell silent.

'That Susan Woods. She told me at school the other day that she really hates me and everything to do with me, and if ever she sees me outside of school, she'll cause trouble for me.'

Sarah understood that some young children could be quite spiteful, and Betty had once told her that when Clemmie and Dorothy were younger they'd been bullied at school. But she had sorted out that problem and moved the girls to a better school. So why was this happening now? Clemmie had never been the friendliest of children, but that could be put down to shyness. Come to think about it, Sarah had never actually seen the girl with anyone other than her sister, and Maisie's daughters. Granted she was almost a grown-up now; but what with Betty keeping her in school longer, hoping to give her the best possible chance of a bright future, she hadn't mixed with many adults in the workplace. Her manner was still very much that of a schoolgirl.

'There must be a reason why somebody hates you, Clemmie. Have you done anything to upset the girl?'

'No, it's not that at all. It's just . . . well, her father died six months ago, and she's changed so much since then. It didn't help that her mother used Daddy's undertaker's business to bury her husband. Now it's as if she blames our family for her dad being dead. I've tried to keep away from her as much as possible, but she knows I work here, and . . .' Her voice cracked with emotion.

'I commend you for that and agree that to keep out of her way is the best course of action. I'm afraid in this life we never quite know how people will react when things aren't going well in their lives. I'm sorry to hear that she's blamed you. Is there anything I can do to help?' As Clemmie only shrugged sadly, she went on: 'I know your mother would very much like you to go to university at some stage, and that means knuckling down and working hard at school. However, if this girl is going to be a thorn in your side, it won't be conducive to learning. Betty has such hopes for your future. Between you and me, she wants your late mother's family to see that she has guided you well on your path to adulthood. So we must do what we can to sort this little problem out, don't you think?'

'That's my other problem,' Clemmie said, looking up at Sarah. Her eyes brimmed with tears. 'I don't want to go to university – I really don't. I want to work in business, and I *do* want to do well for myself. I really do wish that Maisie was my mother. I envy Bessie and Claudette, being able to work in their mother's new business.'

'You too have a mother in business,' Sarah said, trying to appear sympathetic.

'A manager at Woolworths is not quite the same, is it? Besides, Betty is not my mother.'

Sarah had anticipated something like this. From what

Betty had told her, the girls were prone to coming out with such comments whenever life didn't go their way. 'Betty loves you dearly, so please don't deny her the chance to care for you like a daughter. You have no idea how proud she is of you both. Don't you think she'd have refused your father's proposal if she didn't want to be your mother too?'

Clemmie thought about Sarah's words. 'Please don't think I hate Betty. It's just that if my mother had lived, I would have been taken into the family company by my grandparents and would have had a place on the board by the time I was twenty-one, just like Mother did.'

Sarah shook her head, perplexed. 'I understand that your mother's family no longer owns shares in department stores, so it's not as if your father can approach them to offer you a career. Perhaps you should consider another profession? I truly do feel you should speak to Betty about this. Woolworths is a wonderful company to work for and you could go far, just as she has. She's not one to blow her own trumpet, but she had a hard time after her fiancé, who was your father's friend in the trenches during the Great War, died. She is an example of how so many older women have forged a path so that younger women like you and Dorothy can have a brighter working life.'

Clemmie's eyes lit up with interest. 'Was she a suffragette?'

Sarah smiled. 'You need to talk with Betty, as it's not my story to tell. All I can say is, she wants you to value your education and use it to succeed in life. Forget that girl and think of your future.'

An expression of fear crossed Clemmie's face. She reminded Sarah of a wounded animal. 'You don't understand –

Susan is just one of a group who all seem to think they're going into brilliant jobs, courtesy of their fathers. She has been denied that and is turning them all against me because my stepmother works for Woolworths and Daddy is an undertaker. All this talk of how, now the war is over, the world has opened up for women – it's just not true. It all depends on who and what our parents are. I feel as though everyone wants me to do so well . . . but I truly don't know what to do with my life. And that girl coming into the store today, seeing me as nothing but someone selling buttons, was just too much. I had stepped away from the counter so that our customers wouldn't overhear the spiteful things she was saying, and as I tried to ask her to please not be so unkind . . . she attacked me.' Clemmie put her hand to the side of her face, touching a scratch that Sarah had only just noticed. 'She just attacked me. Why would somebody do that? All because I was working in a shop? Can you not imagine what my life will be like if I end up working for Woolworths full time, or if I stay at school? I will never escape those nasty people,' she said, starting to shake before covering her face with her hands. She began sobbing so violently that Sarah got up and hurried round the desk to give her a hug. Clemmie might be close to adulthood, but to all intents and purposes she was simply a child in despair. Sarah's heart ached for her.

'Now, you're probably going to laugh at me, Clemmie, but I'm going to take a leaf out of Betty's book.' She leant back over the desk, opening the top drawer, from where she took out a clean white handkerchief. 'You know, way back when I was only a few years older than you, I sat in

Betty's office sobbing my heart out over a falling-out with my Alan – and Betty gave me one of her clean handkerchiefs. She must have given away hundreds during the time she's worked here. Then she went to fetch a cup of tea for us both. You may laugh, as it's something that Nanny Ruby would do, but it does help, believe me. Especially if there's a biscuit on the saucer.'

Clemmie hiccupped into the handkerchief and nodded, doing her best not to meet Sarah's eyes. 'That would be nice. Nanny Ruby is very wise,' she replied, glancing up for a moment then looking back at the handkerchief, as if taking in Sarah's words.

It warmed Sarah's heart the way all the younger girls called her grandmother Nanny Ruby, even if they weren't related. It showed how much Ruby was loved. 'You stay there and take a few deep breaths to calm yourself and gather your thoughts. I will be back in a couple of ticks, then we can have a chat about your problem . . . what do you say?'

Clemmie scrubbed at her eyes, making them even redder. 'I'd like that, but please don't say anything to Betty. I feel such a fool, and it makes me look so ungrateful when I don't really mean to be. Life can be so difficult . . .'

Sarah promised it would be their secret, and hurried from the room. Although she wanted to help the child, she knew she'd never get any work done at this rate – and there was Betty hoping to have a chat with her later. Although she loved her friend dearly, she could honestly say she'd not managed to clear any of her paperwork today.

She stopped suddenly as a thought came to her, causing somebody behind her in the corridor to almost cannon into her. She apologized, although the thought she'd had made her nod to herself as she entered the staff canteen. Yes, that might be the answer – for now, at least . . .

'Well, I think you're mad,' Freda said as she bit into her corned-beef sandwich. The pair were bundled up in their coats and scarves, but still enjoying their time away from work as they sat huddled on a wooden bench looking out over the River Thames. There were very few people about, and most of them seemed to be hurrying on their way as it was too chilly to hang about at this time of year. 'Whatever made you think of that idea?'

'I just wanted to help the girl. Now that I'm a staff supervisor, it seems right that I should do something to help one of our Saturday girls who's so terribly unhappy. I need to run it past Betty, though.'

'And don't forget you've not discussed your job with Alan yet, coward that you are. He may not be too keen on you taking on more hours.'

'I am a coward; and Alan would be upset if he thought I couldn't talk to him about this. His business is starting to do so well, and now he has James working with him, he can get so much more done. I feel the bad days have passed.'

The two friends fell silent as they stared out over the Thames, remembering the day that James's brother Lemuel had perished in the river. It had been Freda and Tony's wedding day. Lemuel had not long married their friend Sadie, and his death had left her alone with two children.

'He's lucky to have James. He comes up with so many brilliant ideas, but at the same time he keeps Alan's feet firmly on the ground,' Sarah added. 'I agree with you, it's daft of me to even be thinking of taking on more work when all I ever wanted to be was a wife and mother. But this optimism since the end of the war seems to have grabbed hold of me. Why, the other evening, after we listened to Margaret Roberts's speech and Betty started to say how much she admired the woman – well, it had me thinking I should do more with my life than just be a wife and have a family.' She flashed an apologetic look at Freda. 'I'm sorry – you will have your own family one day, and then you'll know how I feel. Which reminds me, what was it you were going to tell me this morning? So much has happened, we never got round to our chat.'

'I just wanted to let you know about something Tony mentioned. You know how he's helping to train the cyclists for the 1952 Olympics, and management have allowed him some time off to do that alongside his job? I suppose it's a feather in their cap to know one of the staff is so heavily involved in the Olympics, and working for our country to gain more medals. Why, he's even thinking of setting up a Woolworths cycling club, and has written to the editor of *The New Bond* asking if he might be able to put a few words about it in next month's issue.' *The New Bond* was Woolworths' staff magazine.

'That's an excellent idea. And if we have a local branch of the group, I'd quite like to join in. Not for racing in the Olympics, you understand,' Sarah chuckled. 'More for the exercise. Alan is talking about the children having bicycles soon, because he has one – which is much safer than riding his motorbike,' she snorted, remembering Freda had also toppled off a few motorcycles in her time. 'It will be a way for us to do something together as a family, don't you agree?'

'Of course I do. I'm always out cycling with Tony. Perhaps I could join you – we could even invite Betty and Maisie and take a picnic, that's when it's a bit warmer.' Freda shivered, screwing up the paper bag that had contained her lunch and putting it in her pocket.

'So, what's the problem? I take it there is one?' Sarah asked, thinking she'd have to get back to her office soon.

'Well, Tony's been informed it's time for him to take over a branch as a full-time manager, since he's done so well working in the team that's been inspecting the stores. It doesn't look as though he will be sharing managerial duties at Erith as he was before.'

'That's marvellous news,' Sarah said, hugging Freda before brushing a few crumbs from her friend's hair. 'Sorry about that – you must be thrilled? I wonder where he'll be sent . . . Crayford, or perhaps Bexleyheath? At least he'll be home more often and not travelling around the country.'

'It is wonderful news. But the chances are he will be moved to another part of the country permanently,' Freda said sadly.

'But you must be so proud of him?' Sarah asked, trying to encourage Freda to see the positive side even though she would miss her friend terribly.

'I am, Sarah. But I don't want to leave Erith and my friends. How can I tell Tony? I can't hold him back, can I?'

6

'That smells good,' Alan said as he squeezed past Sarah in their small kitchen to wash his hands in the deep stone sink.

'It's just a bit of mutton stew and dumplings. I'll be glad when rationing and shortages are a thing of the past and I can put decent food on the table again,' she said, turning to kiss his cheek.

'Sounds good to me. Your dad is visiting later. He wants to chat to us, well, you in particular, about something or other. I thought perhaps afterwards we could go to the Prince of Wales and have a quick pint. Do you fancy coming with us?'

'If you don't mind, I think I'll stay in. My feet are killing me and I've not seen much of the children all day, what with working. Besides, it would be a cheek to ask next door to sit with them at short notice. Actually, Alan, there's something I want to talk to you about . . .'

'Fire away,' he said as he opened the biscuit tin. 'Oh, it's empty.'

'I meant to pick up some broken biscuits from work, but I completely forgot. Do you know, I had to break up a fight this morning on the shop floor. I certainly wasn't expecting anything like that.'

'You should have let one of the warehousemen sort it out. You could have been injured,' he said sharply. 'Breaking up fights – it's not work for a woman.'

'Oh, heavens, it was two young girls fighting. I'd not have stepped in if it had been men brawling. All the same, it was quite stressful; once I'd had a word with the Saturday girl involved I felt quite shaken, so much so I grabbed a sandwich and walked down to the waterfront to take a breather with Freda. She told me Tony's been offered the chance of promotion, to manage a larger store.'

She looked sideways to see how Alan was taking the news. There was a time that he'd been destined for management with Woolworths himself, until war interrupted their lives, and afterwards he'd left the RAF and decided to set up his own motorbike workshop. She often wondered if, deep down, he regretted not staying with the company. She needn't have worried.

'Rather him than me – I wouldn't relish a life where I was at the beck and call of senior management all day and every day. What does the kid say about moving away? I doubt Tony will be given a local store.' 'Kid' was his nickname for Freda; Alan had called her by that name ever since she'd arrived in town at a young age, and he still treated her like a kid sister.

'She's not happy about it and is torn in two. She loves her life here, but she wants to see Tony succeed. Alan, please don't say anything – it's for Freda to share her news. They need to sort it out for themselves. I would hate Tony to think we've been gossiping.'

He ran his hand across his lips. 'Consider them closed,' he laughed before looking serious. 'Are you sure you're up to working Saturdays? I hope it won't be too often, as I like to think of you here at home.'

'Well, the thing is . . .' She stopped speaking as Buster rushed into the kitchen to ask if his dinner was ready.

'It won't be long. I'm just waiting for the dumplings to cook through. Go back in the other room and finish your jigsaw puzzle, I'm trying to talk to your daddy.'

'You were saying?'

'The thing is, Betty has offered me a promotion. It will be more money,' she added quickly, before he had a chance to speak.

Alan was thoughtful. 'I know there was a time when we were chasing every penny, but those days are gone now. We're doing all right at the shop, and with the ideas I have for expanding, we could go far. You've got to think about the children, Sarah; you can't keep passing them from pillar to post just so that you can go to work.'

She was indignant. 'So you want me to stay at home, waiting for when you can spare me a few hours and when the children need me?' she said, feeling slightly better for voicing her point of view. 'That time when we were desperate for every penny could easily return. You're a great provider for our family, but still, I'd like to go out and do something useful. Perhaps if I can't work at Woolworths, I could work for you in the shop? I could reorganize everything, what with having the knowledge from my time working at Woolies.' She crossed her fingers behind her back as she spoke. Alan had often said that a repair shop was no place for a woman.

He shook his head quickly. 'No, no – I don't think it would be right for us to work together. Tell me more about this promotion?'

As she started to take knives and forks from the drawer of the green-painted dresser and polish them on a tea towel, Sarah told him about taking charge of the part-time staff as well as Saturday girls and how it would mean her working on Saturdays. 'Betty reckons I'm good with youngsters. And I know for a fact she's not; she can't even handle her own children, at least not the older girls.'

'What makes you say that?'

'It was her Clemmie, the oldest girl, who was in the catfight at the store today. But I think I've solved the problem with her.'

'You mean the Billingtons' posh eldest daughter was fighting in the store? That has made my day,' Alan chuckled.

'Betty had a lot to learn when she married Douglas and took on his two daughters, considering she'd never cared for children before. I think she's done a pretty good job, to be fair – but Clemmie is now a wilful young woman, and this girl she fought with was quite spiteful about Betty and Douglas being in trade. We can't blame her for fighting back. All in all, I feel Clemmie is a nice girl, and I'm prepared to help. She's had terrible problems at school.'

Alan groaned. 'I should have guessed you would. As long as she doesn't end up living under our roof, you can do as you please.'

'What, you mean I can take the job?' Sarah shrieked, placing the salt and pepper pots on the table in order to give him a hug. 'I promise I won't neglect the family; I can prepare dinner before I go out to work, so that when you come home everything will be the same as usual. Your mum's not going to be working as many hours because of her leg playing up, and she said she can take the kids on more while I'm working. And that was before I told her about the promotion. She thinks we ought to stop relying on Nan quite as much, now she's getting on a bit. She'll be seventy in the summer.'

Alan released his wife from his arms and stroked a wisp of hair back from her face with one finger. 'Mum's right,' he said. 'But will she be taking on too much?'

'The mornings are fine for her. She wants to be home for Dad when he gets back from Vickers in the afternoons, now that he's often out on council business in the evenings. I think it's quite sweet.'

'As long as they're both fine with it. I don't want you tired out of an evening, and I don't want us putting pressure on my mother – or come to that, Ruby either.'

Sarah agreed with him. 'Come on, let's eat this stew before it burns to the bottom of the pan. I want to be cleared up before Dad comes round. Did he say what time he's coming?'

After they'd finished eating and the children were in bed, George Caselton arrived. He gave his daughter a big hug as he came in. 'Something smells good.'

Sarah chuckled. 'What is it with you men? Alan said exactly the same when he came in from work. It's only a bit of mutton stew, would you like some? There's enough left over for tomorrow. I do like to make a big pot.'

'No, love, it's all right. I'm full to the gills with Maureen's fish pie. Just like you, she made enough for another day,' he grimaced. 'Is Alan allowed out for the evening?'

'Oh Dad, you make me sound like his jailer. Alan can do what he wants; he's worked hard all day, so he deserves a pint just like you do. He's having a shave at the moment, so you've got time to tell me what's been going on in the world of politics.' She pointed to a cosy armchair by the fireside where he could sit in comfort.

'I'm sure you don't want me talking about local problems with buildings, drains and dodgy landlords. A lot of my work as a councillor is quite mundane, you know.'

'But you love doing it, Dad. You are so good at helping people by sorting out their problems and putting the other party to rights.'

George chuckled. 'I have to agree with you there, and I much prefer helping people to the council's many committee meetings. I will say the highlight so far has been meeting young Margaret Roberts; you know that woman is going to go far.'

'Do you think she's going to win the seat for Dartford and Erith?'

George rubbed his chin thoughtfully. 'I'm not sure she'll win this time, but mark my words, one day she'll take a seat in parliament – and God help anyone who crosses her then. That woman knows her own mind, and woe betide anyone who treads on her toes.'

'Oh Dad, do you have a soft spot for her? Next you'll be saying she's a future prime minister. Mind you, there's a few women who feel it's about time we took control to sort this country out.'

'Now, love, don't you start talking like the rest of them.

Common sense flies out the window when people get political. Besides, that's not why I came round here.'

'I know – you came to collect Alan for a drink. It's a shame the kiddies are all tucked up in bed. They'd have liked to see their granddad.'

'I'll see them tomorrow. I'll take them for a drive.'

'They'll love that. Buster keeps asking why we haven't got a car instead of that rusty old van Alan uses for the shop. I've refused to go in it as it's so dirty and scruffy.'

'You'll get your car one day, don't you worry. Before then, you've got your dad to act as your chauffeur. You know you've only got to call and I'll come running,' he winked.

'Don't you mean you'll come driving?'

George shook his head. 'You're in a good mood this evening. What cheered you up?' he asked, noticing his daughter's pink cheeks and happy smile. Too often, it seemed as if Sarah carried the world on her shoulders and her delightful smile was dampened.

Sarah explained about her promotion at Woolworths and how Alan had agreed it was a good idea, what with Maureen having the children to taking some pressure off Ruby. 'I can go to work with an easy conscience. But tell me, didn't Alan say there was something you wanted to talk to me about tonight? I'm intrigued.'

'I take it Maureen's told you she wants to throw me a party for my fiftieth birthday? I'm worried she'll go overboard and invite every Tom, Dick and Harry from up the council. I just want you to keep an eye on what's going on. Let's make it a family and friends occasion, shall we?'

'Of course, Dad, I agree with you. It's better that way, isn't it? I'm pretty certain Maureen won't want the mayor

69

and his like arriving – she's as uncomfortable with them as I am. I'm not sure about Nan, though; she quite likes rubbing shoulders with them and pretending she's posh, especially since you bought her that fur stole.' Sarah didn't add that she thought some of the councillors' wives were rather snobbish and not very nice. 'It's so much better to have friends and family come along for a knees-up.'

'Then I'll rely on you to keep an eye on Maureen and make sure she doesn't get carried away.'

'I'll do that, Dad,' she said, before teasing George for being a coward. 'By the way, Maisie took me to see the factory where she's going to run her business. I understand you know all about it, having checked it over for her?'

George looked a little embarrassed. 'I did want to tell you, love, but it wasn't my story to share. I only gave it the once-over to make sure it was a sound investment. She will go far, that girl, considering she only wanted to sew for her friends. It's a good job she's learnt to drive, though, as it's a fair trek down that lane to the marshes. It makes me wonder if she'll get staff to travel down there to work for her?'

Her dad mentioning the marshes made Sarah think of Ruby. 'Dad . . . how come we never knew about Nan working down the munitions factory on the day of the explosion? I was quite shocked at how upset she was when she said she wouldn't be going to visit Maisie's factory.'

'It was a terrible affair, love. Your nan was nearly killed, and if it wasn't for your Granddad Eddie, God knows what would've happened. We'd have lost her for sure, like so many people lost loved ones that day. It's like the soldiers who don't talk about the time they served in the two wars; your nan's never opened up about that place. I put it down to the shock of what she must have seen that day. It was your granddad who told me how he found her. I'll tell you something for nothing: it brought your nan and him closer together. In fact, they never left each other's side until the day he passed away.'

'Oh Dad. It's just like one of those love stories in the magazines I read. I'll not mention it again. And I'll make sure when Georgina is doing her project for the Brownies and Girl Guides that I'm present, so Nan isn't asked a question that makes her feel uncomfortable. Here comes Alan – have a lovely evening, but don't let him come home blotto. He's going in to work tomorrow to catch up with his paperwork.'

Alan joined them, doing up his tie. 'What's that you're saying about work?' he asked.

'I'm saying you'll be busy tomorrow, just like every day,' Sarah smiled, straightening his tie for him.

'And he'll be even busier once he gets his television and wireless sets in the shop,' George grinned.

A silence descended on the room as Sarah gave Alan a questioning look.

As he leant in to kiss her cheek he whispered, 'We can talk later, eh?' before he and George left to go down the pub.

So much for never having secrets from each other, Sarah thought as she returned to the kitchen to clear up after their meal.

Once she'd finished the washing up and checked the children were sleeping soundly, she added a couple of pieces of coal to the fire and settled down with her knitting. At times like these, she relished the silence. She didn't even put the wireless set on, so the only sound came from the fire as the coals settled. Yes, it was good not to have worries – although the thought of Alan and his television sets niggled her, but she'd not fret. No doubt it would all be explained in good time.

Her mind wandered back over the day. She'd been slightly wary about venturing into Betty's office that afternoon to discuss the offered promotion. She felt a little guilty about having jumped the gun and said that she'd take it before talking things over with Alan.

'Oh, I'm delighted,' Betty had said, giving her a warm smile. 'We will make a good team, you and I; it will be such a weight off my mind to know you are taking care of the part-time staff, especially the Saturday girls. There are quite a few of them, and it can eat into my day. Perhaps in time you'd like to take on the hiring and firing of our full-time staff as well?'

'I'm not so sure about the firing side of it,' Sarah replied, 'but I'd quite like to become involved with the hiring of staff. After all, I've been there myself and been taught by an expert. I like to feel I'll be sympathetic to those who are wary about completing application forms and planning their work around their families. We also have men who are still returning to work after call-up, and that's a big change in their lives. Yes, I think I could be sympathetic and also firm,' she added.

'A little bird tells me there was a problem you had to sort out this morning?' Betty asked, raising an eyebrow.

Oh God, Sarah thought, she doesn't miss a thing. However did I think I could get away with not informing Betty about what happened in the store? 'It was something and nothing and has been sorted out, although there could

The Woolworths Saturday Girls

be an ongoing problem in the staff member's life,' she said, trying hard not to intimate that it was Betty's own daughter who had the problem.

'We must always care for the welfare of our employees, and not just think of them as people who are here between opening and closing time each day. What happens in their private lives can affect their work. What do you plan to do?'

Sarah gulped. 'The staff member is being bullied at school, and it seems working on the shop floor each Saturday leaves her open to intimidation by other girls who come here as customers. I sent them packing with a flea in their ear. I thought perhaps a letter to the head-mistress would be in order. It's fine if schoolchildren wish to come into the store to shop, but if they're entering our premises to intimidate one of our workers, something has to be done.'

'I totally agree,' Betty said, 'and if when you've written the letter you would like me to cast my eye over it, I'm here to help. Please don't think for one moment I'm checking up on you, Sarah; I trust you implicitly. However, young girls who have a bee in their bonnet may not stop turning up to pick on a Saturday girl. We may need to think further than just writing a letter to the headmistress. It could make for a tense situation, and again, this could overflow into the staff member's private life.'

'The girl seems to be intimidated because of her family and working in Woolworths. If she could be shown to have a responsible position, it might do much to help her confidence and show these other people that she's more than a Saturday girl working on the shop floor. Of course, there's

73

nothing wrong with that at all – I worked on the shop floor myself for many years.'

'And I too, in my early working life. There is nothing shameful about it at all. I do despair of these little snobs,' Betty said. 'But what can we do about the Saturday girl?'

'I'd like, with your permission, to make her a Saturday supervisor. Mainly she would be assisting me in my office, but she would also be a useful link between management and the Saturday girls on the shop floor. Perhaps we could give her a shilling a week pay rise to reflect the added responsibilities she would be taking on?'

Betty clapped her hands together in delight. 'That is an admirable suggestion. It will show head office that our Saturday girls aren't just here to work a few hours and earn some pocket money before leaving school, but are seen as valued members of staff. Well done, Sarah. Please keep me posted.'

Sarah got up to leave. As she opened the office door, Betty called out to her: 'By the way, what is the name of this girl?'

Sarah turned and gave her a rueful look. 'Her name is Clementine Billington.'

'Oh my,' Betty said, putting her hands to her face as Sarah returned to the desk.

'I didn't want to make a secret of it. I just thought, if you didn't know the name of the staff member, it would . . .'

'. . . It would allow me to think more dispassionately about the situation,' Betty finished for her.

'Yes, that's right. I didn't want to deceive you,' Sarah apologized. 'Does it still stand that I can offer Clemmie the position?'

Betty thought for a moment. 'I do still feel it is an admirable idea, but I'm disappointed in myself for not knowing my own stepdaughter was being bullied. Young girls can be so spiteful,' she murmured to herself. 'Of course, we will deal with that when – or rather, if – it happens again. Why not call Clemmie into your office now and give her the good news? You can say she will have another shilling in her pay packet each week. At least we will have a happy daughter at home over the weekend. That will be a pleasant change,' she smiled.

'I'm so pleased you agree,' Sarah said. 'It will be the making of her. Can I also tell her she doesn't have to wear an overall, and can come to work in a smart skirt and blouse?'

'Of course,' Betty said as her smile grew wider. 'Our poor staff will be groaning at having two Billington women supervising in the store.' She reached across the desk and took Sarah's hand, holding it tightly. 'Thank you for being so conscientious, and for being a good friend to my family. If you have any other ideas, please do bring them to me. I want us both to run a happy ship here at Store 397.'

7

Sarah loved Sundays. She liked to spend the day with Alan and the children, and perhaps go to Nan's or her dad's house for late tea in the afternoon. She wished she could invite all the family to their house, but a two-up, two-down with a small scullery on the back didn't give much room for entertaining – not in the winter months, anyway. When it was warmer at least they could sit out in the small garden at the back of the house, or even pack a picnic and meet up with friends and family at the recreation ground not far away.

Today she overcame the lure of her warm bed and got up early. There was washing to be done and hung out, and an early start meant a leisurely afternoon. She soon had the copper bubbling away and as the children had followed her downstairs she had their sheets washed and on the line before it was even nine o'clock. The children's clothing went out next, although she spent some time with a scrubbing brush and soap flakes cleaning off grass marks on Buster's shorts. Although it was still only late February, the sun was doing its utmost to break through the clouds, and a slight breeze meant the items hanging on the washing line were slowly drying. Sarah loathed damp washing hanging about the house and over the fireguard around the fire. She would often put items on a clotheshorse down in the cellar, which was as clean as the rest of the house; it had been used by Maureen as a shelter during the war.

Sarah had suggested to Alan that perhaps they could kit out the cellar as a bedroom for Buster. At the moment the two children were sharing a room, but it wouldn't be long before Georgina was too old to be sharing with her brother. At the back of her mind, Sarah knew the time was not far off for them to move on and find a house more suitable for their growing family. It was a conversation Alan would fight against, as he'd been born here and grown up being taught how to repair bicycles and motorbikes in the back garden by his father, who'd died when he was still young.

Shaking off her glum thoughts, she made a pot of tea and covered it with a brightly knitted tea cosy made by Freda in the days when she was learning to knit. It was rather out of shape and had been darned in a couple of places where her friend had dropped stitches, but it was much loved and would never be replaced. Sarah only needed to look at the tea cosy and she was back in the days before the war, when the girls didn't have a care in the world and could just enjoy each other's company, going dancing and to the pictures and sharing secrets. It had been a wonderful time in Sarah's life. It was then that she'd met and fallen in love with Alan.

'Pop upstairs and tell your dad there's fresh tea down here, love,' she called to Buster, who was lying on his back on the rug in front of the hearth examining a tin toy car.

As soon as Alan was down she'd collect the sheets from

their bed and get them washed and out on the line as well, she thought with a satisfied sigh. Then the copper could be emptied of the dirty water and the washing would be done for the week, apart from her personal bits and pieces which required hand-washing. Hopefully she could do the ironing this evening while listening to the wireless, once the kids were in bed and Alan had his nose in one of his books. It crossed her mind that he had a couple to be taken back to the Carnegie Library; she could do that in her lunch hour on Monday.

'Good morning, love,' Alan said as he appeared at the kitchen door. 'Is there any sugar for the tea? And I could kill a slice of toast.'

'Just about,' Sarah answered, checking the tin where she kept the sugar dry. 'Just imagine what it'll be like when rationing is over. It will be glorious to be able to spoon sugar into our tea without worrying if we have enough to last the week. Who'd have thought that nigh on five years after the war ended, we would still be counting every grain of sugar and using ration cards?'

Alan laughed. 'You sound just like your nan.'

'That's not a bad thing, is it?' she asked, unsure whether he was criticizing her.

'Not at all, you could do a lot worse than be like her. You just have some of her mannerisms.'

'I'll take that as a compliment,' Sarah said, thinking that she was glad she hadn't taken after her mum, Irene, who had been quite a cold woman.

'Why the sad face?'

'I was thinking of Mum and what might have been.'

'We can't look back, we can only look forward, love.

Remember your dad is married to my mum now, and they're very happy together.'

Sarah nodded, reaching up to tighten the scarf tied round her hair that saved it from going frizzy while she did the washing. Underneath the scarf she'd put in some curlers, hoping that once the washing was done and the scullery free of steam her hair would look half decent. 'I suppose you're right,' she said, rescuing the toasting bread before it burnt and placing it on a plate in front of Alan. 'Here you go – I'll top up your cup in a minute if you finish that.'

Alan seemed fidgety, she thought, as she carried on with her chores. 'Something on your mind?'

'I was just wondering if you'd like to take a walk with me later?'

'I don't know – it's quite a busy day, with our Georgie carrying the flag in the church parade this morning. She can't be late,' Sarah said, looking up at the clock. 'And Buster will be marching with the Cubs – which reminds me, I need to put an iron over Georgie's Brownie dress. After that, dinner will be ready, and don't forget we're going to your mum for tea later. It doesn't leave much time for walking. And it's still a bit chilly out there,' she said, thinking of how cold her fingers had been while pegging out the washing.

'I wasn't meaning a walk as such, more a wander up to the shop. There's something I want to show you. If you're not planning on staying on at the Baptist mission for the service, perhaps we could do it then?'

Sarah sighed. She'd thought that with the children out of the house for a couple of hours, she could tidy their bedroom and polish the furniture without interruptions. But looking at the anticipation on Alan's face made her feel she should agree to his request; besides, she was curious about what he wanted to show her.

'All right, let's do it. The housework can wait until later. Perhaps you can help me?' She smiled as his face went pale. 'I'm only joking,' she laughed. 'Georgie is old enough to cross the two roads to get to the Baptist Church, and I'm always drumming it into Buster to hold her hand, so now we will see if he can be trusted. Georgie will soon tell me if he misbehaves.'

'We could walk up there at the same time. It's on our way, and then we've only got to watch them walk up Queen Street and Freda will be there organizing the children.'

'Yes, and no doubt Akela will be there as well waiting for the Cubs – if not, Freda will keep an eye on Buster until the march starts.' She would have liked to watch, as she felt so proud of her children in their uniforms with their faces scrubbed shiny clean, marching along proudly. With Georgie chosen to carry the Brownie pennant, she was even prouder than usual. 'Dad did say he would walk down and take a photograph of them in their uniforms, so we'll have something to remember of the day. Now, I need to get our sheets washed and out on the line; then I only have your grubby overalls to do and I'm finished.' She always put Alan's overalls in last, as the soapy water was fit for nothing once they'd been through the wash. She could leave the hand-washing of her underwear until later today; it was still something she liked to do while alone.

Sarah and Alan stood watching as the children walked towards the Baptist Church. Up ahead, they could see Freda in her Brown Owl uniform. She waved to them. Now Buster and Georgie were in good hands, they turned and walked along the High Street towards the river, passing Maisie's dress shop, where Sarah stopped to look in the window. She sighed over a beautiful wedding gown arranged on a plaster mannequin.

'She's done so well for herself,' Alan said, 'when you think she always said dressmaking was a hobby, and she would never do anything apart from make garments and do repairs for friends.'

Sarah agreed, although she couldn't help feeling Alan was being more complimentary about Maisie earning a living than he was towards his own wife. 'You do realize that dress is second-hand, don't you? I happen to know she pulled apart three old gowns to make that one. It looks as good as anything you'll find in the fashion magazines.'

'I'll take your word for it, not reading that kind of magazine myself. However, I had no idea, as it looks brand new,' he said admiringly. 'What about the other dresses, are they for bridesmaids?'

'Yes, they're made from new fabric. It's highly unlikely that Maisie could find four dresses exactly the same, as so many people hold onto their frocks after a wedding. Her prices are so reasonable that even with restraints on clothing and Maisie having to be aware of utility clothing, women are able to go to her to be kitted out when we're still being told to make the most of ourselves.'

'She's got a good head on her shoulders. And even if she doesn't talk as common as she used to, she's remained as normal as us,' Alan grinned.

Sarah grinned back at him, thinking of all the times when Maisie's turn of phrase had had her blushing. 'That's why she's done so well. She understands us ordinary women and has no time for snobs. Although I hear that quite a few well-heeled people in this town are known to visit her establishment outside of hours, to have outfits restyled or made from scratch.'

'Do they really?'

'I only know that because Maisie is a friend, so please don't go telling anybody else. I know what you're like when you've got a pint inside you.'

'As if I'd chat in the pub about women's clothing. Who do you think I am?' He chuckled. 'Come on; I'm getting chilly standing here.'

Sarah slid her arm through his and they walked on slowly, passing the funeral director's premises jointly owned by Douglas and David. 'It's never really struck me before that all the businesses along this way are owned and run by family friends,' she said, looking away with a shudder. 'It always gives me the shivers looking in the window at funeral furnishings.'

'Don't tell me: someone has walked over your grave?' Alan asked. It was well known amongst their friends that Sarah had these feelings from time to time.

'No, I'm just a bit chilly,' she lied, hoping that nothing terrible was going to happen to someone she loved. So often, after she'd felt like this, something would happen to one of her loved ones.

'Now, I want you to stand still for a moment,' Alan instructed as he pulled his scarf from around his neck and covered her eyes.

'Oh Alan, don't be so daft. What will people think?' she said as he took her by the shoulders and guided her forward a couple of steps.

'People will say you have a very clever husband who is thinking of the future for his business. It's not just Maisie Carlisle who can expand her business, you know.'

'Alan, whatever are you talking about?' she asked, wondering if her Sunday best hat had been set askew by his scarf as he tied it over her face. 'Can you take this off, please?'

'In a second,' he said, turning her so that she knew she would be facing the shop rather than the road. He gently removed the scarf. 'You can open your eyes now,' he said as he kept hold of her shoulders.

'Oh my goodness! Whatever have you done?' she cried, gazing at the double-fronted shop. Gone was the array of new and second-hand bicycles; the window now displayed three television sets in their polished wood cabinets. On a new shelf at the side stood wireless sets of varying shapes and sizes. As Sarah put her nose against the glass to be able to see everything clearly, she spotted a shiny new vacuum cleaner. 'Gosh, I've dreamt of owning one of those,' she sighed with envy, before turning to give her husband a quizzical look. 'Alan, what's going on – have you sold the shop?' She looked up to see the shop sign was still the same: 'Gilbert and Son'.

Without saying a word, Alan took her by the hand and led her towards the window at the other side of the shop door, where bicycles were lined up close together. Displayed on shelves up the wall were all the parts and gadgets that were required for his bicycle business.

'It was your dad's idea to begin with, and I listened; after all, he has invested so much in my business over the years. What he said about the future being in televisions, radios and gramophones made a lot of sense. With James working here with me since . . . since Lemuel's death' – he looked sad at the thought of his late friend – 'I said let's see if it would work. No doubt your dad will explain it better later, as he's the one with the business head. However, by running two businesses on the same premises, if one fails, we have the other. We can always go back to bicycles and motorbike repairs.'

Sarah remained silent. What he said made sense, and knowing her dad was part of this idea, she believed it would work. George wasn't someone to jump in with both feet without thinking of the consequences. However, it felt as though she'd been excluded from Alan's plans, and that made her a little sad. There had been a time when he'd told her everything and shared his dreams for the future.

But then, hadn't she done the same – accepting her new position at Woolworths without discussing it with him first?

'I think it's wonderful,' she said, giving him a hug. 'Come on, let's go inside so I can look closer. You do realize the children will want a television set, and I'd simply adore that vacuum cleaner and iron . . .'

A look of relief crossed Alan's face as he unlocked the door and led her into the shop. 'If this goes well, you can have whatever you like, as long as we can afford it. This town is thriving, and the Gilberts are going to thrive as well.'

'Who'd have thought, when I first came to live in Erith with my nan, that I'd meet a handsome man who would end up running his own business? Does this mean an end to having to wash your oily overalls?'

'I'll be wearing a white coat to repair the wirelesses and televisions once I've been trained.'

Sarah groaned. 'Then perhaps you should start selling those new-fangled washing machines as well.'

'One day, my love, one day.'

She ran her hand over the polished cabinet of a television set. 'I thought now it was the 1950s, life would get back to normal, like it was before the war; but it's not, is it?' she said wistfully.

Alan swept her up in his arms and swung her round, causing the vacuum cleaner to sway dangerously on its stand. 'Life is better than it has ever been, but if you want a taste of 1939, I can always take you for a ride on my bike,' he suggested with a grin.

'Alan Gilbert, put me down this instant. People will see us through the window. As for me being a pillion on that awful motorbike, you've got another think coming. Perhaps we should consider getting a nice motor car for the family, so we can go out on trips and have picnics,' she said, a dreamy look crossing her face.

'You've been reading those women's magazines again, haven't you?'

'It doesn't hurt to dream,' she sighed, gazing over his shoulder towards the vacuum cleaner with the many attachments.

Claudette Carlisle sat on a wall around the corner from Queen Street Baptist Church, swinging her feet back and forth and being careful not to scuff the leather of her best shoes. She loosened the tie of her Girl Guide uniform before checking her wristwatch. It was a treasured Christmas gift from her parents.

'We have ages before dinner, why don't we go for a walk?

It's cold sitting here,' she said to her sister, who was gazing over towards a group of lads kicking a football about.

'I want to stay here. Besides, weren't Clemmie and Dorothy meeting us after church?'

'I spotted them at the back with their parents when I carried the Girl Guides flag down the aisle at the beginning of the service.'

'I could hear the babies making a racket,' Bessie snorted. 'Honestly, you'd think Mrs Billington would leave them at home. Why, I'd die if I was her age and still having babies. She's ancient. Clemmie and Dorothy must be mortified.'

'Oh, it's lovely that her and Mr Billington have had babies when they didn't meet until a few years ago. Mum was telling me all about it. I don't think Dorothy minds too much, because she looks after the children sometimes, but Clemmie is a bit sniffy about it. There again, she's sniffy about lots of things,' Claudette said. It crossed her mind that her own sister was very much the same, but she wasn't about to voice that opinion, knowing she could end up with a sharp pinch on her arm off Bessie.

She'd often thought it would be nice to have Dorothy as a sister, as the two girls got on very well indeed, both attending Girl Guides together while the older two paired up. During those times, Clemmie didn't try to act so posh.

'Oh look, there they come now,' Claudette said, jumping up and waving as the Billington girls appeared.

'For heaven's sake, watch what you're doing. You'll make us a laughing stock,' Bessie said, seeing the group of boys nudging each other and laughing. 'Where have you been?' she asked Dorothy and Clemmie. 'We'd almost given up and gone home.'

86

Dorothy winked at Claudette. 'Clemmie said she wasn't going to be seen dead with me while I was wearing my Girl Guide uniform. So we had to hurry home so that I could change.' She and Claudette laughed, causing Clemmie to blush.

'Shut up, the pair of you,' Bessie hissed. 'It's about time we let the kids go off on their own, don't you think, Clemmie, as they show us up? There's just one thing I'm going to say to the pair of you now. If any of those lads come over, I want you to button up your coats and walk away. I don't want them having any chance to laugh at us; do you get me?' She glared at the two younger girls. 'And for heaven's sake, take your beret off and stuff it in your pocket, Claudette. Nobody is going to see you here at the rec, so you won't get in trouble for being out of uniform.'

Claudette linked her arm through Dorothy's and they wandered away, towards where a couple of swings moved slowly in the chilly February air. 'Sometimes those two get right up my nose,' she said, as she and Dorothy took a swing each. They kicked with their feet until they swung back and forth, side by side.

'I don't worry about them. Clemmie is a right little madam, or so I overheard my dad saying to Betty,' Dorothy giggled. 'I think he was hoping that she would like the idea of going to university, just so he had a few years without her under his feet – but then, she would probably come back even snobbier than she is now.'

'Why aren't you like her?' Claudette asked as she leant back and swung harder, trying to send the swing a little higher. Her hair flew out behind her and her cheeks were turning pink in the cold air.

'I shouldn't really say, as I keep getting told off for over-hearing what Dad is saying to Betty; but it seems my real mum acted very much like Clemmie, so perhaps she's inherited it? I don't remember much about my mum. Clemmie, being older than me, reckons she remembers her very well. I'm not sure she's telling the truth, though. What about you, do you remember your mum?'

Claudette shrugged her shoulders. 'Not a lot. I can remember living with my nan and not having a pair of shoes to wear, so walking in the street barefoot. And . . .' She trailed off and put both feet on the ground, so the swing came to a sudden halt.

'What do you remember? It's all right, you can tell me,' Dorothy said as she also brought her swing to a standstill, noticing Claudette was close to tears.

'It was the day we came to live with Mum – well, she's not really our mum, but we call her that. Really she is our Auntie Maisie. Our dad was in the army and my mum – I've not got the same mum as Bessie – had gone off somewhere and left us with our gran. I remember hurrying to the underground station when the siren went off . . . there was an awful crush, and Auntie Freda helped us out of the pile of bodies. After that we came to Erith to live with Maisie, and later she adopted us.' Claudette's expression brightened and she managed a smile. 'My dad is dead now,' she added, not looking at all sad, 'but I don't know much about him. Is that wrong of me?'

'No, not at all,' Dorothy said, putting her arm around her friend's shoulders. Although they were of similar ages, Dorothy was slimmer and shorter by a few inches. 'We are both very lucky to have new mums, and you've got a new dad as well. I've still got my dad and I love him very much. Even if he does have a strange job.'

Claudette giggled before nudging Dorothy with her elbow. 'Be thankful we've got Saturday jobs working with Betty, instead of you helping your dad out. Ew, imagine having to work with dead bodies!' She shrieked with laughter.

'I don't know, it sounds like a nice job. We are helping families after they lose someone they love. And don't forget your dad's in the same business too.'

'You'd never get him helping out with the bodies. Mum says he prefers to stay in the office. But doesn't your dad do that too, with them having three funeral parlours? I asked him why the business was growing so quickly, and he told me everyone has to die sometime and that's why undertakers are always so busy.'

The girls looked at each other and grimaced.

'Hello hello, a couple of those lads have gone over to talk with Bessie and Clemmie. Shall we go and listen and embarrass them?' Claudette grinned.

'Yes – but button up your coat. They'll kill us if they see you in your uniform. Look, one of them is offering your sister a cigarette.'

Claudette shook her head. 'She's taken it as well. She's going to cop it if Mum finds out.'

As the younger girls approached, one of the boys glanced over his shoulder and pulled a face. 'Come on, lads, we don't talk to kids.'

'We are fourteen. Not exactly kids, when we can go to work,' Claudette snapped back.

'We'll see you next Saturday in the town,' the leader of the group said to Bessie, ignoring her sister's outburst.

Bessie agreed before throwing the part-smoked cigarette behind a wall. 'That killed our conversation. Trust you two to turn up. Couldn't you see we were chatting to the lads? You could have stayed on the swings and played a bit longer.'

'We weren't playing, we were talking. What are you up to? You know you're not allowed to meet lads without permission,' Dorothy said, glaring at her sister.

'I'm not going. She can go on her own,' Clemmie shrugged. 'They're not my cup of tea.'

'Besides, you're at work on Saturday,' added Claudette.

'He means after work.' Bessie smiled indulgently. 'Why so many questions? Are you jealous?'

'Have you forgotten we're going to the party for Mr Caselton's fiftieth birthday?' Claudette said.

'Blast – I forgot about that. I'll have to let the lads know,' Bessie said thoughtfully. 'I can tell Mum I've got a headache so she doesn't get me to go down her awful factory again; then I can get word to the lads tomorrow.'

'You'll have to get used to that awful factory, as you call it,' Claudette said over her shoulder as she walked away. 'You're going to be working there for a very long time according to Mum's plans.'

'Not if I can help it. And I'm not working in the new shop she's talking about. I can't think of anything worse.'

'This is going to cause trouble, I can feel it in my bones,' Claudette whispered to Dorothy.

'Now you sound like Nanny Ruby,' she whispered back.

'It's no bad thing being like Nan. All hell will break loose if the adults find out what Bessie's up to. Those lads are trouble. I've heard things about them drinking and fighting and such like. They don't even wear ties or look smart.

And the one Bessie likes could do with a good scrub; his hair always looks as though it needs a trim and a wash.'

'He does have lovely green eyes, though,' Dorothy sighed.

'You're bonkers. This is all going to end in tears, as Nanny Ruby would say.'

8

Ruby looked around the room with a smile on her face. There was nothing she liked more than a family gathering, and this was sure to be a wonderful evening. It might only be the hall at the back of the Prince of Wales pub in Erith, but it was where many of her happiest family celebrations had taken place. The hall was a little rough around the edges these days, and like many places it could do with a lick of paint after taking a pounding during the war years – but who noticed that when they had good friends and family around them?

A decent spread of food was on display, with many people having brought along a plate of something, so Maureen wasn't working too hard feeding the guests. There was ale for the men, sherry for the women, and lemonade for the children. If anyone wanted something different, the public bar was open. Ruby approved of the party starting earlier so that the children could enjoy themselves before being packed off over the road to Sarah's house, to be cared for by her neighbour. She must remember to bundle up a bit of food for the lady, to say thank you.

'Is everything to your liking, Mum?' George asked as he

put his arm around her shoulders. 'I must say, you do look smart in your new frock. Did it come from Maisie's shop?'

'No, Bob treated me to it when we went to Dartford; it's from the Co-op,' she said, straightening the navy-blue pleats. 'You don't think it's too young for me, do you? I wasn't sure about the lace collar . . . I'm glad you had your party here. We've had some good times in this hall.'

'You look smashing, Mum, but then you always do. Did you know, my Maureen was all for renting the hall above the electricity showrooms? She thought I'd like to invite my colleagues at the council, and she even asked me for the address of the mayor and the MP Norman Dodds, would you believe?' He laughed. 'I took one look at her list and noticed she'd added that Margaret Roberts. That was when I tackled her and put my foot down. No electricity showrooms, no councillors and no members of parliament. I like it here at the Prince of Wales, and so do my friends and family. There's a time for socializing with people at the council, and there's times for family. This is a family celebration.'

'I agree with you there, George,' Ruby said, stretching up to kiss his cheek, 'although I'd be that proud of you to think you had important people wishing you a happy birthday.'

George chuckled. He knew his mum well, and she'd have been like a queen bee overseeing important guests. 'We've been through a lot, Mum, haven't we? Just think, if you hadn't fought tooth and nail to hang onto number thirteen, we could have been living anywhere right now. Come to think of it, we might not have survived the two wars. And we most certainly would not be married to the loves of our lives.'

'It's not like you to get sentimental, George. You've not had one too many already, have you?'

'Not yet, but perhaps ask me again by the end of the evening. Turning fifty is a bit of a milestone and to my mind, if it wasn't for you, I'd not be here now. Or have a good job down at Vickers.'

'You've amounted to something to be proud of,' she said, patting his hand. 'Wherever you ended up you'd have done just as well. Don't forget, I expect you to have a dance with your old mum before the end of the evening – but make it a slow one. I can't keep up with the fast dances these days.'

'It'll be slow dances most of the evening. This band doesn't go in much for modern songs and dances,' he said, looking towards the small platform at the end of the hall where three musicians were setting up. A woman on the upright piano, a man sitting behind a drum kit and a young lad with a trumpet. 'That's all we need for a bit of dancing and a sing-song.'

'Make sure you get up there and say a few words to everybody, George. You've had enough training speaking at those council meetings, so now you can say something to the people who love you. Make it after the kids have gone, though – you know what it's like. They'll be running round the room shouting their heads off and I won't hear a word you say.'

'I'll do that, Mum,' he said, kissing her cheek for a second time. 'Now, I must go and say hello to a few people. They're arriving thick and fast. Are you sure you're quite comfortable there?'

Ruby nodded. 'Yes, I've saved a seat for Maureen, and the three girls have put their cardigans on their seats to save them while they fuss about with the food.' She smiled indulgently.

'Is your mate Vera here yet?'

'Mark my words, she will be here before too long – she doesn't like to miss a thing. I hope young Sadie comes with her. I like that girl. She's had a tough life, but now it's turned out all right, although she deserves a medal living with her nan for so long and having her two kids to look after. I must say, Maisie's a love, giving Sadie a job taking care of her young kiddies. It gets her away from Vera for a few hours, and it means Maisie knows young Ruby and the twins are being well cared for.'

'Is that Sadie you're talking about?' Sarah asked, sitting down beside her nan after giving her dad a hug. 'Alan says there's a pint with your name on it over at the bar, Dad.'

George was off like a shot, leaving both women to laugh at his departing figure.

'He doesn't seem to like women gossiping, does he? My Alan's the same.'

'Men cease to surprise me these days. Now, Sadie is coming this evening, isn't she?'

'Oh yes, most definitely, she's outside in the public bar. James stopped to talk to someone.'

'Then we'd best get a couple more chairs before these are taken. Here – grab those two over there, and I'll save them for Cynthia and Sadie. I've not seen Cynthia to chat to since she moved up to South Road. That must've been a right job for her, moving to England. I'd have thought she would leave our shores for good after losing Lemuel the way she did.'

'Sadie told me she wants to stay here, especially as James is working for my Alan. Sadie's youngest is her grandson, after all. She has a lot of family here in England, although if I was her, I'd want to stay in sunny Trinidad.'

Ruby moved in close to Sarah and whispered, 'Do you think there's anything going on between James and Sadie?'

'Who knows, Nan, but James is a lovely lad and is the spit of his brother. If there's anything going on between them, I wish them well. I just hope they take their time and no more little ones come along until Sadie has a ring on her finger. He has taken to her in a big way, so we can only cross our fingers and hope for the best. I did tell her that if ever James wants to take her out, I'd babysit for her. She's brought those kiddies up a treat.'

Ruby nodded in agreement, waving across the room to Vera and her family as she spotted them looking around for a seat. 'Over here,' she called out as the band started the first tune of the evening. 'I just hope people are kind to Sadie,' she muttered, as Sarah stood up to make room for the pushchair.

'Why, what do you mean?'

'What I mean is, her two children are like chalk and cheese, the lad being fair-haired and fair-skinned, and the toddler coffee-coloured with those tight curls. People can be nasty, so I hope she grows a thick skin.'

'She's done more than that over the years I've been living in Erith. Don't worry, she'll be fine. She's got friends looking out for her.'

'Well, George, what does it feel like to be fifty?' David Carlisle said as he slapped George on the back. Maisie's tall, broad-shouldered husband grinned good-naturedly with a twinkle in his deep brown eyes.

'No different to being forty-nine, if I'm honest,' George said, raising his glass. 'Cheers.' Douglas Billington and Alan joined them. 'You can't be far off fifty yourself,' George nodded to Douglas. He knew the man had served in the first war like himself, and tried to figure out his age.

'Another year,' Douglas said good-humouredly. 'My Betty's a couple of years behind me. We were lucky to have our two little ones after we married as late as we did.'

'I'm not sure I'd want to be having youngsters at your age,' Alan said. 'It's hard to imagine you and George here are the same age. You look and act so much younger, despite a sprinkling of grey hairs.' He laughed good-naturedly as George, his father-in-law, pretended to box his ears.

'Talking about old men – where's our PC Jackson? I've not seen Mike since we arrived,' George said.

'He had a late shift at the station,' Alan said, looking at the clock over the bar. 'He's collecting Gwyneth and the children and should be here any time now.'

David Carlisle smiled. 'I was just thinking what a mix your family is.'

'It's best to think of us as one happy family,' George said as he raised his glass to the men. 'Family, friends and neighbours: everyone is treated the same in Alexandra Road. Where's your Betty? I want to claim my dance before the evening's out.' George had always had a soft spot for the manageress of the Woolworths store.

'She was with Maisie last time I saw her. They're talking to our eldest girls out by the side door. She was worried they'd wander off on their own.'

'Now you're not to go wandering off,' Betty said as she tightened a bow in Dorothy's hair. Clemmie stepped away quickly in case her stepmother did the same to her hair.

'The same goes for you two,' Maisie said, wagging her

finger at Bessie and Claudette. 'You are not to go any further than this pavement – and don't cross the road. I don't mind that you want to stand outside the hall, but remember, this is George's party and he'd like to see something of you.'

'Mum, we're grown up now. Please don't embarrass us,' Bessie pleaded, aware that the lads they'd spoken to in the park were standing on the other side of the road waiting for the girls to join them.

'I promise we'll all stay here,' Claudette said. 'We'll be coming inside shortly anyway, as Uncle Alan asked me to sing a song with him.'

The older girls burst out laughing and Claudette looked upset. 'Why are you laughing? Is there something wrong with my frock?' she asked, patting the full gathered skirt of her yellow cotton frock with its puffed sleeves.

'Leave her alone, she's got a lovely voice,' Dorothy said, putting an arm round her friend. 'There's nothing wrong with your dress. If there was, then the pair of them would be laughing at me too.' Although not related, both younger girls often wore similar outfits, and this evening Dorothy's frock was identical apart from being in pale blue.

Betty glared at the two older girls. 'All four of you look very pretty,' she said, although she felt the pair looked too grown up in their fitted white blouses and flared skirts. Her Clemmie was of an age to decide for herself what she wore, and Betty didn't want an argument or a sulking child. It could be hard at times, being a stepmother.

Clemmie and Bessie looked embarrassed as the boys called out to them. Fortunately, their mothers didn't notice.

'Make sure you come in and listen to Claudette when

she sings,' Betty insisted. 'Why, you could even hop onto the stage and join in.'

'No fear, we'll leave it to Vera Lynn here,' Bessie said, a hint of sarcasm in her voice.

'Just behave,' Maisie snapped at her, 'or you'll be going home to bed when the little ones go, do you hear me?'

The girls promised they would, and stood silently until Maisie and Betty went back inside the hall.

'You're not going off with those lads, are you?' Dorothy asked, looking worried as Bessie opened her handbag and took out a lipstick and small mirror. She added a touch of red to her pretty lips before pinching her cheeks and checking her reflection.

'That will have to do,' was all she said before turning to Clemmie. 'I take it you've decided not to come? They won't wait much longer.'

'I'm staying here. Be careful, or you'll get in awful trouble.'

Bessie laughed and hurried off to where the lads were waiting.

'There's going to be trouble, and whatever happens, we are going to be sucked into it because we know Bessie's gone with that Tom. He's the leader of the gang. We're going to get told off as well, and it just isn't fair,' Claudette sighed.

They moved over to a bench against the wall of the pub and sat down.

'We've got to do something.' Dorothy looked between the other two.

'But what can we do?' Claudette shot back. 'Bessie is a nightmare to live with and it's bad enough having to share a bedroom with her. She does nothing but moan about not wanting to work with Mum – I think she moans for the sake of moaning. I told her she can't be a Saturday girl at Woolies forever, but she seems to like it there. I'm just happy I'm going to have a job in the factory; I've dreamt about it for ages. Working with Mum is going to be the best job ever, and now I'm old enough to work full time, I can't wait.'

'You are so lucky,' Clemmie sighed. 'In our house Mum and Dad expect me to get more exam passes and do something with my life.'

'Mum's been talking about Clemmie going to university,' Dorothy added, 'but Clemmie doesn't want to. It's been hell at home. I know our parents mean well but in some respects they've got to let us decide what we want to do with our lives. A teacher at school told my class we should be thinking about a career – that we are every bit as good as the men. Isn't that strange?'

Claudette beamed. 'I want a career, and it's going to be wonderful. Because of Mum's clothing business I'll have a better job than any other girl in my class. I don't need to stay on at school or dream about being married. I'm going to be part of Maisie's Modes, and I'm looking forward to that very much. I'll stay on at Woolies as a Saturday girl too, because I like working there. I can ask Mum if you could have a part-time job with her in the holidays, if you like? It would be fun to work together.'

Dorothy's eyes lit up. 'I'd like that very much – although my mum may want me to work the week in the store.'

Claudette smiled. To work the week, as the young girls called it, meant earning a week's wages and having money in their purse during the school holidays. 'We won't be allowed out of the house ever again if Bessie lets us down.'

She nodded towards the end of the street, where her sister had disappeared with the lads.

'Why don't I sneak after them, just to see where they're going?' Dorothy suggested. 'Then I'll come back here to report. If our mums ask where she is, we can say she's gone to the toilet and one of us can go and fetch her back.'

'That sounds like a plan – although I don't like that we have to tell lies,' Claudette said. 'Trust Bessie to spoil our evening. Who'd have a big sister, eh?'

'Perhaps I should be the one to go?' Clemmie suggested.

'No, I can run faster than you,' her younger sister said, before hurrying across the road in the direction the four had headed.

They couldn't have gone far, she thought to herself as she turned into the High Street, breathing a sigh of relief as she spotted Bessie and Tom walking side by side with his two mates trailing behind. She held back a little in case they turned and saw her. She was expecting them to go towards the river, as it was a favourite place they all headed to in their spare time. There were benches where they could sit and watch activity on the water as well as be alone.

But no – they turned into Pier Road. Dorothy increased her pace and peered round the corner. They'd stopped by the front of Woolworths and were sitting on the steps that led up to the main doors. Wondering what they were talking about, as Clemmie and Claudette were bound to ask her, she ducked down a small alley between the shops that would bring her out by the side door used by staff. From there she could eavesdrop and hurry back to the pub if the group made a move. She prayed Bessie would head back before the two mothers came looking for the girls.

She pulled up a wooden crate the warehouse lads sat on when they crept out for a crafty cigarette and huddled down, pulling her coat closely around her, hoping whatever Bessie and the lads had to say was worth listening to. It was already quite dark at six o'clock, with streetlamps casting an orange glow on the road. Dorothy wasn't one for swear words, but at that moment she could think of a few she could use about Bessie's actions.

'So, you work here full time?' one of Tom's mates asked, as he cupped his hands around his eyes to peer in through the darkened Woolworths window.

'No, she's working for her mother. You know, that clothes factory down on the marshes.'

Bessie was surprised Tom even knew about Maisie's Modes and the factory. But it showed he was interested in her, she thought to herself. That made her feel special. He must really like her.

'I do work here, but only on Saturdays at the moment.'

'That mate of yours is a posh one,' a ginger-haired lad said.

'Her family are well off, I believe,' Bessie replied, not wishing to talk about Clemmie. She wanted Tom to talk to her and the other two to shove off.

'Not so well off if she's working in Woolies,' Tom laughed, taking a swig from a bottle of beer and passing it to her.

Bessie hesitated. If she refused, they were bound to mock her. She tried hard not to pull a face in distaste, deciding instead to take the bottle and wipe the top with the cuff of her coat sleeve. Hoping they hadn't noticed, she took a tiny sip and grimaced. It wasn't beer at all, but some kind of spirit.

'Thanks,' she said, passing it back and refusing the cigarette he held out. 'So, do you all work together? It must be somewhere special if you're looking down your nose at Woolworths.' She was doing her best to sound interested in them.

'We work down the Mobo factory in West Street.'

Bessie snorted with laughter. 'You make toys?' She added mockingly, 'What department are you in, dollies or rocking horses?'

Tom threw her a nasty look. 'It's a good job. I could have had an apprenticeship if my old man hadn't refused to sign the papers. He told me to earn proper money and not the pittance they pay apprentices. But I've got plans; I'm not hanging around Erith forever. Once I've got some money behind me, I'm travelling. I want to see America and Canada. There are opportunities in Canada for men like me.'

Bessie's eyes lit up. Now this was something she'd be keen to do. If she hung around with Tom, she might even be able to go with him. Anything was better than her life right now. 'How long before you go off on your travels?'

'Like I said, when I've got the money behind me. I don't want to be watching every penny while I'm seeing the world. Why are you so interested?'

How could Bessie tell him so soon that she longed to escape – that she hated the thought of working in her mum's factory, selling frocks to old ladies? Maisie never stopped explaining in great detail how she was planning for her children's futures, building a business in post-war Britain so that they would all have good prospects later on and not be living from hand to mouth. Bessie just knew it wasn't for her; but how could she explain this to somebody

103

who'd not only taken her in, but adopted her and given her a good life? She wasn't ungrateful. It was more that she genuinely couldn't see her future with Maisie's Modes.

She shrugged. 'I'm not sure, but like you, I know I want to travel. I just need to think more about it.'

Tom gave her a thoughtful look. 'You're my kind of girl,' he said approvingly as he took a deep gulp from the bottle and handed it back to Bessie. She did likewise before giving him a sweet smile. This could be her escape.

Nearby, Dorothy was horrified by what she'd seen and heard. What on earth was going on in Bessie's mind? She squinted at her wristwatch. At any moment, their mothers might come outside and find them missing. She would have to take action.

Ducking back down the alleyway, she turned back into the High Street and hurried to the corner of Pier Road, waving her arms frantically as if she'd been looking for them all along rather than eavesdropping. 'There you are,' she puffed. 'If you don't go back now, you will miss the dancing.' This caused the lads to roar with laughter.

'I'll walk back you back to the pub,' Tom said, putting his arm around Bessie, 'but you, girl, can run on ahead. And you two can sod off,' he instructed his mates. 'You're cramping my style.'

Dorothy didn't need a second bidding. She hurried back to report to the girls, glancing back at the corner to see Bessie turn towards Tom. He pulled her in close and kissed her before whispering in her ear. What was she doing? Dorothy ran all the way back to the pub and told the others, just as Bessie appeared with Tom and he kissed her goodbye.

The three girls' jaws dropped as Bessie, holding her head high, crossed the road looking very much like the cat that had the cream. Walking past them, she looked over her shoulder. 'Well, come along then. Shouldn't we be inside by now?'

9

After joining Maisie to wish George a happy birthday, Bessie tugged at Claudette's sleeve and nodded towards the ladies' toilets. The younger girl followed her sister without question. She really wanted to know what Bessie had to say.

'I need you to keep quiet about what happened just now. And you're not to mention those lads to Mum, do you hear me?' she hissed as she reached into her handbag and pulled out a lipstick. She pouted as she slicked the bright red colour onto her lips, then checked her teeth in the mirror. 'Tell the other two to keep quiet as well.'

Claudette thought it was like watching a mirror image of how their mother applied her make-up. Bessie might not be enamoured with Maisie of late, or her plans for the girls' futures, but she still seemed to copy her mannerisms.

'Are you going to see that lad again?' she asked.

'His name is Tom, and for your information, yes I am. I'm going to the pictures with him tomorrow evening. And you're to tell the parents you're coming with me.'

'Mum won't allow it as she's not met him. And as for Dad – he'd want to meet him and find out all about him too. Don't you think you're a bit young to go courting?'

'I'm sixteen, for goodness' sake. I know of girls who are married at my age and have a baby on the way, and here I am with my future mapped out by our mum without me having a say in it. You may love the idea of playing shops and grafting in the factory, but I want more from life. I want to travel and see the world. My real mum was an American, and I want to see what that country looks like.'

'You don't know that for sure. We've never been told anything about our real mothers or our early years – apart from our real dad not caring for us, and dumping us on his and Maisie's mum. If it wasn't for Maisie and David, I mean Mum and Dad, we'd have nothing right now and would probably be stuck in a children's home. I think you're being more than a bit ungrateful, Bessie.'

'You think being a servant working for Maisie's Modes is a life, do you? I don't, and I've got plans.'

'Gosh, you've met some lad for ten minutes and you've had your head turned with silly ideas. I don't think you know what you want,' Claudette said as she borrowed her sister's hairbrush and ran it through her own hair before Bessie snatched it back.

'Right, this is what I want you to do. You're not to say anything to the parents about Tom, and furthermore, you're going to tell them you're coming to the pictures with me. Do you understand? We're going to see *The Blue Lamp.*'

'Oh, I want to see that. All right, I'll sit on the other side of the cinema.'

'Claudette, I said you're to say you're coming with me. To cover for me. I didn't say you're actually coming with me.' Bessie looked at her sister as if she was daft.

'But what am I going to do while you're in the pictures? And what if someone sees me?'

'Get yourself a bag of chips and find a bench to sit on. When you see me come out you can join me, but not before I've said goodnight to Tom. I'll hang about until you catch me up. Do you get it?'

'But it's cold and could be raining and I'll freeze to death. Can't I still go and see the film? You'll be at the back with all the courting couples, so I'll sit at the front on my own. I'll pay for my own ticket.'

Bessie thought for a moment before giving a big sigh. 'I suppose you can. Now let's get out there before we're missed. Aren't you supposed to be singing a song for George? And I need to speak to Clemmie before she blabs.'

'I promised I'd speak to them, and Clemmie wouldn't do that. She's a good friend.'

Bessie raised her eyebrows. 'I can't take any chances, as I want to see Tom again. I really like him and nothing is going to get in my way. So keep this shut,' she said, running her fingers across her sister's lips.

'She has a voice like an angel,' Ruby said as she watched Claudette on the stage singing 'If You Were the Only Boy in the World' before everybody joined in with the chorus. A few guests dabbed at their eyes as the song finished. Claudette gave a sweet curtsy before being helped down the steps and joining her mum, who was sitting beside Ruby.

'You should be on the stage with a voice like that,' Ruby told her.

'But I've just been on the stage, singing,' Claudette chuckled, accepting a glass of lemonade from Maisie.

'Don't be lippy to your Nanny Ruby, you know very well what she means.'

'And as you know, she is the star turn at the Brownie and Girl Guide concerts,' Freda chipped in as she leant over and kissed the girl's cheek. 'Perhaps Ruby is right. Have you ever thought of taking up singing and dancing as a career?'

Claudette blushed and looked down into her lap. 'If I was as pretty as Bessie, then I might have considered it. But I'm the plain Jane in the family, so I'll stick to singing at family parties,' she said, taking Maisie's hand. 'I really want to be part of Maisie's Modes and work with Mum.'

'My goodness,' Ruby exclaimed, 'you are one of the most beautiful young ladies that I know, both inside and out.'

Maisie could see that her daughter was embarrassed. 'I'm proud to have you on board,' she said. 'You've got a good head on your shoulders. I can see you running one of the shops in a few more years.'

Claudette was horrified. 'Oh no, I don't want to work in the shop – besides, I'm a bit young for that. You need someone older. I want to work in the clothing factory.'

'She'll always need someone sweeping up and making tea for the workers,' Ruby's friend Vera chipped in.

'She's not going to be a tea girl or a cleaner,' Maisie said. 'This girl has plenty to offer, and she knows what she wants to do. Tell them about your drawings, Claudette.'

Claudette wanted to curl up and die. When she sang she could close her eyes and pretend she was somewhere else, but to have her mum and Nanny Ruby's friends all watching her, waiting to hear about her dreams, was just too embarrassing. Perhaps if she quickly explained, then she could go and join her friends and leave the grown-ups to their own devices.

She took a deep breath. 'It's nothing much, honestly. I just thought that Mum should think about having a shop just to sell wedding dresses, and then perhaps a different shop for children's clothing. If women come to buy wedding dresses and bridesmaids' frocks, they don't really want to be in a shop where mums are buying knickers for their daughters and trousers for their sons. Anyway, I drew some pictures of pretty dresses . . . the kind of thing I'd like to wear if I was a bridesmaid.' She shrugged her shoulders as if it was not important. 'I can bring them down to show you sometime, Nanny Ruby, if you like?'

'I'd like that very much, lass. You've got a clever young girl here, Maisie, and I can see more than a bit of you in her,' Ruby said approvingly.

Maisie put an arm around her daughter and gave her a big hug. 'I'm proud of all my kids,' she said. 'We just need to find a suitable job in the business for Bessie. Perhaps once we're up and running, she'd like to learn to manage the shop? I'll have to have a word with her.'

Claudette stayed silent, thinking about what her sister and that boy had been doing earlier on. Nothing good was going to come of it; she could feel it in her bones. As she looked up she saw Ruby watching her closely and averted her eyes, hoping her nan couldn't read her mind.

'How is that handsome husband of yours?' Ruby asked as she joined Freda at the long trestle table, where she and Sarah were busy taking covers off the plates of food and preparing for the guests to start eating.

Freda smiled warmly at her. Ruby had been like family to her ever since Freda first arrived in Erith. 'He's doing fine, thank you for asking, Ruby. I just wish I could see more of him.'

'I must say, it's not how a marriage should be, when the husband isn't home very often. I know it wouldn't have worked for me – and really didn't, with my first marriage to Eddie. My Bob is a lot more trustworthy.'

'Nan, are you saying Granddad Eddie wasn't trustworthy?' Sarah asked as she moved a plate of cheese sandwiches away from the edge of the table, where a toddler was watching with interest.

'There's a lot you don't know about my life, Sarah. Some of it I want buried forever. I loved Eddie more than life itself. We both fought to stay together, the only problem being we fought at different times. That's a long time ago now – it's water under the bridge, as they say. But you, young lady,' she said, nodding towards Freda, 'why, you've not been married two years. It must feel strange to be apart so much.'

'It is, but with Tony travelling around the country for Woolworths, and then when he's back he's out helping train cyclists for the Olympics . . . well, it's difficult. I trust him, though,' she added quickly.

'It must be good when you do meet,' Sarah said, winking at her friend as she bit into a sandwich.

'Why, Mrs Gilbert, I never thought I'd hear you speak like that!' Freda sniggered. 'But you're right; it's lovely when he's back home.'

Ruby looked puzzled. 'I don't understand what Woolworths is doing, sending him off to visit different stores. What's going on?'

'It's only short-term. You must have heard all the talk of shops going self-service? It's ridiculous if you ask me, as Woolworths is known for its "service with a smile" and helpful staff. It wouldn't be the same if they just picked up what they wanted and then paid at the door. It seems Sainsbury's have started trials, so head office has got a bee in their bonnet about seeing if some of our stores could do the same. Tony is part of the team doing the reports.'

'All I can say about that is, why fix what isn't broken?' Ruby huffed. 'Will Tony work back at the Erith store after all this travelling about? Betty is only supposed to be helping out short-term as manageress, isn't she?'

Freda looked over her shoulder to make sure nobody else could hear. 'I've already mentioned this to Sarah, but it's not common knowledge. Tony is probably going to be offered his own Woolworths store to manage. They had him working at Erith to gain experience, and in the job he's doing at the moment they're seeing how he fits into the management team.'

'Well, I think that's marvellous, them thinking so highly of Tony. You must be so proud, my love,' Ruby beamed.

Freda's shoulders started to shake as she put down the plates Sarah had handed to her and turned her back on the party guests. 'I'm sorry – I don't mean to get upset. And the last thing I want to do is hold Tony back in his career . . . but I'm so unhappy about everything,' she said to Ruby as a large tear dropped onto her cheek.

Ruby quickly fished a clean handkerchief from the sleeve of her cardigan. 'Well now, there's no need for tears. You've got us here to help you. I don't know about you, but I'd quite like a breath of fresh air,' she said, nodding to Sarah.

'Why don't we three step outside for a couple of minutes? Sarah, you follow behind and make sure that nosy Vera doesn't notice. We can soon sort all this out, I'm sure.'

When Sarah got outside with Maisie, whom she'd collected on the way, Ruby was sitting on a wooden bench with her arm round Freda as the girl continued to cry.

'I hope you don't mind me coming out with you, but I noticed something wasn't right,' Maisie said as she hurried to the other side of Freda and put an arm round her as well. Sarah bent in front of their young friend and took her hands.

'Now, my love, you've got your friends here and you've got me,' Ruby told her. 'I may be getting on a bit, but I like to think I've still got my uses and can advise you if you've got a problem. I reckon between us we can sort out whatever it is that is worrying you. Don't you, girls?'

The other two agreed, and after a few moments Freda put down the handkerchief and looked at them all. 'The thing is . . . I am very proud of Tony. He works so hard and he's a good husband. There is talk of him getting his own store,' she explained to Maisie, who hadn't known.

'Why, that's blooming wonderful,' Maisie said, giving Freda's shoulders a squeeze before looking at Sarah's sombre face. 'There's more, though, isn't there? Come on, now – cough it up and put us all in the picture.'

Freda sniffed. 'It could very well be a long way away. And if it is . . . I don't think I could cope, if it meant moving. Or worse still, Tony working away from home for a long time. If we move away from Erith, I'll be alone while he's at work and I'll miss you all so much. I realized that watching you all this evening. You are my family, and I don't want to lose you.' She wept into her handkerchief as her friends watched quietly, not sure what to say or do.

After a few moments Freda wiped her nose, put her hands down in her lap and drew a deep breath. With a more confident expression on her face, she looked at the three friends she loved so much. 'So, if it happens, and Tony is given a store in another part of the country – I'm going to ask that we bring our marriage to an end.'

There was a moment of shocked silence. Then Sarah straightened up, hands on her hips, and cried, 'But you can't divorce a man just because you don't like where he's going to work! I thought you were made of stronger stuff, Freda. For heaven's sake, what's going on in your mind?'

'I agree with Sarah,' Maisie said. 'This isn't like you. Come on, kid – spit out the rest. We've all been apart in the past and kept in touch, haven't we? We'll still see each other. Nothing can keep the Three Musketeers apart for long.'

Ruby watched as the two younger women did their best to tell Freda how daft she was being until they ran out of words. Then she spoke.

'Freda, I was there when you said your vows in church, wearing that beautiful frock Maisie made for you. And you know me, I'm not one for religion and all that – but when you stood by Tony's side and promised to love, honour and obey, I'm pretty sure you weren't thinking of changing your mind after less than two years. So come on, let's have the rest of it.'

Freda took a deep, shuddering breath. 'The thing is . . . I'm still not expecting, and I think there's something wrong with me.'

'My God, is that all?' Maisie hooted with laughter, then quickly grew serious as she saw the look on Sarah's face. 'Sorry, love – but you know babies come along when you are least expecting them. And sometimes when you don't want them. With your Tony being away so much, you've probably not had time to practise as much . . .'

Sarah's eye met Freda's and despite everything they exchanged small smiles, remembering the first time they'd met Maisie at their job interviews with Betty. They had both been shocked at the way Maisie spoke about 'practising' for a baby, and here she was saying the same thing.

'At least you've got a smile on your face now,' Ruby said, not sure what had prompted it but pleased that Freda was suddenly looking brighter.

Freda sighed. 'Thank you for your suggestion, Maisie, but it's not through want of trying. I even hoped perhaps we might have had a honeymoon baby. I went to see a doctor the other day.'

Maisie shook her head. 'I bet he sent you away with a flea in your ear, didn't he?'

'He did, he just said it would happen, and to go away and be a good wife for my husband. I don't know whether anyone has ever told him such a thing before. I felt so foolish that I told him I'd really gone there because I had a cough. Then I spent the rest of the appointment coughing as hard as possible, to prove my point.'

The others burst out laughing and Freda eventually joined them.

'In a way, he's right, love,' Ruby said. 'I'm a strong believer in the idea that if you worry about such a thing, it will never happen. You're young and you're fit and healthy.

Spend more time with Tony when he's home and enjoy each other's company; then you can't go wrong. Why don't you go out with him when he's training on his bike? If I remember rightly, you used to cycle everywhere together. Just enjoy your life and have a laugh, and I promise you – something will happen.'

Freda nodded her head, although she was thinking to herself that Ruby could be wrong.

'Besides, you've got the Olympics to look forward to – you must be so excited that Tony is going to be a coach for the cycling team. That will soon come round. Will you go with him?' Ruby asked, warming to the subject. 'It's a shame it's not in London this time, otherwise we could come and watch and cheer his team.'

'By the way, where is it?' Maisie asked.

'Helsinki,' Freda mumbled, not liking to confess she had no idea where that was. She wasn't even sure if she'd be allowed to go with Tony. If not, it would mean more weeks apart – or even months. 'Let's talk about something else, shall we? I don't want to spoil George's party by bawling my eyes out all the time. Tell us more about your factory, Maisie.'

Maisie started to explain where the factory was sited and how much clearing up they'd done. 'The sewing machines will be delivered next week. We've already white-washed the office walls and also the storage areas, so I don't think it will be long before we've got women in there working. I might have a little party there first. But before then I want you all to come down and look around. I'll drive you in my van – you can have the front seat, Ruby,' she added, puzzled by the expression that had passed over the older woman's face while she was talking.

'I'll say no thanks, all the same, but I do wish you well,' Ruby told her. 'I'll wait till you're at this new shop in Bexleyheath that the girls have told me about, then I'll come up there to look about. I might even bake a cake to celebrate.'

Sarah took her nan's hand. 'Please, Nan, can't you tell Maisie and Freda about what happened to you when you worked in the munitions factory? I know the buildings weren't far from where Maisie's factory is now. Dad told me you'd had a bad experience down there, but perhaps we'd all understand more if you could tell us all about it? We won't let it go any further.'

'It seems to be an evening for sharing secrets, doesn't it?' Ruby said, looking sad.

'A trouble shared and all that,' Maisie said, patting Ruby's knee.

'I'm not saying it's a trouble, but when you've lived as many years as I have, you tend to lock things away and forget about them. I never thought what happened to me back in 1924 would make me scared to revisit that part of the marshes. But now I find it brings up memories I'd prefer to bury, even though until it was mentioned where your factory was going to be, I didn't even realize I was frightened. I'm just being a silly old woman.'

'There's nothing silly about your fear at all,' Sarah said. 'And if talking about it would help, then we promise we will understand. Look how many times you've helped us. Crikey, we'd be lost without your wise words.' She perched on the arm of the bench to make herself more comfortable.

'I'll not go into all the ins and outs of it, but it was a time when me and Eddie had parted ways. He'd done some bad things, and then there was the war, and I felt that my life had moved on without him. Would you believe, I refused to have anything to do with him? However, you'll have read about the explosion at the munitions factory – there was even a Pathé News film at the cinema . . .' She stopped speaking to draw a deep breath. 'Those poor, poor girls who perished didn't stand a chance. I'd been talking to some of them only minutes before it happened. I was injured and would most likely have died too, if Eddie hadn't come looking for me. God knows what would have happened. But as it was, he took me home, and suddenly I had my husband back. It changed me, made me value a man I thought I'd lost forever; and it changed him, too. Any badness inside him was gone. We got on with our lives from that day onwards. That's all there is to it, really.'

'I read about what happened,' Freda said. 'Is it right that nearly all the country was in mourning?'

'Yes, that's true, love. Eddie bought all the newspapers, but I didn't want to look at them, so he put them away in the loft. They are still there, unless the mice got at them. I knew most of those women – they worked with me, and some lived in our road. One of the girls had just started work that day . . . if only she'd turned the job down, she'd be alive today. I had to blank it all from my mind or I'd have gone mad with the grief.'

The girls were silent for a while as they digested Ruby's words.

'That's no different to when my mum went with Maureen up to Woolworths in New Cross to buy saucepans, and she died and Maureen survived,' Sarah said at last. 'Maureen has said how guilty she felt. She thought she should have died too.'

'I was there, if you all remember, and yes, things could so easily have been different,' Freda said. 'It makes my problem pale into insignificance.'

They all sat in companionable silence until Ruby spoke. 'I want you to do something for me, Sarah.'

'Anything you say, Nan.'

'I want you to get your Alan to climb up into my loft and find all those newspapers. God knows what state they're in, but if they are fit to read, have him take all of them back to your house and put them away somewhere. It is history, after all, and one day your children will ask about the disaster. You can show them the papers and tell them that was where your grandmother worked.'

'I'll do that, Nan.'

'As for you,' Ruby turned to look at Maisie, 'I don't want to be the one to spoil your big adventure, so what I'm going to do is take you up on your offer. I'd like to visit your new business. Just promise me that if it becomes too much, someone will bring me straight home again. Is that all right?'

'That's more than all right,' Maisie said, leaning over to give her a big hug. 'I'll do anything you want. In fact, if we invite the rest of the family to visit, there will be more than one car to drive you home, and with so many people for you to fuss over you might forget your fears. What do you think?'

'I'll never forget that day, my love, but you mean well, so I'm going to come and see what's going on. You're doing something really special, and I want to be part of it.'

119

It was Maisie's turn to cry. 'Oh, I'm a daft bugger,' she said as she wiped her eyes. 'I've probably ruined my make-up now, and there's a party going on in there. We're supposed to look glamorous,' she sniffed. 'All I want to do is make a future for my children, and any other children that come along,' she said, looking at Freda. 'And with me factory and an extra shop or two, I can do that. Why, by the time my youngest kids are old enough to work we could have as many shops as Woolworths.' She chuckled.

'Just don't go pinching all our staff, that's all I ask,' Sarah smiled. 'Some of those people you're talking about are my Saturday girls. I'll already be losing your Bessie and Claudette before too long.'

Ruby wondered if that was true. Bessie didn't seem like the kind of girl to want to work in a clothing factory, or even a dress shop, come to that. She'd have to keep an eye on that young girl. She was likeable enough, but reminded Ruby very much of what Maisie had been like when she had first come to live in Erith – only without Maisie's pleasant side. Of course, Bessie had been through a lot when she was young . . . Yes, Ruby would keep an eye on her.

She turned to Freda. 'That just leaves you,' she said. 'I don't want you sitting at home brooding while that husband of yours is away working. You're going to come over to me for your meals. Then, when you aren't at work, we can sit and listen to the radio together. All right?'

Freda looked at the expectant faces waiting for her to speak. 'That's a lovely idea – thank you very much. I don't know what I'd do without you all.'

'In that case, before we all start to cry again, why don't we go back inside and enjoy the rest of Dad's party?' Sarah said. 'There's probably no food left by now, but at least we can have a glass of something to wish him a happy birthday.'

10

'For heaven's sake, hurry up,' Bessie snapped at her sister as she broke into a trot. They had just turned the corner of Alexandra Road, with Bessie looking over her shoulder to make sure their parents weren't still watching them. The Carlisles had all walked together down to the bottom of the road, with Maisie and David stopping at Nanny Ruby's house; Ruby had summoned the extended family for a pow-wow.

'Tom won't wait for me forever; I was supposed to meet him fifteen minutes ago outside the main doors. He won't wait, I just know he won't wait for me,' Bessie fretted.

'Of course he will wait for you. There's ten minutes before the B film starts, so stop moaning,' Claudette huffed as she did her best to keep up. 'If you don't mind me saying, your face is turning all red and blotchy like it does when you're getting upset. It's not a very glamorous look for someone who is going out with a boy for the first time.' Claudette liked nothing more than goading her big sister; Bessie was the vainest person she knew. Her words had the desired effect, as Bessie put her hands to her face to pat her cheeks.

'That's all I need,' she hissed. 'He's not my boyfriend yet – he's invited me to go to the pictures with him, that's all. If I'm lucky, he might ask me out again, if he likes me enough. That'll make my friends green with jealousy. Not many of them have boyfriends.'

For all their bickering, Claudette loved her big sister. 'You will be careful, won't you? You'll not do . . . well, you'll not go too far, you know, like Mum explained to us?' She tried not to squirm as she thought about what it took to make a baby. When Maisie had explained about the birds and the bees, it had put her right off her dinner.

Bessie gave a harsh laugh. 'Just you remember to keep out of the way once we see him. And remember not to sit near us. In fact, perhaps you should cross the road now, so it doesn't look as though you're with me. Trust Mum to have us work late today of all days. I've almost run my fingers down to the bone scrubbing that floor, without going in on a Sunday.'

'Oh, stop your moaning,' Claudette retaliated, trying to catch her breath as she struggled to keep up. 'Don't you love seeing the old building turned into somewhere where we're going to make beautiful frocks? I'm so excited I can hardly sleep at night. This time next month, we will be up and running. And only weeks after that the Bexleyheath shop will be open.'

'I can't believe you're getting excited about working in a factory. I'm just grateful we can stay on at Woolworths at the moment with our Saturday jobs. It's going to be hell once we stop working there. We'll hardly see anybody, apart from some miserable women bent over their sewing machines. It's not as if there'll be any decent lads working there.'

'There's young Sam doing all the odd jobs and cleaning – I think he's even going to be making tea for us. And then Granddad Bob is going to be doing a few hours every day, driving stock to the shops, until Mum gets organized.'

Exasperated, Bessie shook her head. 'I mean lads . . . you know, lads who'll talk about music and films and just be friendly. Not some spotty-faced kid or our adopted great-granddad.'

'I like Bob,' Claudette pouted. 'Talking of granddads, isn't that George coming up the road? He must be going to see Nanny Ruby.' She waved her arms until George waved back.

'I'm crossing the road. You stay and talk to him. And it's Great-Granny Ruby, for heaven's sake – get your facts right.'

Claudette ignored her sister; she was used to her moods. Instead she hurried towards George, who gave her a big hug. 'Where are you off to, young lady? Have you fallen out with your sister?'

'Oh, she's in a hurry to meet . . . she wants to get good seats at the pictures.'

'Shouldn't you hurry along too?' George asked. Looking over towards the Odeon, he caught sight of Bessie going into the main entrance with a lad he recognized from somewhere.

'I'll be all right, don't worry about me. I wanted to say hello to you.'

'Then get a move on, you don't want to miss the main picture. Everyone has told me how good *The Blue Lamp* is. I hope to see it myself.'

'I won't,' she said, reaching up on tiptoe to kiss his cheek before hurrying down the road.

George watched until Claudette had crossed the road before he walked on round to Alexandra Road, pulling his scarf tighter around his neck. The cold night air, mixed with coal-fire smoke from many chimneys, was playing havoc with his chest.

He cleared his throat before knocking on the door of number thirteen. He didn't want to start coughing once indoors, otherwise his mother would fuss. She was too old these days to have to keep worrying about her brood.

'Hello, George,' David Carlisle said as he opened the door and shook George warmly by the hand. 'Get yourself inside – it's too chilly to be out. Was that you I heard coughing?'

'Yes, I'm just a bit chesty at the moment; but don't tell Mum, you know what she's like.'

David laughed. 'Don't I know it. With us living at the top end of the road, she doesn't miss a trick. She walked in the other day and caught Maisie wiping her eyes with a handkerchief, and straightaway she thought we'd had a falling out. It took Maisie a long time to convince her it was just a sad story in her magazine. Only after Ruby had read it herself and had a cry did she understand. I don't know, these women will cry over anything . . .'

'Hello, love,' Ruby said as George entered the front room. 'You've only just caught us. Maisie and David are going to the cinema and we've decided to join them!'

'I was only dropping in a seed catalogue for Bob. Where is he?'

'I sent him upstairs to change his shirt and put a tie on. There's no way we're going to the pictures with him looking scruffy. Well, you don't know who you'll meet at these places, do you?'

George tried not to laugh. He knew his mum was a stickler for being dressed right. 'Are you going to see anything good?'

'It's called *The Blue Lamp*, you know, that film about coppers. It's supposed to be very good, although Bob grumbled it'll be like a busman's holiday, what with him being a retired copper.'

Maisie came in from the kitchen. 'I've done the washing up for you, so you haven't got to worry about it when you get home,' she said, wiping her hands on one of Ruby's tea towels. 'Hello, George, what did you think of the local election?'

George grimaced. 'I'm glad it's over and we can get back to the job in hand – helping the local people.'

'I thought it was a terrible shame that Margaret Roberts never got in. I really liked her. I was 'oping she might come and buy some frocks from my shop if she'd been our MP. I can't say the same about that Norman Dodds.'

'Just remember, the MP and councillors all have wives who buy dresses, so you've nothing to fear about losing business. Norman's a good politician; he'll be good for this area and he's a hands-on kind of chap. I did like that young girl, though. I reckon she's got fire in her belly and she will go far, you mark my words.' He turned as he heard Bob come downstairs, grumbling about having to go out at this time of the evening, and walk into the room. George greeted his stepfather warmly. 'I've heard it's a good film, Bob, so don't you worry about it being a busman's holiday,' he said, grinning as Ruby tried not to laugh.

'I've been retired that many years now, things are bound to have changed, so it will be interesting to see it all the same. Now are you ready, Ruby? If you don't hurry up, we will miss the beginning.'

'I'll walk back round the road with you,' George said. 'I

might stop off and have a cuppa with our Sarah before I head home. I want to have a word with Alan as I'm thinking of treating Maureen to a new wireless for her birthday.'

'I reckon she'd like one of those new television sets,' Maisie said. 'I'm hankering after one myself, but with all our money going into the business at the moment it will have to wait a little while. Come on, you lot, let's get cracking,' she called to David and Bob.

As the men followed Ruby and Maisie out of the front door, David Carlisle winked at George and Bob. They both knew he'd arranged for a television set to be installed on a day when Maisie would be out at work. She deserved a treat and he was keen to be able to sit down in front of it and be entertained; besides which, his purchase would support Alan's new venture.

'Everyone seems to be expanding their businesses at the moment,' George said. 'This family is doing very well indeed.'

'The only thing I'm expanding is my waistline,' Bob said as he tugged at the belt on his overcoat.

'Don't worry about that, once the weather improves you'll work that off over the allotment,' George chuckled as they hurried to keep up with Ruby and Maisie.

'It's a shame you can't join us,' Bob said, as they reached the end of the road opposite the Odeon cinema.

'I'm taking Maureen in a few days, so don't you worry about us. You go and have a nice night. Who's looking after the kids this evening, David?'

'Sadie and James are sitting with them. They offered to after our Bessie and Claudette said they'd planned a sisters' night out together.'

George nodded thoughtfully; he remembered the young lad but would keep his own counsel for now. Bessie was sixteen, and of an age to be considered an adult.

Claudette paid for her ticket and entered the dimly lit cinema, the usherette leading her to a side aisle and pointing with the beam of a torch to an empty seat on the left-hand side of the auditorium. She kept her head bent low just in case Tom spotted her. He'd only seen her the once, but it wouldn't do for her to be noticed now; besides, Bessie would give her grief later.

She settled down in her seat and reached into the pocket of her gabardine mac for the small packet of boiled sweets Bessie had begrudgingly given her. As the lights dimmed further she settled back in the plush seat while an advertisement for next week's film – a musical – came up on the screen. Claudette watched it with keen interest. In her heart of hearts she knew she would dearly love to be on the stage, singing in the chorus line and doing a few high kicks. Perhaps, once she'd earned a little money, she could afford to take dancing lessons. She'd not say anything to the family, though, because Bessie would be bound to poke fun at her; that would be the death knell for her hopes and dreams.

Granted, she was thrilled to be working for Maisie's Modes and also be allowed to carry on with her Saturday job at Woolworths. She loved the store dearly, and had grown up listening to tales of her mum working alongside Freda, Sarah and Betty before leaving to set up her own shop. They'd all spoken of Auntie Betty as if she were a tyrant when they first started work there, but now

Claudette only knew Betty to be kind and loving, and the perfect boss.

As the opening titles played, she started to wonder where Bessie was sitting. She'd no doubt be in the back row, where courting couples always sat to have a kiss and a cuddle in the dark. Claudette had never seen this nor experienced it – after all, she was only fourteen – but her curiosity took over and she started to turn in her chair, looking over her shoulder towards the back of the cinema. Someone seated behind her muttered angrily for her to sit still, but after another ten minutes she couldn't resist turning slowly once more.

Thanks to an usherette showing latecomers in by the light of her torch, she spotted her sister sitting bolt upright in her seat while the lad, Tom, lounged back with his arm around her shoulders. Claudette wanted to laugh, because her sister didn't seem to be enjoying herself. However, what could she get up to in the cinema?

She dipped into the paper bag for another sweet and her fingers touched her purse. She had enough money to buy a bag of chips and decided to hurry out of the cinema when everyone stood for the national anthem at the end; that way she'd be ahead of the queue. Yes, that would be lovely, as teatime seemed a while ago now. If she walked slowly, she could eat them before she got home. As this plan came together, she completely forgot that she was supposed to wait for Bessie.

In the interval she decided to visit the ladies' and joined a long queue that led from the toilets out into the aisle. As she stood there gazing about, her stomach gripped with panic. Wasn't that her mum sitting next to Nanny Ruby?

She shuffled behind a rotund woman so as not to be noticed, and was soon inside the toilet cubicle thinking hard about what to do. What if they saw Bessie with Tom? She had to do something – but what?

Deciding not to queue to wash her hands, she headed back to her seat, although she couldn't resist a glance to where her sister was sitting – Bessie seemed to be alone. As the lights started to dim Claudette dashed up the slope and tapped her sister on the shoulder.

'What are you doing here? Go away, before Tom comes back,' Bessie hissed.

'Mum and Nanny Ruby are sitting over there. You might want to tell your boyfriend you may have to leave.'

'I told you, he's not my boyfriend, he's just someone I'm going out with. Go away now.'

'You're welcome,' Claudette muttered, going back to her seat.

When the film finished she slipped out and headed directly to the chip shop, not waiting for the national anthem to be played, and making sure she was not seen by her family in case they asked where Bessie was. She could only hope Bessie had the sense to look out for their parents. Out in the dark night she crossed the High Street to the chip shop and was soon rewarded with a small bag of chips wrapped in newspaper. The small opening allowed the steam to escape and for her to add a generous helping of vinegar and salt. Claudette liked her food and knew the chips would just hit the spot that the boiled sweets hadn't quite reached. She eyed the hot saveloys, wishing she'd bought one, but the chips would do for now.

There was a small wall by the side of the Co-operative

stores on her way home; she could tuck herself there and enjoy her food with no fear of being seen by her mum. She wondered if Tom would walk Bessie to their gate, but doubted he had the manners to do so. She would keep an eye out for her sister so that she could accompany her along the dark streets. Claudette knew, for all her bravado, that Bessie was afraid of the dark, but she herself didn't mind it at all.

A few minutes later, licking her fingers clean and screwing up the paper into a tight ball, she saw that the film had finished. People were streaming out through the now open double doors into the night. Claudette smiled to herself; they were rather like ants running all over the place, hurrying home or catching a bus or, as she had done, going to the chip shop.

When her parents passed by on the other side of the road deep in conversation, Claudette gave a sigh of relief. It could only mean they hadn't spotted Bessie. She couldn't be much longer, could she?

There was hardly anyone in the street now and the lights were dimmed in the foyer of the cinema, meaning everyone apart from the staff had left. She stood up, brushed stray grains of salt from her coat and started to walk back towards the cinema. As she arrived outside, the staff began to leave. Now there was only a single bulb aglow at the back of the foyer, with the manager saying goodnight to a couple of workers as he locked the doors behind him. Where was Bessie?

Claudette headed down a side street and wandered up the road and back. There was a torch in her pocket – being a good Girl Guide, she always carried one – so she shone it down the alleyways, but couldn't see or hear a thing. If

131

she didn't find her sister soon, she'd have to head home alone and face the consequences. Their parents would be worried, as they weren't usually out as late as this.

She stood on the High Street side of the cinema looking up and down the road, growing increasingly panicked. Where the hell had Bessie gone? It was as she stood there, out of her mind with worry, that she heard men's voices from inside the building, behind an emergency exit. That's strange, she thought – she had seen the manager lock up and go home, hadn't she?

She moved aside so she wasn't as close to the doors and watched as three lads rushed out, two of them laughing their heads off. They were followed by her sister, with Tom. He had his arm slung round Bessie's shoulders and pulled her to him, kissing her soundly on the lips.

'What do you think of that? I told you I'd give you a good time,' he laughed, giving her a pack of cigarettes. Bessie put them into her handbag, along with a bar of chocolate from one of the other lads. She seemed to be enjoying the experience as much as they were.

'I'll see you tomorrow to divvy up the rest of what we nicked,' Tom called as the other lads ran off. 'At least we are alone now,' he said, and Bessie laughed.

'That was fun. I've never done anything like that before,' she giggled as they headed off towards the road that led towards her home.

Claudette hung back, following slowly, not wanting them to know she'd spotted what was going on. It was obvious they'd stolen things from the shop inside the foyer as they left, stuffing cigarettes and sweets into their pockets. They must have hidden somewhere inside until the cinema was locked up. She was aware her sister was as involved as these boys were, and if they were caught, then Bessie would be in trouble. She wanted to run home and cry to her parents, but that wasn't an option. No, she'd have to discuss it with Bessie once they were in their bedroom and had some privacy. For now, she'd keep following them towards home, but would have to be careful in case Tom turned back and spotted her after he'd left Bessie.

As they walked over the hump in Manor Road that was part of a bridge over the railway line below, Tom pulled Bessie into the bushes that lay between the line and the back alleyway of nearby houses. Claudette could hear hushed words, and then silence. She put her hands in her pockets, wishing she'd worn her gloves, and stamped her feet to keep them warm, hoping the couple weren't having too much of a kiss and a cuddle. Turning her back on where they were, she took out her torch and quickly shone it on her wristwatch. If they weren't home in ten minutes, they would need to get their excuses sorted out.

It was a quarter of an hour before she heard the bushes rustle. Tom appeared immediately, setting off down the road, whistling a merry tune. Claudette wasn't sure what had happened, but hoped her sister would hurry up out of there. After waiting for a couple of minutes she crept in through the bushes where Tom had exited, pushing her way through until she saw her sister in a small clearing, straightening her coat and doing up her belt. Her hair looked an absolute mess.

'What the hell are you up to? We are really going to be in trouble if we don't get indoors soon,' she said as she shone the torch on Bessie. 'You look a right state! Put a brush through your hair, quickly,' she exclaimed. 'I don't know, hiding in bushes and kissing lads, whatever will you get up to next? I know I sound just like Mum, but you weren't brought up to do things like this. It's not as if he's a great catch, is it?' This was something she'd read in a magazine.

Bessie said nothing, but quickly brushed her hair and followed her sister out into the road. They both looked left and right before crossing and hurrying up Alexandra Road, keeping their heads down in case anyone spotted them. They slipped passed number thirteen as swiftly as possible, but the curtains were drawn tight closed and the light was out in the hall.

As they approached the top end of the road, Claudette took a deep breath. 'Here goes,' she whispered, but still Bessie stayed quiet. Using her key to open the door, she stepped into the hall to be met by Sadie and James.

'Hello girls, we thought it was your mum and dad,' Sadie said cheerfully. 'You've beaten them home. Now you're here we'll slip off, if you don't mind. The little ones are in bed, we've not heard a peep from them all evening.'

'That's fine, you get off home. I can sit up to wait for Mum and Dad. I didn't realize we were so late,' Claudette said, giving Sadie a kiss on the cheek and James a shy smile. 'Are you going to sit up with me, Bessie?' she asked her sister. Bessie pushed past them all without replying, and went upstairs.

When she finally got upstairs herself, after their parents had arrived home and drunk the tea Claudette had prepared, she found her sister huddled in a tight ball in her bed. Claudette thought she was awake, as she could have sworn she heard a small sob from under the blankets.

'Are you all right, Bessie?' she asked quietly. There was no reply.

Claudette lay on her back, chewing her lip. When they weren't falling out they were normally close, sharing secrets their parents wouldn't have understood; however, lately Claudette felt they hadn't been quite as close. Her sister seemed to prefer being with Clemmie Billington. As the moon cast shadows on the bedroom ceiling, Claudette found she couldn't sleep for worrying about Bessie. 'I'm here if you want to talk to me,' she whispered as loud as she dared, in case their parents heard from the next room.

She waited for an answer, but there was silence.

11

'Have I done this right, Mrs Gilbert?' Clemmie asked, holding out a leather-bound ledger to Sarah.

Sarah peered at the neatly listed numbers and the total at the bottom. 'That looks very tidy. Well done, Clemmie – and please, while we are in the office together you may call me Sarah. On the shop floor I'm Mrs Gilbert, and at home I'm Auntie Sarah as normal,' she said, giving the girl a pleasant smile. 'We are colleagues at the moment, so Sarah and Clemmie seems so much more friendly; unless of course you wish to be addressed as Clementine?'

The girl screwed up her face. 'It's a bit of a mouthful, isn't it? Clemmie would be much better,' she said as she looked down at the badge pinned to the jacket of her suit. 'I feel quite important wearing this,' she laughed. 'Miss C. Billington – but I do hope nobody thinks I was awarded promotion because of my mum.'

'Of course they won't. I wouldn't have anyone work for me because of Betty. She has no influence in this office, unless of course she decides to take the best biscuit on the plate rather than share,' Sarah said, giving the girl a wink.

Betty was known to favour certain biscuits. 'Now let me just double-check your figures.'

'I did them three times, and I used that machine over in the corner. I hope you don't mind. It was while you went for your lunch break. I had a look under the cover and pushed a few buttons. It's an adding machine, isn't it?'

Sarah grimaced. 'It's called a comptometer; you can do all kinds of calculations on it. Head office sent it to your mother with a letter to say there would be staff training at some point. Your mother very kindly passed it on to my office. I have no idea when I'm going to get time to be trained to use such a contraption, and I'm not really inclined to touch it. Well done you for taking a look. Why not put it on your desk and see if you can get more use out of it? There's an instruction manual somewhere in here that may help you,' she said, rummaging in her desk drawer.

'I'd like that very much,' Clemmie said. 'You know, I wasn't sure about working in the office. I was afraid it was some kind of punishment, because of my part in that argument on the shop floor. But I'm really enjoying it. There's quite a lot involved, isn't there?'

'You seem very keen. I'm impressed with your tidy approach to the paperwork, and of course your adding skills. This looks perfect,' Sarah said, passing back the ledger. 'Now, I need to go and see your mother. Do you think you could add up the rest of these pages and carry the figures forward to these, please?' she asked, pointing to some official-looking documents from head office. 'Why not do it in pencil to begin with, then when you know it's correct you can ink over it afterwards.'

Clemmie laughed. 'That's what I do with my homework at school. It looks tidier than lots of crossing out.'

'You're a girl after my own heart, Clemmie. Now, once I've had my chat with Betty I'll pop into the canteen and pick us up a cup of tea each.'

'But it's not my tea break yet.'

'Let's call it a perk of working in the office, shall we? Don't be surprised if your mother joins us, though.'

'Perhaps we ought to hide the best biscuits, then,' Clemmie laughed.

Sarah stuck her head around Betty's door, finding her on the telephone. She mimed 'cup of tea' and pointed towards the wall connecting both offices. Betty nodded and put her hand up, waving 'five minutes'.

'Just the woman I want to see,' Maureen said as her daughter-in-law appeared in the canteen. 'I wondered if you could do me a big favour?'

'As long as I can have a tea tray for three people; and as you've made rock buns, may I have three of those as well, please? They're not all for me – we're having a meeting in my office.'

Maureen's eyes glinted. 'Oh, a meeting, is it? Are you sure it's not an excuse for a tea party?'

'No, not at all. We are going over the paperwork to do with staff pay rises that have arrived from head office, so it's thirsty work. What favour was it you wanted me to do for you? I'll help if I can,' Sarah said, pinching a stray currant from the plate.

'Well, I was going to see that film this evening, it's called *The Blue Lamp*.'

'It is supposed to be good; I was hoping to go with Alan, but he's been so busy with those televisions and wirelesses in the shop that we've just not been able to spare the time.'

'I thought as much. Your dad was going to take me to see it, he even bought me a box of chocolates to take. But he's got such a terrible cough that I've told him to stay home and keep warm in front of the fire. I wondered if you'd like to come with me, seeing as how Alan is too busy?'

Sarah thought for a moment. 'I would love to. I do need to sort out someone to sit with the children, but I can't see it being a problem. In fact, when I get back to my office I'll ask young Clemmie if she can help out. Possibly Dorothy will want to come along too.'

Maureen poured boiling water into a teapot and placed it on the tray that already contained three cups, saucers and plates along with the buns. 'Then I'll knock on your door at six o'clock. That way we can watch the B movie first. It's Johnny Johnson in one of his spy movies – quite an old one because he's given up acting now, Freda was telling me recently. I still can't believe our Molly Missons is married to him. It seems quite strange to me – and he's such a nice chap in real life. Does he still work at Butlins?'

'No, no; in fact, I heard a little while ago that he and Molly now have their own small holiday camp on the Kent coast. I must ask Freda about it. She's sure to be visiting before too long.'

'Oh, I could do with a holiday,' Maureen said wistfully. 'And a nice holiday camp would fit the bill, with no cooking and all the entertainment laid on for the choosing. There is something for all age groups, from what I've been told. I'm going to have to speak to your dad about it.'

'It would be lovely to have a family holiday.'

Back in the office, Clemmie had cleared a space on the desk so that Sarah had room to put down the tea tray.

'Here you are,' Sarah said as Betty walked in. 'You must have smelt the tea brewing.'

'I heard the crockery rattle as you walked past my door. How are you getting on, my dear?' she asked, leaning over her stepdaughter's shoulder and looking at the ledger. 'I must say, you have beautiful handwriting – so much better than mine. In fact . . .' She looked up at a long shelf. 'Here it is,' she said, pointing to a ledger that was ten years old. 'When you have a moment, take a look in there. My handwriting isn't half as nice as yours.'

'Please don't look at mine, as it's even worse,' Sarah said. 'All the blots and crossing-outs will be mine – I'm surprised you never sacked me, Betty.'

The women all laughed as they settled down with their tea. Betty laid a couple of sheets of paper on the table. 'I'm afraid it's not very good news. Although our staff will receive a pay rise, it will be very little.'

'I never expected much, the way the country is right now, still trying to get back on its feet after the war. We will do our best like we always do,' Sarah said.

'I just hope the staff understand,' Betty said as she tapped her pen on the desk, thinking. 'I wonder if perhaps, with Maureen's help, we could lower the prices for lunch in the canteen? At least then we will know our staff have at least one filling meal a day and won't go without. So many women do, you know,' she said to Clemmie. 'They'd rather not see their husband and children go without.'

'That's a thought, although we're going to have to find

new food sources.' Sarah was thoughtful. 'During the war, head office were behind us when we spoke to local farmers and even allotment owners about providing supplies. Come to think of it, Bob has hung onto two of his allotments, and even with our family's help he's finding it a strain. I wonder if we could ask to take on one of them? We could have staff lend a hand, and any food that we create could be used in the canteen.'

'That's a thought.' Betty nodded her head. 'But it's rather long-term, isn't it? I was wondering about right now . . .'

'What about speaking to your Aunt Pat?' Clemmie suggested to Sarah. 'With the big farm in Slades Green – might she and her husband offer us a discount?'

'Good thinking, Clemmie. Why I never thought about Pat I don't know. I'll pop in and see Nan and Bob and ask if they will have a word with her when she next visits. I always seem to miss her these days, what with being at work.'

Betty was warming to the subject. 'We could speak to the local butcher and fishmonger as well. We could negotiate a discount of some kind and offer one back – of course head office would have to approve.'

Sarah kept jotting down notes. 'These are all very good ideas. If we keep abreast of this, there may be an article in it for *The New Bond* – that's the staff magazine,' she explained to Clemmie, who was looking puzzled. 'Oh, before I forget, Clemmie: I wondered, would you be able to look after my children this evening? Maureen has invited me to accompany her to the cinema to see *The Blue Lamp*. Dad's not feeling so well and she's making him stay at home, and Maureen's not one for going to the cinema on her own.'

Clemmie looked crestfallen. 'I would love to, but—'

Betty interrupted. 'Douglas's family have invited us to a party. It's his cousins fiftieth wedding anniversary and we don't see them very often, so I couldn't really turn down the invitation even though I've not met most of them.'

'I completely understand,' Sarah said. 'Don't you worry about it – I can ask Bessie and Claudette. I'll catch them before they finish work this afternoon.'

'I hope they can, I'd hate you to miss seeing the film,' Clemmie said politely before turning to Betty. 'I added up all the figures in the ledger using that comp . . . comp . . .'

'Comptometer,' Sarah supplied. 'That's the name of the adding-up machine you moved in here,' she said to Betty.

'Oh well done, you've worked out how to use it?'

'As I only had to add up figures, it wasn't too hard. The booklet shows there's much more the machine can do,' Clemmie explained.

Betty pulled a face. 'I did look at the booklet, but the instructions went over my head, I'm afraid. I applaud you for understanding even a small part of it.'

Clemmie looked at Betty with a hopeful expression. 'Sarah said there's going to be a training course?'

'There is, but it's a matter of Sarah finding time to attend – that's if you really want to?' she asked, seeing the worried look flash over Sarah's face.

'To be honest, Betty, I can't think of anything worse. Just looking at the thing makes me feel uncomfortable. Rows and rows of buttons with numbers on them, and knowing me, I'll probably get my finger stuck between the keys. Do I really have to go? I don't feel it will help me at all with my work.'

'Oh dear; head office is so keen for us to have one here. They've been using mechanized accounts for some time now. The accounts department swears by them. I'm told this is the way forward in business and will be revolutionary.'

Sarah laughed. 'You're not convincing me, Betty.'

Clemmie was looking between the two women, holding her breath until she could butt in. 'May I attend the course?' she asked, looking nervously at Betty. 'I know I've only been working in this office for two weeks, and only on Saturdays, but I really enjoy office work. I'd like to think that when I leave school shortly I could work in an office, as long as I have training. I really don't want to go to university. I've only gone along with that idea so as not to upset you and Daddy.'

Sarah felt uncomfortable. This really ought to be a private conversation between Clemmie and her parents.

Betty was thoughtful. 'I have come to the conclusion, my dear, that your skills lie in directions other than academia. Your father and I have discussed your future at great length. You know I don't wish you to be unhappy. Sarah has shown me that removing you from the shop floor to work here with her was a very good idea. You are a quick learner.'

'She has proved herself worthy of working here,' Sarah agreed.

'I would need to have a word with head office. I'm wondering if we could offer you a part-time job here in the office and perhaps find you a course to attend; that way you wouldn't be beholden to stay with us if you decided to move on with your career. Let us have a chat about it later with your father, shall we?'

Clemmie jumped to her feet and kissed Betty's cheek. 'I did notice something in the local newspaper the other day. There was a copy on one of the tables in the canteen.'

Sarah looked between the two happy faces and made her excuses. 'I need to go down to the shop floor to catch Bessie and Claudette and ask if they're available this evening, if you will excuse me?'

She left the office and Clemmie followed behind, hurrying to fetch the local newspaper before taking it to Betty, who had gone back to her own desk. 'Look, it's here, quite a big advert. It's for the local college, called Erith College of Technology. They have a course that teaches office machinery – I think that means accounting machines and typing – as well as "a grounding in office practice". I don't know what half of that means, but I'd be willing to learn. What do you think?' she said, looking at Betty expectantly.

Betty took the newspaper and slowly read the advertisement. 'I suggest what we do is write to the college and ask for a prospectus; then you can join when the new term starts. But only if you promise to study hard and we can see that it would be a career-enhancing move. For now, let me get on with some work, but I'll make sure that I write the letter before I leave the office today, and we can catch the last post. We can talk to your father once we know the course is what you wish to follow.' She looked up at Clemmie. 'I'm very proud of you,' she smiled.

Clemmie leant over the desk and hugged her stepmother. 'Thank you, oh, thank you so much.'

Betty smiled to herself. Clemmie was coming out of her shell at long last, and was beginning not to be the aloof girl that no one seemed to like. Oh yes, she was aware of what others thought of her stepdaughter.

Downstairs, Sarah found Bessie and Claudette working on the biscuit counter. Even with rationing dominating the country, Woolworths still managed to supply a reasonable number of biscuits to sell in its stores. Broken biscuits were very popular with shoppers, who hoped to find the occasional whole biscuit in amongst the mix.

She quickly explained her predicament in needing somebody to sit with the children that evening, until Alan returned home. 'If you agree, I can put a telephone call through to Maisie. Then you can come straight home with me and have your tea with the children before I go out?'

Claudette was the first to speak. 'We would love to, wouldn't we, Bessie?' she said, nudging her sister, who looked rather petulant. Bessie just nodded without saying a word.

With a sign of relief Sarah headed back to her office, thinking that she really must get on with some work. She had a heap of paperwork to clear as well as placing an advert for new part-time staff. They really could do with replacing Clemmie, now she worked in the office, as they were one Saturday girl down. Sarah did wonder how long she would have Clemmie working for her. Clearly the girl had plans for a career that might not be with Woolworths.

'You could have said no,' Bessie complained to Claudette after serving a customer.

'I like looking after Georgie and Buster. And Uncle Alan lets us use his gramophone to play his records, and we get to have tea with Auntie Sarah as well. She's a much better cook than Mum.'

'You're always thinking of your stomach,' Bessie snapped as she nodded towards a waiting customer. 'It might be all right for you, but I was going out to meet Tom. Now what am I going to do?'

By the time Claudette had helped the customer and returned to her sister's side, Bessie was smiling. 'I have a plan. You're going to agree with it because you've dropped me in this, and you're going to keep your mouth shut, do you hear me?'

A feeling of dread washed over Claudette and she turned away, tidying up a pile of brown paper bags under the counter. What was her sister up to now?

'Why are you on your own? I thought Bessie was coming with you?' Sarah said as she looked past Claudette and could see the road was empty.

'She had to pop home for something. I'm not late, am I?'

'No, no, of course not, come along inside. I'm just about to dish up dinner. It's shepherd's pie, I hope you like it?'

'I love it, it's my favourite food. I'd eat it every day if I could,' Claudette said, bending down to hug Georgina and grab Buster and give him a big kiss before he ran away.

'I hate being kissed,' he complained as he scrubbed at his cheek.

'You wait until you're older, you won't mind girls kissing you then,' she chuckled. 'Is there anything I can do to help, Auntie Sarah?'

'Would you like to put the knives and forks on the table, please, and I've dished up your Uncle Alan's because he's going to be late and put a plate over it on top of the pan of warm water. If he's not in by eight o'clock, would you light the gas under the pan and keep an eye on the water in case it burns low? I asked him to be home by eight, so hopefully he'll be in by half past,' she chuckled, 'but mind you don't burn your fingers. You'll be no good to your mum down at that factory if you've got bandages all over your hands.'

'I'll be very careful,' Claudette promised. 'Besides, Bessie will be here soon. You have got time to eat with us, haven't you?'

'Yes, I have fifteen minutes before Maureen knocks on the door. I do hope Bessie's meal doesn't go cold.'

'She told me she'd be five minutes behind me,' Claudette said with her fingers crossed behind her back. In truth, Bessie had dashed home to pick up her make-up and a frock to change into, for when she met Tom. Claudette hated telling her aunt lies because she liked her so much, and she loved coming round to her house and helping out with the children. They were slightly older than her own brothers and sisters, so she could read to them and play at being a teacher, or practise her first aid; although Buster wriggled quite a bit.

'I've put a plate over Bessie's as well, so it will still be warm when she arrives.'

Claudette set out the places, leaving one empty for her sister. 'I'll kill her if she's late,' she muttered to herself.

'What was that?'

'Nothing. I was just counting I've got enough forks out.'

They were halfway through the meal before there was a knock on the door and Sarah let Bessie into the house. 'That's a large bag. Are you planning to do something this evening?' Sarah asked.

'Yes, I brought some books and a jigsaw puzzle,' Bessie beamed at Sarah before giving her sister a warning look.

They'd no sooner finished their meal than Maureen arrived. Claudette told Sarah to hurry off, promising they would do the washing up and clear away.

'You should move in with me. I'll find somewhere for you to sleep even if it's in the cellar,' Sarah chuckled. 'No one else seems to help with the washing up around here.'

No sooner had the adults left the house than Bessie dashed upstairs to the children's bedroom. She came down minutes later in her best frock and proceeded to sit at the table putting on her make-up.

'You look pretty,' Georgina said. 'Are you taking us out somewhere?'

'No, not this time. I have to go back to work,' Bessie said. 'But you can stay here and play with Claudette.'

'Shall I fetch your bag that's got the books and the jigsaw puzzle in it?' Buster asked.

'Oh no, I forgot them – but you've got plenty of toys here. Claudette will play with all of them with you,' she told him, smiling sweetly. 'However, if your mummy asks, it's our secret and you must say I was here all evening with you. Do you promise me that?'

'I will if you let me have some of your lipstick.' Georgina sidled up to her.

Bessie held the girl's chin in one hand as she quickly touched a little of the red lipstick to the child's lips. 'There, that looks pretty – would you like a little of my perfume as well?' she asked, picking up a small bottle of Miss Dior that Maisie had given her when there was just a drop of it left. She dabbed the tip of her finger onto the little girl's wrist.

Georgina ran off happily to look at herself in the mirror while Claudette followed Bessie to the door.

'What the heck are you playing at? The children are bound to say something, and don't forget Uncle Alan is going to be home by eight o'clock – you'd best be back here by then.'

'The kids will be in bed by then. Just tell him that I had to go home.'

'I don't like telling lies,' Claudette said, looking miserable.

'I will be going home at some point, so it's not exactly a lie, is it?'

'You will be careful, won't you? I'm not sure what you got up to with Tom in those bushes, but you shouldn't encourage him. You know what Mum has told us about boys.'

Bessie gave a harsh laugh. 'Why don't you grow up? You're more like Georgina than a woman of fourteen who can go to work full time and have a good time.'

'But I do have a good time. I thought we'd be having a good time here tonight, looking after the children. And we always have a good time at the Girl Guides, don't we?'

Bessie shook her head as if in despair, then gave a sarcastic laugh. 'It's about time you stopped acting like a child. If you don't start learning about what adults get up to, you're going to be in for a shock in a couple of years,' she said before opening the door and hurrying out into the dark night.

Claudette watched as she crossed the road and hurried to where the pavement widened by the Prince of Wales pub. She just caught a glimpse of Tom standing under a lamp post. He slung his arm around her sister, kissing her soundly before they walked away.

'Nothing good is going to come of this,' Claudette muttered to herself as she went indoors to start the washing up. Handing each of the children a tea towel, she told them, 'If we get this done, we can play a game, what do you think to that?'

They jumped up and down in excitement, and Claudette decided that whatever her sister got up to was no concern of hers. If Bessie got told off for being out late, or for drinking, well, it had nothing to do with her. All the same, she couldn't shake off a small worry that nagged at her throughout the evening. Would Bessie's actions come back to haunt her?

12

Easter 1950

'Would you like a top-up, Mum? It's a nice drop of port,' George said as he hovered by Ruby, holding out a bottle.

Ruby put a hand over her glass. 'I won't, if you don't mind, love. I'm going to toast Maisie's good health and luck with her new business venture, then I'm going to see if someone will drop me off back home.'

George sat down next to his mum. She'd not left her seat all evening and he was concerned she might be feeling unwell. 'This isn't like you, Mum. You're normally the life and soul of a party. This is a big do for Maisie – look at all the people who have turned up to wish her well.'

They both looked at the crowd of people huddled in the main space of the factory, where industrial-sized sewing machines were lined up in a row. Colourful bolts of fabric could be seen propped up in baskets in the corners of the room. The walls had been painted white and there were posters and hand-coloured designs of women's clothing dotted about, creating a bright and inviting place to work.

'She's made it look very cosy, I must say,' Ruby acknowledged. 'It's just that I feel a bit uncomfortable.'

George placed the beer bottle on the floor beside him and reached out to take her hand. 'I'd have thought you'd be in line for a job down here,' he laughed, but she didn't join in with his joke.

'I said I'd come to congratulate Maisie and the girls, and I've done that. But this place, well, it's no more than a few hundred yards from where . . . from where . . .' She looked at George, lost for words.

George understood as the penny finally dropped. 'I should have thought of that, Mum. I do apologize. It's been a long time since that terrible day and it's brave of you to be able to come along.'

'I'm glad you understand, George. I feel a bit daft, to be honest. It's just over twenty-six years since I lost friends in that explosion and fire, but the memories will always hang heavy where we live because of the loss of so many young lives. Like you said, any other time I'd be the life and soul of the party. It just seems disrespectful to be having fun, when . . .'

'I tell you what, Mum, I've got my car outside, so when you're ready I'll drive you back. Maisie will understand, and as Sarah knows, she'll cover for you. But can you tell me one thing? What was on this very spot back in 1924?'

Ruby thought long and hard. 'Why, it was just farmer's fields around here, or marshland. Apart from Gilbert's factory and a couple of other similar buildings.'

'Then why don't you think of Maisie's business as being in the middle of what was once a field? Imagine cows and sheep along with crops being grown. Why, our Pat's farm is only just along the lane from here. Why allow one small munitions factory to scare you away from this area? If you measure the distance from where Gilbert's was back to where your home is in Alexandra Road, it's not much further – and you're not worried about living at number thirteen, are you?'

'You must think I'm a daft old woman,' Ruby said as she gripped his hand tightly before kissing his cheek. 'I've been so focused on that day that it has stayed in my mind ever since. Even during the last war I was aware of that awful day.'

'You've got to remember, that awful day also brought you and my dad back together.'

Ruby took a deep breath and got to her feet. 'I told you I was being a silly old woman. Now, I'm going to look at those posters on the wall, as I do believe our Claudette drew some of them. She's going to be a real bonus to this business. I'm not so sure about Bessie, though; she does seem distracted,' she said, looking over to the other side of the room. Maisie's elder daughter was huddled up with Betty Billington's two daughters, and her own sister. 'Something is going on with her, you mark my words,' Ruby said.

'Why haven't you told us about Tom before?' Clemmie asked as Bessie stopped to draw breath, her face flushed with excitement.

'Because every time I see you, you're either talking about Woolworths or this course you're going on to become a businesswoman,' Bessie replied sarcastically.

Clemmie looked upset. 'That's not fair; you did ask what I was up to now that I'm the Saturday girls' supervisor.'

'I didn't expect an essay, I was being polite,' Bessie sniffed. 'It's not as if you've asked me what I'm up to. Do you even care that I have a boyfriend?' she said, blowing on her fingernails and polishing them on the front of her blouse.

'There's no need to act like that,' Clemmie said crossly.

'I suppose it's what I deserve for speaking with children, now I've grown up.' Bessie gave them a haughty look and strolled away.

Claudette felt her eyes start to water and blinked hard. 'You can see what I mean about how she's changed,' she said miserably to Dorothy and Clemmie. 'I'm so worried about this boy she's courting. I don't think he's any good for her.'

'What do you mean, no good for her?' Dorothy asked, slipping her hand into Claudette's and giving it a squeeze.

'Come on, you can tell us. It will go no further,' Clemmie promised.

'Well, she brags to me about him, and I don't like what I'm hearing. Perhaps it's because I'm only fourteen and I don't understand what goes on in the world. If I tell you, will you promise not to say anything to our parents? And can you tell me if I'm wrong in what I'm thinking?'

'Of course we will,' Clemmie said. 'I can't guarantee I know the answers about what goes on in the world, but being a little older than you, I may have an idea. Come on, spill the beans.'

Dorothy stood up. 'Let me fetch us some food first, because it may have gone before we get to the table. And if we're sitting here eating and chatting, people won't think we're discussing anything important, will they?'

'That's a very good idea. Come on, let's do that – it's a fine spread. Auntie Maureen prepared it.'

'Not Bessie, then?' Clemmie laughed.

'Ha, ha – of course not. When did she ever do anything like that? She said she was washing her hair.'

The three girls piled their plates high with sandwiches and sausage rolls, which were plentiful considering that so much was still rationed.

'Your mum could always lay her hands on things, couldn't she,' Dorothy said.

'This food was sent by my grandmother; you know, my dad's mum,' Claudette explained. 'That's the posh side of the family. She sent a hamper full of nice things for us to prepare, as they couldn't be here with us today. They've always been really supportive of Mum's business. And Dad's, come to that. We don't see them in Erith very often, but on the odd occasion we've managed to visit them in Wiltshire they've been really nice. I like them a lot.'

Claudette was such a pleasant girl, Dorothy thought. She saw the good in everyone, unlike Bessie.

They went back to their seats, each with a plate of food in one hand and a glass of lemonade in the other, and settled down to chat. Claudette swivelled her seat round so that she was facing the Billington sisters. With her back to the room, she felt she could speak more freely without worrying about anyone looking at her.

'She's been seeing him three or four times a week. Sometimes they go to the pictures, but I go as well and have to sit on my own so Bessie can pretend she was with me rather than a lad, in case our parents ask. Other times, I say we are babysitting together when really it's just me. She's even missed going to the Girl Guides, which is a bit dodgy considering Auntie Freda may tell Mum. I've made excuses about her having a sore throat or a headache, but to be honest, they're going to find out before long.'

'Look, why don't we meet up and go to the cinema, or just out for a walk? I know it's still a bit chilly but at least then you won't be on your own, and we can help. You shouldn't have to carry these problems on your own,' Clemmie said. 'So, tell us, what does he do for a living, and how old is he?'

'Bessie told me he's eighteen and he works down at the Mobo factory near the river. That's where they make toys. He's just a labourer, but brags to make himself sound clever to Bessie – but she can't see that.' She hesitated.

'I take it there's more,' Clemmie said, seeing the concern on Claudette's face.

'I know for a fact he is stealing things,' Claudette said, going on to describe the evening she'd caught Bessie and the lads coming out the back door of the Odeon. 'If they get caught for that, Bessie is going to get into trouble as well, because she was part of the gang. From what I saw, she enjoyed it very much.'

The Billington sisters both looked shocked. 'I can see why you're worried,' Dorothy said. 'Goodness knows what else they're getting up to.'

'She's getting up to something else with him as well,' Claudette said, looking each way before moving closer to the girls and whispering.

What they heard shocked them. 'Why would she do such a thing with a lad at her age . . . what if she . . . ?'

Claudette stopped Clemmie in her tracks. 'I've already thought of that. I too wonder what will happen if she is left with a baby.'

Dorothy was about to bite into her sandwich and stopped, a look of distaste crossing her face as she placed it back down on the plate. 'I feel sick,' she said. 'I could understand if the lad was forcing her – do you think he was?' she asked, looking concerned. 'At least then she'd have an excuse, if . . .'

Claudette was doubtful. 'No. I think the first time they did it was as I followed them home after they'd been nicking stuff from the Odeon. I waited for ages while they were in some bushes down the end of the road, and when she came out she wouldn't speak to me. He headed off home in the other direction, looking full of himself. Mum brought us both up properly to understand what can happen if we go with boys. She made it quite clear, but it's a safe bet he doesn't give a damn about the consequences. As for Bessie . . . I reckon she's in love with the idea of having a boyfriend, and she just wants to show off. She's not thinking straight.'

'You really need to spell it out to her and mention that she could get pregnant,' Dorothy insisted as she picked up a sausage roll, sinking her teeth into it. It was a shame to waste good food.

'She treats me like a kid – she's not going to listen to me. I'm just the person who's there to help her with her cover stories.'

'Then perhaps we need to speak to her together. I'm older than her, so she may just listen to me,' Clemmie said. 'Look, why don't we finish our food, grab her and drag her outside? Then we can give her a talking to. Together we may be able to get through to her that you're not going to cover for her any more, so she'll have to tell your mum

157

and dad she's got a boyfriend and do things properly. And then, if anything does happen, the blame won't fall at your feet for covering for her.'

'Thank you, that's a weight off my mind. I wanted to ask for your help weeks ago, but there just wasn't the opportunity when we were at Woolies; there were always other people around, as well as Bessie.'

'I wish you'd been able to,' Clemmie said. 'Goodness knows how many times she's – well, you know, she's been with him. It may already be too late. Come on, eat up, then we will wander around the room, have a chat to a few people, look at your lovely posters on the walls, and then we can grab Bessie.'

'These are wonderful,' Dorothy said, looking up at the hand-painted designs on the walls of the warehouse factory. 'Where did you copy them from?'

Claudette blushed. 'I did copy the style of the mannequins, but the outfits are my own designs. Do you really like them?'

'They are beautiful,' Clemmie said, looking closely at a picture of a bridesmaid's dress. 'What does your mum think of them?'

'She says she's going to have some of them made up as samples to see what they look like in the flesh, so to speak. I hope she doesn't waste the fabric – they were just ideas. I'm really looking forward to when the Bexleyheath shop opens, because it's going to be just wedding dresses and outfits that people wear to weddings, and of course bridesmaid and pageboy outfits as well. Dad says Mum is going too fast and should hold back a little and have a few bridal items in the two shops; but Mum says it's just frocks, and if it doesn't work out, then the Bexleyheath shop can go back to selling all kinds of clothing, like we do in Erith.'

'I do hope it works out,' Clemmie said. 'If I had a boyfriend and he proposed to me, I'd like to buy a wedding dress designed by you and sold in Maisie's Modes.'

Claudette blushed. 'That's really kind of you, but don't rush and find a boyfriend on my account, will you? We don't want another one in trouble like my sister.'

'Oh goodness, no,' Clemmie chuckled. 'I know what I want to do with my future, and Auntie Sarah and Mum have really helped me.'

Claudette frowned. 'I'm sorry – I've been so tied up helping Mum and working at Woolies on Saturdays, let alone this business with Bessie, that I missed that news. We don't get to chat as much now you're in the office, so please tell all.'

Dorothy couldn't contain her excitement about her sister's news. 'She's going to go to college and learn how to work in business.'

Clemmie smiled. 'She means I'm going to learn how to use business machines up at Erith College. Mum reckons I'll find a decent job. I may even go and work in London.'

'That's wonderful. I'm not sure I'd like to go and work in London myself – it's a bit noisy up there for me, and dusty – but it does sound exciting. Perhaps I could meet you there some time and we could go to the theatre, and even see Buckingham Palace?'

'We can do that long before I have a job. Why don't we make some plans for the summer? We can save up and have a day out, just the four of us.'

The girls agreed to this idea before spotting Bessie standing on her own, looking miserable.

'Come on, let's go sort out this problem,' Clemmie said, heading over towards Bessie. The younger two followed and linked arms with Bessie, so she had no choice but to go with them.

'Come with us,' Clemmie said, looking serious. 'We're going to chat with Nanny Ruby, and then we will go outside for some fresh air. So, as my mum would say, pin a smile on your face before anyone guesses what you're thinking.'

Bessie flashed her a questioning look.

'There's no need to look like that,' Clemmie continued, 'we all know what you've been up to. Come on now, this is supposed to be a party to celebrate your mum's business, so let's go and chat as if we don't have a care in the world. One sad face and she will guess there's a problem, so watch yourself,' she hissed, as they walked across the room trying to look nonchalant.

'Hello, girls – don't you look lovely in your new dresses. Maisie has told me you all got new frocks for the occasion. Turn round and let me have a proper look,' Ruby said, and the girls did as they were told and pirouetted on the spot. Claudette pretended she was a ballerina, which made Ruby laugh out loud. 'You're always the joker, my girl. I'm still surprised you're not planning to go on the stage, you've got a beautiful singing voice as well.'

'No, she's going to work for her mum. Did you know she designed some of those frocks on those posters on the wall?' Dorothy said, proud of her friend.

'You must've got your talent from your mum,' Ruby said,

before falling silent. Everyone knew Maisie wasn't really her mother.

'Don't worry, Nanny Ruby – Maisie is my mum really, and I like to think I've learnt a lot from her.'

'What about you, Bessie – are you excited as well?'

Bessie's shoulders drooped and she looked glum until Clemmie gave her a dig in the ribs, making her jump and do her best to speak pleasantly to the old woman. 'Mum is very clever in business, isn't she? But I don't quite know what I want to do yet,' she said, doing her best to put a smile on her face. How could she tell everyone that she wanted to run away from Erith, to travel and see the world alongside Tom? Thinking of him sent a thrill of excitement up her spine. She'd have to go soon because he'd be waiting outside.

'Phew, I feel quite warm,' Clemmie said, flapping her hands in front of her face. 'I think I'll go outside and get a breath of air. Are you three coming?'

The girls agreed with her. Promising to speak to Ruby again before the evening was out, they hurried after Clemmie.

'They seem excited,' Bob said as he joined his wife, holding a glass of port out to her as he tried not to spill his pint of beer.

'They do, don't they? But you know what, Bob, I think those girls are up to something. I can sniff trouble a mile off. You mark my words, something is brewing.'

'If there is, love, at least you will be here to offer them a shoulder to cry on.'

'That goes without saying,' Ruby answered as she watched the door close after the young girls.

*

'What's this all about?' Bessie huffed as she perched herself on some wooden crates that had been stacked against a wall. She straightened the skirt of her dress as she waited for a response. She was rather proud of her appearance tonight: her hair brushed up into a French pleat, making her appear older, and a pale blue dress that hung and clung in just the right places. She couldn't wait for Tom to see her in it, as she knew she looked just like the Hollywood actress in a film they'd seen recently. She licked her lips, which reminded her she would need to top up her lipstick and add a little more perfume to the front of her throat before he arrived. She'd not do it until the last moment, because her excuse for leaving would be that she had a headache.

'You know damn well what I'm going to talk to you about,' Clemmie said sternly. 'It's that Tom, and how you've been using Claudette to cover for you while you go out to see him.'

'So you've been telling tales, have you? Next you'll be telling Mum and Dad,' Bessie flashed at her sister.

'No, it wasn't like that at all,' Claudette said, trying to hold back tears. 'I've been that worried about you and the things you're getting up to . . .'

'What I get up to is no concern of yours. I'm a grown-up now and you're still a kid.'

Dorothy put her arm around Claudette as she started to cry. 'There's no need to speak to her like that. If you think she's a kid, you shouldn't expect her to cover for you and be forced to tell lies. If you are an adult, you should be able to explain to your parents what you're up to,' she spat.

Bessie gave a dramatic sigh, wishing she had a cigarette to light to complete the effect. It was a shame she had to hide them away in case Maisie saw them and asked questions.

'There's no use arguing,' Clemmie said, taking charge as the oldest of the group. She felt responsible and wanted to make sure everything was sorted out satisfactorily. 'We're all worried about you, Bessie. We get the impression that you're fond of this Tom and could have gone too far with him . . .'

'I like him a lot. He makes me feel grown up.' Bessie didn't add that at times she was uncomfortable with what Tom expected her to do when they were alone.

'I take it he's quite keen on doing a bit of stealing with his mates as well, is that right?' Clemmie asked as she put her hands on her hips.

'How would I know what they get up to when they're on their own?'

'But they weren't on their own the night I saw you come out the back of the Odeon,' Claudette said, wiping her eyes. 'You were with them.'

Bessie shook her head in disgust. 'Oh, don't be so dramatic. I'm seeing a lad I like a lot and we have a few laughs. He's got some great mates and that's all there is to it.'

Clemmie decided she couldn't lose her temper with Bessie, or they'd get nowhere. She needed to convince the girl to listen to some common sense. 'Look here, Bessie, stealing even for a laugh is not good. Forget about how your family would feel, how would you feel if you got locked up in prison? From what I've heard, it's not a good place to be. Apart from the stealing, it's what you and Tom get up to when you're on your own. You do realize you could end up pregnant, don't you?'

The colour drained from Bessie's face. She was glad there was only one light outside and that most of them were in shadow.

'Speak to me,' Clemmie said. 'You do understand about all of this? I take it Maisie has explained what can happen to girls that go with lads?'

'Of course I do. You've got no need to worry about that,' Bessie said, crossing her fingers behind her back and thinking it was all too real now. Had she gone too far with Tom? Only time would tell.

A cough from behind a parked car had the girls turn to see Tom standing there.

'Just the woman I want to see,' he said, as Bessie stood up.

It was too late to use her lipstick and perfume now. 'Hello, Tom. I'll just collect my handbag and coat and I'll be with you,' she said, pushing past the others and hurrying back into the factory.

'Hello, girls,' Tom said as he stepped closer to the group. 'Do you work here? I hear it's a good set-up.'

'No, we don't work here,' Clemmie said. 'Claudette will, because it's her mum's business, and you probably know that Bessie will as well; but we are all here for the party to celebrate the opening of the business. What's it to you?' She stared at Tom. 'Have you been listening to what we've been talking about?'

Tom took a cigarette from a box in his pocket and lit it, looking thoughtful as he exhaled the smoke, directing it towards the girls. They wrinkled their noses in distaste.

'I've heard enough to know you don't seem to like me,' he said menacingly. 'I'll ask you all to mind your own business. If any word of what I get up to gets out, or you try to stop me seeing Bessie, then who knows what will happen to this place? It wouldn't take much for it to go up in smoke. Or perhaps all those pretty dresses you'll be making might be stolen ...' He laughed harshly as the door opened and Bessie hurried to his side.

'I'm ready,' she said, slipping her arm through his. 'You might tell Mum that I've got a headache and I have a lift home, so she's not to worry,' she told the girls, struggling to keep up with Tom as he marched away.

'Oh my God, what are we going to do?' Claudette said furiously, scrubbing her eyes in case she started to cry again.

'We are not going to do anything,' Clemmie instructed her. 'Any time Bessie tells you to cover for her, you are to refuse. If she insists, you get in touch with us and we will come and meet you. We're lucky that our parents have telephones in the house, so you can simply call us and come out with us. The last thing we want is you covering for her and walking the streets on your own. Goodness knows what could happen to you. We will take every opportunity to talk to Bessie and tell her what's so wrong about this chap – and with luck, she will start to listen. If not, perhaps we've just got to hang about and pick up the pieces.'

'But what about Mum and Dad?'

Clemmie was silent for a few minutes as she thought. 'For now, we will say nothing. And when you're at home, try not to be alone with Bessie. That way she can't talk you into anything.'

Claudette nodded her head. 'I can do that, yes.'

'And for now, I'll go and give your mum the message, because she won't cross-examine me. I'm prepared to lie enough to say that Bessie told me on my own and although

I offered to go with her, she said I was to stay and enjoy the party. But that's the only lie I'm going to tell to support your sister. From now on, we take charge of this situation, do you understand?'

13

May 1950

'Can't you hurry, we're going to be late,' Claudette snapped at her sister as she poked her head round their bedroom door. 'Honestly, I don't know what's wrong with you lately, you've been like a wet weekend. It's about time you told Mum and Dad that you're courting.'

Bettie snorted. 'I don't honestly think Tom or his mates are the kind of lads that would come round for afternoon tea, or pop down to visit Nanny Ruby, do you? And whatever it is she wants to see us about, she'd better hurry up, because I promised to meet him at six o'clock. I didn't expect to come home and find a note on the table from Mum to say we're to go straight down to number thirteen because of a family announcement.'

'Well, it must be something important, because her note said Dad is down there as well. If everyone's come home from work early because Nanny Ruby has summoned them, it must be serious. I just hope she's not going to tell us she's ill. She's quite old, you know,' Claudette said. Her bottom lip started to tremble. 'I couldn't bear it if she died, I just couldn't.'

'Oh, for heaven's sake, she's not going to sit us all down and make a big announcement about that. She'd probably speak to the parents and keep the rest of us in the dark. They treat us like kids. We're old enough to go to work, so they should respect us more.'

As they reached the gate to number thirteen, Bessie took her younger sister by the arm. 'Don't worry, I'm sure it's nothing nasty. Perhaps they're planning to have a party. Nanny Ruby is seventy this year, so it'll be a really special party.'

Claudette sniffed back her tears and nodded in agreement. This gentleness was more like the old Bessie, but that just made her feel even more tearful. 'A party for Nanny Ruby would be nice, wouldn't it? Come on, let's get inside and find out.'

The girls stepped into the long hallway, being careful not to tread on the younger children as well as their own three siblings, who were being chased back and forth by Auntie Sarah's son, Buster, while his sister scolded them for being noisy. Mike and Gwyneth Jackson's daughter, Myfi, stood shaking her head at the youngsters. Everyone liked Myfi, who was the spitting image of her mother, dark-haired and with a slight Welsh sing-song lilt when she spoke.

'You're going to get told off in a minute. All the grown-ups are trying to be serious about something and you're going to disturb them. Georgina, why don't you take them out into the garden? But don't get dirty,' she instructed in her soft voice.

'Hello, Myfi,' Bessie said as she gave the younger girl a hug. 'Do you know what's going on?' she asked, pulling off her coat.

'Don't ask me. Nanny Ruby seems quite excited about something. My dad wondered if she's won the football pools.'

'That would be something,' Claudette chuckled. 'There would be a big party to celebrate that.'

'Come in here, girls,' Nanny Ruby called from the front room. 'You're just in time to hear our news.'

Bessie nudged Claudette and looked up at the clock on the chimney breast. 'I'm meeting Tom at six, so if I disappear, you've got to cover for me.'

'No, we told you before, I'm not doing it. Or taking the blame for covering for you. I'm not going to be told off because of you and your antics.'

Bessie's response was to poke her in the back as they went into Ruby's front room. It was chock-a-block; the girls had never seen so many people crammed into number thirteen before. Granddad Bob stood in front of the fireplace talking with his son Mike, Uncle Douglas and their own dad; Maisie, Auntie Freda, Auntie Sarah and Betty from Woolworths were squeezed onto the large settee.

'Mind your backs, girls,' Maureen shouted as she came up behind them carrying a tea tray. Her husband, George, brought up the rear with a second tray.

'Hurry up with that cake,' George said as Clemmie and Dorothy appeared, carefully carrying the large plate that Nanny Ruby used every Christmas for the meat. Claudette gave Dorothy a quizzical look and in return Dorothy shrugged her shoulders to indicate she had no idea what was going on.

'That's it, girls, all squeeze in. Make room for a little one,' George said as the tea tray was taken from him and the men served drinks to the ladies.

'I wanted to call you all together to tell you something important,' Ruby said.

The room fell silent as everyone waited with bated breath to hear what it was they'd been summoned for. It was all too much for Claudette, who burst into tears. 'You're not ill, are you, Nanny Ruby? Please don't tell us you're poorly.'

Maisie slung her arm around Claudette and kissed her cheek. 'Your Nanny Ruby is fighting fit, so you just wipe your face and listen to what she has to say,' she said, brushing a few stray hairs from her daughter's face and kissing her cheek a second time. Claudette leant against her in relief. She wasn't worried about what was going to be said, as long as Nanny Ruby was healthy; that was all she cared about.

'What I've got to say is about me, but there's nothing wrong,' Ruby added quickly. 'As you all know, I've got a big birthday coming up this year – and I've decided I don't want a party.'

'But we've started to think about a par . . .' Sarah said before clamping her mouth shut tightly as she noticed Freda and Maisie glaring at her.

'What I meant was, we had a party recently for George's fiftieth, and it came to me while you were all up on the floor doing the "Knees Up Mother Brown". I love a party but it's such a lot of organizing, and none of us are getting any younger. Not even you three,' Ruby said, laughing at Sarah and her friends' shocked faces. 'I want us to just have a nice time, without people being up the night before making sandwiches and baking cakes and collecting barrels of beer and sending out invitations and all that malarkey. So I've been thinking.'

Bob looked around the room. 'And when Ruby's been thinking we've all got to listen,' he said seriously before giving her a big wink.

'The reason I'm calling you together now,' she continued as she slapped his arm, 'is so that you can all make plans. I want you all to take a week off work – there's plenty of time, so no excuses. You are all working far too hard anyway. We're all going to take the week off, so find someone to look after your cats and your dogs – and that includes you, Bob, because that greyhound is not coming with us.'

'But where are we going, Nan?' Sarah asked. She knew Alan would be none too keen to close his shop for the week, and as for Maisie and her factory business and Douglas and David with a chain of undertaker's shops to run, it could be difficult to arrange. Whatever Ruby was up to, it was going to take a lot of planning.

'We're all going on holiday. I've been corresponding with Molly and Johnny Johnson. Me and Bob have booked a row of chalets at their holiday camp for the end of July.'

'We're going to Butlins?' Bessie asked.

'No, they have their own holiday camp now. It's not as big as the Butlins where they used to work at Skegness, but going by the brochure she sent me and all the information, it will suit families of all ages – from our youngsters, who are running amok in my garden right now,' she said, as screams and shrieks were heard from the back garden, 'to the old fogeys like me and Bob.'

'And me and George,' Maureen chipped in.

'That's very generous of you,' Betty Billington said, 'but I insist we pay for ourselves. It's not as if we are really your family, and there are six of us.'

171

'Betty, my love, you are as much a part of my family as George and Sarah are. I wouldn't dream of this special occasion without you and your children being part of it.' Ruby leant forward and pulled a colourful brochure from under the cushion of her seat. 'This tells us all about the Sunny Days holiday camp. It's on the other side of Kent, so we've not got too far to travel to the coast, and July will be lovely and warm. I've pencilled the date on the back. I want all you grown-ups to make note of it, I don't want any excuses about work. Each family will have their own chalet and we can meet together for the events and our meals, and in the evening in the ballroom we can sit together. It will be wonderful. Oh, and before you four start pulling faces about sleeping with your younger brothers and sisters: I've booked a chalet for the girls to stay together. That's as long as you behave yourselves,' she added, giving Claudette, Bessie, Clemmie and Dorothy one of her looks.

Everyone burst into excited chatter, and the four girls sidled out of the front room and stood together in the hallway. 'This will be fun,' Dorothy said.

Bessie pulled a face. 'I don't know what Tom will have to say about me going away for a week. I'll have to have a word with him about it.'

'You can't have a lad dictate to you about going on a family holiday. He will just have to pine away in Erith for the week,' Clemmie grinned.

'He's not exactly one for pining,' Bessie sniffed as she headed to the front door. 'Cover for me, you lot, I'm off to see him now.' She stuck her chin in the air, ignoring their protests.

'Well, I for one am going to really enjoy myself,' Clemmie said.

'It will be wonderful – and the bonus being, we get to see Johnny Johnson,' Claudette added, smiling at the thought of her Auntie Freda's best friend's husband. Johnny had been a matinee idol during the war; some of his films still appeared at the Odeon cinema, and women still swooned at the mention of his name. Although the younger girls giggled at the way their mothers reacted when he was mentioned, they too had taken a shine to the tall, handsome man who had fallen in love with a local woman.

Sarah, draped in her nan's crossover pinny, was up to her elbows in washing up while Maisie was busy drying the crockery. Freda joined them, laden down with more cups and saucers. 'Thank you, Freda, that must be all of them now,' Sarah said as she relieved her friend of the crocks and placed them in the hot water. 'Thank goodness Nan always has a good stock of cups and saucers. We've not descended on her like this in ages – even at Christmas we don't all get to be together. At least then we use more glasses than cups.'

'That's true,' Maisie chuckled as she passed a clean tea towel to Freda. 'I did say if we didn't have enough I could run up the road and collect some of mine, but she seems to have done all right. I see she's brought out her best stuff as well.'

Sarah watched as Maisie carefully dried a pale green cup patterned with delicate flowers. 'You know, she had very little left to her by her mum. These few cups and saucers and the teapot that's still in the cabinet are about all that's left from the Tompkins side of the family. Nan's two aunts never left her anything, even though they were on talking terms towards the end of their lives. I don't remember Dad saying much about them, either. I ought to make some notes while he still remembers.'

'But men aren't the same as women – they don't seem to want to know as much,' Freda said. 'Well, that's what I've found, anyway. Tony hardly ever speaks of his childhood in the children's home.' She took the cup from Maisie and went through to the living room, where she gently placed it back in the cabinet. As she returned to the kitchen and took some saucers to dry, she looked at her two friends, who were staring at her. 'What's up, have I got a smudge on my nose or something?'

'No, it's just that you've never told us much about Tony's life. We both must have talked for England about our husbands.'

'There's not much to tell, really. Tony grew up in a children's home, and then he worked for Woolworths, and then he met me.' Freda smiled as she thought of her handsome husband.

'Even I know more than that,' Maisie scoffed. 'His great passion in life, apart from you, is cycling and he entered the Olympics in 1948.'

'And he's not home enough at present,' Sarah added.

'Do yer know what? We are becoming too grown up and worrying too much,' Maisie announced, throwing down her tea towel.

'But we are grown up,' Sarah argued. 'What else should we be doing?'

'Enjoying ourselves and doing something we've not done fer years. Let's go out for a bike ride.'

'It's a bit on the chilly side for that. Can't we wait until the summer?' Sarah had never been very keen on cycling.

'I agree with Maisie,' Freda said as a smile crossed her face. 'Let's just go and do it. What about after work tomorrow? It's half day at Woolies, we could bring a picnic.'

'I'm at the shop tomorrow but will finish early,' Maisie said as they started to plan their trip.

Freda grinned at her friends. She knew they were doing this to cheer her up. 'It will be like old times, when it was just the three of us enjoying ourselves.'

14

'I'd just about given up on you,' Tom said, looking at his watch. 'You know I don't hang around for any girl.'

Bessie stopped to catch her breath; she'd run all the way from Alexandra Road to where he was waiting, at the corner by the Prince of Wales. 'I'm sorry — it's just that they were talking, and I couldn't really get away until just now. We were all at Nanny Ruby's house . . .'

'Nanny Ruby?' he scoffed, pulling out a comb from the pocket of his jacket and running it through his jet-black hair.

'I mean Ruby, she's an old lady that lives down the road from my mum and dad,' Bessie said, cursing herself for using childish words. She was no longer a kid and had to stop talking like her sister.

'I'm not competing with an old lady,' he said, throwing his cigarette stub to the floor and stamping on it. 'Are we going to the flicks or not?'

'I'd rather go for a walk, if you don't mind. I've got things to tell you,' she grinned as she held out her hand for him to take it.

He ignored her hand and started walking. 'Let's go down by the river. It's a bit more private this time of day.'

Bessie hurried to catch up with him, thinking it might have been a better idea to go the cinema, as she could have popped into the ladies' to comb her hair and put on some lipstick.

'So, what's this news? I've not seen you for days and now you're jumping up and down with excitement like some little kid,' he said, pulling her down beside him on a wooden bench.

'We're all going to have a family holiday together. My Auntie Fr . . . I mean, our neighbour Freda's best friend, Molly, runs a holiday camp with her husband across the other side of Kent. Quite near to Ramsgate. They used to work at Butlins but set up their own camp a couple of years ago. It's just for a week,' she added, seeing a scowl cross his face. 'It's in July. The family's rented a row of chalets. I'm really looking forward to it, but I'll miss you,' she said, slipping her hand into his and holding it tight so he couldn't shake her off. 'I promise to send you a postcard.'

He looked at her for a moment and then laughed out loud, putting his arm around her shoulders and squeezing her tightly. 'Who knows, I might go off on my own holiday. I may just take someone with me, or perhaps go with my mates.'

Bessie wasn't sure who else he'd take with him; would it be another girl? 'We're not going until July, why don't you come to the holiday camp as well? It's called Sunny Days. I could see you in the evenings. Here,' she said, pulling the brochure out of her pocket, 'this is where it is. I can get another copy, there were plenty at . . . Ruby's.'

He pulled her to him, kissing her until she could hardly breathe. She kissed him back, not wanting him to think he was the only boy who had kissed her. His hands started to roam roughly over her body, but then he stopped to lead her to another bench set behind a wall, out of sight of passers-by.

'You'll need to convince me it's worth going, or I might just take another girl with me,' he said huskily.

Bessie pulled back for a moment. Would he really do that? She liked having a boyfriend; it was something she could brag about to the girls at Woolworths, and it made her feel more grown up. But she wasn't sure she should have done what she had with him, several times now. Her mum had read the riot act to both girls many a time about what happened to girls who went with boys.

Still, she liked Tom. She liked being around him, even if she was uncomfortable with what they did. And if that's what it took to keep him, then so be it, she thought, as she melted against him and accepted his advances.

'Tony, you're home early!' Freda shrieked with joy, throwing herself into her husband's arms.

'I finished earlier than expected and ran to catch the last train rather than wait until the morning.'

'Just to be home with me?' she sighed.

'Of course,' he smiled, gazing into the face he'd missed so much. 'I could kill for a cup of tea,' he grinned.

'You old romantic,' she giggled, pulling him indoors and through to the kitchen. 'I have cake and sandwiches, courtesy of Ruby's get-together to tell us her news. I'll explain later, but you missed a lovely party,' she added. 'At least I can tell you about it rather than write a letter. There's so much to tell.'

Tony came up behind her and slid his arms around her waist. 'You'd have managed somehow. Freda, you don't know how much I look forward to your letters. It can be lonely travelling around so much.'

'But it's good for your future with F. W. Woolworth for you to be able to visit all those different stores and write up reports on how they can be modernized. I just hope you don't have to write a report about our branch. I love the store so much and would hate it to change; I owe so much to Woolies. I'd not have met you, either,' she added quickly.

'We have a lot to be thankful for,' he said, giving her a gentle kiss. 'For people like us to have a home and jobs we love, we're truly lucky. Life has been good to us.'

Freda lowered her head. 'I wish we were just a little luckier. I can't help but think I've let you down. By now we should have our own child, or at least one on the way. I don't know what's wrong with me; I'd do anything to have your baby.'

Tony placed a finger under her chin and raised her face until she was looking at him. 'You have nothing to apologize for. As far as I'm concerned, I have all I want in life. If a baby comes along, or three or four babies, they will be the icing on the cake. But if it doesn't happen, I won't be sad, because I'll still have you.'

Freda didn't know what to say. Thankfully, she was saved by the kettle whistling on the stove.

She knew she didn't agree with her husband. As the months passed by with no sign of a baby on the way, she had been growing more and more desolate. Granted, she reminded herself of Betty's instructions to all Woolies sales staff, to pin a smile to her face regardless; but inside she was distraught that she apparently couldn't produce a child.

Taking a deep breath, she decided to make the most of having her husband home. 'How long are you here for? Will you be coming into the office?'

'I'm only back home for three days, then I'm up to Liverpool, and I expect to be there for a couple of weeks.'

'I thought you'd worked with the team in Liverpool a couple of months ago?'

'We did. It seems the manager there has been taken ill, and I was asked to step into the breach.'

'You don't think . . .' Freda couldn't voice her fear that one day, very soon, Tony would be given a store to manage far away from Erith and their home, and that she would have to contemplate selling up and moving.

He didn't seem to hear as he peered into the pantry and came back with a plate covered with a tea towel. 'These look good. Are they the sandwiches and cake from Ruby?'

She shook her head and smiled as he dived into the food like a ravenous schoolboy. 'I've made a sausage plait for your dinner tomorrow. It only needs to be warmed through, and the spuds and cabbage cooked. Do you want to do it midday, before you go out?'

'Food fit for a king,' he said as he rubbed his hands together. 'I've missed your cooking. Being put up in rooms is not quite the same. This past week in Wolverhampton was so dire I had lunch in the staff canteen, which can be a little bit awkward with so many workers wanting to know what I'm doing there. You know, it's not easy to eat with people watching you so closely.'

Freda giggled. 'I can imagine, knowing what our staff room can be like whenever there's anyone unfamiliar there. I'm surprised you didn't find a pub and have a pie and a pint?'

'Once or twice I did, and then someone pointed out a cafe. Perhaps I should bring you with me on these trips so you can look after me,' he laughed.

'I would if I could,' she smiled, thinking that perhaps she could pack some food up for him to take with him when he went to Liverpool. She started to wonder what she had in the cupboard. Rationing was still a problem, and she and her friends regularly discussed how they were managing to put food on the table for their families.

'What do you have planned for tomorrow?'

'I'm working a half day, and I did promise Maisie and Sarah I'd go for a bike ride afterwards. But if you'd rather I didn't, I can come straight home.'

'No, that's fine. I thought I'd pop in and see the lads from the cycle club and catch up on news. I'll do my washing as well, so you don't have to worry about that.'

'I do have another half day due to me. Perhaps we could do something . . . what do you think?'

He looked up from eating a third corned beef sandwich. 'I say, what about a trip down the coast? We've not done that for a while, have we? We could take the train,' he added quickly.

Freda breathed a sigh of relief. Although she had always enjoyed a trip on the paddle steamer down the Thames to the seaside, ever since the terrible accident on their wedding day, the idea put the fear of God in her heart.

Tony gave her a close look. 'You know we're going to have to face your fear one day, don't you? Just remember all the times we've been on the river and enjoyed ourselves.'

'You're right; but not just yet. I'll face it another time.'

Tony put down his plate and swept her up in his arms.

'I promise I'll never let anything happen to you. You're worth more than life itself to me. You know, I watch your sad face sometimes and I don't know what you're thinking, but believe me, you could never let me down, Freda. If for one moment you're thinking that by not having a baby you've made me unhappy, you can stop that right now.'

'But how did you . . . ? Did Ruby say something?'

'No, she didn't, but I know you so well, it didn't take much for me to guess.'

'Tony . . . I . . .'

He ran his finger across her lips to stop her speaking. 'When you agreed to marry me, you made me the happiest man in the world. Growing up in a children's home as I did, I'd always wondered about living as part of a family and what it would be like to have my own. I know now having children isn't as important as what it's made out to be – it's all about being loved. And I feel so much love when I'm here, in our house, that at times I could burst. Besides, little did I know that when I married you I'd be taking on your extended family as well. There are enough children in the family to keep us busy for a while, don't you think?' He smiled, took her by the hand and led her towards the staircase. 'I don't really fancy that tea, do you?' he said. 'Ruby's cake can wait.'

Together, they ran up the stairs to their bedroom. As they embraced, Freda prayed that perhaps this time, before he went away again, she might fall for the baby that she wanted so much. She couldn't tell Tony that for her, life would never be complete unless she was able to hold a child of her own in her arms.

*

182

'Phew – I'm exhausted,' Maisie said as she climbed off her bicycle and propped it against a fence. 'I'm glad you suggested cycling down towards the marshes.' She stretched her arms out before running her fingers through her hair. 'Just smell that sea air.'

'It's river air, not sea, Maisie,' Sarah laughed. 'You've got a fair way to cycle before we reach the estuary and the sea.' She looked at Freda and slipped her arm around the younger woman's shoulders. 'Are you all right? We can cycle somewhere else, if you prefer?'

'Don't be daft. Tony said to me only last night it was about time I got over my fear of the river. One day – really soon, I promise – I'll get onto the *Kentish Queen* and take a trip down the river to the seaside; and you can both come too, if you like? Actually, Tony is taking me on Wednesday, but we're catching the train. I'm going to leave work at midday. So don't offer me a cup of tea or one of Maureen's sticky buns at lunchtime, or I'll be late,' Freda grinned. 'He's meeting me from work and we're going straight up to the station.'

'Why don't you leave earlier?' Sarah suggested. 'It'll give you longer, and it's not as if you see as much of Tony as you should these days. I have a shift that day in the office, so if you want, I'll pull on an overall and come down to the shop floor and stand in for you for a couple of hours. I'm almost up to date with my work now that I have Clemmie helping me out.'

'But she's a Saturday girl – surely she won't be in?' Freda said, even though she was sorely tempted to accept Sarah's offer and spend more time with her husband.

'She is coming into work for the day before she goes up to the college for an appointment in the afternoon, to find out more about her course and look around. I must say, I quite envy her learning about how to work in an office. Everything I've learnt came from Betty.'

'Well, I for one say you've done a bloody good job,' Maisie told her. 'I always thought you was good enough to run a store.'

'I don't run Woolworths, Betty does – and so does Tony when he's here. I just supervise the Saturday staff and the part-time workers, as well as doing some paperwork for Betty. Thinking about it, I'd hate to manage a store. Since the war ended and so many men have come back to work, it doesn't seem the same as the days when we had more female staff. You've only got to read *The New Bond* to see life at Woolies has changed.'

'You can blame Tony for that,' Maisie said. 'After all, he's one of the team that's going round trying to come up with ideas to update the stores. Someone I was talking to in my shop reckoned that Sainsbury's are going to go self-service – whatever that means.'

'Tony told me his team are just looking into changes, and that could mean things like new counters and redecorating the store. We probably won't be self-service,' Freda said, feeling quite important as for once she could explain something to her two friends. 'But you're right about Sainsbury's; I've heard the same. Self-service means customers would walk round with a basket on their arm and pick up all the goods they want to buy, and then pay at the door before they leave. It all sounds rather strange to me,' she said, shaking her head.

'I'm wondering how many women are going to be put out of work. Because mark my words, it will be the women that lose their jobs, not the men,' Maisie huffed. 'I just thank God I can do something to employ people once I'm up and running, and if I hear of any Woolies women put out of work, they'll be first on my list for a job at the factory. I hope your Tony is kind to women employees and doesn't favour men over us women?'

Freda bristled. 'Oh, come on, Maisie, you know my Tony. He's a good man – he treats everybody individually and takes no notice of whether they are man or woman when it comes down to doing a job for Woolworths. I like to think he's rather like Betty, who has always been a fair manager. In some ways, head office are to blame for telling every man who went off to war that they had a job waiting for them when they returned. That has caused real problems, as many of those men have seen the world and are no longer content to work in a shop.'

'What do you mean by that?' Sarah asked. Her Alan had not been at all interested in returning to work for Woolworths after being a Spitfire pilot.

'Haven't you noticed how some of the warehouse staff don't seem to be as on the ball as they used to be? I'm hoping these men do find satisfactory employment, because in that respect the war has done them no favours.'

'You've made a good point there,' Maisie agreed. 'Of course, in my line of work, I couldn't say whether these people were good workers before they went off to fight for the country, as I didn't employ them then. But it's something worth considering. Perhaps I should mention it when I interview people?'

'Oh, you've got to be careful, Maisie,' Freda said. 'You can't be too blunt and ask, will you work hard because if not you'll be given the sack?'

It was Maisie's turn to be annoyed. 'Of course I bloody can. I'll make it quite clear that if anyone doesn't pull their weight when I'm paying their wages, they'll be given their cards. It's as simple as that, be they man, woman or child.'

'Including your daughters?'

Maisie pulled a wry face. 'That's a bit of a sore point, as my Bessie's turned into a right lazy cow. I could've clipped her ears the other day when she mouthed back at me in front of one of the men making repairs to the building.'

'Crikey, what did she do? Or should I be asking what you did?' Sarah asked, knowing Maisie had brought her daughters up to be polite in front of others.

'I asked her to accompany me to the storeroom to check some supplies. And as soon as the door was closed I nigh on pinned her to the wall and told her to mind her Ps & Qs in front of other people, or she'd find herself working at Woolworths full time. She wouldn't get away with being rude to people like that on a Saturday under Betty's watch.'

'You've made it sound like working at Woolworths is a prison sentence. I think it's a lovely job,' Sarah said, with Freda quickly agreeing.

'Oh gawd – now I've annoyed you too. I didn't mean it like that. You know I've loved my time working in Woolies, and if my business ever went pear-shaped, I'd be back there like a shot, believe me. It's just that I thought my girls would love working for me and be as excited as I am about the factory and the new shop.'

'She's only sixteen,' Sarah reminded her. 'Give her a little time.'

'I suppose you're right,' Maisie said thoughtfully. 'I just wish she was as good at her work as Claudette.'

As they munched away companionably, Freda looked at her two best friends. 'Can I tell you both something?'

Sarah looked up expectantly.

'No, it's nothing like that – there is definitely no baby on the way.'

'Give it time,' Maisie smiled.

'I will – but that's not what I want to talk about. Tony's going up to Liverpool soon to take over the store while the manager is poorly. He's not said much, but I've got to face the truth that this is Tony's career we have to focus on, and that would mean us moving away.'

Maisie swore loudly. 'Blimey, here was me thinking we were going out for a pleasant bike ride, and now we're talking about our lives changing. You've not got any news you want to share, have you, Sarah?'

'No, you're safe this time,' Sarah smiled, although she was thinking that with her friends' lives changing so much, it could easily affect their friendship.

'Come on, you two. I've had enough of miserable faces,' Maisie said as she got to her feet and threw her part-eaten apple into a nearby hedgerow. 'I'll race you to the lighthouse.'

Sarah laughed out loud. 'We can't stay glum for long with you about, can we? Come on, Freda – we mustn't let her win.'

15

June 1950

'Good morning, Betty. I didn't expect to see you in work today,' Sarah said, as Betty Billington passed her in the corridor outside their offices.

'I'd rather be at home sitting in our garden,' Betty smiled. 'Who knew the weather would take such a pleasant turn? It's been such a wet June so far, and sod's law, just when I decide to come in and have a chat with Freda, the sun comes out. Just typical! Anyway, at least it will be a pleasant walk home, and no need for my umbrella.'

'I know what you mean – we only have a small back garden, but it's so pleasant to take a garden chair out there and sit for a while with the sun on my face. I have peas to shuck from the allotment, so I will sit outside with Georgina when I'm home and sort out the peas while it's pleasant. But you mention Freda; is there a problem?'

A cloud crossed Betty's face for a moment. 'Would you come into my office?' she asked, looking left and right. 'I hate to use an old saying, but you know – walls have ears.'

Sarah was intrigued, and followed Betty into her small office, closing the door behind her. 'She's not poorly, is she?'

'Goodness, no; she's bright as a button, as usual. I simply want to have time to sit and chat with her and look at the sketches she's designed for the window display. Freda comes up with such lovely ideas. I still smile when I think of what she managed to achieve during the war with limited supplies. Do you remember the time we had an Easter display and the Brownies helped us out?'

'I do indeed; it's amazing what she can think of. I wonder if it has something to do with her childhood. She had so very little, and must have relied on her imagination.'

'It could well be that. It was Freda who suggested we have a window display dedicated to babies, knitting and sewing, what with our Princess Elizabeth expecting her second child in a few months' time. The eyes of the world are on her, and many women who shop at Woolworths will also like their babies to be dressed like young princes or princesses.'

'A little girl would be lovely; then she will have one of each. I'm so pleased to have a boy and a girl myself,' Sarah sighed.

'I know just what you mean; I couldn't be prouder of my brood if I tried. If you can come up with anything to help the display, please do chip in. In fact, please do join us if you're not overworked.'

'I'd love to – I'll make sure to find the time. After all, there's nothing better than talking about little ones, although . . .'

'What is it, my dear?'

'We should tread carefully talking about babies, with Freda not yet falling pregnant.'

Betty was thoughtful. 'Look how long I waited, and then our Charles came along when I least expected it – and to be honest, thought I was past all that. And then I had a second,' she smiled, thinking of her youngest child, Elizabeth. 'I'm most fortunate indeed, although I'm very grateful we have a housekeeper who takes the youngsters off my hands so that I can work. That sounds quite shameful, doesn't it?'

Sarah, who had been up most of the night because Buster had toothache, could only wish she had room in her house to have a housekeeper, let alone the funds to be able to pay her wages.

'You were lucky on all counts,' she smiled. Betty was such a lovely person, no one could be jealous of her good fortune. 'But you asked me to come in here, when we could have spoken about the window display in the corridor. Is there something else?'

'Well, yes – you may think it's silly of me, but . . . Tony is back.'

'Oh, that's wonderful!' Sarah clapped her hands together. 'Freda has missed him these past weeks while he's been in Liverpool. That manager he covered for must have been extremely poorly to need a replacement for so long.'

'Sadly, the man has passed away. I heard it on the grapevine yesterday. That's why I find it rather strange that Tony's back here so soon, when it would seem he must be needed even more now.'

Sarah was puzzled by how troubled she sounded. 'But why are you concerned?' she asked, noticing the shadows around Betty's eyes.

'Well, Tony is popping in here later today to see me. As

you know, his job, when he's not here, is mainly to help out the team who inspect all the stores. I have a feeling that perhaps it's Erith's turn to be inspected. Will we have changes ahead of us? I hope not, as we are a happy team here, even if the store is a little shabby and world-weary since the war. There's all this talk about self-service and modernization . . . I'm not certain I'm young enough to cope with changes like that.'

'If it should happen, we will weather the storm together,' Sarah said. 'Now, I've got to get back to my office – I want to check on the uniforms. Some of the girls have started shortening the skirts of their overalls, would you believe! Have you ever heard anything like it?'

Betty laughed. 'It wasn't so long ago I was checking on your uniform to make sure you didn't break the rules. The world may have moved on, but there will always be younger girls trying to change the style of their outfits,' she chuckled.

As Sarah got up to leave, there was a knock on the door. Before she could reach it, it flew open to reveal Bessie standing there, looking rather pale, with Clemmie Billington holding an arm around her.

'I'm sorry, Mrs Gilbert – I did go to your office first, but you weren't there, so I thought it best to tell Mum – I mean, Mrs Billington. Bessie passed out behind the counter just now. I was nearby, checking on the paper bag stock for you, and thought it best to bring her upstairs. Look at her – I've never seen anyone so poorly.'

Sarah helped Bessie to the chair she'd just vacated. 'You poor child,' she said, placing the back of her hand on the girl's forehead. She felt hot, although she looked so pale and weak. 'I bet you missed your breakfast; I know what you girls are like, getting out of your beds at the last minute and rushing to get here. Is that what happened?'

Bessie nodded in agreement, before putting her hand to mouth and muttering 'Excuse me' as she ran from the room.

Clemmie went to follow, but Sarah held her back. 'I'll take care of this, Clemmie. I've had a little more experience with sickly youngsters.'

Clemmie turned to look at her mother as Betty raised her eyebrows. 'How was she yesterday, my dear, when you met the girls to go to the cinema?'

'We only met Claudette; Bessie wasn't there.'

'Ah – perhaps she was poorly even then,' Betty said. 'When she's feeling slightly better, would you walk her home? I don't think she should stay in work today, do you?'

Clemmie agreed, although from what she'd been told, Bessie had been as right as rain the night before when she'd gone off to meet Tom.

'Why are you in this state?' Clemmie hissed, as the two girls left Woolworths and headed down Pier Road towards Bessie's home. 'I take it you preferred to meet Tom rather than come with us to the pictures? You missed a good film – *The Happiest Days of Your Life* was so funny.'

Bessie shrugged her shoulders and didn't answer.

'He must have given you a lot of alcohol for you to be like this. Goodness knows why you accepted it. Why, anything could happen, and you'd not know a thing about it,' Clemmie lectured, not realizing that she sounded just like her mother. 'You could get a bad name for yourself,' she added, as Bessie suddenly fled up the alley beside the Co-op and was violently sick.

'You, silly, silly girl,' Clemmie admonished her as she followed, fishing a clean handkerchief from her pocket. 'I don't want it back,' she added, grimacing as Bessie wiped her mouth. 'I hope you've learnt a lesson from this before it happens again and your parents discover what's been going on. Why, they might think I'm involved,' she said in a shocked voice.

Bessie fell into step beside her. 'I only had a couple of swigs from Tom's bottle of ale.'

'That wouldn't make you as sick as this. Are you sure it was just a sip?' Clemmie asked as she held Bessie's arm to cross the busy road. 'Something else must have caused this. I'm going to take you to Nanny Ruby's house, so you have someone to look after you until your mum gets home.'

'No,' Bessie said, stopping so suddenly that Clemmie had to step back to join her. 'Mum said she'll be home in the middle of the day. Besides, Sadie is there looking after the little ones. I'm just going to wash my face and go to bed for a while. I'll be fine,' she insisted, before retching into the handkerchief. 'Look, I've only got to walk a few yards up the road. You go back to work.'

'If you're sure,' Clemmie said, not convinced she should leave her.

'Just go . . . and thank you.'

Clemmie would usually have given her friend a hug, but on this occasion she thought better of it as her stomach heaved at the stench from Bessie's sick-splattered coat.

Bessie hurried up the road towards her home, planning what to say to avoid Sadie so she could clean herself up and slip out to see Tom. She hoped what she had to tell him wouldn't cause an argument.

'I don't usually see you home at this time of the day,' Sadie called out from the kitchen. 'I'm just preparing a bite of food for the little ones – can I get you something?'

'I had some time off due,' Bessie muttered, rushing upstairs before Sadie noticed how poorly she looked or smelt the sick on her coat.

In the bedroom she shared with Claudette she pulled off the offending garment and looked at the marks. Thankfully the flower-painted bowl and jug the girls used each morning to wash was still on the washstand. Checking the jug, she found some water in the bottom and wiped her face over after dunking her face flannel in the cold water. Opening the wardrobe, she pulled out a cotton dress and felt much better once she'd pulled it on and dabbed her lips with bright red lipstick and run a comb through her hair. She frowned at her reflection in the mirror; she looked so pale. Touching each cheek with her lipstick, she rubbed it in until there was a rosy glow and covered it with a pat of face powder. 'That will have to do,' she muttered, peering closer into the mirror and backing away quickly, the smell of her breath making her flinch. She tapped a finger into a tin of tooth powder and sipped at the remaining water in the jug, swishing it around in her mouth. She realized she should have done this before applying her lipstick, but she had been in a rush to get out of the house before anyone questioned her. She wanted to catch Tom in his dinner break and spend some time with him.

Grimacing as she gulped the water down rather than spit it out, she reached for her coat. No, she really couldn't wear it without trying to clean off the marks. Taking a clean handkerchief from the top drawer of the dressing table, she dipped it into the remaining cold water in the jug and scrubbed at the coat before dabbing it with the perfume she saved for best. Even then it wasn't as fresh as it should be. Pulling open the sash window, she hung the coat on the curtain wire; perhaps the light breeze would air it out, but she didn't have time to wait. There was nothing for it but to borrow her sister's best coat. Thank goodness Claudette, although younger, was a stockily built girl for her age.

She pulled on the red woollen garment, which seem to match the pattern on her dress. Deciding not to wear a hat, she headed downstairs and quickly called out goodbye as she slammed the front door closed behind her.

The thought of meeting Tom as he came out of work was uppermost in her mind as she hurried down the High Street towards where the Mobo factory stood, near the river. Her earlier nausea was all but gone. She was just in time; as she drew near, the hooter sounded announcing the dinner break, quickly followed by a crowd of men and women hurrying from the building. Bessie stood on tiptoe so she could see above the heads of the workers, hoping Tom wasn't staying in the works canteen for his meal. From what he'd said in the past, he liked to escape the factory, and sometimes went for a sneaky pint and a cigarette before returning for the afternoon shift.

She was just about to give up when she spotted him with a couple of his mates, heads together, talking earnestly as they headed out of the gates. She pushed through the crowd towards him. 'I'm so glad I've seen you, Tom.'

Tom frowned. 'What are you doing here?'

'I was sent home because I wasn't well, so I thought I'd

come down to talk to you in your dinner break. Is there somewhere we can be alone?'

His mates jostled him and made ribald comments about being alone with his girlfriend, which angered Tom somewhat. 'It'll have to wait till later, I've got things to discuss with me mates,' he said sharply.

Bessie wasn't going to be shaken off that easily. She slipped her arm through his, clinging on tight. 'I'll come with you,' she said, and it wasn't a question.

Tom smelt different. When they were out in the evenings, she could usually smell his Brylcreem and the cologne he used liberally. To be honest, she preferred the oily works smell from his overalls now; his cologne often made her eyes water. It crossed her mind that her father and uncles were not so generous with their toiletries. Perhaps it was because they were older, and Tom was young and handsome. She sighed, holding him tighter.

'We're going down the pub, so keep your head down in case they realize you're too young to be in there.'

'I'll sit in the corner and drink lemonade,' she promised, determined he wasn't going to shake her off that easily just because he was with his friends.

They went into the Ship public house, and Tom nodded towards a table in the corner of the dark interior. Bessie looked around her. It was nothing like the Prince of Wales, which was a welcoming kind of place. The Ship was dusty, the tables sticky, and the men drinking looked kind of foreign, she thought to herself. No doubt they were off the ships from the nearby docks.

Along with his mates, Tony went to the bar and stood there chatting for a while even after the drinks were served.

Eventually they went to join Bessie and Tom slid a glass of lemonade across the table to her, which she sipped gratefully. She was quite thirsty after being so sick earlier, but prayed she would keep it down.

'Is it all right to talk in front of her?' one of the lads asked.

'Yeah, she's fine. She knows to keep her mouth shut, or she'll have me to answer to,' he said, throwing her a steely look before starting to talk to the other two men. They were planning to meet that evening at ten o'clock, after the late shift clocked off. 'Make it the side gate. Will you have all the gear, Chalky?' he asked a younger, curly-haired lad.

'Yep, all packed and ready in my new tool bag,' he grinned.

'What about you, Derek? Do you know where we're going and what's to be done?'

'Don't worry about me, I've done this kind of thing before,' the older lad replied.

Bessie frowned. Whatever they were doing, it all sounded rather strange. 'What's happening?' she asked brightly. 'Can I come along?' Even though she knew she should be home and in bed by that time, she wasn't going to miss out on what seemed to be a bit of excitement.

The two men looked at Tom and frowned.

'Tell her to mind her own business,' Derek said, and Chalky nodded in agreement.

Tom thought for a moment as he stared at Bessie across the table. 'No, I won't. She can come with us and be our lookout. As I said before, she knows to keep her gob shut or she'll have me to answer to. Don't you?' he snarled at her.

'Whatever is happening, it's fine by me. I just want to be with you, Tom,' she smiled, which caused much merriment amongst his mates.

Reaching into their pockets, they pulled out packs of sandwiches wrapped in greaseproof paper and started to eat. Bessie's stomach growled with hunger. 'Can I pinch a bit, please? I missed my breakfast,' she said to Tom, and he begrudgingly tore off part of his cheese sandwich and handed it to her.

'Shall I meet you after you finish work?' she asked him, not knowing what to do for the afternoon. She dared not go back home in case Sadie asked questions about her coat hanging in the bedroom, or her mum came home early – as she'd mentioned that morning she would, before going on to the Erith branch of Maisie's Modes.

'Yeah, you can if you want. Perhaps we can go to the flicks. We have a few hours to spare. You can treat me to a bag of chips for tea, as you've eaten half my sandwich.'

Bessie agreed; thankfully she'd taken some money from her hiding place in the chest of drawers she shared with Claudette, and put the coins into her purse before she came out. She liked to treat Tom occasionally, as she was sure that was what girls did for their boyfriends. She'd have to be more careful, though, as she was saving up to go on holiday, which was only weeks away now.

The men got up to return to work, and Bessie went to follow them.

'You can't come with me, can you?' Tom laughed. 'I'll see you back outside the gates at half past five.' He did have the good grace to kiss her quickly on the lips. 'You look nice,' he winked before leaving to catch up with his friends.

Bessie had the afternoon to kill and decided to go for a walk. Thank goodness it wasn't raining, and the afternoon was bright. She didn't want to go back into town in case someone from Woolworths spotted her and asked how she was feeling. Also, her sister might see her, and then she'd want to know why Bessie had borrowed her best coat.

16

'Hello Tony, it's nice to see you back,' Sarah said, her face lighting up as she spotted Freda's husband standing at the open door of her office. 'Have you been home yet?'

'No, I've just arrived – I thought I'd check in here first. Have you seen Freda?'

Sarah looked up at the clock. 'The second tea break has just started, so you'll probably find her in the staff canteen. I'm going that way myself.'

Tony faltered. 'I wonder, can I borrow your office while you're not using it?'

Sarah raised her eyebrows and smiled gently. 'Of course you can. I know you've not been working here for a while, but you are still our manager. Shall I send Freda in? I'll not say you are here,' she said, starting to grin as he thanked her.

As she headed to the staff room, she thought how lovely it was to be young and in love. It seemed an age since she and Alan had been like that. Their marriage was good, but sometimes she yearned for the days when it was only the two of them; then the war had intervened and then Georgina and Buster had come along, and life got in the way. Perhaps I should try to spend more time alone with him, she thought.

Reaching the canteen, she collected a cup of tea at the counter from Maureen, refusing one of her oatcakes while patting her stomach. 'I'm starting to fill out a little bit, so I'll say no this time, thanks Maureen.'

She went over to the small Formica-topped table where Freda sat chatting with Claudette and Dorothy. 'Sorry to interrupt you ladies,' she said. 'I wonder if you could pop up to my office for a moment, Freda? There's something in there you need to see.'

'Whatever do you mean? I'll wait for you and then we can go together. I have ten minutes left of my break.'

'No, I'd prefer you to go right now. It's quite important,' Sarah said mysteriously.

Freda got to her feet to take her empty cup back to the counter. 'If you say so, but I'd rather have had another five minutes sitting here resting my feet.'

'You can always come back; it probably won't take long,' Claudette suggested.

Sarah watched her young friend leave the room and smiled to herself.

'Is there something going on, Auntie Sarah?'

'Tony has just arrived, and I thought it would be nice if Freda spoke to him alone,' she replied. 'What have I told you about calling me Auntie Sarah at work? You and the other girls can call me Mrs Gilbert on the shop floor, and Sarah at any other time,' she said, giving the girl a friendly smile. 'And perhaps when you see your sister you can remind her. I do hope she's feeling better soon,' she added.

'She's not well? I had no idea – I've not seen her all

morning. We're working on different counters at the moment. It'll only be a few more days, then we won't be able to work during the week and will return to being Saturday girls. Mum is almost ready to start work at the factory full time.'

'I'm so pleased for Maisie; you must be so proud of her. I hope Bessie is back on her feet by then, as she was quite poorly this morning. Clemmie Billington walked her home. She's probably tucked up in bed by now.'

'She wasn't quite the ticket this morning, but insisted on coming in to work. I hate it when people are sick. It's so . . . icky.'

'I used to think the same as you, but once you've had children you get used to things like that.'

'I'm never going to have children. I'm going to be a businesswoman,' Claudette said indignantly. 'If it wasn't for Sadie helping Mum out, she'd not be able to run a business and have young children.'

Sarah agreed and tried not to laugh. Oh, the innocence of youth, she thought to herself. 'It's early days, Claudette, and a woman can change her mind. Your mother has coped admirably and there are five of you.'

'But two of us are grown up, and we work now. It's the little kids that seem to cause the most problems,' Claudette said, although it occurred to her that her big sister was a complete pain these days. 'Mind you, it would be quite nice if we lived in a bigger house and I could have my own bedroom,' she added without thinking.

'Is it hard sharing a bedroom? Before I married, I was lucky and had my own room, until I shared a room with Freda. But now I just share with my husband,' Sarah grinned.

'Oh, that must be awful – it's not as if Uncle Alan is going to grow up and leave home, is it? You're stuck with him for life,' the girl said seriously.

Sarah's face twitched as she tried not to laugh. Fourteen was such an innocent age. 'It can be a problem, as he's a terrible snorer,' was all she could think of to say.

Freda walked into Sarah's office and shrieked in delight as she saw her husband standing there chatting with Betty. She threw herself into Tony's arms. 'I'm so pleased to see you! I didn't expect you home for a couple more days.'

Tony held her tight and swung her around before kissing her soundly. 'I had some extra staff cover, so decided I might as well shoot home and spend some time with my wife. Besides, I have news, and I wanted time for us to talk it over properly.'

'I should leave,' Betty said, feeling like a gooseberry. 'I only came in for this file.'

'No, please stay,' Tony said. 'You will hear this soon enough.'

'Then I'll use Sarah's desk and leave you to your conversation,' she said, sitting on the other side of the room and trying to ignore what was being said.

'It's happened, hasn't it?' Freda said, releasing herself from his arms. 'They've offered you your own store?'

'Yes. It's much larger than this one and quite a step up the ladder for me,' he said, studying her face closely. 'But I'm afraid, my love, it means moving to Liverpool.'

Freda felt her heart plummet into her shoes; this had been her worst fear. In her dreams she'd expected him to settle down at home and run the Erith store, assisted by

Betty. But then, dreams don't often come true, do they, she thought to herself, fighting the desire to scream and cry. Instead she fixed a smile onto her face and gave him a gentle kiss.

'I'm so proud of you, Tony. You've worked so hard. The company must think so much of you to offer this promotion before you've even turned thirty.'

Tony gave her a close look, placing a finger under her chin and lifting her face so he could look into her eyes. 'I know this isn't perfect for you. I feel as though I've walked into your life and shaken it up so much. But in time, when we have our own home in Liverpool and you've made new friends – perhaps helping out with the Brownies and Girl Guides in the area, and bringing up our own little family there – you'll truly love the area and feel at home.'

It wasn't what Freda wanted at all, and she knew that if she had a child, she wouldn't want to take it away from everything she loved about this town and her friends. But then, it was a woman's job to follow her husband's career, so she took a deep breath, suppressed her disappointment and gave him a brilliant smile. 'I'm sure I can. And I'll even be able to find a job in your branch, so we may even see more of each other than we did before.'

'I'm sorry, Freda, but I don't feel that's a good idea,' he said gently. 'It just wouldn't be fair to the other staff for their manager to have his wife working with him. I'm not sure my superiors would approve, either. Why not just enjoy your new life caring for our home and take up a few hobbies?' He folded her into his arms, feeling her tremble under his touch.

Freda stood still for a few seconds, enjoying his embrace and doing her utmost to keep her feelings in check. 'This will never do,' she said eventually, pulling away and straightening her uniform. 'The staff will complain if I ignore the bell for the end of my tea break, and it rang a couple of minutes ago.' She kissed him on the cheek. 'I'll see you at home later.'

Sarah came back into her office after seeing Freda hurry down the hallway towards the stairs. 'You look pleased with yourself,' she said to Tony. 'Here, I've brought you a cup of tea.' She placed it on the desk. 'There's one of Maureen's buns, too. I can fetch a cup for you if you like, Betty?'

'Not for me, thanks. I've not long had one.'

'Cheers,' Tony said as he sat down in the spare chair and bit into the bun. 'I'm starving. I wanted to get back here to give Freda my news, so didn't stop to eat.'

'News? Is it a secret, or can you share?'

'You'll hear soon enough. I've been given my own store at last; I didn't expect it quite so soon, and it's quite a large store too.'

'Oh, I'm so pleased for you. You've worked so hard, and I know it's meant long times apart for you and Freda – but to have your dream come true like this is truly wonderful. Freda must be thrilled.'

'I hope she is. It's going to be a big move for her, after living here in Erith since 1938, but I'm sure we'll soon make a new life in Liverpool.'

'Liverpool? That's a long way away,' Sarah said, not letting on that Betty had hinted this might happen. What with Freda being so fragile at the moment with her worries over having a child, it didn't feel as if this was the right time for her to move so far away from everything she knew.

'I'm going to miss you both,' Sarah continued. 'It will be strange not to see you round and about; and living just over the road from Nan's, I do see a lot of Freda. You're going to have a lot to sort out – when do you take over?'

'Almost immediately. I was told yesterday afternoon that the job was mine. I'm going back after the weekend, so it means leaving Freda to sort out the sale of the house and moving everything north; but I'm sure she'll cope.'

'We will all help as much as we can. You will be coming back before you move away for good?' she said, thinking how nice it would be to throw a party for the couple. 'And of course we're all going on holiday together.'

'I'm not sure that's going to be possible now,' Tony said. 'I can't very well take holiday leave when I've only just taken on a new job managing the store – and by then, Freda will be in Liverpool with me. Perhaps another time, eh?'

Sarah couldn't believe what she was hearing and looked towards Betty. Surely she felt the same? But no; she was writing in her notebook, and looked just as controlled and professional as she did when dealing with tradesmen. Perhaps she was better at hiding her feelings?

Betty looked up and gave Sarah a gentle smile of encouragement.

She understood then. Betty was hurting as much as she was. She turned to Tony and nodded. 'Yes, there will always be another time,' she said, trying to appear positive, but inside her heart was breaking. She'd be losing one of her best friends, and she wasn't sure Freda would be able to cope on her own.

*

Bessie was back at the gate of the factory exactly on time. She didn't want to upset Tom by being late, and the last thing she needed was for people to see her hanging about outside for an age and wonder what she was up to.

The hours had dragged since he went back to work. She'd not wanted to stay in the pub on her own – at her age she shouldn't have been in there anyway. Instead she had wandered further down the road, away from Erith, to see what the area was like, never having explored so far from home before. She came to St John's Church, where she spent a little while walking around looking at old graves until someone came out to speak to her. Bessie politely said she'd been told a relative was buried there, and had come to look around. When the woman offered to go inside and check the register, Bessie gave the surname as Smith – the first common name she could think of – and then hurried away as quickly as she could while the woman went inside.

Aware that the red coat she wore stood out a mile, and with just a few shops and rows of houses round about, she decided she was bored and wandered back towards the town. She told herself that as long as she stayed away from Pier Road, where Woolies was, then she'd be safe and not bump into anyone who knew her. God forbid a customer of her mother's would report back that she'd seen one of her daughters wandering the streets. Even though the comment would more than likely be innocent, Maisie would ask questions.

She stood looking out over the riverfront for a while, watching boats and larger ships as they moved up and down the Thames. The nearby docks were busy with cranes loading and unloading ships. She spotted the *Kentish Queen* paddle steamer going downstream and shuddered. It was very similar to the one they'd been on celebrating Freda and Tony's wedding, when Sadie's husband had died. Bessie knew she wasn't the only one who didn't fancy another trip on the river, even if it was to go downstream to the seaside towns of Ramsgate and Margate. She thought for a moment of Lemuel, the handsome, dark-skinned man who had worked with her Uncle Alan, and how his family had now moved to Erith so that they could be close to Sadie and her youngest child. It made Bessie wonder how she would feel if she ever lost Tom. She knew that she would do anything to keep him.

The sickness she'd felt earlier had stayed away, and now she was ravenously hungry. The small portion of Tom's sandwich had done nothing to assuage her hunger. Knowing there was a chip shop nearby, she hurried up the street to buy a portion of chips, drenching them in vinegar and salt before wrapping them up tightly in the newspaper and going back to sit by the river and eat them slowly, one by one. Someone had left a newspaper on the bench and she picked it up to read it.

Flicking past the news until she came across the page that mentioned women's fashions, she started to read. This was the kind of thing her mother read, so she was used to seeing the newspaper in their home. Although Bessie was not keen to work at the factory or in her mother's shops, she could see that Maisie's Modes would indeed be at the forefront of women's fashion in the town. It was her mother's plan to have whatever was worn by royalty as well as Hollywood stars in the shop windows within a week of being seen on the silver screen or in the papers and magazines. Perhaps one day her mum's garments would be in the magazines and newspapers? They should at least be covered in the *Erith Observer*, she thought to herself, flipping over the page to see a column about women's health.

It wasn't something that interested her very much, but mention of Princess Elizabeth's pregnancy and how she was in good health made her stop and frown. She put her hand to her stomach. Tom had told her she'd put on a little weight and perhaps shouldn't eat so many chips. She'd been rather upset at the time but, until today, had been avoiding the tasty food.

Could she be expecting a baby? Hadn't she overhead women talking about morning sickness when she was serving them in Woolworths? A wave of fear swept through her; she was sixteen, for heaven's sake, her mother would kill her. She shut the idea from her mind; no, she just had an upset stomach, that was all. Her monthlies had always been irregular, so she had no way of remembering when the last one had been, not that she ever took note of such things.

The final page before the sports pages was an article surrounded by adverts for bridal wear. She dreamt of walking down the aisle in sparkling white lace and seeing Tom waiting for her at the altar. If she was expecting, perhaps he would do the honourable thing and ask her to be his bride. After all, there were girls she'd heard of at Woolworths who'd married at her age. It wasn't her choice, because she wanted to see the world, but if Tom married her, what did it matter? She threw the newspaper aside and sat there, thinking. An idea came to her – yes, it was certainly worth trying.

As the hooter sounded for the end of the afternoon shift Bessie started looking for Tom, this time not being so obvious about it. She stood back and waited rather than jump up and down waving. He had said he'd be there, so why make a fuss? She was disappointed when he arrived with his mates again, as she'd hoped they would have some time alone.

'Aren't we going to the pictures?' she asked, sidling up to him and hanging onto his arm.

'We all are,' he said to her, 'once you've bought those chips for our tea.'

'But . . .' She was about to say she'd already had some and really would prefer to go into the cafe and perhaps have sausage and mash, but seeing the look on his face, she didn't like to argue. Besides, if she was paying for them both, she wouldn't have much money left in her purse.

'Yeah, we'll have some chips with you as well,' the other two lads said.

'Come on, then,' Tom said, 'and this one can pay for them, as I'm forever taking her out. It's time she paid me back.'

Bessie was miserable as she trailed after the men up the High Street to the chip shop opposite the Odeon. She was frightened of bumping into someone she knew, so kept looking around all the time until they were inside the chip shop. Not only did Tom's friends want chips but they asked for sausages as well, while Tom suggested a bit of fish wouldn't go amiss. 'I'll have a pickled onion as well,' Chalky said.

210

Bessie didn't fancy chips again and chose a sausage, asking for it to be wrapped separately to the rest of the order. She breathed a sigh of relief after counting all the pennies and coins to hand over the counter, finding she was left with sixpence in her purse. If he expected her to pay for them to get into the pictures, he was out of luck. She prepared herself for another argument. They argued quite a lot these days.

They walked round to the side of the Odeon, leaning against the wall to eat their food. Bessie took a couple of mouthfuls of her sausage and couldn't face any more. She was about to throw it to a stray dog who was sniffing nearby, when Tom stopped her. 'Don't go wasting decent grub,' he said, snatching it from her hand.

'What's the film?' she asked, and was disappointed to hear it was a cowboy picture. 'I think perhaps I might go home rather than stay with you,' she said.

'Please yourself,' Chalky said. 'We didn't want no girl hanging about with us anyway.'

'No, you stay with us. You might come in handy later,' Tom said through a mouthful of food.

'I should get off home after the pictures or I'll be in trouble with my mum,' Bessie said. She was aware that earlier she'd agreed to join in with whatever they were up to tonight, but surely they didn't really need her around for that. She didn't feel very well. But the three lads started laughing at her, pulling her leg about being a little kid who had to answer to her parents. She brazened it out and laughed with them, deciding to stay after all. She didn't want to lose Tom, at least not now; so she'd best do as he said.

Once inside, she went to the ladies' and cleaned herself up a little then joined them. Thankfully she had an aisle seat next to Tom, so she was able to snuggle up against him. As the lights went down he put his arms around her and kissed her.

'Tom, I'd like to ask you something, but don't go getting angry,' she said as he gazed up at the screen while the opening titles played.

'What's that, babe?'

'If I was pregnant, would you marry me?' She sucked in her breath, relieved she'd voiced her thoughts.

He snatched his arm away quickly. 'What the fuck are you talking about? What makes you think I want to marry anyone?'

Bessie forced herself to laugh. 'I was only joking,' she said, snuggling back up to him. 'Let's watch the film.'

They hung back once it was over and were the last to leave the cinema before heading back towards West Street and the factory where the men worked.

'You know what you're doing?' Tom said to the other two, looking around him at the empty streets.

'Yeah, it's all sorted. What about her?' Derek asked, pointing a finger towards Bessie.

'She's going to be our lookout,' Tom said.

Bessie stopped walking. 'Yes . . . about that,' she said uneasily. 'What do you mean, Tom? I'm not so sure I can do it. What if I get caught?'

'If you do as you're told, it will be fine. But if you don't do the job properly and we get caught, you'll never hear the end of it,' he said in a menacing voice. 'I'll beat you until you are black and blue.'

Bessie swallowed hard and nodded. If she was expecting a baby, she dared not fall out with Tom now. She needed him to be a good father, so that they could all live together and be happy . . .

It felt as if an age had passed while she'd been crouching behind the fence near where the men had gone in through a side door of the building. Someone had cycled by, but she'd shrunk back so they couldn't see her. Now she spotted a familiar figure walking towards her on the other side of the road. She almost fainted with fear: it was Sergeant Mike Jackson. What should she do?

Mike carried on and turned the corner of the road. He was walking away from her, but even so, he might come back at any time – and on this side of the road, she thought. Looking around quickly to make sure she was still alone, she went to the door, tapping on it hard. 'Tom, it's time you left,' she called in a low voice before banging on the door a second time.

The door opened a crack and Derek's face appeared. 'Why are you making all that noise, you silly cow? You'll wake the neighbourhood up.'

'I've just seen a policeman walking down the other side of the road. He might come back this way.'

It was hard to tell how he reacted to this; it was dark, and he had a scarf covering most of his face. 'Get back outside. I'll call the others,' he snapped.

Very shortly after that Chalky and Tom came out. Tom had two duffel bags over his shoulder while the other men carried holdalls.

'Where did you get those from?' she asked. 'What's in the bags?'

'Ask no questions and you'll be told no lies,' Tom hissed. 'Now, you'd better sod off home. I've got things to do with these two.'

'But it's dark. Something might happen to me,' she said fearfully.

'Just go – and if anyone asks what you've been up to, remember to say you've not been with me. You haven't seen me, got it?'

'Yes, Tom.'

Bessie hurried along as fast as she could, keeping to the shadows and constantly checking to make sure nobody was following her. The roads down by the river didn't feel like the safest of places even in the daytime; her dad had often told her to keep away from the area, even if she was with her sister and her friends. Beads of sweat broke out on her forehead as she made her way along. Soon she had a stitch in her side, which started to make her feel sick again.

By the time she reached the end of Alexandra Road she was fighting not to pass out with the fear of what she'd been through. Stopping to lean on a wall, she gasped for breath, looking about like a frightened animal in case someone should see her. She only had to get to the top end of the road where her home was, but how was she going to explain to her parents why she was so late? They were bound to hear her put her key in the door. It was then that she had an idea . . .

Taking deep breaths to try and control her rapid heart-beat, she slipped down the alley at the side of number one and followed the dirt track that ran the full length of the gardens on that side of the road. No one was likely to hear or see her.

*

Ruby couldn't settle in bed, with her back aching and Bob snoring. The bedroom felt stuffy and dry. She decided a cup of water would help, along with a breath of fresh air.

Of course, the moment she entered the kitchen, Nellie the dog wanted to go outside. Ruby opened the back door and watched the dog run around the garden as she sipped the cool water. She thanked her lucky stars that Bob's greyhound hadn't decided to join in, but then, it was a lazy bugger.

'What's she up to?' she muttered quietly, watching as Nellie stood dead still. The dog was staring at the high gate at the end of the garden. Then she turned and rushed back to Ruby, yipping excitedly and wagging her tail.

'Come in now,' she said, grabbing hold of Nellie's collar and pulling her through the open doorway, concerned about waking the neighbours. The dog kept looking back towards the alley beyond the garden, making Ruby wonder if someone was out there.

Who's out and about this time of night? It's nigh on midnight, she thought, as she walked to the end of the house to look up and down the gardens. She caught a flash of red scurrying away. Why, that looked like Claudette in her best coat. Whatever was the kid doing up at this time of night?

Now wasn't the time to go up to Maisie's house to find out, because if she was wrong, it would make her look daft. Instead, she decided to keep an eye on the girl and see what she was getting up to.

Bessie let herself in through the gate. The house was in darkness. Bending down, she picked up a handful of earth and threw it up at the back bedroom window. It took a few tries before Claudette appeared and pulled up the sash window to look out.

'Claude, it's me, Bessie,' she hissed. 'Come down and let me in – but bring my nightdress with you.'

Claudette shook her head but did as she was told, appearing a couple of minutes later and letting her in through the back door. As Bessie pulled off her coat and dragged the nightie over her head, Claudette started to ask her what she'd been up to and why their bedroom smelt of sick. 'I had to put a few pillows into your bed to make it look like you were asleep, otherwise Mum would have gone nuts. Thankfully she'd been told you'd come home sick and as she had a visitor, she left you alone to sleep it off.'

'Be quiet. I'll explain later. Let's get to bed, shall we?'

They were halfway up the stairs when the lights came on and Maisie stood on the top step, hands on hips. 'What on earth are the pair of you up to?'

17

'Goodness knows how you got away with that last night,' Claudette huffed as she straightened her bed after getting dressed. Work today meant being at her mum's factory, where they would be interviewing staff. She had dressed a little more smartly than usual, wearing a tartan kilt Maisie had made for her last Christmas and a cream knitted twinset that she usually kept for best. She would be assisting her mum, chatting to the women and showing them around. 'Why are you lying there like that? You can't be ill again, because you were OK to go out last night. And please can you do something about that stinking coat of yours?' she said, pushing up the sash window to let in more air.

'Just go away and leave me alone, will you? I don't feel right.'

Claudette grabbed hold of her sister's blankets and pulled them off her body. 'Get out of bed now, we're going to be late.'

'I'm not coming with you, I'm going into Woolworths today. Not only have I not picked up my pay packet because I went home early, but I'm also going in to make up the hours I lost through being ill.'

'Ill? You were with that Tom, weren't you? Whatever were you up to . . . No, don't tell me. I don't want to know,' Claudette said with a disgusted look on her face. 'Whatever it was, Mum and Dad don't deserve a daughter like you. All I will say is if you get yourself into trouble, don't expect me to cover for you. Now, I'm going downstairs to help with breakfast. Get your backside out of bed, clean yourself up and clean that coat of yours – it stinks. And another thing,' she said, as Bessie groaned. 'Never, ever touch my things again, do you hear me?' She wagged her finger at Bessie before leaving the room, slamming the door behind her.

As she helped Maisie prepare breakfast and get the little ones dressed and ready for Sadie, she noticed her mum keep looking towards the stairs as if waiting for Bessie to appear. Claudette feared her mum was about to have a row with Bessie for being up last night. Perhaps she knew Bessie had been out all the time.

'Give Bessie a call, will you, or we're going to be late,' Maisie said.

Claudette hurried to the bottom of the staircase and bellowed, 'Get yourself down here now, Mum wants you.'

A few minutes later, a sheepish Bessie came downstairs and joined them. 'Can I just have a piece of toast, please, Mum? I can't face anything else,' she said, all but collapsing into a chair and putting her head in her hands.

'Oh, my poor darling, are you still feeling rough?'

Claudette had to admit Bessie did look rather sick. But it served her right, pinching her best coat as she had.

Maisie hurried out to the small kitchen, giving Bessie time to grab hold of Claudette's sleeve and pull her close. 'Don't you dare say anything about me being out last night, do you hear? As far as you're concerned, I was in bed asleep all evening. In fact, if you do say anything, I'm going to tell Mum that I've decided I will come and work in the factory, but I want the job you're going to do. I'm the oldest, so she'll let me do it,' she sneered, causing Claudette to agree at once. She'd do anything to hold onto the job that her mum had promised her. It was all she thought about, all she dreamt about; Bessie wasn't going to spoil that for her.

Maisie came back into the room. 'Don't eat that if you don't want to – we can always whip something up for you in the little staff room. It's been painted and equipped now.'

Bessie gave her mother a forced smile. 'I'm sorry, Mum, I just don't think I can go with you today. I might just get back into bed.'

Maisie ran her hand across Bessie's forehead. 'You do feel warm. Don't bother eating that toast, as you'll only bring it up again. I don't know what you've got; I just hope the little ones don't catch it. Try to keep out of their way, will you?'

'If I feel better this afternoon, I need to go into Woolworths and apologize for having to leave early. And I need to collect my pay packet.'

Maisie sat down opposite the two girls. 'I've been thinking about Woolworths, and about the family holiday. I'm afraid I've got some bad news for both of you.'

Claudette looked anxious. 'Please don't say the holiday has been cancelled?' She'd done nothing but chat about it with the two Billington girls, from what clothes they would wear to how exactly they'd spend their time while they were there. Claudette planned to enter the sports competitions, while Clemmie Billington was pondering whether to enter the beauty queen competition. She was old enough, but needed the right kind of swimwear – and she wasn't sure whether her mother would even allow her to do it.

Seeing Claudette's downturned face, Maisie was quick to assure her it wasn't that sort of bad news, or not exactly.

'Darlings, your dad and I can't really spare the time to go to the holiday camp, as much as we would love to; I've heard such great things about the place, and it's been an age since I've seen Molly. I've been speaking to Sarah and Betty, and it seems Betty is in the same boat as me: she can't leave work at the moment. However, Freda will surely go. After all, Molly is her good friend.'

'Does that mean Clemmie and Dorothy can't go either?' Claudette asked.

'No, they can still go, of course; Sarah and Freda will be there to keep an eye on you. But for the most part you will have to look after yourselves. I'm trusting you both,' she said, giving them a stern look. 'Of course, Nanny Ruby will be there with Granddad Bob, but remember, they're elderly people and this is supposed to be a nice holiday for them. I don't want any squabbling or anything that will have Nanny Ruby upset, do you hear me? Which reminds me – I've altered a couple of dresses for her. Claudette, would you run them down to her before we set off for work?'

'I can do it, Mum,' said Bessie, who was delighted by her mum's news. It meant that if Tom did come along to the holiday camp for the week, she'd be able to slip off and see him without her parents knowing anything about it.

'No, you can't. You get yourself up to bed for a couple of hours at least. Only if you feel better can you walk round to Woolies this afternoon,' Maisie cautioned her. 'Now, I've been wondering whether you are responsible enough to take baby Ruby along with you on this holiday – the twins are far too young.' She chuckled at their horrified expressions. 'I'm only joking with you,' she said. 'She can stay at home with me and yer dad. Perhaps we can all have a holiday later in the year, once work has settled down.'

Bessie grinned to herself as she went upstairs to bed. Things were getting better all the time. If only she didn't feel so sick, she'd be on top of the world.

Claudette hurried down the road with the parcel her mum had given her tucked under one arm. She was so excited about the prospect of sharing a chalet with her friends and her sister. If only Bessie was more like her old self, they would have a wonderful week.

'Good morning, Nanny Ruby, Mum asked me to give you this. It's the two frocks she altered for you. She said if there's any problems to send them back and she'll have another go.'

'I'm sure they'll be fine. Come in a minute while I get my purse.'

'Mum said there's no charge. Not to you, anyway.'

'You're a chip off the old block, aren't you? I bet you're going to enjoy working with your mum down that factory. I reckon we'll have somebody taking over her business one day and making it as big as Woolworths.'

Somebody? Claudette wondered if that meant her mum was taking on someone else to do her job.

'There's no need to look glum, you silly girl; I meant you'll be the one running Maisie's business empire. That's why what I'm going to say needs to be listened to,' Ruby said suddenly, looking serious.

Claudette frowned. Ruby was known for being wise; everyone went to her with their problems. Whatever did she mean?

'I spotted you last night creeping up the alley at the back of the house. I'm not going to ask what you was up to – but don't do anything to let us down, will you?'

'But I wasn't—'

Ruby raised a hand. 'I don't want to hear excuses, my love. You were wearing your best coat. Even in the dark I spotted that red coat.'

Claudette was in a quandary. If she explained to Nanny Ruby it was actually Bessie she'd seen, she'd be getting her sister into trouble. Bessie had threatened to stop her having her dream job working with her mum . . . However, Claudette hated the idea of Nanny Ruby thinking she was a disappointment to her.

'I promise you I'll never do anything to disgrace you,' she said, leaning over to give Ruby a quick kiss on the cheek. 'I must go; we've got lots of work to do at the factory today. I'm helping Mum interview staff.'

'Then I mustn't keep you, my love. And tell your mum thank you for altering my frocks. They are going to do me a treat on our holiday.'

'Thanks, love, that'll hit the spot,' Maisie said as Claudette placed a cup of tea in front of her with two biscuits on the saucer. They had set up a table at one end of the main room, where the seamstresses would be working. From there they'd be able to see how the women being interviewed worked on the test pieces, and they were only a few yards from the staff room, where others could wait to be seen.

'I've picked the best two out from the broken biscuits, so it gives the right impression to the people we interview,' Claudette said seriously as she sat down next to Maisie and looked at the list of names in front of them. She flicked through a small pile of letters that had been sent enquiring about the seamstress positions Maisie had advertised in the local newspaper.

Maisie chuckled. 'I'm hoping it's our set-up that will impress them, rather than our unbroken biscuits. But thanks for all your help, love. I'd never have thought of writing back to those ladies and giving them times to come along to see us. Thank goodness your dad gave us that old type-writer.'

'It did take me a while to write the letters, using two fingers and having to peer at the keyboard. But I'll get better with practice. I did wonder if I should do a course or something at the college, just so that I'm a bit better at typing and things, until we can afford to have somebody work in the office? Clemmie might be able to advise me about courses, with her going up there to learn all that complicated stuff. Rather her than me – I much prefer to work with fabrics and fashions.'

'Funny you should say that, because I've been wondering if Bessie might like to learn some secretarial skills, since she's not interested in the fashion side of the business. What do you think?'

'I think that's a bad idea, Mum. She's really not inter-ested, and you know when she's got one of her moods on her, she can be downright rude at times. We don't want her on the phone to potential customers and putting them off, do we?'

Maisie ruffled her daughter's hair. 'If only Bessie was more like you. I could retire early and leave you lot to keep me in luxury.'

'Not just yet, eh?' Claudette smiled at her. 'I'll go outside and see if anybody is hanging about. I'm surprised we've had a few that have just turned up on the off chance there's a job available.'

'We can invite them in and make them a cuppa in the staff room while they're waiting.'

'Do you think that's a good idea?' Claudette asked, not having done this kind of thing before.

'I do,' Maisie smiled knowingly. 'It will show us in a good light. We need something to entice them to come down here to work, since it's off the beaten track.'

'I'll even leave out a plate of biscuits, but it'll have to be the broken ones,' Claudette said as she hurried outside, holding a clutch of application forms and a few pencils. It had been her dad's idea to use the forms, and he had helped her design them. It was a jolly good idea, because then she and Mum could look over them after they'd met the applicants. She'd also put a bench outside so the women had somewhere to sit, if they preferred to wait there rather than come into the staff room.

There were three women waiting. Two looked rather nervous and it was obvious to Claudette that they were wearing their best clothes. The third was a bit flash and puffing frantically on a cigarette. She stubbed it out when she spotted Claudette.

'Oi, kid, how much longer have I got to wait? I haven't got all day to stand about down here, my fella's coming to collect me in half an hour.'

'It won't be long, and if all of you would like to come through to the staff room, you can have a cup of tea while you complete the application form. It will save time,' she added as the rude woman opened her mouth to answer back. 'May I ask if any of you applied in advance?' The two nervous women had, so she ticked their names off the list she was holding.

'Please come through, I'll be calling you both first,' she smiled as she led the ladies through the factory to the staff room.

Maisie had decided to give a sample of sewing to each applicant to see how they performed. She'd set their table up in such a way that it was facing away from the entrance door, so as not to intimidate anyone coming into the large room. This also meant that she could talk privately to each applicant while others sat at the sewing machines to work.

'Here, I didn't know we had to do some sewing. I hope you're going to pay us for it,' the rude woman remarked.

'It's just a sample, so that we can check you know how to sew in a straight line and use a sewing machine.'

One of the shyer women spoke out. 'I've brought a couple of samples of my work with me. I thought perhaps you'd like to see that I can set pleats and sew buttonholes.'

'Thank you, Miss Dawson, that's very helpful. Now I've just made a fresh pot of tea and there are some biscuits on the table, so help yourself, ladies. If I may remind you all, this is the only room in the building where you are allowed to smoke. I'll call you shortly, Mrs Jones – please feel free to bring your tea with you. We don't want to rush you.' She smiled politely and hurried back to her mum.

'What are they like?' Maisie whispered as she checked her face in a small compact mirror. She reapplied her lipstick and began powdering her nose.

'I can't speak for the sewing because we've not given them the test yet, but one lady has brought some samples along to show us, which I thought was extremely conscientious of her. One of the three I couldn't take to . . . she seemed a bit full of herself. But then, she could be the best seamstress . . .'

'That's true, and to be honest, if looks and the way someone speaks were taken into account, I'd never have been hired in a million years. At least I've tried to improve the way I speak,' Maisie said. 'I just hope we can find some good workers, and quickly. We need to be up and running as soon as possible.'

Claudette looked at Maisie. She seemed worried. 'Why the rush?'

'The Bexleyheath shop opens in just under four weeks. I need enough stock to fill it by then, and I want to focus on wedding clothes and smart outfits for the mums. I'm hoping these women can start work next week.'

The smile left Claudette's face. She knew they were going to be hard pushed to be up and running by then; they couldn't expect her dad to fund the business for too long. She looked at a large calendar hanging on the wall. 'Do you realize what that week is, Mum? It's the week we're all on holiday. Perhaps I should stay here with you?'

'No, no, no – you are having your holiday. I want you to have fun,' Maisie said, leaning over and kissing her cheek.

'Besides, I want you to take your notebook and have a look while you're there, see what beachwear women are wearing. You might get some good ideas. And don't forget to check out their party clothes as well – which reminds me, we must sort out some nice dresses for you and Bessie to wear in the evenings, when you go dancing.'

Claudette smiled at her mum. 'I'll do all I can to help you before we go. I'll sort out the fabric, and me and Bessie can measure each other to make sure the dresses fit. Perhaps we could get one of the women to run them up? That way, if they make a few mistakes, it won't matter as much as it won't be shop stock.'

Maisie roared with laughter. 'You're a crafty one, aren't you? I wonder where you get that from?'

'I learnt from the best,' was the answer. 'Now, I'll go and get Mrs Jones and we can hear what she has to say.'

'Good idea. And the next one we think is any good, we can ask her to start as soon as possible. There's no time like the present. Why wait till next week?'

Mrs Jones – or Fiona, as she asked to be called – was a very pleasant woman. Maisie looked down at the application form and noted that she was forty-two and a widow. She explained she'd lost her husband in a factory accident several years before and had come from the East End, but now lived in Slades Green with her mother and three children.

'Mum is a cleaner down the pub, and she also does a bit of private work for a few people in the big houses in Erith. She's a hard worker, just like I am,' she said. 'I didn't think to bring anything with me like the other lady. Will that go against me? I really do need this job, and I've worked as a seamstress before – but in the East End. It was more like a sweatshop, but I'm a hard worker,' she assured them.

'Don't you worry about that, love. I'd have asked if we needed you to bring something,' Maisie said. 'What I'm going to do is have Claudette here – she's my daughter, by the way – take you over to the machine. I would think you'll know this model, because they're all second-hand from a factory that was closing down in the East End, but shout if you don't. There's no need to worry about anything here; I want a friendly ship. Claudette, would you give Fiona the machine over there?' She pointed to the corner. 'It's a child's summer skirt. If you could stitch the seams together and add the waistband; there's no need to hem it or anything like that. It'll give me a good idea of what your work is like. Take your time, there's no rush, and if you want, you can go and have another cup of tea.'

Fiona Jones looked relieved. 'Thank you, I'll do my best and I won't take too long. Besides, I've got to cycle back for the kids before Mum has to go off to her next job,' she said, following Claudette, who quickly pointed out what was to be done and then returned to Maisie.

'I like her,' Claudette whispered as she put a big tick beside Fiona's name on the application form.

'I agree with you, but there's one glaring problem.'

Claudette thought for a moment. 'Do you mean her having to rush off?'

'Yes; how can she hold down a full-time job if she's running after her kiddies? We can try to be accommodating, but even so, if there is someone who can work full time, they'll go above Fiona on the list, and that will be a shame. Go and call the next candidate in while I have a think about this.'

228

When Claudette returned with Miss Dawson, she could see her mum was scribbling on a piece of paper which she turned over before she gave a welcoming smile to the older woman.

'Hello, love, how are you?' she said, holding her hand out and giving the lady a firm handshake. 'My name is Maisie Carlisle of Maisie's Modes, and this here is my daughter, Claudette, who will be working here with us. She might look young, but she's got it all up there,' she grinned, tapping on her own head. 'Now, what's your first name . . . let me see . . . ah, you are Miss Eleanor Dawson. And I can see that you've worked as a seamstress in the past. Can you tell me something about that?'

'I'm in my fifties,' the lady apologized. 'I hope that won't go against me, but I've always worked – that's when I wasn't looking after my parents. They have now departed this earth.'

'I'm sorry to hear that,' Maisie said. 'Do you live alone?'

'Yes, I have a small house that my parents left me near Crayford, but I can get here very easily as I have a small run-around car. It's not much, but it gets me where I need to be.'

'Mum has just learnt to drive. She has a van for factory use. Perhaps when I'm old enough, I can learn,' Claudette said.

'I'm pleased I learnt – it was something I did during the war. I was left a little money by my parents and I put it to good use. I did wonder, but no, perhaps now's not the time to say . . .'

'Go ahead, love,' Maisie smiled.

'Well, if I'm fortunate enough to gain a position here, I would be able to offer a lift to any ladies who live between

229

here and where I live. I know you're a bit out of the way, but with my vehicle it's not a problem for me.'

Maisie took to the woman at once. She was already thinking of her colleagues and she'd not even got the position.

'That's very generous of you, Eleanor, most generous indeed. Now, what sort of sewing have you done?'

Eleanor reached into her handbag and pulled out several letters. 'I have some references from when I used to work in London for the fashion houses. It was a couple of years ago now, as I've only just taken up looking for work again after stopping when my parents were poorly. I hope that doesn't matter,' she said, chewing her lip nervously.

'It doesn't matter at all, my love. I always say sewing is like riding a bike. If you fall off, you can always get back on again, can't you?' Maisie winked. 'This is very interesting,' she said, sliding one of the letters across the table to show Claudette. 'I see there is mention here of you being a skilled embroiderer as well as a seamstress. That could be very handy for our wedding gowns.'

Eleanor clapped her hands together. 'You are making wedding gowns? How wonderful. I've always enjoyed helping brides to find the perfect dress. Will you be offering a made-to-measure service, something special for those special brides, or is it all off the peg?'

Maisie raised her eyebrows. There were so many new ideas coming in today. She hadn't thought of bespoke gowns, but now that Eleanor mentioned it, why not?

'Tell me, Eleanor – have you ever supervised staff?'

'Yes, I have. Because of my age and not having a family, I managed to work my way up in the profession; that is, until the war years and the time I spent caring for my parents. But before that, I was helping younger girls to train for the job.'

'And although I advertised the job here, since you drive, would you be prepared to travel to my shop in Bexleyheath, to measure and speak to any bride who wanted a special gown? I would of course pay travel expenses and a little extra; I wouldn't expect any staff member to be out of pocket.'

Eleanor reached into her handbag again and pulled out a handkerchief, dabbing her eyes.

'Please do forgive me,' she said with a little laugh. 'It's just that the kind of job you're talking about has been my dream. I would simply adore to work for you; that's if you'll have me. I do have a few examples of my sewing as well as my embroidery,' she added, pulling out the samples she'd shown Claudette earlier as well as an envelope containing samples of delicate stitching and beadwork. 'I've also worked in pattern cutting, something I picked up along the way, although my skills might be a little rusty. But like you say, I can climb back on that bike and start cycling again very easily.'

'Eleanor, I could kiss you,' Maisie grinned. 'When can you start?'

'This afternoon, if you wish,' Eleanor said, 'assuming of course that the wages and hours are suitable, not that I'd probably argue, even though I shouldn't say that.'

'I'll tell you what, Eleanor. If you want to go out to the staff room again, make yourself a fresh pot of tea, I'll just see this other lady that's waiting and then we can have a nice long chat about Maisie's Modes and bridal gowns.'

'Gosh,' Claudette said when Eleanor had left them. 'She's a find, isn't she? But what was that you were scribbling when I came back to the table just now?'

Maisie turned the page over and pointed to the heading 'homeworkers'. 'I'm going to make a suggestion to Mrs Jones when she's finished her sample, to see if she'd prefer to work from home. It may fit in around her children very nicely – or perhaps she could be part time?'

'How about part time and a homeworker?' Claudette asked. 'I'm really looking forward to this, aren't you?'

'I am indeed, my love. I just need somebody to manage the Bexleyheath shop, or I'll be popping backwards and forwards far too much. But I need people I can rely on to do that job. The Erith shop is ticking over nicely, and with it being down the road and close to home, it's not a problem. Bexleyheath is a bit further off, and being a bridalwear shop we need someone that little bit special, don't you agree?'

'I do; but I can tell you right now, this is not the right person,' Claudette said, tapping on the remaining application form. 'So if you were thinking of her, strike her off the list right now. You need someone a bit older, someone who has been married and knows what an exciting time it is for the bride and her mother.'

'Blimey, Claudette. You may only be fourteen, but you've got your head screwed on right, haven't you?'

'As I said before, Mum, I've learnt from the best.'

18

Claudette showed the final interviewee through to where her mother sat. As far as Maisie was concerned, she had a list of seamstresses to be proud of. Miss Dawson was a find, and she knew she'd not get many of them to the pound; and as for poor Mrs Jones, she almost cried when Maisie offered her a job and the opportunity to work from home if she couldn't manage the hours at the factory.

'I don't want lose a good seamstress just because she's got children. I've got youngsters at home myself and it can be a worry, so I do sympathize with you. If you ever have a problem, you come and talk to me – especially if it's about kiddies. My Claudette is a bit on the young side to advise you, but the girl's got a heart of gold, so don't worry about her age, will you?'

Eleanor Dawson offered Fiona Jones a lift home and they went off the best of friends, chattering excitedly about their jobs. Maisie looked up as Claudette ushered in the final candidate, then down at the scribbled application form, trying to make out the spidery writing. 'Doris Andrews?'

'Yep, that's me, darling,' the woman said, sitting down opposite Maisie.

Maisie wrinkled her nose at the smell of cigarettes. That could be a problem if she hired Doris. Maisie like a cigarette herself, but she knew that the smell of smoke could linger on clothing, which wouldn't give a good impression when she was trying to sell garments. 'Have you worked as a seamstress before?'

'Yeah, but not making fancy clothes like those,' Doris said, looking at the pictures on the wall. 'I've been working down at Sebel's, where they make the Mobo toys. There's lots of things need sewing there – it's not quite up to what you're looking for, but I thought I'd chance me arm. I've been down there a while now and, well, it's a bit boring.'

'Do you make your own clothes?' Maisie asked, trying to find a reason to hire the woman.

'Yeah, I always have, right through the war. It was the only way to get any decent clobber. I was always first in line if there was a bit of parachute silk going begging.'

Maisie nodded, reminding herself to look past the brashness to see if there was someone she could employ underneath. 'What I'd like you to do is go over to the machine – my daughter Claudette will show you which one – and you will find some strips of fabric. I'd like you to join them together so that I can see the finished seams. Then I'd like you to use the needle and thread provided to hem the bottom, so that I can check how neat your hand stitching is. Do you think you can do that?'

'It will be a doddle,' Doris said, ignoring Claudette and going straight to the machine.

'What do you think?' Maisie asked in a low voice.

Claudette wrinkled her nose. 'I don't know, I suppose it all depends on what her sewing is like, but you'll have to have a word about the smoking. I did point out earlier that the staff room is the only place in the factory where she could smoke, but at the moment she smells like a kipper. I'm not being rude, am I?' she asked her mum, expecting to be reprimanded.

Maisie shook her head. 'You've hit the nail on the head there, and even if it makes me sound like a snob, I'm going to have to mention it. Have you seen her application?'

Claudette sat next to her mum and took the form. She frowned at the name; why did that surname ring a bell? It was a common enough name, but for some reason . . . She busied herself sorting out the pile of applicants who'd definitely not got a job. 'That's ten letters to write,' she said. 'I'll get started on them when I get home. I know if it was me, I'd like to know whether I'd got the job or not.'

'Your dad is home tonight. Perhaps we can ask him to help out. He's better on a typewriter than we are. I say let's give it a couple of months and then if we're ticking over OK, we'll get someone to work in the office, even if it's part time.'

'Thank goodness for that,' Claudette said.

'Here you are, ducks, all done and dusted,' Doris said, returning to the table and throwing the piece of work in front of Maisie, who lifted it up and inspected the stitching.

'I must say, it's very neat, both the machine and the hand stitching.' She looked the woman in the face. 'I do have one reservation about employing you.'

'Don't worry, love, I know what you're going to say. It's me smoking, isn't it? I've been told about it before. But I like this place,' she said, looking around, 'so I'm prepared not to smoke while I'm at work.'

'But it does linger,' Maisie said.

'I expected you to say you'd be supplying an overall, that way you wouldn't smell any smoke on me,' the woman said wisely.

Maisie picked up a pencil and added this idea to her list. She'd source the fabric and have the women make their own. 'Do you have any questions, Claudette?'

'I wondered if you had any family,' Claudette asked.

'No one that would come and work here.' The woman cackled at her own joke. 'I've got a brother, Tom. He's working down the toy factory as well.'

Claudette felt her heart thump in her chest; could that be Bessie's Tom? She'd best not ask anything else, in case the woman put two and two together and realized that her brother's girlfriend was linked to them. Her mum would go through the roof.

Clemmie Billington could hardly contain her excitement. Today she was going to meet the women leading the course she was taking at Erith College, and would also meet the other nine girls on her course. She'd been asked to bring along her examination certificates from school and was carrying them in a large envelope tucked under her arm.

Stepping off the bus outside the college, she looked up at the old building. She'd not been in this part of the town before, even though it was only four stops on the bus from Pier Road and Woolworths. The road bordered Belvedere and from where she stood she could see a great part of the town below her as well as the Seaman's Home and the edge of Franks Park. The few houses dotted along the road were bigger than her home and stood detached from each other with large front gardens.

She took a deep breath as she gazed up at the tall red-brick building with its deep windows. To think that in a year from now, she would be leaving with professional qualifications that could lead to her working in London – or anywhere else she chose. Her father had intimated she could work for him afterwards, as he always needed competent office staff, but she shied away from the idea of working with dead people. She knew her dad and his staff were respectful of the people they looked after, but even so, she found it creepy. How could she tell anyone she worked for an undertaker? It just wasn't something that you talked about when you met people for the first time. She couldn't even laugh when Betty told a joke about the day her dad had fallen asleep and been trapped inside a coffin. It just wasn't funny, was it?

As she stepped down from the bus she was followed by another girl who looked to be around the same age as herself. Both headed towards the large entrance at the side of the building.

'You're not by chance going to the office machine meeting, are you?'

Clemmie gave a polite smile. 'Yes, I am. It's the first time I've been here apart from my interview, but then I just went into the one room and then left. I believe we're going to be shown around today as well as meet the machines?'

'It's rather daunting, isn't it? I applied for this course a couple of years ago after a neighbour recommended it to me. She has a really good job in London at the moment. But things got in the way and I've been unable to contemplate starting until this year,' the girl said. 'We are early – would you like to go for a cup of tea before we go to the meeting place? I'm a bag of nerves.'

237

'Me too,' Clemmie agreed. 'I'm Clemmie Billington, by the way.'

'And I'm Jane Wheatley, pleased to meet you,' the mousey-haired girl smiled, holding out her hand, which Clemmie shook straight away. She could see the girl had tried to dress smartly, although her dark brown coat and matching hat had seen better days. Then she chided herself for thinking such a thing.

'Already I don't feel so nervous, now that I've met someone else who's on the course. It's strange how knowing somebody, even briefly, makes one feel more at ease,' she replied as they headed towards the student refectory.

'I'm finding it all rather strange,' Clemmie confided as she carried two cups of tea to a table that Jane had found in the corner of the busy room. It reminded her of the Woolworths staff room, but must have been at least four times larger. Large scrubbed wooden tables were scattered around, with earnest-looking students grouped at some of them chatting excitedly. At one end was a serving hatch where they could purchase food and drinks. 'In a way it's like going back to school at the start of a new term, and in other ways it's completely different. I do have a new notebook and pencil case, though. Does that sound childish?'

'No, not at all,' Jane laughed, reaching into her bag to pull out a new notebook and a pencil case. 'My younger sister bought these for me for good luck. I know we don't start properly for another week, but I just felt I ought to bring them along in case we have to take notes.'

'I was thinking the same. I'm wondering if I'm going to

be older than some of the other people on the course. Would some of the students be more like fifteen or sixteen years of age?'

'Oh, I doubt it. When I started the course a couple of years ago . . .' She stopped as she saw the look on Clemmie's face.

'So you did start it before? Why did you stop – was it very difficult?' she asked, feeling that perhaps she'd bitten off more than she could chew.

'No; something happened in my life that meant I couldn't continue. Our main tutor promised to hold a place open for me, and here I am back again. I was eighteen last month.'

'Oh, you poor thing, were you ill?' Clemmie asked, thinking that could be the only reason. 'I'm eighteen too and have only ever had a part-time job at Woolworths on Saturdays. I didn't know what I wanted to do with my life, so my stepmother and my dad said I might as well continue at school until I decided. They did have some grand ideas about me going to university, but to be honest that's not my cup of tea at all. I don't think I'm bright enough, for one thing.'

'Don't put yourself down. There are times when I never thought I'd get back here, but my parents have been marvellous, even though I let them down in so many ways. They stepped in to help out, so hopefully my future is a lot brighter now.'

Clemmie was dying to know what Jane meant, but as she'd only met the girl in the last hour, it seemed rather rude to push her too much. No doubt in time she would explain. 'So, do you think the other students will be our age?'

'Well, they need to have obtained some exam results to show their competence, so I would think the youngest will be around sixteen.'

'Not much difference, then, that's good. I didn't want anyone pointing the finger at me for being the oldest student and wondering why.'

Jane laughed. 'If there are any fingers being pointed, they'll be aimed in my direction. Don't you worry, there won't be many girls there with one of these on their finger,' she said, holding up her left hand and showing a gleaming gold band.

'Oh my, you're married, how wonderful. No wonder you took some time off. Did you have a lovely wedding?'

Jane screwed up her face before she spoke. 'I need to place my cards on the table and explain, if we're to be friends. It's unfair of me to keep things back . . . and then you may not want to be my friend after all.'

'Oh, I'm sure that—'

'Let me explain first, please. I had a boyfriend; we've known each other since we were thirteen. We went to school together and always talked about getting married. Our parents know each other and we planned for a future where we would have children and a home. It's just that we were rather foolish, and the baby came along first. We had a rushed wedding. Even though both families were overjoyed about the baby, he wasn't happy. He was called up for his national service and, looking back, I know he was relieved to be going into the army. The day after we had a romantic farewell together, with my mum looking after the baby, he must have posted a letter to me. It arrived by the second post on the morning I'd waved him off. There was me wondering where he was and what he was doing, as well as already missing him like hell – and he was asking to be released from our marriage.

'My dad was livid, and all my mum could say was, at least I was married. But I was seventeen, I had a baby – and I'm sorry to say, only a couple of months later I realized I was expecting a second child. It was a right mess. And if it wasn't for my parents and my in-laws, who have been marvellous, I'd have a right old problem on my hands.'

Clemmie felt so sorry for Jane. She seemed a decent sort, and she was pretty certain what had happened to her could happen to any girl who had fallen in love.

'So, you're back at college and that's a positive step, isn't it?' she said, hoping she wasn't preaching to the girl. 'Tell me about your children. Will your mum be able to look after them all the time? What about when you go to work after we finish the course?'

'I have two little boys, John and David, and I love them to distraction. Mum and my mother-in-law are helping me look after them, and once I'm working I'll be able to pay them back for everything they've done for us. So, you see, I haven't got a husband, I'm young, and I've got two kiddies. I'll understand if after today you really don't want to know me.'

'Not want to know you! You don't know me very well, do you?' Clemmie chuckled. 'Well, I think you're wonderful with how you've coped, and perhaps one day you'll allow me to meet your children. I hope we'll become really good friends,' she said. Something about this conversation was helping her to realize that she could now put her old life, and all her problems from school, behind her. This was what proper friendship was about – even a new friendship. It was about supporting each other through thick and thin and sticking up for each other. She hoped that she and Jane would be friends for a very long time.

Jane beamed back. 'Tell me about yourself – what made you want to do this course?'

Clemmie explained how unhappy she'd been at school and how things had come to a head on the day she'd had a fight in Woolworths with one of the bullies, leading to her supervisor recognizing her interest in business machines and encouraging her to take a course.

'I know that store very well. I don't live far from the town; we are in South Road up near Britannia Bridge.'

'Oh my goodness, we've probably walked past each other without knowing,' Clemmie chuckled. 'Why don't we plan to catch the bus together in town to go up to the college and come home together in the evenings? My stepmother's going to drop me off in town each day on her way to work, so I can catch the right bus.'

Jane reached across the table and squeezed her hand. 'It's as if fate has brought us together,' she smiled.

The two girls spent the afternoon following their tutor from room to room while the different accounting and calculating machines were explained to them. They were given schedules of the lessons, along with a list of books that they needed to read on subjects such as office practice and commerce. There would also be English and arithmetic lessons, and both girls sighed with delight when they learnt they were expected to study *Romeo and Juliet*.

'Not that I want anything to do with boys or romance for the rest of my life,' Jane explained, as they pored over their notes during the short bus journey back to their part of Erith. 'I'm just so grateful that Miss Marks fought my corner for me to be able to return to the course. It's a shame I don't still have the books; I'll have to purchase them all over again.'

'That is a shame – what happened to them?'

'My bloke, Pete, burnt them not long after we married. He reckoned my place would be in the home with the kids, and we only had the one then. He said I'd have no time for learning.'

'What did he do for a job?'

'A bit of labouring, nothing much. I think perhaps he was frightened of me improving myself and wanting to get a decent job to support us. I cried when he burnt those books.'

'It sounds a bit like Hitler, doesn't it? He was supposed to have burnt books before the war.'

'Pete turned into a bit of a Hitler, to be honest. However, that part of my life is now over. I know I'm better off without him. I just need to be able to buy these new books – I don't like to keep asking my parents for money.'

'Look, you can tell me to mind my own business, but have you thought about getting a part-time job? I know it would only be Saturdays at the moment because of us going to college, but would your mum have the kids for another day? I only ask as Woolies are advertising for Saturday girls and part-time staff. I know when I've been on holiday from school, they allow me to work extra days. The money always comes in handy. I could put in a word for you, if you like. It would only be for the next year or so while you do the course, and then after that you can find a really good job. Hopefully you'll be working fewer hours than you would at college. Scribble down your address here – I'll ask, and then I can let you know. I'm pretty sure you'd hear something before I see you when we start attending college.'

'That would be a godsend, thank you. I'm pretty certain my mum would say yes. She wants me to be able to stand on my own two feet. She shops in Woolworths all the time and is always saying how nice the staff are.'

Clemmie felt as though she might burst with pride at the thought that Betty managed a store people liked so much. She felt guilty that she'd given her mum a bad time in the past and vowed she would be a model daughter from now on.

'Bessie, get off your backside and make us both a cup of tea, will you? We've been working all day. I know you were sick this morning, but you look right as rain now,' Maisie said.

Bessie scowled. 'I was thinking that now I feel all right, I might go out this evening.'

'Oh no you're not, you're going to stay home and help your sister. You know how to use your dad's typewriter, and there are letters to be written to the people we've interviewed today. Once we've had a bit of tea I'll clear the table and while I'm putting the kids to bed you can get stuck in between you, do you hear me?' she said to Bessie, whose scowl became darker. 'Let me just remind you that if you want a new dress to wear when you go on holiday, you've got to start pulling your weight more. Otherwise I won't bother asking my new staff to run it up for you, once me and Claudette have chosen the fabric and cut it out. Which reminds me – the pair of you need to note down each other's measurements. You've both filled out and shot up a bit since I last made you an outfit.'

Later, with their tea finished, Claudette brought out the typewriter and placed her notes next to it. She then pulled a tape measure from her pocket. 'Let's do our measurements now, shall we?' she said, getting Bessie to stand still and hold her arms out while she took several measurements around her bust and waist. 'Mum is right, you have filled out a bit. You might have been sick lately but it hasn't stopped you putting weight on. Have you been dipping into the broken biscuits at work?'

'You've probably taken the measurements wrong. Here, let me check,' Bessie replied, sliding the tape measure around her waist. She could see straight away that Claudette was spot-on with her numbers. 'Oh well. I look good for it and my boyfriend hasn't made any complaints.'

'Talking of your boyfriend, I think it was his sister who came for an interview today. She works down that place where Tom works, and they've got the same surname. It is Andrews, isn't it?'

'It's a common enough name,' Bessie said. For some reason she didn't feel like talking about Tom's family with her sister, or any of her personal business. It was bad enough that Claudette had covered for her when she'd come home late a few times. Then there was Nanny Ruby, who'd thought she saw Claudette running up the back alleyway that night, meaning Claudette could be in trouble for something Bessie had done. Yes, thought Bessie, it was better that she didn't share anything with anyone.

She shrugged her shoulders and added: 'I've got no idea about Tom's family and I'm not really interested, so don't you go saying anything to this woman if she starts work at the factory.'

'You'll see her yourself when you're working there.'

We'll see about that, Bessie thought to herself as she sat at the typewriter. 'You read out what you want to put in this letter, and I'll type,' she said, placing a clean sheet of paper into the machine and winding it through the roller. If she kept talking about the letters, it wouldn't give her sister time to ask questions about Tom.

19

July 1950

'How can she be a Saturday girl?' Bessie sneered as she stood at her counter along with Claudette and Dorothy. They were looking across the aisle to where Sarah was introducing Jane Wheatley to the assistants on the childrenswear counter. 'I heard she had two children. Saturday girls are schoolgirls, not older women with kids.'

'I like her,' Dorothy said. 'I was with Clemmie when we met her at the bus stop. She is going to be attending college with Clemmie and they're the same age, so you can't really call her an older woman, can you? And college is kind of like school, isn't it? I think it's good that she's trying to earn some money to help bring up her children. Did you know her husband left her?'

Bessie shrugged her shoulders. She didn't really want to hear this; as far as she was concerned, the woman shouldn't be a Saturday girl because she had children. She turned her back on Dorothy and continued to speak to her sister instead. 'I suppose Clemmie spoke to her mum and got a job for her friend; talk about sticking together,' she said, before quickly picking up a feather duster to dust the display of crockery in front of her as Sarah moved over to them.

'We don't need three Saturday girls on this counter, ladies. Bessie, could you move over to groceries and help out today? It's heavy work and you're better suited to it than the younger girls.'

Bessie all but snarled at Sarah, but did as she was told.

'Oh dear, Auntie Sarah, I have a feeling my sister is going to be grumpy for the rest of the day. She doesn't like getting her hands dirty, and those potatoes are pretty muddy.'

Sarah felt her mouth twitch, but tried to remain professional as she was on the shop floor and in view of other staff and customers. 'It's nice to be moved around from counter to counter, and I wouldn't worry about your sister. After all, we're off on holiday soon. Are you both looking forward to it?'

'I can't wait,' Dorothy said as she picked up a cloth and rubbed it over a row of Brown Betty teapots. 'Claudette and I are going to enter the talent competition and we've been practising our songs. We did wonder if Mrs Caselton would play the piano for us?'

Sarah was confused for a moment before she realized it was Maureen the girl was talking about. 'Why don't you ask her?' she suggested. 'She's on her last shift up in the staff room, you can catch her when you both go for your tea break.' She looked behind the counter to see if the area was tidy and ticked it off her list. 'Why don't you arrange it so that you can go together?' Both girls might be too shy to speak to Maureen on their own, but together they could do it. 'My Alan may be able to help you as well, he likes to sing. I'll leave you to your work,' she said, giving them a warm smile before moving on to check on another counter.

'She's nice, isn't she?' Dorothy said. 'It will be fun going on holiday with them, but it's such a shame my parents can't go because of work.'

'It is. I would have liked to see my parents at the holiday camp too, but as my mum said, there'll be other opportunities. And at the moment, the factory comes first. I'm just glad she didn't ask me to stay behind and work as well. It's so busy there at the moment.'

'I was grateful to have a dress made similar to yours, it was so good of your mum. I really enjoyed myself when you showed me around the factory. I quite like sewing.'

'Well, if you're ever looking for a job when you leave school – and that won't be long – why not consider working for Maisie's Modes? Mum is very good at training people, and you could do a lot worse.'

'I might just stay at Woolworths for now,' Dorothy said with a smile. 'I like meeting the customers and helping them with their purchases. But I'll keep it in mind; thank you very much.' She popped the lids back onto the teapots and lined them up so that the spouts all pointed the same way. 'So, how's it going now that you're up and running?'

Claudette looked around her; it was still quiet in the shop. 'Look, let's unpack that box of cutlery – it needs polishing before it's displayed on the counter. If we do that, we can chat at the same time; but make sure you've got eyes in your back of your head, in case the supervisor comes round or a customer needs serving. After all, that's what we're here for.'

'I will,' Dorothy promised, helping to rip the top off the

case and pulling aside straw in order to lift out smaller boxes containing knives, forks and spoons. Passing Claudette a clean cloth so they could polish the items as they went out on display, she looked around her. 'It's all right to talk now.'

'We've picked some really good ladies to work for us. I helped Mum with the interviews. One lady used to work making wedding gowns and she does the most beautiful embroidery. Straightaway Mum snapped her up, and although she will be working in the factory she is to work solely on wedding and bridesmaid's dresses; although there will be times when she'll drive up to the new shop at Bexleyheath, which is opening in a couple of weeks, so she can measure brides for their special dresses.' Claudette grinned as she displayed a selection of polished spoons. 'Are there any more tablespoons in the crate?'

Dorothy rummaged in the straw and pulled out a bundle. 'Here you are.'

Claudette took the spoons and started to buff them. 'We need some more apostle teaspoons as well,' she pointed out before continuing to talk about Maisie's Modes. 'Did you know the brides will be able to have gowns designed to their specification? This lady – Eleanor, her name is – has even promised to show me how to do some embroidery. I'm looking forward to that, as it's something I've never tried. When I get it right perhaps I could embroider our names onto our cardigans?'

'That would be lovely. Do you think you could show me how to do it as well? It will look so glamorous.'

'Of course I will.'

The two girls looked over towards the haberdashery counter on the other side of the store.

'We'll be able to buy what we need from Woolies,' Dorothy grinned. 'Do you like the rest of your mum's new staff?'

Claudette thought for a moment. 'There is one woman I'm not sure about. I did tell Mum when she came for the interview that I had reservations. Already, after being there one week, I can see she doesn't seem to fit in. She's quite, what would you say . . . loud? And when Mum is not about she talks to me like I'm a little kid, not a fellow worker. I'm just thankful that I'm not sitting at a sewing machine next to her all day long. I couldn't cope with it.'

'If she upsets you, you should tell your mum,' Dorothy said. 'Is it possible she's picking on you because she knows your mum owns the business?'

Claudette was thoughtful. 'You could be right. She's just one of those brash women that opens her mouth and speaks without thinking. There's something else about her as well: she's the older sister of that Tom who our Bessie is knocking about with.'

Dorothy rolled her eyes skywards dramatically. 'Oh no. I hope you don't mind me saying, but I don't think he's the right chap for your sister. He is so uncouth. I've only seen him a few times but when we were in the cinema and she was there with him, we could hear him and his mates talking and laughing over the film. I don't know why they've not been kicked out.'

Claudette couldn't help but laugh. 'Uncouth? You sound just like your mum. Not that it's a bad thing,' she added, seeing that Dorothy looked hurt. 'I think I'll use that word in future, I like it.'

'At least for the next week we won't have Bessie mooning over him while we're away. It will be a good week.'

'I'm afraid not. Tom is going to the holiday camp as well. Him and two of his mates. Bessie's already told me she expects me to make excuses for her so she can see him. Even though Mum and Dad won't be there, she doesn't want Nanny Ruby or anyone else finding out about him.'

'That's what I don't understand,' Dorothy said. 'If I was going out with a lad, I'd be proud to introduce him to my family. Why does she need to lie about seeing him? Is it because she's ashamed of him and she secretly knows he's not good enough for her?'

'You've hit the nail on the head there,' Claudette said, 'and that's one of my mum's sayings. Look out – we have a customer.' She brushed pieces of straw off her uniform and gave the lady a big smile.

Sarah headed upstairs towards her office, but before she started work, she thought she'd put her head round the door and let Betty know how the latest recruit was doing – especially as Jane was a friend of her daughter's. She tapped on the door and entered when Betty called out to come in, but drew up short as she saw Tony and Freda sitting together opposite Betty.

'I'm sorry – I can come back later,' she said. This didn't seem like a social visit, as neither Tony nor Freda was on duty today.

'No, please come in,' Betty said. 'This is something you need to hear.'

Tony gave her a weak smile while Freda kept her head bowed, looking into her lap as she twisted a handkerchief between her fingers.

'I just wanted to let you know that the new Saturday girl seems to be fitting in all right,' Sarah explained. 'I'll have Clemmie take her break with Jane to check she's coping. I thought she could be her mentor – in fact, I thought perhaps we could do that for all new staff, so that they don't feel they have to come to management for every little thing.'

'Another excellent idea, Sarah. I knew I'd done right to offer you the part-time staff manager's job. Now, pull over that stool and sit down.'

Sarah did as she was told, looking between their three faces. A feeling of dread washed over her. Somehow, she knew that whatever she was about to hear would not be good news.

'We've received official confirmation that Tony is to take on management of a larger store in Liverpool,' Betty said, pointing to a letter on her desk with the F. W. Woolworth heading.

'Oh dear,' Sarah said without thinking. 'I know you told us, but to see it in writing . . .' She felt like crying. 'When will you be starting work there?'

'It will probably be a few weeks before I leave, I would think, with so much to do. Tony is going sooner, and he'll try to find us a house to rent close to where he works. There's no point in buying all the time we own our house down here,' Freda said, looking at her friends through red-rimmed eyes. 'I'm very proud of Tony,' she said. 'I just don't know where to start . . .'

Sarah reached over and took Freda's hand. 'I'm here to help you as much as possible. Everybody will help. When are you going up there, Tony?'

'I'm catching the train tomorrow,' he said, a serious look on his face. He was completely aware of how the news had affected his wife. 'I'm hoping Freda can come up with me for a week, just to look around and see what it's like. I appreciate it's very hard for her to be going to an unknown part of the country to start a new life.'

'I've done it once before,' Freda mumbled. 'When I came here.'

They all fell silent until Sarah exclaimed, 'But what about the holiday? We will be going the day after tomorrow. Won't Molly be expecting to see you?'

Freda looked at her and shook her head slowly, not able to speak.

'There seem to be so many of us dropping out of this holiday,' Betty said, 'what with Douglas and me, and of course Maisie and David – and all because of work. I can't help but feel that some of us have our priorities wrong. Perhaps in the future we should all do something together, wherever we are living in the country.'

'I was looking forward to seeing Molly, and of course Johnny. I have such happy memories of when they worked at Butlins,' Freda said, before bursting into tears. Tony put his arm around his wife and hugged her until the tears stopped. 'Of course, my own husband comes first,' she said.

Sarah had been thinking, and decided to speak up regardless of how much she might offend her friends. 'I personally feel that Freda should come with us on holiday. In the great scheme of things, Tony, how will one week make any difference to you moving away? With us all mucking in and helping when we get back, it won't take long. Besides, if you're just shutting down the house, then you'll need someone to keep an eye on it. And what about Winston Churchill?'

Betty looked puzzled. 'What does Churchill have to do with this?' she asked.

That did make Freda laugh. 'He's our cat, Betty. We adopted him just after we married. He was quite a chubby kitten and Tony remarked he looked like Winston Churchill, and the name stuck.'

'Oh dear,' Betty said, chuckling, 'I do feel Sarah has the right idea. I know it is only a week's grace, but Freda would have a chance to say goodbye to her friends as well as spend time with them and think about your plans for the future.'

Freda looked at Tony, waiting for him to speak. 'Perhaps you'd prefer to discuss it when we go home?' she said. 'Although, if you are catching the train tomorrow . . .'

Tony gently kissed her cheek. 'I don't need to make up my mind; it's already been made for me. I was a fool to expect you to go with me – I'm used to travelling alone. Although I will say I'll miss our home here in Erith. Don't forget, I've only got this job for a year; head office are going to decide after that whether I stay or whether I move on to another store. We may even find ourselves moving south again.' He smiled gently, obviously upset to see his wife in such a state. 'Yes, you take your holiday with my blessing and enjoy yourself, my love. In fact, don't come to join me for two weeks – that will give you plenty of time, when you come back, to choose what will go north with you and what's to stay locked up in the house.'

'And who is going to care for Winston Churchill,' Betty added with a smile. 'I'm going to see what I can do to find you a suitable position in another Woolworths store, close to where you will be living. I know Tony has said he prefers you not to work with him, and I can appreciate that, but Liverpool is a large place with several stores. At least then you will have something to fill your days – and what could be better than Woolworths?'

'Thank you all for your help and advice,' Freda said. 'I am looking forward to moving north with Tony; at least I'll get to see him more often.' She smiled as she took his hand. 'And a job in Woolworths, even part time, would be very nice while I settle in. Now, my dear, we ought to go home and pack your suitcase, and you can also tell me which clothes you no longer require. There just happens to be a jumble sale at the church hall, so they'll be receiving quite a few items from us as I sort out our home.'

'All right,' Tony said. 'But first I'm taking you over the road to Maisie's Modes to buy you a lovely dress to wear on your holiday. I may not be there to waltz you around the dance floor, but at least I'll know that you're the belle of the ball.'

'Oh my.' Betty dabbed at her eyes as she returned to her office after seeing Tony and Freda out. 'It's lovely to see a young couple moving on with their lives, but I'll miss Freda so dreadfully. I'm sure you will too, Sarah . . . Sarah?'

Sarah had taken one of the vacated seats and had her head in her arms on the desk. She was sobbing her heart out. When she was able to speak, she looked up at Betty.

'Why do things have to change?'

'Oh Sarah – there's no need to get so upset,' Betty said as she leant over to hug her. 'You know, I've seen so many changes since I've worked here, and at times I desperately miss staff and friends when they move on. Why, I still have a tear in my eye when I remember that Maisie no longer works with us; I'm so proud of how she's moved on with her work. She's a shining example of what a woman can accomplish these days when she puts her mind to something. I fought for most of my life to be independent and to be able to earn my own living, and that's what all women should be able to do. Yes, we are both going to grieve as we lose the Freda we love; but just for a moment, think back to how we first knew her.'

'Time has certainly changed us all,' Sarah said.

'My first memory of Freda is of looking up from my desk on the day you three girls arrived for your interview and seeing a small mouse of a girl with old clothes and a scared face. She desperately wanted a job and was keen and eager to live in Erith. None of us knew back then how that young girl's life would pan out,' Betty smiled. 'But look at her now: she's made a good marriage, and Tony is the happiest man on earth. We both know that she will cope with her sadness at leaving us and will work hard to help him in his career. I am certain she will do well – and who can say? A change of direction may be just what the doctor ordered.'

Sarah digested Betty's words. 'But she wants to stay here. And above anything else she wants to give Tony a child, so they have their own family.'

'And that's going to happen, my dear – and it's not as if we'll never see her again. Granted, you won't be able to have lunch with her or chat over a cup of tea during your tea breaks; but with so many people having telephones these days, it will be easy to chat with her just the same. And letter-writing can be so therapeutic.'

Sarah wiped her eyes. 'I will do my best to be a good letter-writer. You know, when Maisie was sent to live with her in-laws while she was carrying baby Ruby, we all got so caught up in our lives we forgot to write to her . . .'

'I remember – and look what happened. She found her way back to us and gave birth in Erith. You're Freda's closest friend, so perhaps you two are the ones who will hold everybody together, keep the friendships alive and arrange to visit each other. I know Liverpool is a long way away, so perhaps you could meet midway and have a weekend somewhere in a little hotel to keep in touch? Your friendship will survive whatever life throws at you. Perhaps one day when she's expecting that baby, she will come back to Erith to have her child in the bosom of all her friends.'

'That's a lovely thought,' Sarah said, brightening up. 'And she still owns her house in Alexandra Road, so that will be her link to us. Tony did say his contract is for one year; maybe they will decide he's not good enough to run the store. Although that's unlikely, isn't it?'

'My dear, I believe you are clutching at straws now,' Betty chuckled. 'Tony is a rising star within the Woolworths company, and with a woman like Freda at his side he can certainly go places.'

'You're right, Betty, I'm being silly. Why, I've mentioned to your Clemmie how you've propped me up through life's ups and downs with a plentiful supply of handkerchiefs and cups of tea.'

'And now it's your turn to carry on the tradition. I know you're already doing a splendid job. I had a little chat with Clemmie the other day, and she told me how good you've been to her.'

'I'm so pleased you spoke to each other. She's a bright girl; you should be proud of her. She's settling down now and will enjoy her college course. Like you say, none of us will lose touch completely. We've all grown up under the Woolworths umbrella, and that's thanks to you, Betty. You're the matriarch of the Woolworths family.'

'Now you're making me feel older than I am,' Betty laughed. 'Be off with you, back to your work.' She flapped her hands at Sarah to dismiss her.

Sarah smiled and kissed Betty's cheek. 'Yes, boss,' she grinned.

'Thank you, Sarah.'

'Whatever for?'

'For giving me back my eldest daughter. She's a different girl these days, and you made that happen.'

Tom released Bessie from his arms and gave a satisfied smile. 'I've got a chalet to myself at the holiday camp. I've told the lads they can share. That means we can be together all the time and not have you worrying about getting back home before your curfew, even if it is another chalet.'

Bessie had expected something like this to happen. 'I'm not so sure, Tom. It's going to be very hard to get away to be with you. I know my mum and dad aren't coming with us, but I've still got Nanny Ruby and Granddad Bob and my aunts, as well as the three girls that I'm supposed to be sharing with. I'll be able to slip away occasionally, but I can't be with you as much as I would like,' she added sadly. 'Do you know, Tom – my family might think kind-lier towards you if . . . if . . .' She looked down at her left hand, and then looked him in the face. 'We've been going together a while now, and just sometimes, a girl expects a ring on her finger. After all, we are very close now.'

Tom pushed her away and reached into his leather jacket for a cigarette packet, not even offering one to her as he lit up. 'You girls expect too much from us blokes. Why can't we just have a bit of fun?'

'We've done more than have a bit of fun. I've covered for you and your mates on a few occasions now, and if you get caught, that means I'm in trouble as well. Besides, you said you loved me when . . .'

'A bloke says anything when he wants to get his way with a girl,' he sneered. 'It's just one of those things. So don't go all soppy on me like the actors in those films you like watching. I'm no Johnny Johnson,' he laughed. The girls all loved watching Johnny when he'd been a matinee idol in so many spy movies playing the secret agent Clive Danvers. Even at her age, when she thought she'd be seeing him soon at the holiday camp a small shiver of excitement ran through her. Why, even her Nanny Ruby was a little in love with the man.

'Tom, I'm just saying I like being with you – but sometimes you've got to think about me and not only yourself.'

He shook his head and gave her a hard stare. 'You're too clingy at times, Bessie Carlisle. If you aren't careful, I might find a replacement. There are plenty of other girls who'd like to go out with me.'

Bessie felt her stomach lurch and a wave of sickness washed over her. Why was it she was feeling sick all the time? As usual, she pushed any niggling worries about the most likely reason firmly aside. Perhaps she was seriously ill. Well, if Tom was going to drop her, she'd rather die anyway. She shrugged off the sickness and reached out to kiss him. If that was what it took, so be it.

'I'll see you as much as I can. I'll even sneak out when the three girls are asleep. Is that all right?'

'It will have to be. But don't be surprised if you see me having a bit of fun on my own while we're there. There might also be the chance to pick up a few bob here and there.' He nodded to himself. 'Yeah . . . I don't expect to come home after a week without some extra dough in my pocket.'

'Please, no, don't go thieving there,' Bessie pleaded. 'I know the people who own the holiday camp. It's a new venture for them and it would be awful if there were robberies while we were there. It would give their business a bad name, and it would upset my Auntie Freda.' She didn't like to add that she hated how much he enjoyed stealing from others. It went against everything she'd been taught since being adopted by Maisie and David.

Tom laughed out loud. 'You and your bloody family. I'm going out with you, not them. And think on: if I was ever to marry you, I most certainly wouldn't be marrying your family as well. You'll be expecting me to go round your nan's house for tea on a Sunday, and I ain't that sort of bloke. You need to get that into your head, are you listening to me?'

'Yes, Tom, I'm listening,' she said meekly. There was no arguing with him, but inside Bessie was miserable. Her dream of Tom becoming part of her family one day was starting to fade.

20

'It's wonderful to see you,' Freda exclaimed as she hugged Molly Johnson before spinning round to look at the Sunny Days holiday camp. Molly hadn't changed at all: her curly blonde hair still bounced around her face as her blue eyes shone in delight. The camp reminded Freda very much of Butlins, where the two girls had worked just after the end of the war. Even though Sunny Days was on a much smaller scale, it had cheerful rows of flower beds and the buildings were painted a bright, clean white. Excited chatter came from groups of holidaymakers carrying their suitcases towards the rows of chalets.

'And look at you,' Freda added, stepping back to indicate the pronounced swell of Molly's stomach. 'You need to tell me when the baby is due and what you have planned . . . will the baby live here at the camp? Why, you've hardly said a thing in your letters.'

'I wanted to wait until we were face to face,' Molly said, linking arms with Freda and heading towards the reception area. 'I'm not sure this is exactly the right time for our baby to come into the world, what with our business only just getting off the ground, but it's welcome just the same.'

'What do you mean, the right time?'

'Well, this is the first full season for Sunny Days, and we made quite a few changes over the winter months. Johnny is up to his neck working for his father's talent agency as well. Thank goodness our house is on the site, otherwise I don't know how we'd have managed. Now that we've settled in, you must come and visit often. We have two guest bedrooms, would you believe – isn't that posh?' She chuckled.

Freda stopped in her tracks. 'I've got something to tell you, too, and it's why Tony isn't with me. He's been offered his own store at last.'

'Well, that's wonderful news! You must be so pleased,' Molly said.

'I am, and I'm so proud of him. The only problem is, it means moving away from Erith and our lovely home,' Freda said. It was Molly who had generously given her the house in Alexandra Road, at a time when Freda had desperately needed somewhere to live. 'If we sell the house, Molly, I'm going to make sure that the money comes to you. It wouldn't be fair for us to keep it.'

'Don't be daft, the house is yours; it's all in your name. We are doing more than all right here, with my inheritance from my parents. I just know that my gift to you went to the right person. Besides, who knows – if I have a tiff with Johnny, I might very well come knocking on your door for the spare bedroom,' she chuckled.

Freda gasped in mock horror before laughing. 'I don't reckon that's going to happen; you're the only one of my friends who married a matinee idol. Besides, I dine out on telling people that my friend is married to none other than

Johnny Johnson – so I'm afraid, my dear, you're going to have to stay with him until you are in your dotage.'

'If you're moving, will you be closer to us here? I'd so love a close friend, especially now,' Molly said, patting her tummy.

'I'm afraid not; the store is in Liverpool.'

'Liverpool!' Molly shrieked. 'Why, that's miles away.'

'Don't worry, the girls have told me we must meet up often, and I'm including you in that. Bring children, babies, cats and dogs – the more the merrier. Betty mentioned we could rent somewhere, then we could all be together and have a good chinwag.'

'Or they could all come here, if it's out of season. I wouldn't dream of charging for the chalets, and we can eat in my house.'

Freda hugged her mate. 'That's so generous of you. And as for the baby coming along, I'm a little jealous but excited for you all the same. I'd best start knitting now.' Freda knew she could never really be jealous of Molly, despite her yearning for her own child. 'Your mum and dad would have been so proud,' she added gently. Molly's parents had died in a car accident just after the end of the war.

'Don't get me started,' Molly said. 'I've done nothing but blub ever since I've been carrying this little one. Honestly, I've even wept over some of Johnny's old films, and I've seen them a dozen times or more.'

The girls laughed together as they entered the reception area, where Freda's friends and family were gathering too. Molly stepped forward and addressed the whole group.

'Now, you'll be pleased to know that I've put you all in the same row of chalets, so that you can see each other whenever you feel like it. There's lots going on, so I would expect that some of you will be heading towards the pool and others to the ballroom to join in with the fun. If you prefer a quiet day, you will find the garden is a tranquil place to sit. Plus, we're not far from the beach, so you are free to come and go as you please.' She handed out guides to the week ahead, as well as keys on large wooden tags with chalet numbers painted on them. 'Everything is in the guide, but if you have any questions, track me down, or speak to Tina here behind the desk. She knows everything there is to know and is my trusted right-hand girl.'

Tina beamed at the guests. 'Yes, please ask me anything. I'm also in charge of this,' she said, pointing to a microphone, 'so you will hear my voice over the tannoy system throughout the day, announcing what's happening.'

'Rather like it was at Butlins,' Freda said, remembering her exciting trip there in 1946.

'Yes, and like Warner's holiday camp, and some of the others. So many are built around the same business model – although ours is smaller and more select,' she winked.

'I simply adore the uniform,' Sarah said, coming forward to kiss Molly on the cheek. They'd met a few times over the years and exchanged Christmas cards. 'That orange is so cheerful.'

'I designed it myself,' Molly said as she gave them a twirl and chuckled. 'If any of you young girls ever want a summer job, please just let me know,' she added.

Dorothy beamed back at her. 'Do you ever want people who sing and entertain?' she asked. 'Claudette here has a beautiful singing voice.'

'I believe Claudette will be too busy working for her

265

mum; that's why Maisie couldn't be with us today, which has quite annoyed her,' Ruby said. She stepped forward to give Molly a hug. 'I popped into Missons' the other day and Mr Jones said to send you his best. He and his missus will be down in a few weeks for their annual holiday.'

'I do miss Erith,' Molly said, 'and it's just lovely that everyone can come and visit me. Please, none of you ever be strangers, will you? We're hoping to be open all year round eventually, once we get the heating fixed. Now, why don't you go and get yourselves settled in, then I'll treat you all to afternoon tea. There's an old-fashioned tea room just past the ballroom. I was rather crafty and designed it on the model of the Lyons teashops, so it will feel familiar to you – but please don't tell Joe Lyons, or he'll be after me with a lawsuit,' she giggled. After pointing them in the direction of their chalets she said, 'I'll see you all later on.'

'I claim the bed by the door and window,' Bessie said, throwing her suitcase onto the bed. If she wanted to slip out to see Tom during the night, it would be easier not to have to climb past the others and risk waking them up.

'That's fine by me,' Clemmie said. 'I'll have the one over by the wall and the washbasin. That way I'll get first dibs on washing in the morning.'

'Looks like you and I have the bunks,' Claudette grinned at Dorothy. 'I'll go on top,' she added, quickly jumping onto the ladder to check out her bed.

'That suits me. I'd probably fall off; you know how clumsy I can be,' Dorothy said.

'Shall we unpack and get settled, or go out and explore?' Clemmie asked.

'I'd quite like to go for a swim in the pool, it looks lovely,'

Claudette said. 'I could have jumped in as we walked past earlier, it was so hot travelling down on the train. Do you want to join me, Dorothy?'

The two younger girls pulled out their bathing suits and towels and hurried from the chalet towards the pool, waving to Ruby and Bob as they passed by. Ruby had already settled in a deckchair and placed a sunhat on her head. 'This is going to be a wonderful holiday,' she said before dropping off to sleep.

Back in the chalet, Clemmie kept an eye on Bessie as they unpacked their suitcases and slipped them under their beds. She'd been waiting to get Bessie on her own because of something that her friend Jane had told her. It had been eating her up inside all week, but she hadn't wanted to worry anyone else, so thought it best to wait until they were alone and wouldn't be disturbed.

'Can I ask you something, Bessie?'

'Depends on what it is,' Bessie replied, looking out of the window for the tenth time since they'd entered the chalet.

'I know you've been seeing that Tom for quite a while now, and I hope you don't think I'm being nosey, but have you . . .' Clemmie started to colour up as she tried to think of the right words to use.

'Have I what?'

'Well, you know . . . have you done it with him?' she all but whispered, turning away to hang up her best dress on one of the hangers on the wall.

'I'm old enough,' Bessie snapped back.

'So am I, but I haven't,' Clemmie said, wishing she'd not asked.

'You've never had a boyfriend, have you?' Bessie smirked.

267

'I don't want to get into an argument about it and the last thing I want to do is fall out with you. But I've noticed you're filling out quite a bit, and this past couple of months you've been so sick. Do you happen to know the reason why?'

Clemmie had fully expected Bessie to argue with her. Instead the girl suddenly sat down on her bed, not caring that she was crushing her clothes, and started to cry.

'I have, you know . . . I mean, I've done what you mentioned. Oh Clemmie . . . I think I might be pregnant.'

Clemmie joined her, moving the dresses to the other side of the bed, and put her arm around Bessie. 'Have you told anybody? Does Tom know?'

'No. I did say to Tom about getting married, or even engaged. But he laughed at me and said there was no point as we got along fine as we were.'

That's how he would answer, Clemmie thought, as she silently fumed. Now wasn't the time to tell Bessie that Tom was a bad lot; it might just alienate her further. Then there'd be no getting through to her. What Bessie needed right now was a friend, and Clemmie was determined to be that friend. 'Do you happen to know when you had your last monthly?'

'Four months ago, from what I can remember.'

'How come your mum, or even Claudette, hasn't noticed that you've not had your, er . . . visitor? Betty buys sanitary napkins for me to save my embarrassment asking the chemist for them. She'd know if I wasn't using any.'

'As soon as I thought that I might be, you know . . . I started to sneak them out of the packet, so it looked as though I was using them. In our house we wrap used ones in newspaper and burn them in the boiler in the kitchen.

I carried on doing it, so mum was none the wiser. Or nosy Claudette, as she now uses them.'

'So they aren't aware, not even with you being under the weather?'

'Mum's been so busy with everything, I don't think she's had time to stop and look at me, which suited me down to the ground. I'm quite thankful she's not coming this week in case she questioned me about my clothes not fitting properly. I've managed to let a few out, and when we had new dresses made for the holiday, it was Claudette who measured me. She did notice I'd grown, though. It's not going to be long before it really shows and I can't hide it,' Bessie said, looking down at her tummy without touching it. 'I don't know how that Molly can be so excited about being pregnant and showing off her bump.'

'It's because Molly is married and she loves her husband, and that's the natural progression of things. Sadly, for you and Tom it's just been a bit of fun and the lad led you on when he shouldn't have done. You're only sixteen, for heaven's sake. Whatever are your mum and dad going to say?'

'I dread to think what Dad will do. What do they call it, a shotgun wedding? At least Tom would marry me then.'

'Yes, and Maisie would be right behind with a pitchfork, prodding the pair of you up the aisle. Will you be happy to marry Tom, if they insist on it?'

Bessie shook her head violently. 'No . . . no, I realize now he's not a decent lad. But he's got things over me, so I can't leave him. Mind you, if I am pregnant, it would be nice to be married . . .'

'What do you mean, he's "got things over you"?'

'I've helped him a couple of times when he's been out robbing.'

Clemmie groaned. 'Oh Bessie, whatever have you done?'

Bessie looked glum. 'I thought you'd be more sympathetic.'

Clemmie shook her head, not realizing she looked rather like her stepmother when she was disappointed in something the girls had done. 'Sympathetic? You could end up in prison if you've been helping him do such things. Didn't you think about that before you joined in with his antics?'

'I thought it would be fun to begin with. After that, I didn't want to be a spoilsport, or have him turn on me.' She rubbed her arm as she spoke, remembering the way Tom had grabbed her the previous week.

Clemmie felt sorry for Bessie and angry with her at the same time. 'At least you've got a week away from him. It will help you clear your head. We can use that time to make plans for your future. We're going to have to tell our sisters, though; otherwise they might guess and let it slip out, and drop you in it with your parents.'

Bessie nodded in agreement. 'Thank you,' was all she could mutter, as her throat tightened. She thought she might burst into tears again. That would never do.

'Now, why don't you wash your face and we can go for a walk and look around the camp?' Clemmie said. 'If Nanny Ruby or the aunts ask why we've not gone swimming with the others, I'll tell them it's my time of the month and you're keeping me company.'

Bessie hugged Clemmie. She had always thought the Billington girls were on the posh side, but here Clemmie was going above and beyond to help her out; and all of a sudden she didn't feel so afraid any more. She cleared her throat.

'Thank you, Clemmie, you don't know how much this means to me. I've been an utter fool. I don't want Mum and Dad to know I've let them down so terribly.'

'They're going to find out eventually,' Clemmie said, giving her a sympathetic smile.

'No, they won't – because I've decided I'm going to go away somewhere. I don't know where and I don't know how, but I think it's the best plan. That way I won't bring any shame upon my family.'

'I'm not sure that's the right thing to do, but as I said, we've got a week here on our own so we can make plans together, all right?'

Bessie took a deep breath. 'I'm not quite on my own. Tom is here with his two mates. He wants me to meet up with him in the evenings, after you've all gone to bed. I dread to think what the three of them are going to get up to this week.'

Clemmie was thoughtful. She knew pretty well what Tom wanted to get up to with Bessie; but as for the three lads together, if they thought they were going to rob Molly and Johnny Johnson's business, they had another think coming. Clemmie would do her utmost to stop them.

'Have you had an enjoyable afternoon?' Freda asked the four girls as they sat down next to her at dinner. There was fish and chips on the menu, and everyone was ravenous despite some of the adults having enjoyed an afternoon tea with Molly.

'It's a wonderful place,' Claudette said as she tucked a napkin into the neckline of her new dress to protect it. 'I'm

271

going to look at the competition boards after dinner so that I can put my name down for as much as possible. Did you know they hand out medals at the end of the week?'

Bessie laughed out loud. 'Next you'll be entering the bathing costume competition to be queen of the camp.'

Claudette frowned. She was aware she was on the tubby side, although Maisie had assured her it was puppy fat and would go in time. 'I'm not interested in that sort of thing, and besides, at my age I would still be eligible for the camp princess. Why don't you enter the holiday camp queen competition? After all, you love prancing around in your swimsuit as a rule, not that I saw you in the pool this afternoon. I thought you both would have joined us,' she said, looking at her sister and Clemmie.

'Oh, I agree,' Freda said, 'you two older girls really ought to enter; you're both so pretty.'

'I'll think about it,' Clemmie smiled. Bessie hugged her thick cardigan around herself and stuck a fork into a chip. No one quite heard what she mumbled.

'I'm going to miss you when you move away, Auntie Freda,' Claudette said. 'May I write to you?'

'That would be wonderful. You can tell me all about the Brownies and what you're all up to, and how much you like the new leader. You will stay on to help her, won't you?'

'Yes, but it won't be the same without you,' Claudette pouted. 'It's not as if I can go over the road and visit you; and I'll miss our bicycle rides. Who is going to live in your house?'

Freda always felt that chatting with Claudette was like talking to another adult, and was happy to answer her questions. 'It's been so quick that we're thinking we will just close up the house for now. I'll take anything that we need with us and Tony's arranging a van to collect it all next week. Perhaps you could come and help me pack a few boxes?'

'I'd love to. It will have to be evenings, though, as we're busy at the factory now Mum's second shop has opened. What will happen to Winston Churchill?'

Freda's smile disappeared. 'I'd like him to come with us eventually, but until we find a home it's going to be hard to keep him safe. I think for the time being, he's best left at the house. I'll have to ask a neighbour to pop in and feed him and check he's all right.'

'I could do that. And I could I play with him as well. He knows me, so he won't be afraid. I can make sure he doesn't bring any mice into the house too; that's as long as you don't think I'm too young to help you?'

Claudette was quite grown up for her years and such a trustworthy girl; besides, she lived at the top end of the road, so it wasn't as if she had to make a special trip. 'I'll have to check with Maisie,' Freda said, 'but yes, that would be really helpful. I can write down exactly what Winston likes and doesn't like, and if you can find time to play with him, that would be super. And I'll leave you some money as well, for his food. That's a weight off my mind, thank you.'

They chatted for a while about the house and Freda living in Liverpool before their plates were taken away and a dish of jelly and blancmange was placed in front of each of them.

'I don't think I can face this. I'm full up,' Bessie said as she pushed her dish away, whereupon the other three girls divided it between them.

'Honestly, you girls, you'd think no one has fed you for a week,' Freda laughed.

'Being on holiday makes you hungry,' Claudette grinned. 'Are you sure you don't want some?'

'No thank you, I've had sufficient.' Freda looked across to the next table, where Sarah was sitting with Alan. 'Should we go into the hall and save our seats? Ruby wants to play bingo before the dancing starts. It'll be better for her to be near the front so that she can hear all the numbers being called.'

'Are you saying I'm going Mutt and Jeff?' Ruby called from her table close by.

'No, we're not, Nan,' Sarah said, 'it's just that when we play bingo in the church hall, you're always saying you can't hear the caller. And then you tell him to shake up his balls all the time.'

'Perhaps it would be a good idea,' Ruby agreed.

The adults started to move away, leaving the girls to finish their dessert and promising to save their seats in the ballroom. It was then that Bessie looked up and spotted Tom and his two mates on the other side of the dining room, chatting to some waitresses who were giggling over whatever they were saying.

'I'll catch you all later,' she said, pushing back her chair and hurrying in Tom's direction as fast as she could. She shoved chairs aside, weaving around tables until she reached his side. 'Hello Tom,' she said, kissing his cheek before glaring at the other girls. 'Do you fancy going for a walk?'

Tom leant back in his chair and stretched his arms above his head. 'I suppose I could. I'll see you guys in the bar later,' he said, before getting to his feet and slinging an arm around Bessie's shoulders as they left the dining hall.

'She really ought to be careful,' Claudette said as she watched the scene unfold. 'Mum and Dad might not be here, but plenty of their friends are and will soon notice if she's with some lad – especially him.'

'Do you know much about him?' Clemmie asked, not wishing to tell them just yet what was happening with Bessie. Despite what she had said to her friend earlier, she felt the girls were too young to know about such things.

'Only what I've said before. He's a bad lot and I know he goes nicking things. You'd think with him having a good job, he'd stop being a thief, but I have a feeling it runs in the family,' Claudette said, removing the napkin from the front of her dress and wiping her mouth.

'You talk as if you know something,' Clemmie frowned.

'I know that in the week since Tom's sister started working at the factory, our stockroom is a bit lighter on scissors and other small items. I'm sure it's her doing it.'

'What has your mum said?'

'I've not told her yet. I was hoping she might notice and sack her while we're away. But I do have a plan, if she's still there when we return.'

Claudette outlined how she planned to count the stock that was kept in one cupboard and make a careful note. Then she would check each evening, and if she noticed a big difference, only then would she report back to her mum. Maisie had a lot to contend with as it was and seemed quite stressed at times, so if she had some proof, it would help bring the thieving to an end.

'That's a good idea,' Dorothy said. 'Don't forget, if you ever want help at the factory, I can always come down and help you. I'd love to see how everything works – I don't want paying,' she added quickly.

'Remind me when we get back, or I may forget. It would be lots of fun to show you round and see what you think about my ideas. Mum's been so generous, allowing me to have some of my designs made up. They could be in the shop before too long.'

Clemmie was quiet as they left the table and walked towards the large ballroom on the other side of the camp. What was Bessie letting herself in for? Tom was a bad lot, and although she'd asked for help, there she was rushing after him just because he chatted to a few waitresses. Clemmie doubted he would hang around if he knew Bessie was expecting his baby. She'd learnt a lot from her new friend Jane, and wondered if Tom was cut from the same cloth as Jane's husband. However, unlike Jane, Bessie wouldn't be able to rely on Tom's family – not if what Claudette said about his sister was anything to go by.

It was hard to believe Bessie was nearly two years younger than she was and had got herself into so much trouble. Family and friends were the answer, and Bessie needed their support just now.

'I suggest we make an excuse for Bessie,' Clemmie said to the other two. 'Someone is bound to ask where she's gone.'

'Let's say she has a headache,' Dorothy suggested, and they all agreed.

They found seats close to where Nanny Ruby was sitting and were soon joined by Myfi, the daughter of Mike Jackson, their local police sergeant. All the girls liked Mike because he could be such fun. Gwyneth, his wife, was a little younger than him and was always pleasant to talk with. It was a shame Myfi was younger than Claudette and Dorothy, as they got on well with the girl. She wasn't allowed to go out in the evenings, otherwise they would have welcomed her as a fifth member of their little group. As it was, they played cards with her and joined in with the bingo game, all the time looking out for Bessie.

It was quite late in the evening when Clemmie noticed Bessie enter the ballroom and look around for her friends. They were on the dance floor doing the Hokey-Cokey at the time, and she slipped from the large circle and hurried to Bessie. 'Crikey, you've been a long time, what have you been up to?'

Bessie giggled and gave her a wink. 'That would be telling, wouldn't it?' she said, wobbling so much she needed to grab the back of a chair to steady herself.

'You've been drinking with him, haven't you?'

'So what if I have? You're not my mother.'

'I may not be, but you've already got yourself in a right old mess with Tom and you're going to make it worse. Don't you realize there are plenty of people here who will see the state you're in and report back to Maisie – or worse still, your dad?'

Bessie stood still for a moment, as if thinking about what Clemmie had said. 'It's not as if I can get pregnant, if I'm already pregnant, is it?' she sniggered.

Clemmie felt so sad. She'd really thought she was starting to gain Bessie's trust and would be able to help her. At the same time, she felt a familiar surge of irritation at the younger girl's behaviour.

'You disgust me, Bessie Carlisle,' she said as she turned

away. 'I wanted to help you. But I'm not sure I can, if you can't help yourself by keeping away from him.' She started to walk away.

'Please, Clemmie, I didn't mean what I said. It's just – I'm so frightened of what's going to happen to me . . .'

Clemmie's heart went out to Bessie. She was only a kid really. She turned back.

'You know Tom is no good for you, don't you? Let me fetch our bags and cardigans from the table and we can walk back to the chalet. I'll let the other two know.' She went over to the two younger girls and whispered to them, nodding back to where Bessie was waiting. Claudette and Dorothy decided to leave with her.

'Come on, let's get going,' Clemmie said, linking arms with Bessie and leading her outside into the darkness. 'I've got a torch,' she said, reaching into her pocket. 'It's a bit creepy out here after being in that brightly lit ballroom.'

'They never have many lights on around the chalets,' Claudette said. 'It's so the younger children don't wake up, I heard someone talking about it.'

They walked on slowly, enjoying the warm air and the silence after the noise of hundreds of people having a jolly time. As they approached their row of chalets, several shadowy figures stepped out. Clemmie caught her breath in surprise before directing the torch towards them. She sighed with relief when she recognized the lads.

'What are you three doing here?' she asked, taking the key to the chalet from her pocket ready to open the door. 'I think Bessie's had enough of you for this evening, don't you, Tom?'

'We thought we'd come and see what your chalet looks

like. I hope there are plenty of beds?' he grinned, taking the key from her.

Clemmie flinched at the smell of alcohol on his breath. 'It will be no different to yours, so be on your way, you're not coming in.' Snatching back the key, she put it in the lock. Before she knew what was happening he had pushed past her, shoving the door open. The three lads went in ahead of them. Claudette and Dorothy began to follow, but Clemmie was quick to stop them. 'Stay out here and keep away from them – we don't want any trouble.'

The boys started laughing and bouncing on the beds. Tom found a nightdress beneath Claudette's pillow and waved it above his head.

Clemmie knew the last thing they should do was to enter the chalet and be alone with the lads. It could put them all in danger. She pushed Bessie towards a deckchair that had been left on the grass in front of the chalet. 'Go and sit down. Keep out of the way,' she instructed her. Bessie, too fuddle-minded to argue, did as she was told.

Hands on hips, Clemmie stood on the step of the chalet and raised her voice so it could be heard over the merry-making. 'Come out of there immediately. Otherwise I'm going to call for help.'

'If you do, I'll tell everyone me and Bessie are a couple. They'll know exactly what I mean,' Tom laughed.

'I don't think you really want to say anything about Bessie, do you? Not in her state, anyway?'

Tom stood still, and put his hand out to his mates to do the same. 'What do you mean about Bessie? What's she been saying to you?'

'You seem to see enough of her. Haven't you noticed

how her shape is changing?' Clemmie said, nodding over her shoulder to where Bessie had closed her eyes, oblivious to what was going on.

Tom shrugged his shoulders. 'She has put on a bit. I told her as much myself, but she will keep scoffing chips. I told her if she doesn't start looking after herself, I'll be dropping her.'

'Oh, it's more than that,' Clemmie said, feeling she had the upper hand. 'You want to start behaving yourself, Tom, and acting like a responsible father and potential husband. Because when Bessie's family find out the condition she's in, and the part you've played in this, you'll be marched down the aisle before you can wipe your nose.'

In the torchlight, she could see Tom had turned rather pale.

'You're lying. You're just jealous because I'm not going out with you. Not that I would.'

Clemmie laughed scornfully. 'What makes you think you're some great catch? I'd not touch you with a bargepole. Have you looked at yourself in the mirror lately?' she snapped back. 'There's one on that wall, so take a look now.'

'Is there a problem here, Clementine?' a familiar voice asked.

Clemmie turned to see Mike Jackson as well as his wife and daughter standing there. 'We were coming back early because our Robert is asleep in the chalet. Can we help?'

'I think they're just leaving, Sergeant Jackson,' Clemmie said, making sure the lads still inside the chalet caught Mike's full title. They were on their feet and left quickly with sullen looks on their faces.

'We must have left the key in the door,' Dorothy said,

retrieving the key from the lock. 'Silly us. I promise it won't happen again.'

'Who are those lads?' Mike asked.

'I have no idea,' Dorothy answered. She yawned. 'I'm ready for my bed, I don't know about you. And Bessie is as well, look – she's fallen asleep,' she said, forcing a laugh in an attempt to cover for her friend.

Mike Jackson frowned. The taller of those three lads had looked familiar; he couldn't help feeling he'd seen him before. He wished the girls goodnight and they went on their way.

Clemmie took a deep breath. 'Hopefully we got away with that,' she muttered to Bessie, who was still in the deckchair, dead to the world.

21

'This holiday has sped by so fast,' Dorothy said as the girls stretched out on the grass in front of their chalet, sunning themselves. 'It takes twice as long for a week to pass by when we're at school or work.'

The girls chuckled at her comments, although they all agreed she was right. 'At least we have the dance tonight as well as the awards ceremony. You'll be in line for a few medals, Claudette. I've never known anyone enter so many competitions.'

'I've enjoyed entering them. I have a few matches to play later this afternoon to determine if I'm a winner or a runner-up, but there is a prize for each, so I don't really mind. It was just fun playing and moving up the leader board.'

'I'll come and watch you,' Dorothy said. 'Which ones are you playing?'

'I'm in the final for putting, ladies' darts, and also crib. It's a good job Granddad Bob gave me a few lessons on crib and darts before we came on holiday – it's really helped.'

'He's in the final for the men's darts and George is in the final for men's crib; he beat Granddad Bob in the semi-final. It's going to be a big family event, with you all standing

282

up on the stage with your medals and prizes,' Dorothy said. 'Although it's a shame we never won the talent competition. I do hope Auntie Sarah takes photographs.'

'Auntie Sarah will be on the stage herself, to help Nanny Ruby collect her prize as Glamorous Grandmother. She's still astonished to have been announced the winner. I think it had a lot to do with the dress Maisie made for her – she looked as pretty as a picture,' Clemmie smiled.

'She brushed it all off as a load of nonsense, but I think she was secretly very pleased,' Dorothy said. 'I know I cheated like anything when the compere put his hand over her head for people to vote and clap. I'd asked people on the tables close to us to clap for her. Claudette, shall I ask Auntie Sarah if I can borrow the camera to take the photographs? I have used it before.'

'That's a good idea,' Claudette said, 'although it's such a shame you were runner-up in the children's athletic events. At least you're free to help out with photographs. The camp photographer will be taking them, but with the amount of us up on stage it'll cost a bomb to buy copies. This way it will be much cheaper.'

Dorothy got to her feet, brushing grass from her skirt. 'I'll go and ask Sarah now before I forget. I'd like to ask her for a few tips. She's very good at taking photographs, you know – I think that's why George lets her use the camera so often.'

The day drifted by, with the girls walking to the beach to have a final paddle and throw stale bread to the seagulls. 'I hope we can come back again, it's such a lovely place,' Clemmie said. 'Why don't the four of us save up and book to come next year on our own? I'm sure our parents would allow us, because we've been good this year – well, most of us, anyway,' she amended, glancing towards where Bessie was dipping her toes into the sea. 'We'd best get ready for dinner. Being the last night, I want to make sure my hair looks nice. I'll help with yours if you like?' she said to the younger girls as they all headed back to their chalet.

As they turned the corner into their row of chalets, they spotted Tom and his mates up ahead. They'd been remarkably quiet this week after almost getting caught by Mike Jackson.

'Hi, Bessie, come over here,' Tom called out.

'I'll come with you,' Clemmie said, and held onto Bessie's arm as they walked over to where the boy stood.

'I didn't invite you over here,' Tom glared at Clemmie. 'I just want to speak to her.'

'Where Bessie goes, I go too. She's not very well these days, and if you don't realize why, then you're a bigger fool than I put you down to be.' Clemmie had no time for the lad, and she wasn't intimidated by him either. She knew if he got up to anything, or upset Bessie, she'd go to Mike Jackson for help. He might not be a blood relative, but he was as good as, and he was a decent man, so he'd help them.

'I've got a little job on tonight,' he said, ignoring Clemmie and speaking directly to Bessie. 'I need you to help. Me and the lads are going to be busy, and we need a lookout. Be outside the reception office at midnight, and don't bring her.' He nodded towards Clemmie. 'If you don't come, I'll be having a word with my sister and telling her what we've been up to.' With a wink, he added, 'She's got a loud enough mouth that everyone in that factory of your mother's will soon know all the details.'

284

Bessie was in tears as they went back to the chalet. 'What can I do?' she cried.

Clemmie stood with her arms folded in front of her. 'You're going to do as you've been told to do. You are going to be his lookout.'

'How can you say that?' Bessie asked. 'You know he's bound to be robbing the reception office, and I don't want to be involved. I don't want to end up going to prison just for helping him.'

'No, you won't. I have a plan. I'm going to need your help too,' Clemmie said to the two younger girls. 'And hang onto that camera, whatever you do. It could come in handy.'

'Are you going to tell Molly?' Dorothy asked.

'Not at the moment, because there's nothing we can do before it happens. If they change their mind, then we're going to look idiots, aren't we? Besides, Molly is expecting a baby and she shouldn't be upset too much.'

Claudette came up with a suggestion. 'Then tell Mike Jackson.'

Clemmie chewed her lip as she thought carefully. 'I don't feel we should at the moment, because it's going to mean explaining how Bessie knows Tom, and the hold he has over her. Also, he could still spill the beans about what you've both been up to,' she said, raising her eyebrows at Bessie.

'There's no need to continue talking,' Bessie said. 'My problem is going to come out before too long. I too have a plan for my future, but I'll tell you at the right time. For now, though, I agree – let's not tell anyone yet. Please, Clemmie, tell us what we should do?' The girls sat on their beds and listened to what Clemmie had to say.

*

285

'Come on, girls, finish your meal up,' Ruby said, stopping by their table. 'I'm relying on you to save us good seats tonight. It's the big bingo game before the dancing starts and there are lots of big money prizes to win. I'm determined to win something,' she chuckled. 'Everyone buys tickets for the last game of the week. I'm told it's the highlight of the holiday.'

'I see you're wearing your glamorous gran outfit,' Claudette smiled back. She loved her Nanny Ruby, and she looked so smart in her grey crepe frock trimmed with white lace collar and cuffs.

'Are you biased or are you after some of my winnings?' Ruby laughed as she stroked the girl's head. 'You know that if I win one of the big money prizes, I'll treat you all. I think we should purchase extra bingo books this evening, as so many people seem to be saying they will. There must have been a fortune spent in reception on those books of tickets just to be in with a chance to win. Then there's the gala raffle . . . I must say, this holiday camp is far better than where Molly and Johnny used to work. It's beautifully clean, the food is plentiful and it's been sunny all week.'

'I don't think Molly has anything to do with the sunshine, but even if it rained, there would have been enough indoor activities to keep us all busy,' Sarah said as she joined them. 'However, I packed my mac and if it had rained, I'd still have gone out for walks and visited the beach. It's a bit different to rain back home in Erith, if you know what I mean?'

Ruby agreed. 'It certainly is. Now come along, girls, let's get cracking.'

Ruby was more than happy with where they sat on the

edge of the ballroom. They weren't far from the stage, so she could easily hear as the numbers were called for each game. At one point she became so excited she shouted 'House!' only to find she had made a mistake, as she still had one number outstanding. She blushed bright red with embarrassment, but the entertainment staff were cheerful about the matter and everyone returned to the game. When Ruby's number was pulled out, everyone in the ballroom cheered with delight.

'That'll be spent on a treat for all the kiddies once I get home,' Ruby said as she slipped a five-pound note into her handbag. 'This is the icing on the cake for me. I think I'll have a port and lemon later, just to celebrate,' she told Bob.

Once the bingo game was finished, the stage was cleared and the band took their places. One by one, the week's competition winners were invited onto the stage to be presented with their prizes and medals. Everybody cheered when Sarah assisted Ruby to collect a bunch of flowers and a sash, along with a voucher for a holiday the following year. 'There is something to be said about being a glamorous granny,' Ruby whispered to Sarah as they posed for the photographs. 'I'd better start having my hair done more often,' she chuckled.

Claudette won the most medals. She'd come first in the putting and darts as well as some of the team games, and she was a runner-up in the crib tournament. When George and Bob also appeared on the stage there were some good-humoured comments from the compere as it became clear how many of the same extended family had won prizes. He insisted on a group photograph, along with Molly and the entertainment staff in their smart orange jackets.

Dorothy pushed towards the front of the crowd to make sure she'd taken enough photographs. This was certainly a holiday to remember.

After all the excitement, they relaxed with their drinks until the band started up and people began to drift onto the dance floor to enjoy the last evening of their holiday. The four girls danced with each other, which seemed to be a common thing: there were plenty of other women also dancing together. All of the girls had taken ballroom dancing lessons at the Erith Dance Studio when they were younger, and knew enough of the basic steps to be able to do a waltz and a foxtrot.

'It does my heart good to see you girls enjoying yourselves,' Ruby said as Claudette and Dorothy came back to collect Myfi and young Georgina to dance with them.

'It's getting rather late for the youngsters to be on the dance floor,' Gwyneth remarked as she shuffled along the seats to sit next to Ruby and Sarah.

'Oh, it's once in a blue moon,' Ruby said. 'Let them enjoy the end of their holiday; if they're tired tomorrow, they can sleep on the train going home.'

They sat back, watching the girls as they danced around the ballroom.

'They all look so pretty in their new frocks,' Ruby said. 'But I do think Bessie is putting a little weight on, which is unlike her as she's always been a slim girl.'

Gwyneth glanced at Sarah, who raised her eyebrows. 'I've been thinking the same. She's been seeing a lot of one particular lad, hasn't she? I've spotted her a few times around the town. You don't think . . . ?'

Sarah took a deep breath. 'I pray to God she's not, but

you know, I'm inclined to believe that perhaps she is expecting. We're going to have to have a word with Maisie when we get back.'

Ruby shook her head. 'Whatever you do, don't speak to Maisie,' she said. 'This is one time when we need to let the girl speak for herself. I intend just to be here when she wants to talk. Being an old woman, I like to think I can ask a few more questions than you two. So, let sleeping dogs lie for now.' She turned in her seat and glanced towards the bar. 'Now, who wants another drink before closing time? Let me give a shout to Bob.'

Gwyneth and Sarah exchanged a look. Both of them understood that the discussion was at an end once Ruby had spoken.

'Make sure you lock the door,' Clemmie whispered to the younger girls as they crept quietly from the chalet. 'And if you use your torch, keep it pointed to the ground; we don't want anybody recognizing us.'

'I'm not sure about this,' Dorothy said. 'If we get caught, then they might think it's us that's going to do the robbing.'

'No, they won't, and to be on the safe side, I've written a letter,' Clemmie said as she put her hand on her sister's shoulder. 'Would you rather not come with us? You can go back to the chalet if you like?'

'No, I'll be all right,' Dorothy insisted.

'What have you written in this letter? You've not dropped anyone in it, have you?' Bessie asked, giving Clemmie a sharp look.

'No, it's nothing like that at all,' Clemmie assured her. 'I just felt that I wanted to write a few things down, and you're not to worry. If nothing happens, I'll tear it up as soon as we get back so that nobody reads it.'

'I've got the camera ready,' Dorothy said, 'but I'm worried that if the pictures are taken in darkness, there will be nothing to see when the film's developed.'

'Don't worry about that – just have the camera ready. Promise me you won't panic and run away?'

'No, no, I won't do that,' Dorothy said bravely. 'Where will we hide?'

'There's a foyer in front of the reception area; Bessie, you and I are going to stand there and wait for the lads. You two should stand behind that wall over there – no one will see you as they approach. Once the lads have gone into the building, go to the side of that large window. When I shout, you take your photograph – and then you run like crazy back to our chalet and lock yourself in. Here's the key,' she said, handing it to Dorothy. 'Make sure it's safely in your pocket . . . Blast, I've forgotten something. Give me the key back for a moment,' she said, and rushed away. 'I'll be back in a couple of ticks,' she called over her shoulder, keeping her voice low.

The three girls stood and waited until a breathless Clemmie returned and gave the key back to her sister. 'Right, I'm ready. Has anything happened yet?'

'No, not a thing,' Bessie said. 'Hang on a minute . . . yes, I can hear voices. You two, go and hide now,' she instructed the younger girls, while taking Clemmie's arm and dragging her towards the foyer.

When the lads appeared, there was some grumbling from Tom's friends as they saw that Clemmie was with Bessie.

Tom, however, was quite laid-back. 'That's all right, no

one worry about it. That means we've got two pairs of eyes to look out for us,' he said. 'You both stay here, and let us know if you hear anybody approaching.'

'And what are you going to do?' Clemmie asked. She felt brave, and with what she had in the large pocket of her coat, she wasn't worried about things getting rough.

'Never mind about that. I'll see you all right afterwards, but only if you do as you're told. Come on, lads,' he said, before bending at the door and fiddling with the lock until the door swung open.

'I think he's picked the lock,' Clemmie whispered to Bessie.

'Keep quiet, you're making more noise than they are.'

Bessie peered up and down the gravel pathway that led to the office block from the main holiday camp complex. Surely if anyone approached, they'd hear their footsteps crunching on the gravel. It would give them time to hide.

There was a creak and then the sound of the door opening as the lads got into the reception office. Clemmie took a couple of steps further into the darkened corridor, followed by Bessie, to watch what the lads were doing. Her heart was thumping so loudly she thought they'd hear her. Taking deep breaths, she tried to listen to what was happening.

'Well done,' Tom said, as there was the sound of splintering wood and a small crash. Clemmie guessed this meant they'd broken into a cupboard, or perhaps a drawer.

Any time now, she thought to herself, wiping her damp hands down the sides of her coat.

'There's hundreds of quid here,' one of the lads cheered loudly.

'Shush, keep the noise down,' Tom told them. 'Put the

bags of coins and the notes into this holdall. We're going to have to scarper pretty quick.'

Five . . . four . . . three . . . two . . . Clemmie counted under her breath. When she reached *one*, she put her hand round the side of the door to the office and flicked on the light switch. 'Now,' she screamed out loud, praying that Dorothy heard her call out and managed to take at least one photograph before the light was switched off again, temporarily blinding them all.

'What are you doing? They're going to be livid! Come on, we've got to get out of here,' Bessie hissed.

'What the . . .' Tom said as he turned and lunged for Bessie, grabbing hold of her by the hair. She struggled to get away from him, but he held on tight. 'Quick – get going,' he called to the other lads. 'I'll take the holdall.'

'Let go of me,' Bessie cried as his grip became tighter. His two mates pushed past them and ran out into the dark night.

'Let go of her now,' Clemmie commanded as she reached into her pocket.

'Ouch, ouch,' Bessie screamed as Tom laughed before giving out a loud groan. There was a clatter of coins falling and rolling across the floor, followed by the sound of his body crumpling to the ground.

Clemmie switched the light back on to see Tom out cold on the floor of the passageway. 'Did he hurt you, Bessie?' she asked.

'No, I'm all right,' Bessie panted, 'but what did you do?'

'I put some of those coins we won from the penny machine into my sock. I saw the trick once in a Johnny Johnson film. He knocked out two Nazi spies in one fell swoop.'

She helped Bessie up and they stood there together, wondering what to do next. A few moments later, Molly appeared, with Mike Jackson not far behind.

'Johnny would be proud of you,' Molly said, as she stood in the doorway wrapped in a dressing gown and still wearing her slippers. 'Thank you for putting a note through my door.'

'That goes for me, too,' Mike Jackson said, gesturing to a security guard, who was close behind, to cuff Tom's wrists before the lad could come round. 'I may not be on duty, but I'm still a policeman.'

'But what about the two other lads who helped him?' Bessie asked.

'We clobbered them,' Dorothy chuckled, as she and Claudette joined them. 'It was quite simple really: when they ran out of the doorway, we stuck our feet out and they tripped over them. Then we sat on them and called for help. Two of the Orange Coats are taking care of them.'

Very soon, other helpers arrived to hold onto the men. They were followed by the local constabulary, who, after taking a few notes, put the three lads into a car and drove away, promising to return the next morning to take statements. Molly led the girls and Mike over to the nearby tea room and made a pot of tea, along with milkshakes for the girls.

'We've got some evidence,' Claudette said as Dorothy handed over the camera. 'It's Uncle George's camera, so please don't lose it, will you?' she said to Mike.

'The police will probably want the film, not the camera,' he assured her. 'However, what I'd like to know is, how did you four girls get involved with all of this?'

The girls looked at each other. Bessie could be dropped

right in it if they let the cat out of the bag about her being Tom's girlfriend.

It was Claudette who spoke first. 'I suppose it was my fault really. I overheard them talking round by the pool as I went back to the chalet for my cardigan. We decided it would be a good idea if we could stop them.'

'You should have come to me,' Molly said. 'I would have arranged for our security staff to be here in wait.'

'We did think of that, but if we were wrong, we could have been reporting innocent people, so it was best that we did it ourselves.'

'What made you slip the note under my door?' Mike Jackson asked Clemmie.

Clemmie had expected this question and tried to look nervous. 'I became frightened and was worried about someone getting hurt, so I scribbled notes to you and Molly very quickly and put them under your doors. I didn't want to knock and speak to you in case I woke the children,' she added, giving herself a pat on the back for coming up with that thought so quickly.

Mike considered all of this while they finished their milkshakes, but if he had any doubts about it, he didn't express them. 'Well done, girls. I think perhaps you ought to get back to your beds now. However, promise me that if you come across a crime in future, you will inform the police rather than take things into your own hands.'

The girls were silent apart from Clemmie, who promised that they would be more careful in future.

Molly was grateful for what they'd done and gave them all a big hug before walking them back to their chalet, saying that she hoped all the excitement wouldn't mean they slept in in the morning and missed their last camp breakfast.

They wished her goodnight and went into the chalet, locking the door behind them. Pulling off their coats, they collapsed onto the beds and started to giggle.

'We pulled it off, just like in the movies,' Claudette laughed. 'I think we ought to celebrate.' She rummaged in the drawer by her bed. 'Good, there's four of them.'

'I'm not sure the good guys in the movies toasted each other with sherbet dip-dabs, did they?' Clemmie chuckled.

Bessie looked miserable. 'We might have stopped them,' she said, 'but what if they let Tom go? He's going to be so angry, and it will be me he comes looking for. I've got a feeling I haven't got a boyfriend any more.' She looked down at her tummy and placed a hand there. 'And there's me carrying his baby.'

22

It was a subdued group of friends who climbed onto the train to head home the next morning. Freda hugged Molly tightly.

'A week doesn't seem enough to catch up,' she said. 'I'll write and give you my new address. I should be there in a week or so, and I promise that we will keep in touch more; I want to come down here to meet the little one when it is born.'

'October will soon be here, and my baby wants to meet its godmother. I insist you are here for the christening.'

'I promise I will be; and thank you so much for inviting me. It means so much, especially at the moment,' Freda said, trying hard not to cry.

Molly secretly prayed that Freda would soon have her own child and the little ones could grow up as friends. 'Safe journey, everyone,' she called as the train pulled out of the station.

The four girls found themselves sitting in a carriage with Mike Jackson, Gwyneth and their two children. Baby Robert was too young to understand anything that was being talked about, but everyone was aware that Myfi was at an impressionable age, so they were careful about how they discussed the goings-on of the night before.

Bessie, her face pale, stared out of the window. She was afraid that if she looked directly at Mike Jackson, he would be able to read her mind and know there was a little more between her and Tom than the girls were letting on.

'What do you think will happen to them?' Clemmie asked as she bounced young Robert on her knee.

'I'll be on duty tomorrow so will make enquiries, but I'm pretty certain that by then they will have been charged with theft. Are you absolutely sure you don't know these lads?'

'No, I don't, sorry,' Dorothy said while the others remained silent.

Mike had a feeling they were keeping something from him. 'This won't be the first time these lads have been up to something. I'll do some digging about in our records. If they aren't charged, the three of them should be receiving their call-up papers before too long, going by their ages.' Perhaps a spell in the army will sort them, he thought as he picked up his newspaper.

Before long Robert dozed off and was handed back to his mum's arms, where he slept soundly. The day was hot and the sun beat through the carriage window, making it feel quite stuffy. 'Why don't we wander along the corridor?' Clemmie suggested to the other girls.

They stepped out of their compartment and wandered along a little way to where the outside door of the train had its window open, letting in a welcome breeze.

'It's such a mess,' Bessie whispered. 'I've decided I'm not going to tell Mum and Dad.'

'Don't you think they're going to guess before too long?' Clemmie said in a low voice. 'Why not confess to everything and get it over with? Your parents are decent people – they may tell you off, but they will understand.'

'But what if they send me away to one of those mother and baby homes?'

'Do you mean where they take the baby away afterwards and it goes up for adoption?' Claudette asked, looking horrified. 'You might never see the baby, and I might not see it, and I would never be an auntie, and mum would never be a grandmother . . .'

'I feel as though I need more advice,' Bessie said. 'It's not as if I've ever known a girl who's had a baby by herself – well, apart from people like Gwyneth, and I can't really speak to her because she's a grown-up and a friend of Mum's. I need someone my own age, someone who knows more about it all and can tell me how she coped.'

Dorothy nudged Clemmie, who was staring out of the open window with her hair blowing in the breeze. 'What about the new girl – you know, the one you met at your college who started work at Woolies the other day? She's not much older than you, and she's got two children.'

'That's right,' Clemmie said. 'Why didn't I think of Jane? She will be at work on Saturday – why don't we make sure we've all got the same lunch hour? I can arrange it, because I have to set the charts up for the day. We can go out, away from the store, and then you can ask her lots of questions.'

'Better still, why don't we see if she'll meet us up the rec on Bank Holiday Monday?' Claudette suggested. 'Most of the town will be there, so we can slip away to talk with her. I know it's a few weeks off but I can't think of any other time where you can meet and chat without people wondering what we're up to?'

Bessie gave them a smile. 'You'd do that for me, and after I've been such a cow to you all? I don't know what to say.'

Claudette put her arm around her sister. 'I'm just happy my sister's come back to us and isn't the awful person we've known these last months. Promise me you'll have nothing to do with that Tom again.'

'I promise. I've learnt my lesson, even though it's too late,' Bessie said, laying a hand on her tummy. 'I also need to hide this from Mum . . . for now. Can I rely on you to help, Claudette? I need to find some looser clothing, and perhaps we can engineer it so Mum never quite gets to see much of me. It'll give me time to think more about the future.'

'Then that's a plan; but what about when you're working down at the factory? Tom's sister is working there, and she may well know that you were his girlfriend.'

'Maybe I should offer to help out at the Bexleyheath shop? Then I won't have to cross paths with her.'

Claudette shook her head. 'I have a feeling you're too late. Mum's been interviewing for more staff this past week, and it'll all be sorted out. Why don't you come and work with me in the stockroom? At least it'll keep us away from the sewing room. We'll just have to duck and dive for now.'

'Here you are, Claudette,' Freda said, dropping a bunch of keys into the young girl's hands. 'Are you sure you'll be able to come in and feed Winston Churchill and look after him while I'm away? I'm hoping, once we've settled into a new house, he can be collected and come to live with us.'

'That's a good idea, Auntie Freda, but until then be assured that I'll be his mummy. I plan to spoil him rotten and will play with him and keep him company as much as possible. Now, have you packed everything? Are you sure there's nothing else you need to take?' She looked around Freda's front room. 'Have you got enough clothes?'

'Yes, I have; my suitcase can't hold another thing. If there's anything in my wardrobe you want to borrow, feel free to do so. I trust you implicitly to look after everything here – but remember, if there are any problems at all, you can rely on Mike Jackson. He's only a few doors down the road. Or you could pop over the road to Ruby, or even speak to your mum; that's if she's not too busy. I'd hate to burden her at the moment.'

'I can also speak to Auntie Sarah or Uncle Alan. We're all here to look after your house until you come home again,' Claudette said. 'And also help out at the Girl Guides and Brownies while our new Brown Owl is learning the ropes.'

'What would I do without you?' Freda said, giving her a hug and kissing her forehead. 'Once Tony and I are settled in, I insist that you and Bessie come up and visit. I can give you the grand tour of Liverpool; not that I know anything about it at the moment,' she grinned as a car tooted its horn out the front. 'That will be my taxi cab to get me to the station,' she said, reaching for her smart hat and matching bag. Taking a deep breath, she went to the front door and headed out to the vehicle, surprised to see friends and neighbours standing in front of their houses waving her off. The last they saw of Freda was her smiling face as she turned the corner of Alexandra Road to begin her new journey.

'It's just you and me, Winston, so please be a good pussycat,' Claudette said as she picked him up and hugged him. 'I'm your new mummy for now.'

*

'I'm sorry that we've had to come to work before I could find time to speak to you,' Maisie said to her two daughters as they sat in her office. 'Aren't you warm in that large overall, Bessie?'

'No, I'm fine. And it's good to cover my clothes, because I'm cutting up fabric at the moment. I don't want pieces of cotton stuck all over my summer frock.'

'Well, that's sensible, but you don't need to wear it all the time,' Maisie smiled. She was so pleased that Bessie seemed to have returned from her holiday a changed girl – or rather, the girl she used to be. Perhaps all she'd really needed was a break and a proper rest. After all, life for the Carlisle family had been pretty busy for quite a while.

'Have you met all of our seamstresses now? I've explained to them that both of you will be working here, and made it clear that I don't want you treated like trainees. I know you're not sure what you want to do yet, Bessie, but I'm behind you whatever you decide. Claudette, I want you to learn as much as you can about pattern cutting; but even so, you must find time to sit in here and work on your own designs. Don't forget, Bessie, if you have any ideas, please let me know.'

'I will,' Bessie said. 'One thing I'm quite interested in is the embroidery for the wedding dresses. Eleanor showed me how she stitches fine beads onto gowns. I'd like to give that a go, if I can?'

'Then you shall. I'll make sure we have some pieces of fabric that you can practise on, and when Eleanor isn't busy, perhaps she can teach you a little more. What do you say to that?'

'I'd like that very much,' Bessie replied, as her mother smiled back at her. She did wonder how Maisie would treat her once she knew Bessie was carrying a child.

After their meeting Bessie hurried back to the stockroom, where Maisie had set up extra workspace for the girls.

'That was harder than I thought,' she said to Claudette. 'I felt as though at any moment Mum would pull open my overall and point at my tummy and demand to know what was happening.'

'You're safe now,' Claudette said, although she didn't like to point out that Bessie had also filled out around the face. Questions were bound to be asked – especially if they bumped into Nanny Ruby, who didn't miss a thing. 'Do you fancy a drink? We can sit in the staff kitchen. Or if we're careful, we can bring it in here, as long as we're not working near the fabric.'

'I'll go and get it and be back before the break starts,' Bessie said.

In the kitchen, Bessie was shocked to find Doris standing with a cigarette in her hand.

'I was hoping to see you,' she said, glaring at Bessie. 'Have you heard about my brother Tom?'

'I have no idea what you're talking about,' Bessie said, busying herself filling up the kettle and putting it on a small gas ring.

'Well, you've been seeing him, haven't you? He told me you've been helping him with a few bits and pieces, shall we say?' She gave Bessie a sly wink. 'And with him having his collar felt at the same holiday camp where you both were until the other day, it stands to reason you're involved with whatever was going on.'

302

Bessie spun on her heel and glared at the woman. She needed to put her in her place now, before things got worse.

'Now look here: I did go out with your brother a couple of times, but that was all. If he decided to go to the holiday camp while I was there, that was his choice. I never saw anything of him while I was there. Got it?'

'Yeah, but . . . it's funny how you were there when he got his collar felt by your copper friend.'

'It was pure coincidence,' Bessie replied as the kettle started to boil. It gave her a reason to turn away from Doris to carry on making the tea. She felt the woman poke her in the back.

'Don't turn your back on me. I know you're behind my brother getting nicked, and I don't like it. If he goes down, and it sounds like he will, I'm going to tell your precious mother and all your family exactly what you've been up to, because Tom told me everything.'

Bessie felt her bravery slip away from her. She was going to be in so much trouble. If this woman knew everything that had been going on, Bessie could be arrested. She was just about to tell the woman to mind her own business when a stern voice came from the doorway.

'What's going on here?' Maisie asked.

'We were just chatting,' Doris said. 'Nothing for you to worry about, Mrs Carlisle.'

'Oh, but I am worried, because I've been standing outside listening to you threatening my daughter. So you'd better sit down there and tell me exactly what's been going on.'

Bessie felt her legs turn to jelly as she gripped the nearby sink to keep her balance.

'You too, Bessie,' Maisie said, giving her a gentle smile.

She turned to Doris, her expression severe again. 'First of all, how do you know my daughter? You never mentioned it when you came for your interview,' she said.

It was Bessie who answered. 'I went out with her brother Tom a couple of times, that's all.'

'But I heard you threaten my daughter. What exactly is it you're going to tell people about her? Because I don't like anyone trying to blacken any member of my family's character.' Before Doris could reply, she went on, 'And in fact, I was going to have a word with you anyway. I'm not happy with your work. It's not satisfactory and your time-keeping is abysmal. To be honest, I don't think you fit in around here – so collect your things and go. I'll have your money and your cards made up and sent on to you. Consider yourself sacked.'

The woman ran from the room, swearing and calling them the kind of names that had even Maisie blushing. When she'd gone, Maisie sat down in the vacated chair.

'I'm sorry you had to put up with that, Bessie. I shouldn't have employed the woman to begin with. Now, what's this about you seeing her brother?'

Bessie took a deep breath. 'I went out with him a couple of times, Mum; I know I should have told you, but I was a bit frightened. In fact, I done worse than that because I asked Claudette to cover for me and that wasn't fair of me, was it? I split up with him because I knew he was a bad lot, but he followed me to the holiday camp.' She thought she ought to say something about that, because it was bound to come out very soon. 'I never even saw him while we were there; he was with his mates. Uncle Mike can tell you more, but – well, he was the one they caught robbing on the last night we were there. I promise you, I'm not seeing him again, and I was quite shocked to meet his sister here.'

Maisie nodded slowly. 'Well, it's all over now, love; but will you promise me one thing? You're an age to go with lads, but we'd quite like to meet them. Nothing formal – you don't have to be worried about it. Blimey, I was going out with lads long before I was your age, so I'm not one to talk. But just tell me about it, OK? Let's not have any secrets.'

'I promise, Mum,' Bessie said, feeling a wave of regret that she already had such a big secret to keep from her parents. The idea of telling them about it filled her with dread.

She and Claudette were helping Maisie prepare dinner that evening when there was a knock at the door. 'Go and see who that is, please,' Maisie said to Claudette, who hurried to open the door. Bessie turned away from her mother, glad she was wearing a baggy jumper to hide her bump. She had to be careful.

'Hello, Uncle Mike. Come in,' Claudette said, surprised to find him on their doorstep in his sergeant's uniform.

'I hope I'm not interrupting your dinner?'

'No, we're still getting it ready. We've not long got home, please come through,' she said, leading him to the living room, where he removed his helmet.

Maisie glanced through from the kitchen in surprise. 'Hello Mike, you've not come to arrest me, have you?' She chuckled. 'Everything is above board down at my factory. There's not one bolt of dodgy fabric picked up from the docks.'

Mike didn't laugh, although he was usually up for a joke. 'I'm afraid I'm here on official business. Maisie, do you mind if we sit down and have a chat with your two girls?'

Maisie frowned, but pointed to a seat at the table. 'Sit yourself down there. Come on, girls, put the veg down and let's see what Mike's got to say. I take it it's got something to do with that robbery at the holiday camp?'

Bessie's hands were shaking as she pulled a chair out and sat herself down, wondering what Tom had told the police. The more she thought about him, the more she realized what an idiot she'd been; but even so, part of her knew she had been blindly in love with him. Hopefully absence would be a great healer, and she'd make sure she didn't bump into him again.

'I wanted to let you girls know that Tom Andrews and his two friends have been charged with breaking into the holiday camp office and attempting to steal money. I just want to make a few notes that can go on the file about this.'

'Ask away,' Claudette said as she reached under the table to hold Bessie's hand and give it a squeeze. 'We've got nothing to hide.'

'I take it both of you knew this Tom Andrews, and that's why he followed you to the holiday camp?'

Bessie took a deep breath. 'Claudette didn't know him, it was me. I've been out with him a couple of times, and I did mention that I would be going to the holiday camp for the week with my family. He never told me he was going,' she added. After all, he hadn't told her he'd booked – he'd just made a sarcastic comment about it. 'I was as surprised as anyone when I saw him there.'

'Did you meet up with him alone while you were there?'

'I spent most of the time with Claudette and the two Billington girls.'

'There was so much going on, we hardly even saw the family,' Claudette chipped in, hoping it would help.

Mike Jackson scribbled in his notebook for a little while and then looked up at Bessie. 'So why, then, was he in your chalet that first night?'

Maisie looked between the girls. 'What's all this about?'

Bessie turned bright pink and couldn't speak.

'The three of them were drunk. They could have picked on anybody in that row of chalets. Mum, you don't need to worry – we were all together, and nothing happened,' Claudette assured her. 'It was as Clemmie was opening the chalet door that the three lads barged in. We made sure not to go in and follow them as we knew it wouldn't be safe. We were asking them to leave when Uncle Mike came along with Auntie Gwyneth, and he saw them off. It was something and nothing – it was dealt with, and to be honest, it had gone right out of my mind. I don't think I even spoke to them because Clemmie took control.'

'Thank goodness Clemmie had the sense to sort it out,' Bessie added.

'And did you see them after that?'

'No, not on my own,' Bessie said, 'but the girls did see them and overheard them saying what they were going to get up to that night. That's why we decided we ought to do something.'

Mike outlined what had happened for Maisie's benefit. 'Clemmie dropped a note through my chalet door to say she thought a robbery was in progress. She didn't want to knock on the door in case it woke up our Robert. The girls took it upon themselves to apprehend the thieves.'

307

Maisie clutched her hand to her cheek. 'Oh my goodness – if I'd known all this was going to go on, I'd never have allowed you to go on holiday on your own.'

'Mum, we didn't do anything daft. In fact, all that Dorothy and I did was stay out of the way and take a photograph of the thieves. We gave the roll of film to Uncle Mike. I wish I could have done more, but Clemmie again took control, and Bessie and I along with Dorothy did as we were told. At no time were we in danger. Uncle Mike and some of the security staff were there before the men could escape.'

'And you say you were going out with this lad, Bessie? I think, young lady, you want to choose your friends a little more carefully.'

'Bessie wasn't to know, Mum,' Claudette said, being rewarded with a thank you squeeze by Bessie.

'The roll of film has been developed,' Mike said, taking a packet of photographs from his pocket. 'I've taken the liberty of removing the four photographs you took – they are rather grainy, but they will be used in evidence to prove he was there and show what he was doing. I'll leave the rest here, although I believe Sarah took them?'

'Dorothy borrowed the camera, but we can return the photographs to Aunt Sarah to save you time. I'm just glad we were able to help,' Claudette said seriously.

'At least one of the girls had some sense,' Maisie said through pursed lips. 'I'm sorry that you've had to waste time coming to speak to them, Mike.'

'Not at all. In fact, the girls are all up for a reward. Mr and Mrs Johnson were very impressed with how they helped, and they'll be receiving a letter very soon. Now I must be on my way. It's the end of my shift and I thought I would pop in and see you on my way home. Gwyneth is making a steam pudding, so I don't want to be late,' he said, rubbing his stomach.

Maisie saw him to the door, thanking him for his time, before returning to where the girls were looking at the photographs.

'Why is it I get the feeling you were more involved with this Tom than I'm being led to believe?' she said, giving Bessie a hard stare before dashing into the kitchen with an exclamation as they heard a pan of potatoes boiling over on the cooker top.

'She's going to find out soon. God help me then,' Bessie whispered to Claudette.

23

August Bank Holiday 1950

Bessie stood in front of the long mirror fixed inside the wardrobe door. She turned from left to right, peering closely at herself. Whatever she did, there was no avoiding the fact that she was obviously pregnant.

She sank down onto her bed and put her hands over her face. 'What am I going to do?' she muttered to herself.

Even with Claudette letting out the seams of her clothes and Clemmie craftily swapping her Woolworths overall for a larger size, she could no longer hide the fact that there was a baby on the way. She was glad of her friends and her sister, who'd stood by her these past few months; at times it had felt like they were conducting a military campaign, shielding her and making excuses so as few people as possible had a chance to look at her widening girth.

She knew the time had come to put her plan into action, and went back to the wardrobe, pulling out a small bag of money that was tucked away behind her winter jumpers. She tipped it out onto her bed, lining up the few notes and many coins, and was chewing her lip thoughtfully when Claudette burst into the room.

'Mum says you're to hurry up as they're about to go. Dad wants to watch the athletics, and Mum promised to meet Auntie Sarah at the recreation ground. You know how much she likes to watch all the events while we have our picnic. Have you found something to wear?' she asked urgently.

Bessie had been sent to her room to find something summery to put on. Her parents had pointed out that the skirt and cardigan she was wearing didn't quite fit the bill for a family outing to Erith recreation ground on Bank Holiday Monday.

'I can't find a thing that fits me, unless I go in my work overall. Everything else is now bursting at the seams. I can't even think of an excuse why I should stay here. What am I going to do, Claudette?'

Claudette went to the wardrobe and started rummaging through all the hangers, holding up garment after garment only for Bessie to say she'd tried it on, or that it was too tight, or to just laugh in despair. Once she'd exhausted every item of her sister's clothing, she turned to look at her own dresses hanging at the other side of the rail before pouncing on a dress she'd made for herself before their holiday. She had agreed with her friends that the colour didn't suit her and hadn't bothered wearing it again.

'I've always been podgier than you,' she said, showing no embarrassment, 'and as I only wore it while on holiday and Mum didn't come with us, the chances are that it will fit you, and Mum won't realize it's mine and wonder why you are wearing it. Now wipe that glum look off your face and try it on,' she said, throwing the pale blue dress towards

311

Bessie. She had to admit the colour suited her sister better than it had her.

'It's still too tight, I can't do up the zip at the side,' Bessie said, holding up her left arm to show the dress gaping open. Claudette stepped forward and gave it a tug, but it didn't help.

'It's a shame as the style does cover up quite a bit, and we don't have time to make alterations. I know,' she said, after staring for a moment at Bessie stuffed into the frock. 'It's not that hot outside yet. Why don't you wear a thin white cardigan and carry my handbag that matches the colour of the frock? If you tuck it under your arm, no one will see the gap in the dress. It does mean if it gets any warmer, you'll have to just sit and sweat, but needs must,' she added, passing Bessie a cardigan and then her bag.

Bessie did as she was told and went back to the mirror. 'You're right. No one would guess, would they?'

'Also, if you brushed your hair back into a ponytail it would lift your face and not make you look so . . .'

'Fat?'

'It's only the baby. Once you've had it, you'll go back to being slimmer than me again.'

'That's the least of my worries. If Mum kills me, I'll not have to worry what size I am,' Bessie said with a bitter laugh. 'I wish I could make an excuse and stay here but I promised to meet Clemmie and her friend Jane up at the rec; Jane is going to tell me a little more about what to expect.'

'Then I'll come with you,' Claudette said. 'I can be your lookout in case there's anybody around who knows us. Are you ready to go?'

312

Bessie checked her lipstick and made sure her purse was in the handbag Claudette had loaned her. 'That's as good as I'll get,' she said, then reached out and touched her sister's arm. 'Thank you, Claudette.'

'Don't thank me just yet; we need to get out of the house before Mum or Dad sees you. When I go into the front room, you wait for me out the front. But keep in front of our wall so they can't see all of you from the window.'

'What are you going to do?'

'I'll make an excuse about going on our own, and then we're going to scarper,' Claudette said, giving a wink. 'Let me go downstairs first, and you follow.'

They got to the bottom, and Claudette stuck her head through the door. 'We're going on ahead to meet Clemmie and her friends,' she called out before hurrying out to join Bessie. 'We can go this way,' she said, pointing to the top of the road. 'If we walk over Britannia Bridge and down Thanet Road, we can get into the rec by the side gate. It'll save us going down our road and risking bumping into Nanny Ruby and the rest of the family.'

'Quick, turn left,' Claudette said, dragging her sister away from the main arena at the recreation ground towards a row of trees that bordered the footpath.

'I thought we were going to meet Clemmie,' Bessie protested as they stopped behind a tree.

'I just spotted nosy Vera from up the road. She's got eyes like a hawk. You stay here and rest in the shade while I go and collect Clemmie and Jane. Don't go anywhere or I might never find you again, as it's so crowded around the arena. It's unlikely the family will walk up this way since the footpath doesn't lead anywhere.'

Bessie sat down under a tree and fanned herself with a leaflet they'd been handed at the gate. It had just gone midday and the sun was right overhead. She was finding the heat unbearable. Leaning her head against the tree trunk, she closed her eyes, unaware of someone slowly, silently approaching.

'Fancy seeing you here,' said a voice immediately in front of her.

Bessie opened her eyes and blinked. She recognized the woman's voice but couldn't quite think who she was. The sun behind her threw her into silhouette, making her difficult to see properly.

'No need to look so confused. I'm Tom's sister, remember? Your mother sacked me.'

For a moment Bessie wondered if Tom was with her, and looked to either side – but no, the woman was with a man she didn't recognize. He was pushing a pram with a couple of youngsters sitting in it.

'If you're looking for Tom, he's not here. Not that he'd want to speak to you after all the trouble you got him into.'

'But I didn't . . .' Bessie started to say as she struggled to her feet. She felt too vulnerable sitting on the ground.

'So, the rumours are true – you are up the duff? Your mother must be so proud of you,' Doris laughed sarcastically. 'Don't worry, I've told people it can't be Tom's, as he didn't know you long enough.'

Bessie was shocked – how could anyone think that she slept around? Tom had been the only one. As she opened her mouth to say so, Doris reached out and pushed her sharply. Bessie reeled back against the tree, lost her balance and slid to the ground.

'Ouch!' she cried as she landed on a large root protruding from the grass. 'There was no reason to do that.'

'There was every reason,' the woman snarled. Suddenly she reminded Bessie of Tom when he was angry. 'Because of you, my brother is locked up. It seems some nosy copper started digging about and found him guilty of several crimes. And it's all your fault, because you were with him at the time. He told me so when I visited.'

'I . . . no, I mean . . . I didn't do anything.'

Doris stepped closer, waving her fist in Bessie's face. 'You'd better get out of Erith,' she spat, 'because when Tom comes out of prison, I reckon he'll be looking for you.' Then she walked off, laughing with the chap pushing the pram.

'Oh my God, Bessie, what's happened?' Clemmie came running up to her, with Dorothy and Claudette just behind. They helped her to her feet and brushed down her skirt. 'You're not hurt, are you?' Clemmie asked, reaching out to touch Bessie's tummy.

'No, I'm fine – she didn't hurt the baby. Although I may have a bruise on my backside,' Bessie said, cradling her bump in her hands. It was the first time she'd felt any love for the child she was carrying.

'I tried to catch you up,' Jane said as she arrived with a pram, 'but it was a bit bumpy on the grass, and I didn't want to eject the kids.' She smiled. 'How are you, Bessie?'

'I'm fine, thank you for asking, Jane,' Bessie said. She was aware that she hadn't been very pleasant to Jane when they'd first met at Woolworths. Over the weeks since then, they'd chatted during their breaks, and Bessie had found her to be a most affable woman. She sympathized with the fact that Jane was now alone with two children after her husband had scarpered.

They all settled down on the grass and Jane lifted her two children out of the pram. The older one, a little girl, was toddling about, while her son was still a babe in arms.

'Can I hold him?' Bessie asked, and the girls watched as she cuddled the baby. It was something Bessie wouldn't have been seen dead doing six months ago.

'You've changed,' Clemmie smiled.

'I've got no choice, have I?' she said as she passed the baby to Claudette to hold. 'Thank you all for meeting me. Especially you, Jane, because you don't really know me that well, or my problem.'

'I know enough to realize that you need help. I'm only a few years older than you, and I've been through what you're about to go through. I know I had no choice but to marry when my parents found out about my condition, and that didn't work out; but even so, I've learnt a lot during the past few years. I'm told you won't even see a doctor, so the least I can do is try and explain some of what you can expect.'

'I'll go and collect some food,' Dorothy said, looking a little squeamish. 'My mum's sitting with your mum and Auntie Sarah, and they've got a big picnic basket. I won't say where you are. I'll bring back some food for all of us.'

'I'll help you,' Claudette said, and the two younger girls scurried away.

'It's probably best they don't listen,' Clemmie said. 'I think they're a bit young for some of this.'

'I am, too, but it's a little late for me,' Bessie said.

They sat for half an hour while Jane asked Bessie countless questions and gave her advice. She reached into the pram and pulled out a small book from under the mattress. 'Here, you can have this. It was given to me by a nurse at the hospital and I found it really helpful.'

'Thank you so much,' Bessie said as she flicked through the pages. 'This is really going to be useful.'

Jane glanced at Clemmie before asking, 'You're quite sure you're not going to tell anybody?'

'I'm quite sure. I've made some important decisions these last few days.'

'I'm still at a loss to understand how you're going to have this baby without your mother finding out. It's not just going to pop out one night when you're in bed, you know? Even then, what will your mother say? It'll be an awful shock if you don't talk to her soon. How will she feel?'

'No, I'm adamant I'm not saying anything. Please don't think badly of me. I've disappointed them and I've turned out as bad as my real dad and mum. Maisie tried so hard to bring me up right.'

'Having a baby doesn't make you a bad person, Bessie,' Jane said. 'You made a mistake, that's all. And believe me, in time you're going to love your little mistake – that's if you're planning to keep it?'

'I don't know what I'm going to do yet, but . . . I'm glad Claudette's not here, because I've made the decision to go away. I'm not sure where, but I've got a bit of money saved up to be able to pay rent somewhere – hopefully until the baby is born.'

'I thought you'd say that,' a voice said from behind

317

them, and Claudette and Dorothy appeared. 'That's why you were counting your money before we left, wasn't it? What were you going to do, run away and not tell any of us where you were?'

'It's best to keep somebody informed, even if you don't tell your parents,' Jane advised.

'And you'll need all the money you can get hold of,' Clemmie said. 'That's where the three of us can help you.'

'What do you mean? It's me that's got myself into this mess; it's not right for any of you to be helping me. I'm grateful for Jane's advice – having this baby frightens the hell out of me – but I know I've got to face it, and I'll face it alone.'

'But you won't be alone,' Clemmie said. 'I want to give you my share of the reward money from Molly and Johnny.'

'But that's ten pounds,' Bessie gasped.

'I'll add my share to that,' Claudette said.

Dorothy wasn't going to be left out, and quickly offered her money as well. 'And I have three pounds in my piggybank you can have, too.'

'I'll draw everything out of my post office savings account for you. But you've got to promise to stay in touch, wherever you go,' Claudette told her.

'But how am I going to do that?' Bessie asked. 'I can't write to any of you because your parents would tell Mum; and even if I telephone home, or to work, how do I know who will answer? It's best if I just disappear for a while.'

'Oh no you don't,' Claudette said. 'I'll come with you.'

'Gosh, think of the stink that would cause,' Dorothy said.

'Then this is what you're going to do,' Clemmie explained. 'I've been thinking about your predicament; I had a feeling you would want to disappear, and I was worried you'd do it without telling us. Thank goodness you didn't. There's a telephone box close to the Prince of Wales. What you can do is ring us at certain arranged times when one of us will be waiting outside the box. When you get to wherever you are going, find a local telephone box and write down the number. If we do need to get in touch with you in an emergency, we can ring that – and whoever answers, we can ask them to give you a message.'

'There is no need for that,' Bessie said. 'I'm going to rent a room somewhere on the coast and find a little job to tide me over until I'm too far gone to work.'

'Then you need to make up a story to tell the people who rent the room to you. Buy yourself a wedding ring; you can get one in Woolies. Say your husband died in an accident and add a couple of years to your age,' Jane advised. 'If people think you're respectable, they will be much more helpful than if they knew you were a pregnant, unmarried sixteen-year-old who's run away from home.'

Bessie rubbed the side of her face thoughtfully. 'Gosh, this is going to be harder than I thought; but you're right. I'll have to do that.'

Claudette had never been more proud of her sister than she was at that moment. 'I'm not happy that you're going to leave home, and I can't begin to think what it will be like for Mum and Dad, but perhaps it's for the best. You are an adult, even if some people won't think so with you only being sixteen. I'm proud of you, now you're rid of that Tom. Only positive things can happen in your life from now on. But let's make sure all your plans are in order. You have the money, but you can't just turn up somewhere and expect to find a place to live within a couple of hours of arriving in town. And the last thing you want to do is to be walking the streets after it gets dark, looking for a room.'

'You're right,' Bessie agreed, 'and I'm grateful to all of you for helping me with my plans. However, I'm going to ask a really big favour of you now: that you never tell the parents, or even the police, where I've gone or that I'm expecting a baby. In my own time, I will write to Mum and Dad just to let them know that I'm all right, but I don't want them coming to look for me. Not until I'm ready to return to Erith with my baby.'

Every one of the girls sitting there agreed, even Jane, although she acknowledged no one was likely to ask her about Bessie. She also promised that she would sort out some baby clothes and send them on to her.

Bessie was touched. 'I'm so grateful,' she said, giving the girl a smile. 'Considering I was acting like such a cow when you first started at Woolworths, you've been a true friend.'

Jane squeezed Bessie's hand. 'I'll always be here to answer any questions you've got about babies. I don't have a phone number, but I'll give you my address and perhaps we could exchange letters? Anything that scares you, just write to me. In fact,' she said, looking to the other girls, 'why don't you all use my address to exchange letters with Bessie? I'll not tell my parents what it's about, although to be honest, I'm sure my mum would support this – but I promise not to tell her,' she added, looking at the alarmed faces. 'So when you send a letter, put it inside another envelope with my name and address on the front and no one will be any the wiser.'

'That's awfully good of you,' Clemmie said, 'and it makes it much easier than hanging around outside telephone boxes.'

'Although you could always write and say when you'll be ringing the telephone box, and then we can have a proper chat as well, all squeezed into the phone box together,' Dorothy giggled.

'Now, let's be practical,' Clemmie said. 'We need to find somewhere for you to live that's far enough away that you won't be recognized, but close enough that if there is a problem, one of us can jump onto a train or bus and be with you the same day. What do you think?'

'I'd already thought of that,' Bessie said, 'and decided that I'm going to move to a seaside town. There's bound to be work, if only for a few weeks, and then I'll have the money that you've given me to fall back on.' She pulled out a couple of pages from a newspaper that had been folded in her pocket and spread them on the grass in front of her.

'I'm going to go to Ramsgate. We know it well from when we've taken trips down the river on the *Kentish Queen* – but I'm not going to travel that way, because one of the Sayers family would recognize me. I'll catch a train, it's easier. However, I'm going to get off the train a few stops before Ramsgate and then go by bus for the last bit of the journey. That way, if any questions are asked, everyone will think I got off the train and must be staying in Whitstable – that's where I'll get off the train,' she explained to a puzzled Claudette. 'Look at these,' she added, passing the newspaper pages to the girls.

Dorothy didn't understand. 'These are adverts for guesthouses for holidays – you're not going on holiday. And you might find them a little bit expensive if you stay longer than a fortnight.'

'No; I mean these,' Bessie said, pointing to a couple of smaller classified adverts. 'They also offer out-of-season accommodation that will suit me up till Christmas.'

'Why Christmas?' Jane asked.

'Because my baby will be with me by Christmas.'

'A Christmas baby,' Jane sighed. 'Regardless of the circumstances, that makes it extra special.'

'Then you'll come home?' Claudette asked.

'I don't know; we'll have to wait and see. But knowing that you're all rooting for me will keep me strong during the months ahead.'

Clemmie stabbed her finger at one of the smaller advertisements. 'This looks perfect,' she said. 'Sea View Guesthouse in Ramsgate – I know you'll be there in the winter months but if you're going to be at the seaside, you might as well be near the sea. It seems it's close to the harbour and the landlady is looking for long-term residents in a house of just women, any age considered. There is an address below it as well; why don't you write a letter and give Jane's address?'

'I'll keep an eye out for the post,' Jane said. 'I'm normally up early with the children anyway so that I can have them washed, dressed and fed, so as soon as a reply arrives, I'll pass it on to you.'

Clemmie hugged Jane. 'You are a true friend to us all.'

Jane smiled at the girls. 'It's been hard for me these past few years. I'm just grateful to have new friends and be able to help.'

'Well, thank you,' Bessie said. 'I don't deserve your help, or anyone else's come to that. I've been a fool, and still you all stood by me. Now why don't we go and enjoy the rest of the day? Goodness knows when we'll be able to do it again. And no crying,' she told Claudette, giving her a smile. 'I want to make memories of today to hang onto through the dark days ahead.'

24

September 1950

Bessie waved from the window as the train pulled out of Erith station. A tearful Claudette waved back as she stood beside Clemmie Billington, who had her arm around the younger girl's shoulders, while Dorothy ran alongside the train frantically waving until she reached the end of the platform.

'It's just you and me now,' Bessie said gently, stroking her tummy. In the two weeks since she'd announced her decision on that Bank Holiday Monday, her friends had worked wonders to prepare for today. In her suitcase she had three dresses that would see her through her pregnancy. Claudette had joked that they looked like tents, but Jane, who had lent them to her, pointed out they would do her very well until the last days of her pregnancy. There were also two smocks which she could wear over her skirts, even though she'd not be able to do them up and would use a piece of elastic between the buttonhole and the button.

At the bottom of the suitcase, wrapped in tissue paper, was a hand-knitted layette for the baby, as between them the girls had been knitting all the hours possible while their parents weren't watching. They'd scoured second-hand shops and visited a jumble sale for other essential items. Bessie had looked at the baby clothes that were for sale in Woolworths and, rather than be seen purchasing them herself, had asked Jane to collect them for her after she'd handed her the money. No one would think twice about a young woman who already had two youngsters buying more clothing. Jane had also purchased a brass ring, which Bessie now slipped onto the third finger of her left hand. For all intents and purposes she looked like a young bride – the only problem being that her pretend groom was languishing in jail. Sergeant Mike had informed them that Tom had gone down for three years.

Clemmie had handed Bessie a card at the station and told her not to open it until the train pulled out. Settling back in her seat, she carefully opened the envelope and pulled out a letter.

Her friend had written how brave she thought Bessie was to go ahead with her plans and reminded her that she only had to contact them and the three girls would be there in a flash to bring her home, regardless of what her parents would say. As Bessie read the last lines, four ten-shilling notes fell out, and it was then she saw that Clemmie had written she was to use the money to buy nappies – some-thing Bessie had yet to purchase because she didn't have the space in her suitcase.

She allowed herself a few tears before giving herself a talking to and reaching for the book about motherhood Jane had given her. Try as she might, she couldn't concen-trate and kept checking her watch. It would be an hour before the train pulled into the station at Whitstable.

She already knew there was a bus stop just the other side of the road from the station where she could catch a bus to Ramsgate. At least then, when her parents found the letter she had left for them and made enquiries at the station about a young girl purchasing a ticket, they would only be able to find out she'd travelled to Whitstable. She hated deceiving them, but in her letter she'd only said that she needed to leave Erith and was travelling alone, and that they weren't to worry. She had promised to write to them again soon to say she was safe. She also made a point of mentioning that Claudette knew nothing about her plans, in case her sister was blamed for keeping her secret; and she finished by telling Maisie and David how grateful she was for all they'd done bringing her up, and that she hoped one day they would be able to forgive her.

Bessie hadn't shown the letter to her sister, so that if Maisie were to read it out to the family Claudette's response would be genuine. She kept telling herself she'd done right, but she did find it hard to pretend, even in a letter, that she'd planned all this herself. She knew that if it hadn't been for Clemmie, Dorothy, Claudette and Jane, it would not have been possible for her to leave home and be financially secure for the time being.

The reply from the landlady at Sea View Guesthouse had come promptly back. Her terms for the room were reasonable and with what money Bessie had and what she'd been given, she should be able to cope until at least February. By then, with the baby a few months old, she would either have found employment or decided what she intended to do next. She'd made a point of mentioning in her letter to the landlady that being alone in the world and having lost her husband, she felt it only right to explain that she was expecting his child. Bessie wanted to be upfront about her pregnancy, just in case the woman took one look at her and she found herself out on the street. As it was, the landlady, Mrs Neville, was most welcoming and mentioned that there were already other children living in the guesthouse.

Apart from knowing she was going to cause heartache to her loved ones later in the day when they discovered she'd gone, Bessie felt as though she was finally at peace. She allowed herself to rest her head back for a while and close her eyes.

When the train pulled into Whitstable, she collected her suitcase from the guard's van and left the station. It was late morning, with very few people about, and the bus was already sitting at the stop waiting for train passengers.

The conductor helped her on board, taking her suitcase and making it secure on a luggage shelf. He promised to tell her the best stop for the guesthouse, and she settled down to enjoy the view as the bus trundled through small villages with occasional glimpses of the sea. If she hadn't been in such a serious situation, she would have been like a child again, calling out 'It's the sea!' as she had when her parents took her to the seaside.

'How far gone are you, love?' a woman asked as she sat down close by.

'I'm due in December,' she smiled back, realizing that it was the first time she'd spoken to a stranger about expecting a baby. It felt good. Thank goodness her mum was so tied up with the factory she'd not drawn breath to speak to Bessie for weeks, let alone spend time noticing her changing shape. In turn, Bessie had done everything possible to keep away from the adults who would question her. She'd felt guilty for not going to tea with Nanny Ruby when she'd been invited, but she'd had a feeling Ruby would have asked too many questions.

When the bus stopped close to the harbourfront in Ramsgate, the bus conductor pointed to the road she should take to walk to Sea View. Bessie gave a sigh as she saw what a steep climb she faced. Seeing her condition and the size of her suitcase, the conductor climbed down from the bus, shouting to the driver to wait.

'You can't go carrying that up there,' he said, looking around him until he spotted a couple of young lads. He called them over, instructing them to help Bessie with her suitcase.

They set off at quite a pace. The lads, sharing the handle of the case, reached the doorstep several minutes before a red-faced Bessie. 'Thank you so much,' she said. 'I'd never have managed that on my own.' She reached into her purse and gave them sixpence. 'Please treat yourselves.'

The boys thanked her profusely and went on their way just as the front door opened and a rosy-cheeked woman, with salt-and-pepper hair fastened back in a bun, invited her inside, insisting she could manage Bessie's suitcase.

'I'm Flora, and you must be Bessie,' she beamed. 'Come down to the kitchen and rest your feet while I make you a nice cup of tea. It was fortuitous that you answered my advertisement, as I don't place them very often. I've had the room empty for quite a while now, and it has been used for storage since one of my long-term lodgers moved away. But recently my daughter pointed out to me that I might as well clear it out, give it a lick of paint and rent it out, as it's such a nice room. There's a lovely view of the sea from the small window. It's not overly large, but there is room for a bed and a cot. And there's already a chest of drawers and a wardrobe in there.'

'That reminds me, I need to organize a cot,' Bessie said as she followed Flora into the room. She looked around for a moment before turning to her new landlady with a smile and declaring that it was perfect.

'There is no need – we already have one here, from when my grandchildren were younger. It comes in handy sometimes. You are welcome to use it for as long as you wish – it has a very good mattress and is very clean.' She led Bessie back into the kitchen. 'You'll find this a homely place to live, and I hope you will be happy here. Now, are you hungry? It's nearly lunchtime, and I can rustle us up something to eat.'

Bessie thought of her money. She knew that her weekly board covered breakfast and a hot evening meal. The woman saw her falter and, guessing what was in her mind, raised a hand before Bessie could utter a word.

'I'm inviting you to lunch – there is no money involved. In fact, you'll find here at Sea View that we don't stand on formality; after all, what's a bit of food amongst friends? You're part of the Sea View family now, Bessie Davis.'

'Crikey, and I've not even taken off my coat,' was all Bessie could say. She couldn't believe her luck, although she had to remind herself her surname was now Davis and hoped that Flora Neville never asked for any formal identification. Clemmie had written a reference for her, as had Jane, which had been sent with the letter enquiring about board. She prayed that would be enough, at least until she'd had the baby and could decide how her future was going to pan out.

Maisie felt as though the bottom had fallen out of her world. She sat down quickly at the dining table before her legs gave way beneath her.

'It's not bad news, is it?' Sadie asked. 'When I spotted the envelope on the table I wasn't sure whether to phone you at the factory. But then I thought, that's Bessie's handwriting, so it couldn't be urgent, could it – otherwise she'd have told you this morning?'

'There is nothing you could've done, Sadie, even if you'd rung me,' Maisie said, reaching for the cup of tea Sadie had just put on the table. 'I wonder, would you use my telephone to put a call through to Sarah and ask her to come here straight away? You'll find her number in the little book next to the telephone.'

Sadie said she would, although she was frowning with concern. 'Are you sure there's nothing wrong?'

'Nothing that can't be sorted, thank you, Sadie. You can get off after you've spoken to Sarah; and thanks for all you've done today,' she added, looking at a neat pile of ironing on the side of the table. 'I don't know what I'd do without you.'

'It's a pleasure. If there's anything else I can ever do, please ask. I'm grateful for the opportunity to be able to work while the children are still young.'

After Sadie had left, Maisie walked through to look out of the kitchen window. The twins were playing nicely in the garden along with their older sister. She went to the staircase and called up to Claudette, 'Could you come down, please?' It occurred to her that the reason Claudette had dashed straight upstairs when she came in might be because she knew what was in the envelope.

'I'll just be a couple of minutes,' Claudette called back. 'I'm changing out of my work clothes.'

Maisie returned to the table to read the letter again. Bessie had always been a problem child; perhaps she should've sat with her and asked what she wanted to do with her life. She had always assumed the girl would enjoy working in the family business. Instead, with so much going on at the factory and the second shop – not forgetting the possibility of a third in the not-too-distant future – she'd let the girl get on with things, and now it was too late.

When Claudette came downstairs she tried to act as normally as possible, but could see the envelope had been opened. 'What was it you wanted, Mum, do you want me to start dinner?'

'Not for now. Now, sit yourself down, I want to talk to you.' Maisie slid the letter across the table. 'Do you know anything about this?'

Claudette read every word, and then read it again. She hadn't known Bessie had it in her to write such a letter explaining how she loved her family and had no choice but to go away. It tore at her heart.

'Oh Mum,' was all she could say before bursting into tears.

Maisie knew how easily Claudette could dissolve into tears, but this was clearly a genuine reaction, and it convinced her the girl knew nothing of Bessie's plans.

'What are you going to do, Mum?' Claudette asked when she could finally talk.

'I don't know, love. I'm going to have a word with your

dad when he comes home, and your Auntie Sarah is on her way round. Bessie should've been working at Woolworths today, with it being a Saturday, and I wanted to ask you if there's been any problems at work? Did you not wonder why Bessie wasn't working at Woolies?'

This was where Claudette was going to have to lie to her mother. 'She told us she was using up a day off she was owed, and was going to meet a girl from school,' she replied, crossing her fingers under the table and hoping her mother believed her. 'Auntie Sarah should know if that's true, because it will be on the staff board in her office where she records all our leave and overtime.'

There was a knock at the door.

'Go and make a fresh pot of tea for your Auntie Sarah while I let her in.'

Claudette stayed in the kitchen pottering about until the tea was made, then put it on a tray with clean cups and saucers ready to take into the living room. She walked into the room just as Sarah said, 'You need to speak to the police about this. Isn't she under age?'

'I won't go to the police; it might only make things worse. She's sixteen, after all, so she's old enough to do most things. Perhaps I'll just have a word with Mike Jackson and see what he advises. I don't know how David is going to take this, I really don't, he idolizes our girls.' She smiled at Claudette as she placed the tea tray onto the table.

'Is it all right if I still meet Clemmie and Dorothy this evening, or would you rather I stayed home with you?' Claudette asked as she poured the tea and put it in front of both the women. 'If you need to speak to Dad, perhaps I should look after the little ones . . .'

'That's good of you, love, but there's no need for you to change your plans. It won't bring our Bessie back. Besides, your dad won't be in until late; he has a meeting to attend, and by then the kids will be in bed and I can speak to him in peace. Why don't you pop out into the garden and get the kids in, and I can feed them before they have their bath?'

Claudette did as she was told, glad to be out of the room. She didn't like to see her mum so upset.

Sarah looked at Maisie's face. There was no visible expression. 'You've taken this very well,' she said, looking at the letter again. 'If it was my Georgina, I'd be screaming the place down.'

'Do you think so? Then I've done well to hide it in front of our Claudette. I'm so angry with Bessie I could scream, and probably louder than you ever would. How dare she do such a thing to disrupt this family? There can't be a problem so bad that she needs to run away. I wonder if it's got anything to do with that lad she was knocking about with a few months ago. If I didn't know he was locked up in prison, I'd think she'd run off with him; but that can't be the reason, can it?'

Sarah didn't know what to say to help Maisie. She'd voiced her concerns about Bessie to Gwyneth and Ruby, but perhaps she should have been braver and spoken to Maisie, even if her friend had told her to mind her own business. Her heart ached for Maisie. It wasn't fair that the woman, who was such a good mother, had to face such a thing.

'Perhaps you should let David know now,' she suggested, keeping her thoughts to herself.

*

333

Sergeant Mike Jackson sat down in Ruby's front room, balancing his notebook on one knee and a cup of tea on the other.

'Well, Mike, or should I say Sergeant Jackson? What have you found out, love?'

Mike smiled. Only Ruby could summon the family for a conference about what to do with regard to the missing Bessie Carlisle. He knew there were few actions he could take in an unofficial capacity, but this was a family matter, and he planned to help as much as possible. If that meant reporting anything untoward, it would have to be done, whether Ruby liked it or not. The girl had been gone three days now and they were none the wiser about where she'd disappeared to.

However, there was no sign that Bessie had been abducted and she seemed, going by the letter to Maisie, to have left of her own accord. As he looked up at Maisie and her husband, David, he felt a profound sadness for them. This kind of thing could happen to any parent.

'Do you mind me speaking in front of everybody, Maisie, David?'

'We've got nothing to hide, Mike. I just can't help feeling that we've missed something. I need to know that she's all right. If for any reason she doesn't want to live at home with us . . .' Maisie's voice cracked as she spoke. 'I just . . . I just want to know . . .'

David took over as he held Maisie's hand tightly. 'Can I just say, or should I say can I beg, that if anyone in this room hears from Bessie, please tell her that she can come home any time she chooses. If there's a reason she has run away, we forgive her. Nothing can be that bad that she can't come back to us.'

'I'll second that,' Ruby said as Sarah, Bob, Alan, Betty and Gwyneth agreed. 'Now, come on, Mike: tell us what you've found out.'

'You do all realize that as she left of her own accord it's not an official police problem, and in a way, my being in uniform when I asked at the station wasn't quite the right thing to do? However, I'm prepared to have my knuckles rapped for that; it's more important we find out where Bessie is right now. I do have some news,' he said, giving Maisie and David a warm smile. 'A young woman fitting Bessie's description did purchase a one-way train ticket to Whitstable on the morning in question. The ticket seller said she was alone and because she had a suitcase he asked if she was going on holiday, although he does not recall her reply. It had been a quiet day and he'd been pondering on his own holiday; that's why he recalled the conversation. He did wonder afterwards because as a rule, people going on holiday would normally purchase a return ticket. He never saw her on the platform, so is unsure whether she was alone.'

Clemmie felt dreadful. She couldn't look at Dorothy or Claudette in case it showed on their faces that they knew something about Bessie's disappearance. They'd sat quietly so far, hoping not to be the target of any questions. Thank goodness they'd thought to tell Bessie she should purchase her ticket on her own, for the very reason that someone might recall seeing her at the station. It was fortunate they'd not been spotted seeing Bessie off – but there again, if platform staff had observed, they would also have seen three young ladies with return tickets to nearby Slades Green. The girls had planned Bessie's escape in minute detail.

Beside her, she heard a quiet sob – it was Dorothy. She reached out and put her arm around her sister. 'This is too much for Dorothy, she's been so worried about Bessie. May I take her out into the garden?' she asked. 'Mum will tell me if there's anything else,' she added, looking directly at Mike Jackson.

'That's all I've got to say,' Mike said. 'She's obviously in the Whitstable area, but I wonder why she chose that town?'

'It could just have been that the train was going that way, and she could only afford a certain amount of money for her ticket,' Bob said, drawing on his knowledge as a retired policeman.

'She had plenty of money,' Claudette blurted out, before going quiet.

'Well, cough it up, Claudette, you can't stop after saying something like that,' Ruby said. 'Do you know anything, girl?'

'I only know how much she had in her post office savings book, and that was about twenty pounds. I've been with her when we went to the post office and paid in our reward money from Molly, and I noticed that she had five pounds and ten shillings apart from that. She's not very good at saving, and we had been on holiday,' Claudette smiled, recalling the fun they'd had. 'Apart from that her piggybank is empty; I checked it the day she went away when Dad asked me. That's all I know about her money, sorry.'

Betty cleared her throat. 'I can add something to that, and Sarah can confirm. It was only two days before she disappeared that she collected her pay packet for her Saturday job and a few extra hours she'd worked. The total amount in the envelope was nine shillings. I know, if it had been our Clemmie who had run away, that it would hearten me to know she had enough money to survive until, I assume, finding herself a job. Your daughter is a sensible girl, and you should keep that in mind,' she said, giving the Carlisles a supportive look.

'Well, I for one believe the child won't starve. Going by what our Claudette and Betty have told us, she's also got enough money for a train ticket home for when she decides what to do. She's not a daft kid and knows what's what, so stop looking so miserable,' Ruby huffed. 'I had much less and no one to support me when I wasn't much older than she is now. I coped. There's nothing else a woman can do. We just need to wait.'

'Oh, there's plenty we can do,' Maisie said. 'Now Mike's confirmed where she got off the train, we can go down to Whitstable and look around and see if we can find anyone who saw her that day. We may even find her working in a cafe or somewhere like that. She can't have just disappeared off the face of the earth.'

Claudette was thankful Bessie had decided to get off the train where she did. As long as nobody had spotted her getting on the bus, she would be safe. However, she planned to write a letter to her, just to let her know what was happening here at home. She'd not put too much about her parents being upset; that could only make Bessie feel worse, and she needed to think about herself and her baby right now.

The adults chatted on, making plans to drive down to Whitstable, with Sarah offering to go too on her day off.

'Perhaps I could go down for the day and take Clemmie and Dorothy with me? Clemmie would look after us,' Claudette said. Before Maisie could speak, she added, 'We would be able to speak to younger people when you grown-ups couldn't.'

Maisie looked at her husband. 'What do you think, David? Claudette may have a point there.'

'If you wanted to wait and come with us on Sunday . . .' Claudette started to suggest, looking at her mum.

'No, I think the three of you on your own may do much better. I trust you all to behave,' Maisie said, and Betty agreed. 'I'll give you the money for your train tickets and your lunch while you're down there,' she added. 'Thank you, Claudette. You're truly a good sister to Bessie.'

25

30 November 1950

'Why can't we go to the Lyons teashop?' Dorothy asked as they sat in a small cafe overlooking the harbour at Ramsgate.

'I've explained to you before,' Bessie said as she tried to make herself more comfortable in her seat. 'My land-lady's friends work in the Ramsgate and Margate teashops. If I go into either of them, not only will they recognize me but they'll be bound to ask about my friends. It would go against the story I told them when I arrived, about not knowing anyone down here. I came here as it had been my husband's wish to live here before he died. I must say, it's a lot easier living here on my own than I expected. Mrs Neville is so nice, as are the other residents. I wish I could show you my bedroom – I've set up a cot, and a couple of the ladies have knitted for me. I feel such a fraud at times.'

'Pick what you want,' Claudette said, 'I'm paying for this. Mum thinks we are down this way looking for you again – don't worry, we didn't buy tickets to Ramsgate, we did the same as you and went to Whitstable then caught the

339

bus. Saying that, on the way home, why don't we go by train and buy another ticket from Ramsgate to Whitstable, and just stay on the same train all the way home? It's getting a bit chilly out there,' she said, as spots of rain hit the cafe window. 'Mum is starting to suggest we don't come looking any more as our searches have been futile.'

'Just make sure that when we get off the train at Erith, we get rid of our tickets just in case one of our parents finds them and asks questions,' Clemmie added. 'I will say it's getting hard to be able to find time to come down here at the moment. I've not got any more days off college until the Christmas holidays. And then, of course, Betty will be asking us to work extra days because of the Christmas rush.'

'I'm sorry to inconvenience you,' Bessie pouted. 'Don't come if it makes it too hard for you. I'd hate any of you to suffer.'

'Oh, it's not like that at all, I'm just trying to be practical. All I'm thinking is it will have to be a Sunday, and we'll just have to pray that Mum and Dad don't offer to drive us down,' Clemmie said, looking hurt.

'I'm sorry; I'm feeling rather miserable today. I didn't sleep well. I feel so uncomfortable,' Bessie said, wriggling on the seat. 'This chair is awfully hard.'

Clemmie looked at the menu. 'Let's eat up quickly and go for a walk, shall we? I've got some things in my bag for you – don't let me take them home with me.'

'That's very good of you,' Bessie said. 'I'm sorry for being grumpy.'

'We all would in your situation,' Claudette said. 'Is there anything else you want me to bring from home, like your winter coat perhaps?'

'Mum would notice it had gone, so best not to. There's a second-hand shop up the road; I'm going to have a look and see if they've got a coat in there that would fit me. I need a larger size at the moment,' she chuckled, rubbing her tummy.

'It won't be long now, will it?' Dorothy asked.

'Just a couple of weeks, working on what I read in Jane's book. I must say, she's been a diamond. She's written me so many letters, and any question I've asked, she's put me straight.'

'Where are you going to have the baby?' Dorothy asked.

Bessie didn't like to admit that she'd not booked in or even seen a doctor. Her landlady, Flora, had mentioned that there was a midwife living up the road from Sea View who came out to ladies who were having their babies at home. Although Bessie had not continued the conversation, she at least knew that when the time came, she could ask one of the residents of Sea View to call on the midwife to help her. She just prayed that everything would be straightforward, because going into a hospital could mean them asking questions about who she was. The less she had to lie, the better.

'Have you decided what to do afterwards?'

'Not really; I know I'm going to see how I feel, and if the baby is a good sleeper. Jane reckons one of hers slept through the night and was very good, whereas the other one was a nightmare to live with and she was fit for nothing. Flora did mention that if I wanted to work, some of the ladies at Sea View might be able to look after the baby; then I could stay there afterwards.'

'What – forever?' Claudette asked.

'To be honest, I don't know what to do,' Bessie said, trying to pin a smile on her face, although inside her mind was in turmoil. 'Tell me, how is everybody back home?'

'I still miss you, and I swear Mum looks ten years older. As Dad would say, she's going through the motions. She's so worried about you.'

'Perhaps one day I'll come home, but for now you can post this,' Bessie said as she delved into her bag and pulled out an envelope. 'I've not mentioned the baby, or that I'm living in Ramsgate. I'd be grateful if you could post it on your way home.'

Clemmie took the letter and tucked it into her pocket. 'In that case, we will get off the train at Whitstable and post it there to keep up the pretence you live in that area.'

'I'm truly grateful,' Bessie said as she gave them all a wide smile. 'I couldn't have done this without the three of you – four, as I should include Jane. Please give her my thanks. I'll make it up to you all one day. Now, let's order, shall we? I'm famished; and then we must go for a walk before I seize up in this chair.'

Half an hour later, they left the cafe and paused to look out over the harbour.

'This is a lovely town,' Dorothy said. 'Under different circumstances, I would love to have a holiday here. I read about Ramsgate in a travel book I found in the library. Don't worry – I never took it home,' she assured the other girls, as she saw their alarmed expressions. 'That pretty harbour was where many of the small ships sailed from the rescue of the troops at Dunkirk. And to think we're only a few miles away from Sunny Days holiday camp.'

'That did worry me,' Clemmie said.

'Molly's had her baby, so she's not likely to be popping down to Ramsgate for the day; so you're all right for a while. It's just a case of having eyes in the back of your head. If she does bump into you after you've had the baby, you could say you're working there as a nanny. That's if you're out pushing the pram.' Dorothy was pleased with her suggestions.

'Hopefully I'll not bump into Molly or Johnny before I've had the baby. I can't really hide this, can I,' Bessie said, looking down at her large stomach.

'You could always walk straight past them as if you don't know them. Then they might believe they were mistaken and it's not you after all.'

'I'll try to remember that, Dorothy, but it could be hard. Do you think we could walk a bit faster? I'm terribly chilly; the wind off the sea is quite blustery today.'

'Yes, it is,' Claudette said, taking the scarf from around her neck and wrapping it around her sister's shoulders. 'That will help, but why don't we come with you to the second-hand shop? Then we can help you find a suitable coat.'

'That's a good idea. With the four of us together, we can have a good dig about and see if there's anything else worth picking up,' Clemmie said.

'I've got to be careful with my money,' Bessie said, 'it won't last forever. I've budgeted very tightly for this.'

'Then we shall have to haggle,' Clemmie said. She linked arms with Bessie and they walked away from the seafront, up the sloping road to where she pointed out the shop.

'Crikey, I'd kill for a shop like this in Erith,' Claudette said as she looked at the large double-fronted building with rack upon rack of clothing, as well as household items and other paraphernalia.

'I suggest we split up, otherwise we'll never cover every rail before our train leaves,' Clemmie said.

'How can I help you?' a lady asked, appearing from behind a curtained-off doorway inside the shop.

'My friend is looking for a winter coat; the one she has doesn't fit very well at the moment.' Clemmie smiled politely.

'I can understand why, my dear,' the lady beamed. 'When is the happy event?'

'A couple more weeks yet, and the way the weather is at present, I just need to keep warm. I'm not fussy about the colour,' Bessie replied.

'Crikey, you have changed,' Claudette giggled, earning a short look from her sister.

'You've come to the right place. If you come over to this rail, I have several that would suit you and keep that baby snug as well.'

The girls followed the woman and exclaimed over the coats that she pulled out.

'They don't even smell musty,' Dorothy said without thinking.

'I pride myself on all the garments being clean and fresh-smelling,' the lady said, not taking offence, 'but I do know what you mean. Some other establishments are not quite as fussy. However, you can come here anytime and leave with complete satisfaction. If not, you're welcome to bring it back. Once you don't have use of this coat, when the baby comes along, you're welcome to come back and exchange it for something more suitable for your size – no charge, of course.'

'That's very kind of you,' Bessie smiled. 'Money is tight at the moment.'

'It is, my dear. I wonder if you'd be interested in one of these?' the woman asked, crossing to the other side of the shop, where there were several prams lined up. 'They've all had a good scrub, and everything is in working order,' she said, putting her hands on the handles of a Silver Cross pram and bouncing it gently up and down. 'It's almost as good as new. I'll even throw in a sun canopy and some blankets.'

'You'd definitely look like one of those posh London nannies pushing that up and down the road,' Dorothy said as she picked up the blankets and checked them through. 'This is all as good as new.'

'Once the owner finished having her family, she had no need of such things and generously donated her baby equipment to us. The money we raise here goes to a local children's charity,' the woman added just in case the girls hadn't noticed the details of the sign over the shop.

'Oh, I adore it,' Bessie said. 'My baby would be so cosy in this.' She bent to look at the price label hanging from the handle. Clemmie saw a despondent look cross her face as she said that perhaps she'd return another day, before the baby was born.

'A deposit secures,' the woman said with a smile. 'Five shillings should do it.'

'I'll have to think about it. I'm not sure if my husband's family are treating us to a pram,' Bessie said, not meeting her friends' eyes after making such a blatant lie.

After she had picked out a warm forest green woollen coat and pulled it on with help from Claudette, the lady bundled up her thin coat, wrapping it in brown paper and tying it with string. 'Don't forget, my dear, come back here anytime and I'll see you all right. I like to help the young mothers,' she said.

'I don't know about you,' Clemmie said, 'but all that shopping has made me dry. I spotted a little teashop down the road.' She pulled out a couple of shillings from her purse. 'Here, Dorothy, take this and buy us all some tea. I don't need the change,' she added, looking at her sister pointedly, which meant Dorothy had permission to buy a cake or a bun as well. 'You all go on together and I'll catch you up – I just need to do something. I'll be no more than ten minutes.'

She watched as her three friends walked down the road, Claudette and Dorothy linking arms with Bessie. Once they'd gone into the teashop, she returned to the second-hand shop and went up to the assistant. 'I'd like to purchase the pram, please, as a surprise for my friend. I'll also have those,' she said, pointing to several bundles of baby clothes that were neatly tied up with ribbon.

The lady packed everything into the pram and clipped the pram cover over, so nothing would get wet in the fine drizzle. 'Your friend is very lucky; I wish her well. It's hard bringing up a baby,' she added. 'I was in the same position once and had to give my baby up for adoption. You tell your friend, when she's had the baby, to come in and see me – it's always quiet in here on a Monday. I can offer a cup of tea and a chat to break up her day.'

Clemmie left the shop, thinking how kind people could be to complete strangers and how the lady had guessed Bessie's situation. She carefully pushed the pram along the road towards the teashop, excited about what Bessie would think when she saw it. She stopped in front of a large picture window and was careful to put on the brakes. Claudette spotted her and nudged Bessie. The beaming smile that lit up her face was something that would stay with Clemmie forever.

'Is this for me?' Bessie asked as they all stepped outside. She ran her hands over the pram, almost stroking it. 'But how . . . Why . . . ?'

'It's my gift to you. I know traditionally women don't have a pram in the house till after the baby is born, from what I've heard in Woolworths; but I don't think any of us should worry about superstitions, do you? Especially when this was such a bargain. I wanted you to have it. And these,' she said as she pulled back the cover to reveal bundles of baby clothes and nappies. 'I'm not sure how you are for nappies, but the lady did tell me you can never have enough. I wouldn't know,' she giggled. 'If there's anything that's the wrong size, or you don't like, you can take it back. She also said to pop in and show her the baby when it's born.'

'Gosh,' was all Bessie could say before she flung her arms around Clemmie and hugged her. 'I don't deserve this at all.'

'Of course you do. Now, let's just check these brakes again – we don't want it careering down the road and into the harbour,' Clemmie chuckled. 'Then we can have that tea, and after that I'm afraid we're going to need to be heading to the station. But not before we've walked this as close as we can to Sea View without us being seen. I'm afraid from there on you will have to knock on the door and ask someone to help you up the steps. I hope your landlady is amenable to having a pram in the hallway?'

'Oh, she's a sweetheart,' Bessie said, not taking her eyes

off the pram. 'Who'd have thought a year ago that I would have got so excited about such things?'

'A year is a long time, isn't it?' Claudette smiled. 'Now come on, let's get cracking or we're going to miss the train. And we mustn't forget to post your letter, either,' she said to Clemmie, who patted her pocket to check it was still there.

They bid Bessie goodbye at the corner of her road. Clemmie held Bessie as tight as she could as she whispered in her ear, 'I hope it goes all right. Once you've had the baby, put a telephone call through to Woolworths. If I'm not there, leave a message for me. I'm sure you can think of something suitable in case Mum or Sarah answer.'

'I'll do that,' Bessie smiled. 'That's if I can't get through to Claudette at the factory.'

'Perhaps it would be worth ringing direct to the factory after all. You could always say "I have a message for Claudette Douglas; it's Mrs Murchison to say thank you, the frock fitted perfectly." If you have a boy, say it's a blue frock, and if it's a girl, it's a pink frock. At least then we will know,' Clemmie suggested, biting her lip and fighting hard to keep a smile on her face.

Bessie stood at the door of Sea View and watched as the girls walked out of sight before letting herself in and calling to Flora Neville to help her bring the pram inside. It was as she stood talking to Flora and several of the other residents that the uncomfortable feeling she'd had all day suddenly became more intense. 'Ouch,' she said as she reached to hold onto the pram.

'How long has this been going on?' Flora asked as she nodded for one of the women to pull a seat over.

'Most of the day – but I've been walking. I thought I was just stiff . . . but now I'm not so sure,' Bessie said, clutching her stomach. 'It's too early for my baby to come.'

'Babies come when they are ready to come, and not before,' Flora said. 'Why don't we get you up to your bedroom? I'll have someone go for the midwife – that's what you want, isn't it?' she asked with a knowing look.

'Yes, that's what I want,' Bessie replied breathlessly. She cried out in pain, biting her lip to stop herself calling out for her mum.

The post arrived just as Maisie was setting out for work. She'd already waved off Sadie, who had loaded the children into the large pram she still kept and attached walking reins to the older ones.

'Rather you than me,' she chuckled as she helped them down the step and out of the gate.

'It's easy once I'm organized,' Sadie said. 'Besides, I'll be meeting James very soon, so if any of them are playing up, one look from him and they'll behave.'

'Bless him, he wouldn't hurt a fly. Have a lovely time,' Maisie called after them. 'I could do with a morning at the park myself – perhaps I'll join you another day.' Smiling to herself, she went back indoors to collect her bags. A letter had landed on the doormat and she picked it up, thinking it would be something for work. As she went to put it into her pocket, she recognized the handwriting and returned to the living room, leaving her bags where she'd dropped them in the hall.

Maisie had dreamt of the day she would hear from Bessie. It had been over two months now, and all kinds of things had gone through her mind. Perhaps Bessie would tell her where she was; if that was the case, Maisie would jump into her van and drive there straight away. If it was bad news, then her child needed to be at home.

She tore open the envelope and straightened out the single page. Scanning the few lines, she felt a wave of emotion building up inside her. Then she screwed the letter into a ball and threw it onto the table, laid her head on her arms and started to cry; not large, angry sobs, but gentle tears of loss. She was beginning to believe she would never see her eldest child again. And she knew that if she had to go through life not knowing what had happened to Bessie, it would eat her up inside, making her a bitter angry, woman.

As her tears subsided she reached for the letter, starting to straighten it out again to see if she'd missed anything. Just then, there was a knock at the door. Not caring what state her face was in, Maisie opened it to find Ruby standing there.

'I was just off to the shops when I spotted your van still parked in front of the house and wondered if there was a problem? You've usually left by now,' she started to say before noticing Maisie's tear-streaked face. 'I can see something has happened. Quick, love, let me in, before Vera notices I'm on your doorstep and follows me.'

Maisie nodded and stood back for Ruby to enter the house.

'I've never seen you look such a state, if you don't mind my saying so. I don't mean that in a rude way,' Ruby said as she sat in Maisie's recently vacated seat, nodding to Maisie to sit down. 'Now, what's going on?'

'I've had a letter from Bessie,' Maisie replied, showing no emotion.

'Well, it can't be good news,' Ruby said, noticing the crumpled page in her hand. 'May I?'

'Be my guest.' Maisie slid the letter across the table to Ruby, who sat and read it slowly.

'My opinion, for what it's worth, is that this is good news,' she said after a few moments.

'How can you say that?'

'It's good news because the girl is still alive and hasn't done anything daft. Or should I say, she was alive at five o'clock yesterday, when she posted this letter,' Ruby said, pointing to the postmark, 'and it looks as though you were all correct when you said she was in the Whitstable area.'

Maisie thought for a moment. Trust Ruby to talk sense. 'I never thought of it like that. But I wonder why she's taken until now to write to me – and then hardly told me anything about what she's been up to? I expected so much more after all this time.'

'My guess is, she's settled where she is, and isn't on the run, and whatever is on her mind she is now facing it square on and realizes it's time to write to you. It's been on her conscience, no doubt. It's not as if she's a bad child. Look,' Ruby said, pointing to the page, 'there's no aggression in her words. She doesn't blame anyone else. She just apologizes for leaving without explaining properly, and says that she is well. I know there's no address, so you can't reply or go looking for her at the moment. Perhaps when the next letter comes – and it will – she'll tell you a little more. What do you think?'

'That's the problem, Ruby: I can't think straight. I know she could be a little mare at times, but like you say, she's a good kid at heart, and I miss her like hell.'

Ruby got up and went into the kitchen to fill the kettle.

'I don't know about you, but I need something to drink with all this talking,' she said as she returned to her seat. 'Now, I'm older than you, Maisie, and I've seen a lot in my years. Sometimes there's a small signal or two as to what's going on; it's something us mums get to learn as we go through life.' She chuckled gently. 'There were times when my George was a youngster, I wished I could read what was going on in his mind, I can tell you. As for Bessie, I have a feeling there was something that put her in a position where she couldn't stay. My gut tells me it has something to do with a lad. George said he'd spotted her once going into the cinema on the arm of a lad; and then there was that business at the holiday camp, when the girls stopped that burglary. I've got a feeling Claudette knows more than she's letting on.'

Maisie looked shocked. 'I'm her mother – I should've known these things. Sarah said as much, but did I listen? I do wonder if I'm putting work in front of my children these days. Well, that's going to change. If it means I'm losing touch with my kids, I'll stop it by selling the business.'

'Now you're talking daft,' Ruby said, wagging her finger. 'I expected better of you. This could've happened even if you'd stayed at home all day long. Kids are kids, and at that age they are still learning about life.'

'But what can I do?' Maisie asked. 'I want my daughter back home.'

'There's nothing you can do, apart from take heart that Bessie has reached out to you with this letter. Keep your ears open. You never know – there may be someone who knows where she is.'

Maisie frowned. 'Do you think my Claudette knows?'

'If she does know something, it's not your place to cross-examine her. You don't want to alienate another of your daughters, do you?'

'Then what . . . ?'

'You've got to stay strong to help keep a happy home for your other children and David, but above all . . . try to prepare yourself for the day when Bessie returns home. You might just discover that things have changed.'

'What do you mean? You don't think she's married that Tom, do you? Oh God.' Maisie was anguished.

'There you go, worrying about things that haven't happened,' Ruby tutted. 'How can she have married him, when he's in prison? Besides, my thoughts are that she came to her senses over that lad; otherwise she wouldn't have helped the other girls stop the robbery.'

'You're right,' Maisie sighed, 'I'm making something out of nothing again. I'll do as you say and try not to allow it to eat me up inside. Now let me make that tea.'

Ruby looked up at the clock. 'I'll say no to that after all, thanks all the same. I'd better be on my way. I'm supposed to have met Vera to go down the Co-op, and she'll be on the warpath.'

Maisie chuckled as she helped her to the door. 'Thank you, Ruby. As always, you've come up trumps. You always have the answers to everything.'

Ruby kissed her cheek and headed to the gate.

There's something I've not mentioned, she thought to herself as she clicked it shut behind her. As sure as eggs is eggs, that girl is expecting a baby.

26

~

21 December 1950

'Here, let me help you down the steps with your pram,' Flora Neville said to Bessie. 'How is little Jenny today?'

'She's very well. I wouldn't say she slept through the night, but she went four hours. In fact, I was so worried there was something wrong, I couldn't sleep and sat watching her,' Bessie said as her landlady leant over to brush the sleeping baby's cheek with the tip of her finger.

'She is adorable. Will you be receiving any visitors to see the baby?' she asked.

'No, I don't think so. I've written to everybody, but my late husband's family live so far away,' Bessie said. She was getting used to telling lies about her situation. Flora had been so helpful, especially after Jenny's birth, when Bessie wasn't up to doing much herself, that now she'd started to help out around Sea View. In the past few weeks she had been making trips to the shops for Flora, and also prepared some meals.

'What horrid weather,' Flora said as she opened the front door. The sky had turned a deep grey with icy spits of rain.

'I'm not a fan of the cold weather, but how I dream of snow over this awful rain. It would be lovely to have a white Christmas,' she added, before pausing to listen. 'Oh, that's the telephone – stay right there, Bessie. I'll help you in just a moment when I've answered it.'

Bessie buttoned up her coat, wrapping a warm scarf around her neck. At least she knew Jenny was comfortably tucked up in her pram, under a crochet blanket sent to her by Clemmie. The girls had yet to come down to see the baby, as they would only have been able to meet outside of Sea View; Bessie hoped to see them shortly after Christmas, when everyone was a little less busy.

She was still fussing around the pram when her ears pricked up at the mention of a familiar name.

'Mr Caselton! How are you and Maureen? Oh dear, I'm sorry to hear that. Let me check my diary . . .'

Bessie didn't like to turn to watch Flora on the telephone, although she was eager to hear the conversation. Surely that must be George Caselton; but why was he ringing here?

It was then that the penny dropped. Hadn't George and Maureen spent a few days here after their wedding? She vaguely recalled that they'd come to Ramsgate. What rotten luck, she thought to herself, that they'd decided to visit Sea View again.

When Flora finished the call she disappeared briefly into the kitchen, and Bessie quickly peeked into the bookings diary beside the hall telephone.

'That was the Caseltons from Erith. They're coming here the day after Boxing Day – that's less than a week away,' Flora said as she returned. She went on to explain that during the off season she normally took in female lodgers rather than family groups, but as the Caseltons were old customers, they were more than welcome.

Bessie knew then that she would have to find somewhere else to live, and do it quickly, otherwise her family would know where to find her, and she was not ready for that.

She needed to ask somebody if they knew of any digs available at short notice, but the only person she ever talked to was Mrs Charles, who ran the second-hand shop. The woman had been so helpful to her with baby clothes, and of course this lovely pram that Clemmie had purchased as a present. Bessie decided to walk down to the shop immediately.

She opened the front door and managed to bump the pram down the steps on her own, calling back over her shoulder, 'There's no problem, Flora, I've managed it myself. We'll see you later.' Then she headed into town at a brisk pace.

By the time she reached the shop, Jenny was still asleep in her pram. Bessie turned it away from the wind coming up the street from the seafront and made sure the brakes were secure before going into the shop, turning back to check she could still see the pram from inside.

'Can I help you?' asked a young woman behind the counter.

'I was hoping to see Mrs Charles,' Bessie said, looking towards the door to the back room where the woman would usually be busy sorting out donations of goods.

'I'm afraid she's not very well and is taking time off until the new year; it's her chest,' the girl explained when she saw the worried look on Bessie's face. 'May I help instead?'

'I only came to visit with my baby. I'll return in the new year,' Bessie said. As she reached the door she turned back.

It was silly not to ask. 'I wonder, would you know anyone who has a room available? I'm going to have to move from where I'm staying at the moment as my landlady has family problems,' she said, wishing she didn't have to tell lies quite so often. It was becoming far too easy for her these days.

'As it happens, I spotted a card in the newsagent's window close to where I live, although I can't remember the details . . .'

'Perhaps I could look there,' Bessie replied. 'Where is it?'

The woman gave her the name of the shop and explained where she'd find the street. It was quite a walk, but Bessie didn't have anywhere else to go, so after thanking the girl profusely she headed off towards the other side of town, away from the seafront and the shops and hotels.

This part of Ramsgate didn't seem quite as pleasant, but Bessie reminded herself that Erith too was different in some areas. She kept on walking until she turned into a narrow side street with no pavements. Up ahead was a small group of men standing about talking; for some reason Tom and his mates crossed her mind, as they seemed to be of a similar age and swarthy appearance. She wondered what she'd ever seen in Tom and shuddered; but at least that unfortunate experience had produced her darling daughter, Jenny.

As she tried to pass the men, they stood in front of the pram and threw questions at her.

'Where are you going, darling? Can I come with you?'

She put her head down and kept walking until she was grabbed by the shoulder.

'Please don't do that,' she begged as one of them pulled the pram from her hands and lifted the cover.

'Leave her alone,' Bessie screamed. 'Help! help!' She

looked around desperately, but there was nobody else in sight.

'Look what I found,' one of the men shouted, pulling out her handbag from where she'd hidden it under the blankets.

'Please give it back to me. I won't tell anybody,' she begged.

They ignored her and ran off, shouting and shoving each other, until they disappeared at the end of the road.

In shock, Bessie turned the pram and walked rapidly back to a part of town that she recognized before sitting down on a bench, shaking profusely. There was a cafe over the road and a strong cup of tea would have put her to rights, but in her distressed state it was only just sinking in that her handbag had contained her purse, and in there had been every penny she possessed.

This gave rise to another realization. Was this how people had felt after Tom and his mates had stolen from them? And she'd been party to that. Perhaps she deserved what had happened. Thank goodness they hadn't hurt Jenny. It was silly of her, she knew, but whenever she went out she carried her money with her, even though she knew that no resident of Sea View would ever have taken anything from her room. The small amount she had left had been her security blanket against being on the streets. Now what would happen? There was no point in looking for new digs, as she couldn't afford to pay rent; come to think of it, she already owed a few weeks to Flora. What with having the baby and everything else, she simply hadn't got round to handing over her money. What could she do now? she thought, as Jenny stirred and started to cry.

'The poor little thing needs feeding,' a woman said from the doorway of the cafe. 'Why don't you bring her in here, love? It's very quiet and warm. You can sit at the back and feed her without being disturbed.'

Bessie knew that she wouldn't be able to pay for a cup of tea. It felt wrong to use the cafe to care for her baby; but like it or not, Jenny needed feeding. So she accepted the woman's invitation and went into the warmth. Leaving the pram in a corner, she sat down to feed Jenny.

Holding the baby to her breast, she tried to take comfort in the knowledge that at least she wouldn't need to buy food for her at the moment. But even so, their situation was dire. They couldn't go back to Flora's, even if Bessie explained that she'd had her handbag stolen. There was no way she could find money anywhere else, and it would be wrong to ask her sister and friends to send more money when they'd already given her so much. On top of everything else, it would only be a few days before the Caseltons' visit — and she couldn't face them.

The cafe owner came over to the table and placed a cup of tea in front of Bessie.

'I'm sorry, I came out without my purse. I can't afford . . .'

'Oh, there's no need to pay me, lovie. I always have a cup of tea about now before the rush starts, and there's plenty in the pot that would be wasted, so it would be nice to join you,' she said as Jenny finished feeding. Bessie settled the baby back into her pram after she managed a satisfactory burp.

They chatted for a while about the town and the cafe, with Bessie feeling calmer in the woman's company. It was a small place with just a dozen tables covered in clean oilcloth, but it was cosy and she was grateful to be out of the chill.

'Oh well, no peace for the wicked,' the woman said as a family group came in and ordered a meal. 'There was me with my bad back, thinking I could have a quiet day,' she sighed.

'I could help you for a few hours, if you like?' Bessie offered shyly. 'As long as you don't mind the pram being here, Jenny is very good.'

'Well, if you don't mind, I'd be ever so grateful,' the woman said in surprise. 'But I'd hate to think there was somebody at home waiting for you.'

'No, it's fine, honestly. I could do three hours, if you like?'

'Like? I'd love it. My name's Beryl, by the way. Right, let me run through what we sell, and then I'll be able to put my feet up for a little bit. My doctor warned me I shouldn't overdo things, but would I listen,' she cackled.

Bessie pulled on a large white apron and wrapped it around herself. Soon she was frying eggs, making sand-wiches and thoroughly enjoying herself. The hours flew by. She was checking on Jenny when Beryl called her over to the counter and gave her a used envelope containing coins. 'I can't afford a lot, love, but there's a bit in here to help you, and before you go, I'll make us some grub.'

Bessie tried hard to hide how grateful she was and murmured, 'There was no need,' although she was clasping the envelope tightly in her hand, fearful it would be taken away from her.

She enjoyed a plate of egg and chips before waving goodbye, with Beryl calling from the doorway that she should drop in any time she was passing. Once she was away from the shop and further down the road, she found another bench and sat down to peer into the envelope. It was all loose change and a bit of silver – probably from the tip jar, she thought, but welcome all the same.

An idea came to her, and with a determined attitude she walked the pram to a nearby telephone box. It was a Thursday, so Claudette would be at the factory. She'd take a chance and hope her sister answered the telephone. If she didn't, Bessie would simply put the receiver down; thank goodness she knew the number off by heart, she thought to herself as she started to dial.

Hearing her sister answer, she quickly pushed the buttons and within seconds was speaking. 'Claudette, it's me, Bessie.'

'It's lovely to hear from you, how is Jenny?'

'She's fine, but something has happened . . . I can't tell you everything now because I've got very little money for the phone. It's just that I need to come home right away. Don't ask any questions – I'll explain later. I have a feeling I won't have enough to get me all the way back to Erith. If I travel as far as I can on the train, can I meet you there? I'll find a telephone box at the station and ring you again. I'll be about twenty minutes.'

'Of course I will. But Bessie, are you in danger?' Claudette sounded anxious.

'Only in danger of being found out. I'll explain when I see you.'

She put the receiver down and counted the change she had left, wondering how far it would take her by train.

The rain started in earnest as she headed towards the station. It was early afternoon by now and the station was empty; she didn't even have to queue at the ticket office.

Pushing the envelope of coins across the counter, she asked, 'How far can I go on the up line with this money?'

She didn't want to ask if the money would get her to Erith; she still felt as though she should share as little information about herself as possible. In the past months, it had become a way of life to lie and keep her own counsel.

The man studiously counted the money and stacked the coins evenly before checking a board on the wall. 'How does Gravesend sound to you?'

Bessie wasn't sure how far Gravesend was from home, but it was closer to Erith than Ramsgate. 'It will do me nicely, thank you.'

The man slid a ticket back across the counter and peered at the pram by her side. 'That will have to go into the guard's van,' he said, 'but it won't be a problem. My wife travels that way quite a lot with our kiddies. I'll call a porter to help you to the right platform.' He gave Bessie a smile.

'I just need to make a telephone call; is there a telephone box nearby?'

'Just over there,' he nodded to the waiting room, 'but be quick, as your train goes in ten minutes.'

'Thank you, do you know what time the train pulls into Gravesend?'

He looked at his watch and then a chart, running his finger down a row of numbers. 'Twenty minutes after three.'

She thanked him and hurried to the telephone box, where she rang the factory again. Claudette answered straight away. 'I'll be at Gravesend station at twenty past three – can you meet me? I don't mind waiting.'

'Don't worry, I'll be there. Do be careful, won't you? You sound worried.'

'I'm fine now that I know I'm going to meet you. Thank you, Claudette. I hope I've not got you into trouble?'

'Of course you haven't,' her sister said. In the background, Bessie could hear Maisie's voice saying 'Is that for me?'

'I'd best go. See you soon,' she said, and hung up as a porter approached her. The young man was more than helpful as he guided her to the right platform, then helped the guard lift the pram onto the train. Bessie followed close behind, worried the train would go without her.

'Park yourself down there,' the guard said, pointing to a small wooden pull-down seat again the wall. 'I'll tell you when we get to Gravesend and help you off.'

Bessie sat down gratefully, relieved to be on her way after her stressful day. Whatever happened after this, she would just have to deal with it. She'd never felt so tired and worried in her life, but at the moment at least she and her daughter were safe.

Claudette was waiting on the platform as the train pulled in, having asked a delivery driver to drop her at Slades Green station so she didn't have as far to travel. It had been her half day, and she was glad not to have to walk far – or to explain to her mum why she had to dash off.

The guard had hardly opened his door before she was pushing forward to help him take the pram down onto the platform. Then she hugged her sister tightly. 'I've been dying to come and see you both, but with everybody being so busy I've not been able to make an excuse to take time off. I've not even seen my little niece,' she said, as Bessie thanked the train guard and then pulled back the covers so her sister could look at the sleeping Jenny.

'She's adorable,' Claudette sighed, 'just like a little doll.'

'I can assure you Jenny is much noisier than a little doll, especially in the middle of the night if she wants feeding,'

Bessie smiled. 'Already she's got me twisted round her little finger.'

Claudette stepped back and looked at Bessie thoughtfully. 'You've changed,' she said. 'You look so much more peaceful . . . more like a mother.'

'You'd not have said that if you'd seen me this morning after some men pinched my handbag. I just didn't know what to do.'

Claudette was horrified at this news. 'But why didn't you go back to your landlady and explain what happened? You could have used her telephone to get through to one of us, and we'd have sent some postal orders to tide you over?'

'If only it was that simple,' Bessie said before explaining about overhearing that George and Maureen would be visiting the guesthouse very soon.

'Crikey – that was a bit of hard luck. But thinking about it, I do remember them saying they've been to Ramsgate, as have Mike and Gwyneth. No doubt George spotted the advert just like we did in the *Erith Observer*. It's such a shame. By the way, where is your suitcase – where are your things?'

'I've not been back there. Everything is still in my room. I feel awful about it because Mrs Neville and the other residents have been so lovely to me. Perhaps I ought to telephone her and say that I've been called away urgently, and would she pack all my things into a suitcase and I'll arrange for somebody to collect it; what do you think?'

'I don't know . . . the problem the way I see it is, where are you going to go now? Or are you coming back home with me to Mum and Dad's, and introduce them to Jenny?'

Bessie felt herself turn clammy and hot at the idea.

'I don't know what to do,' she confessed, moving the pram over to a bench where she was able to sit down for a moment. 'All I could think about was running away from Ramsgate and ringing you for help. I'm sorry to land all this on your shoulders. I just don't feel as though I can suddenly turn up on the doorstep and say, "Hello, you are grandparents" – it seems so unfair.'

'Well, I think you're wrong. Mum has been a total mess since you've left, and Dad won't even talk about it,' Claudette said frankly. Seeing Bessie's shocked expression, she added, 'It's more that he's very sad.'

'I did wonder if perhaps I should stay here in Gravesend, but then, I still need some money and to find a job, and of course now I haven't got anyone to look after Jenny for me while I work. Gosh, what an awful mess I'm in,' Bessie sighed. 'Do you have any idea what I can do?'

'I do have one thought, but it's awfully dangerous.'

'Whatever do you mean? I can't put Jenny in danger,' she said, reaching out to place a hand on the cover of the pram as if to protect her daughter.

'Not endangering your lives – I just mean, you'll be very close to our house in Alexandra Road and you could bump into someone who knows you at any time.'

'How close?' Bessie asked.

'You'd be staying in number fourteen. I have the keys to Freda's house while she's away because I look after Winston Churchill, remember? Plus, it's dead opposite Nanny Ruby's house, so she'd be bound to notice, never mind her friend Vera from up the road. Look, it's getting dark already – I hate these dark afternoons. We've got to make a decision soon.'

Bessie thought for a moment as a porter stepped onto the platform, calling out the names of stations being visited by a train that was just pulling in. Amongst them were Dartford, Slade Green and Erith.

'It would be so lovely just to jump on that train and go home. Oh, if only. . .'

'I've got it,' Claudette said, jumping to her feet. 'I have the key to the back door. If we catch a train in the early part of the evening, we can go the back way into number fourteen in the dark. You could stay there for a couple of days, at least until we sort something out. I can have a word with the other girls to see if they can come up with anything else.'

'What about the neighbours? Won't Nanny Ruby see a light? She might even think it's a burglar. Goodness, what would happen then? Also, Mike Jackson lives just down the road. If there's any movement in the back gardens, one of the neighbours might point it out to him.'

'Look, we've only got to get you into the house. Freda has high walls each side, so the next-door neighbours aren't going to notice somebody going in – and once you are there, you won't have to come out again anytime soon. You'll have to avoid putting the lights on and perhaps not use the front bedroom or the front room, because if the curtains are closed all day it will look strange, and Nanny Ruby will notice. But you have the kitchen and the living room and there are two back bedrooms, which Freda uses for guests and where her lodgers used to sleep. It would give you that breathing space while we sort out what's going to happen next. Shall we get out of the station for now and go for a walk?

We could find somewhere to eat as it's almost teatime; I've got an hour before Woolworths closes.'

'Why do you need to go to Woolworths?'

'No, silly, I mean telephoning Clemmie at Woolworths. Don't forget her college is closed now, so she's working at Woolies until January. I think we're going to need her and Jane's help, don't you?'

'I certainly do,' Bessie said, thinking that at last she had some help thanks to her sister and their friends.

Clemmie raced up the stairs to the staff room alongside Jane. 'If we're not quick, we're going to miss out, and this is the last tea break of the afternoon; Maureen will be putting a tea towel over the tea urn and not taking any more orders. Gosh, I've never known it so busy! I was quite glad to go downstairs and help out in the Christmas rush, but I must say, I miss the peace and quiet of the office.'

'I know what you mean, it's like bedlam down there,' Jane agreed. 'But I do like working on the Christmas counter. Everybody seems to be so happy; that's when they're not elbowing each other out of the way to grab the last calendar or a bunch of tinsel. I'll not moan, though, because it means I'm bringing some money in. I can put some aside for the new term at college and also treat the kids and my mum and family at Christmas. I must say, everybody is so friendly here – I was quite surprised they even threw a party for the pensioners and retired employees, that was such fun.'

'I love the annual Christmas party. Everybody is so happy, and to think all our guests go away with a gift after eating a lovely meal and having a sing-song as well. If you get the chance to talk to my Auntie Sarah, ask her about the old days during the war and what they got up to at the parties. In some ways I wish I'd been old enough and living in Erith at that time.'

As they passed the office, Sarah stuck her head out. 'Oh Clemmie, just the person I'm looking for. Claudette's on the telephone and it sounds rather urgent. I hope nothing is wrong,' she said, looking worried.

Jane and Clemmie exchanged a glance. 'I'll go and get your cup of tea and wait for you in the staff room,' Jane said.

'I'll leave you alone to have your conversation,' Sarah replied. 'I need to speak to Betty about something.' She gave the girls a smile and left them.

'I hope there's nothing wrong with Bessie,' Jane whispered before she headed away.

Clemmie's heart was beating rapidly as she sat down and picked up the receiver. 'Claudette? What's going on, and where are you?'

'I'm in Gravesend, but don't ask why because I'm in a telephone box and it's eating up my coins. Bessie is with me, she had to leave Ramsgate really quickly and she's lost all her money. We've got a plan, or I should say I have a plan, as Bessie's not so sure. Please listen, because I need you and the girls to help . . .'

27

23 December 1950

'It's only me!' Claudette called out quietly as she entered Freda's house pushing Jane's pram.

'My goodness, whatever are you doing with that pram?' Bessie giggled from the end of the hall as she ducked out of view of the front door. She didn't want to step forward and help Claudette in case she was spotted. 'Have you pinched somebody's baby?'

Claudette reached in under the hood and, peeling back the blankets, she held up a cabbage. 'There's no baby in this pram, just some food and other items from the girls. It was Jane's idea to lend me her pram to carry the shopping, and I've told Mum and Nanny Ruby that I'm looking after Jane's youngest for the day. Otherwise somebody might notice I was going in and out of here with a lot of bags – which would be strange, as I'm only supposed to be here to feed Winston Churchill.'

Bessie shook her head. 'Whatever will you girls come up with next? Already you've found me somewhere to stay

369

and you've put some coins in the meter so I can use the gas stove, and there's food on the table . . .'

'Most of this is Clemmie's doing. Honestly, I feel she could turn to a life of crime, perhaps even mastermind a bank robbery. She is so clever with all the details.'

A shadow crossed Bessie's face for a moment.

'Oh, I'm so sorry! I didn't mean anything by it. You were thinking of Tom, weren't you?'

'I was, but just for a moment; honestly, it doesn't matter, it was just me being silly. Let me put the kettle on and you can tell me all about your day.'

'Now we sound like an old married couple,' Claudette said as she lifted out a shopping basket from under the covers, along with a bundle of clean nappies and some other items for baby Jenny.

'These came from Jane,' she said, 'and until we retrieve your clothes and the baby's things from Ramsgate, you will need them, as you can't have much here for Jenny. It's not as if you can hang anything out on the line in this weather, so at least now you should be able to manage.'

'You've thought of everything. I'm afraid if it had been one of you three in trouble, I doubt I would have been able to come up with anything so useful to help out.'

'Of course you would – we just think about it as we go along,' Claudette said. 'There is a new issue of the local paper coming out after Christmas. Clemmie's going to get a copy and check out the advertisements for any places you can rent. Her suggestion is to find somewhere where they can look after Jenny, so that you can work, even part time, just to pay your way. I'll continue helping you out, and I've managed to put a bit by in my post office book, so I'll draw that out for you.'

'No, honestly, you've done enough, Claudette. I can't keep taking your money.'

'You'd do the same for me,' she said. 'Besides, I can't see my little niece going without. It's a shame we can't turn the light on, it's a bit dim in here, isn't it?'

'I know. I'm being careful when I light the stove because with next door's kitchen facing us, even with a high brick wall between us, you never know if they'll notice something. I've kept the curtains closed all the time and gone to bed early.'

'Thank goodness Auntie Freda said I could use her clothes that are in the wardrobe; so at least you have a few items to wear.'

'Well, I feel quite awful about it, but I intend to make sure everything is cleaned so she won't know I've been here once I leave.'

'I like to think Auntie Freda would have helped us. I do miss her. We've not received a letter yet this week, it's probably held up in the Christmas post – hopefully something will come by Christmas Eve. The good thing is, I can pop in and out of here all over Christmas and when I'm not at work, because everyone knows I'm looking after Winston Churchill. I've been talking about how I'm sad he's on his own at Christmas, so I'll be spending longer with him. Look, by the way – if ever you really need to go out, you can use this,' she said, pulling out her own red coat and hat. 'You borrowed it once before and Nanny Ruby thought it was me, so hopefully you can get away with it again. In the dim December light, they may well think it's me pushing this pram; what do you think?'

'I'm amazed at the things you come up with,' Bessie said. 'Now, can I give you something to eat? With all this dashing about, you'll be starving.'

'What are you cooking?' Claudette asked, peering over her shoulder. 'It does smell good.'

'It's bubble and squeak and a slice of Spam.'

'That will do me fine. After I've eaten, I'll have to scoot off, as I need to get the pram back. If I'm wandering about with it too late, people will wonder why the baby hasn't been put to bed.'

'When you see Clemmie, please thank her for me. I'm not sure I said thank you enough times the other night when she helped me.'

'You never stop thanking her, and she knows, so there's no need to worry about that. By the way, Clemmie said that when she spoke to your landlady, Mrs Neville understood that you had to dash off because a family member was taken ill. If, come the new year, you wish to rent the room again, she won't charge you for the time you've been away. But if you decide not to return, she can arrange to have your suitcase put on the Ramsgate train and we can collect it at the other end.'

'Gosh, I've not thought about returning to Sea View. I'd jump at it like a shot – but who's to know if any other family members will visit and find me there?'

'That's true, but let's think about it later, shall we? I'll make sure Clemmie says the right thing to Mrs Neville. It was quite easy for her to say you don't have a telephone where you are and Clemmie had permission to speak on your behalf.'

'There's so much to remember,' Bessie said. 'Now eat

this up before you have to head back and return that baby to Jane,' she chuckled.

'Just one other thing I've got to do first,' Claudette said, picking up Mr Churchill and giving him a good hug.

'He's been getting plenty of fuss,' Bessie said.

'Actually, this is really about what I need,' Claudette said, pointing to the loose cat hairs that were now on her coat. 'Mum grumbled the other day about the number of cat hairs I had on my clothing. It would be strange if I went and didn't have any on this coat.'

As Bessie kissed her sister goodbye, Claudette took a small parcel from the pram. 'This is for Jenny – I designed it myself. Open it when I've gone.'

After she had left, Bessie carefully opened the parcel. Claudette had always been embarrassed if anyone complimented her designs; no wonder she'd wanted Bessie to open this on her own. She gasped as she unfolded a layer of tissue paper folded around the garment and lifted out a delicate pale pink dress. Running her fingers over the perfect smocking, she smiled to see *Jenny* embroidered inside a heart on the edge of the white collar. She couldn't resist looking inside the dress to admire the perfect seams. Claudette's dressmaking skills were remarkable. Her fingers touched a small ribbon, and peering closer, she read the words *Maisie's Modes*. To think her daughter was going to wear a dress from her grandmother's own company, stitched by her auntie. What a lucky little girl she was.

'I think it's time for bed, don't you, young Jenny?' she said as she carried her baby upstairs to the back bedroom. Once Jenny was settled into her bed, which for the moment was a large bottom drawer taken from the chest of drawers in their bedroom, Bessie pulled on a voluminous white cotton nightdress and climbed into bed.

Lying there, she did her best to count her blessings; after all, she had a healthy daughter and good friends. But it was sad to think that in the same street she had family and loved ones she couldn't see. Would she ever be welcomed by them again, after what she'd put them through? Worrying about Jenny's future and her own, Bessie fell into a troubled sleep.

Some time later, she woke with a start. She heard the front door close and footsteps move down the hall, heading towards the kitchen. Knowing Claudette had left money on the table and not wanting anyone to steal from her a second time, she was filled with rage, and not thinking of the consequences, she crept silently from the bedroom and down the stairs in her bare feet, turning towards the living room. In the hallway was an umbrella stand. She reached for one of Uncle Tony's walking sticks, which he'd used after his accident when he'd first worked at Woolworths. Raising the stick above her head, she raced into the room, shrieking loudly in the hope of scaring off the intruder.

The person in the living room also shrieked.

'Bessie?'

'Auntie Freda?'

The noise woke Jenny, whose cries drifted down to where the two women stood staring at each other in shock.

'Surely that's not . . . Winston Churchill?' Freda asked uncertainly, and was answered by the purring cat rubbing against her legs. She frowned. 'I think we need to talk, don't you, Bessie?'

'I'd like that,' Bessie said, knowing at once that the game was up. She couldn't talk her way out of this even if she tried. 'But first – can I go and collect my daughter, please?'

Freda pursed her lips and nodded. She was absolutely exhausted, having missed her train connection, and had been hoping to climb into bed and just sleep. The last thing she had expected was to see an apparition in white screaming at her, and then to find it was Bessie Carlisle. Maisie and Sarah had corresponded with Freda, so she knew something of the situation – including the fact that they believed Bessie to be living in the Whitstable area. So to find Bessie sleeping here was confusing enough; and what was this about a baby?

She stood by the table waiting until Bessie appeared, this time wearing a dressing gown Freda recognized as her own, although she hardly noticed. All her attention was on the mewling infant in Bessie's arms, wrapped up in a white shawl.

Freda reached out and took the red-faced baby. 'Oh, you poor little mite. Are you hungry?' she asked.

'It's more the noise we made. She's usually quite good around this time. It's often the early hours of the morning when she will wake me – she likes her food.' Bessie smiled to see the baby in Auntie Freda's arms. 'Do you mind if I feed her while we talk?' she asked, loosening her gown slightly and taking the baby to put to her breast.

'I don't mind at all,' Freda smiled. How could she be angry with Bessie when she had such an adorable baby in her arms? 'Do you mind me being in the room? I can go into the kitchen and make a hot drink, if you like?'

'Please stay, it would be good to talk to someone. First, I need to apologize for being here in your home. After all,

375

you trusted Claudette to take care of it; please don't blame her. I've only been here for two nights.'

'There will be time for explanations shortly, but first attend to this darling baby. I don't even know her name,' Freda said, mesmerized by what she saw.

'This is Jenny. Jenny, meet your Auntie Freda,' Bessie smiled. 'I'm sorry to involve you. I know babies are a touchy subject, and I'd honestly rather this was your baby than mine – not that she's going anywhere now. I'll never allow her out of my sight.'

Freda reached across and took one of Jenny's tiny hands, which clutched her finger tightly. 'I don't blame you, either. I will be the same with my own. I'm going to rely on you so much in the next few months.'

'Do you mean . . . ?'

'Yes, Tony and I are expecting our own child. That's why I'm here – I wanted to share my news with the family. Tony can't get away until late Christmas Eve, after his store closes. He plans to drive down, and I don't know what you were like, but I couldn't face a long journey in the car in this condition. It was all I could cope with sitting on the train for so long.'

Bessie chuckled. 'We're going to have a lot in common, Auntie Freda.'

'I think it's time you dropped the "auntie", don't you?'

Once Jenny was settled and Freda had made cocoa and found some biscuits in the cupboard, they settled down while Bessie told her the whole story, including her time with Tom and how frightened she'd been.

'I'm so torn, Bessie. On one hand I can sympathize with your mum, and I have been kept up to date with letters from them; do you know, Sarah and Nanny Ruby have guessed your little secret, but have said very little to your mum. I don't feel she could cope if she knew what was happening to you and she wasn't there to hold your hand. If it is any consolation, I feel that if I were in your position, I'd have done the same. I suppose the cat would have been out of the bag if you'd come face to face with George and Maureen at Sea View. Goodness, I don't know who would have been more surprised! As for those men stealing your handbag – well, it just shows that there may be nasty people about, but there are many more kind people in the world. And we should hang onto that thought in darker times.'

'I can never say sorry enough times. So many people have been kind to me. It has taken it out of me, having a baby; it's such a relief to be able to talk to someone other than my sister and my friends. They've been amazing, but,' she chuckled, 'they are still only children. I really needed to confide in an adult.'

'Now you have. And come tomorrow, or should I say today, we're going to have to make some decisions. I'll be popping over to see Ruby after breakfast and I want to share my news with them. The chances are there will be people coming in and out of this house tomorrow, so it's time we planned ahead, don't you think?'

'Yes, I do. When you go over to speak to Nanny Ruby, would you bring her back here, please? I know she'll have the right advice for me.'

Next morning, neither Freda nor Bessie could face breakfast. Both of them nervously watched the clock until Freda decided it was time for her to cross the road to number thirteen to speak to Ruby.

'It will all be fine,' she said, taking Bessie's hands and kissing her cheek. 'You've got nothing to worry about. I'm convinced Ruby will give you her words of wisdom – she may do it with a sharp tongue, but we're just going to have to stomach that. I will be here with you, and whatever happens, I'll support you. Let's hope this little lady behaves herself when she meets the rest of her family,' she smiled, looking at the child, who was sleeping soundly in her pram.

'That's a pretty dress she's wearing,' Freda smiled. 'I hope if I have a little girl, she will be as beautifully dressed. I'll have to take fashion tips from her.'

'If you have a daughter, she will probably be wearing this frock, because Jenny will have outgrown it by then.'

Freda's eyes lit up. 'Oh, how marvellous: hand-me-downs! That's one thing that's so lovely about our big extended family. Where did you get this?'

'Claudette made it; isn't she clever? I must say, my sister has done so much to support me – and she's not even fifteen yet. I hope she never finds herself in the same situation as me, but if ever she needs me, I'll be there for her. Now, please can you go over to Ruby's? We need to get this over and done with. I'll be dashing off to the loo again, I've never been so nervous in my life.'

Freda picked up the front door key and put it in the pocket of her smart suit. 'I reckon half an hour should do it. I just hope she doesn't offer me a cup of tea – I'm awash with it. Why does our family drink so much tea?' she laughed before she left, quietly closing the door behind her in case it woke the baby.

Bessie paced the floor. Each time she reached the large

bay window she quickly looked across the road before backing away in case she was spotted. It must have been twenty minutes before she saw movement in the doorway of number thirteen. No doubt she'd have the telling off of her life, but as Freda had said she'd be there by her side, she felt calmer. If only Claudette could be here, as well as the Billington girls and Jane; but they were busy at Woolworths, it being the last shopping day before Christmas. Bessie knew from last year that it would be a busy day for them with all staff manning the counters; this was not the time to ring them. Even if Freda had had a telephone, which she didn't.

She held her breath as the front door opened and heard Freda say, 'After you, Ruby.' Turning to the front room door, she watched as that slowly opened as well . . . and then she was face to face with Nanny Ruby. Bessie placed a protective hand on the pram as the old woman looked between her and the sleeping child.

'Oh, you silly, silly, girl – we've been so worried,' she said as she opened her arms, and Bessie rushed to her.

Once the crying had stopped, and Ruby had put an arm around Freda, she insisted on holding the baby. 'This is my first great-great-grandchild,' she said proudly as Jenny woke and stared into Ruby's face. 'I don't want to know anything about her father; as far as I'm concerned, the future starts here. We're going to look forward, not back, my love.'

'I don't deserve this,' Bessie sniffed. 'I've put all of you through hell.'

'I knew you'd be safe; you've had three little guardian angels looking after you, haven't you?'

Bessie was confused. 'How did you know . . . ?'

'I guessed, my love; you girls are too close for you to be able to disappear into thin air the way you seemed to. Not to mention that you've managed to return and get into Freda's house, when Claudette held the key.'

Bessie looked at the two women and laughed. 'I thought we were being so clever,' she said.

'It would take a month of Sundays for you to fool me. Now, why haven't you got the kettle on yet? This old woman needs a cuppa; and as for this young lady,' she said, beaming at Freda, 'now that she's expecting my great-grandchild, she needs looking after.'

Bessie got up to make the tea. She turned at the door to say, 'You do realize, Nanny Ruby, that we aren't blood related to you – don't you?'

Ruby gave her a wink. 'We don't need to be blood relations for you to be one of my family,' she said. 'It's what's in here that counts.' She put her hand to her heart. 'Now, hurry up, because we've got to make plans to inform your mother.'

Christmas Eve at number thirteen was always a busy affair, with people coming and going, dropping off presents for the children for Ruby to distribute. There would be time to have a glass of something and a bit of a chat, with Ruby tuning in the wireless so she could listen to a church service and sing along with the carols. This year was slightly different, with her sitting by the telephone, address book open as she started to ring her family, even calling some of them who were still at work, instructing them not to arrive until seven o'clock. George did question her, but she told him all would be revealed in good time.

At six o'clock, Bessie, assisted by Freda, crossed the road to number thirteen. It was already dark in the street, and many curtains were closed against the inclement weather as families prepared to celebrate Christmas.

'You know, at this time every year, with the doors to Woolworths finally closed, I've always felt as though I could suddenly relax. We'd served all the customers, had our staff celebrations and entertained the old folk at their special party; and now all that was left was to put on our coats and wish everybody a happy Christmas before we went home,' Freda said. 'It is always a special feeling.'

'It's funny, I felt like that last year. There was always the anticipation of what would happen Christmas Day. Even if Nanny Ruby burnt the dinner or Granddad Bob got tiddly, it was still the tradition to go to number thirteen to enjoy each other's company and toast the King after his speech. It's all about tradition, isn't it?' Bessie replied.

'It is, and it's all about family,' Freda smiled. 'Gosh, the pair of us are going to surprise everybody, aren't we?' she added as they walked up the path to number thirteen and knocked on the door.

'I was just about to send Bob to get you. I thought, I've made all these plans and the pair of you are going to be late and mess it up,' Ruby muttered, straightening her best crossover pinny and patting her freshly curled hair.

'You look very nice,' Freda said, kissing her cheek. 'Now – what are the plans?'

'Well, first off, I want you all in the living room, and I'll close the door so you aren't spotted. Do try to keep the baby quiet; I know as a rule I don't mind them crying, but at the moment it's important she's not heard before the allotted time.'

Bob looked into the pram. 'Are you listening, young lady? Don't you defy your Great-Granny Ruby, or you'll be in trouble.'

'Please, Bob, leave that child alone or you'll upset it.' Ruby wagged her finger at him. 'Your job is to make sure everybody has a drink, because even if there are tears and upset, if you shove a drink in their hands, it will give them something to do. Oh, and while you're out in the kitchen, make sure you check the oven – I don't want anything burning, do you hear me?'

'Yes, love,' Bob said, giving the girls a wink. 'Come along with me,' he said, leading them into the living room.

At that moment there was a knock on the front door. Ruby felt hot and fanned her face; she'd been rushing about non-stop today, organizing everything. It would be good when Christmas Day came and she could relax and enjoy the festivities.

Opening the door, she greeted Maisie, David, Claudette and the three younger children. 'Come along in – quick, quick, before you let the cold in. Claudette, take all the coats into the living room and put them in the cupboard under the stairs.'

'We can do that,' Maisie said as she went to take her husband's overcoat.

'Oh no, I want you all to stay here. And Claudette is to come straight back into the front room, because what I've got to say includes you as well.'

Claudette could not look anyone in the eye and hurried from the room. She had a feeling Nanny Ruby had discovered their secret.

'Now, park your backsides down there: I've got something

to say to you. And you three,' she said, giving the younger children a hug, 'can sit yourselves down on the rug in front of the fire and play with your toys while us grown-ups talk.'

Ruby sat in her favourite armchair and waited until Claudette returned; the girl was trying hard not to smile. Ruby noticed, and gave her a stern look.

'Now, I've got one question for you, Maisie Carlisle. If I could grant you one wish in the whole world for Christmas, what would it be?'

'Gawd, Ruby, that's asking something, isn't it? I just want all my family home for Christmas, but that's not going to happen, is it?' she said, as David took her hand.

'Miracles can happen at Christmas, love, but it might not be quite the miracle we expected. I just want you to know that whatever Bessie did was done with the best of intentions; I don't want you to be upset.'

Maisie frowned. 'Are you telling me Bessie is here?' She started to get up. 'Where is she?'

'Sit down and listen to me. Now, I don't want to shock young Claudette by saying that when you arrived here, Maisie, you were hiding quite a few secrets. Don't worry – I won't say any more,' she went on, looking at Maisie's alarmed face. 'That's for you to tell your daughter. But everything turned out for the good in the end, didn't it?'

It was David who spoke. 'Yes, everything has worked out for the best. And whatever happens,' he said, looking towards the door, 'we can cope with it together, Maisie.'

'So, what you're telling me is . . . to watch my mouth?'

'In a way, yes,' Ruby said. 'Now, you sit there until I come back. I'll be two ticks.'

Claudette deliberately sat down with her back to her parents, in case they guessed from her face that she knew what was going to happen. As the door started to open, she thought better of it and got up and sat on the arm of the settee next to Maisie, in case she became upset.

'Oh my God,' Maisie cried out as she rushed to Bessie, engulfing her in her arms while being careful not to crush the small bundle. 'You naughty, naughty, girl! Why did you leave us like that?'

'I'm sorry, Mum,' Bessie said. 'I hope you can forgive me?'

David went to his wife and daughter and gently took the baby so mother and daughter could hug properly. 'Who are you?' he asked as he stroked her tiny cheek with one large finger.

Claudette couldn't keep quiet and joined her dad. 'This is Jenny. She's your granddaughter, Dad.'

David looked at Bessie with unshed tears glistening in his eyes. 'I know I should be angry with you, but I can't think of the words right now. I'm just so grateful we have you home with us once more. As for this little one, words fail me . . .'

Ruby looked at the Carlisle family. All she could see was an outpouring of love.

'I take it your Christmas is complete?' she asked as Bob pulled out his handkerchief and blew his nose loudly, overcome with emotion. 'Oh, you silly bugger,' she exclaimed fondly, giving him a kiss on the cheek.

Maisie reached for her granddaughter and held her close. Looking around the room, she took in the expectant faces. Whatever she said next would set the mood for the rest of the day.

'This will be our best Christmas ever.'

Acknowledgements

I must first say a big thank you to the whole team at Pan Macmillan for polishing my books until they shine. Susan Opie for her thoughtful input to the story structure; Samantha Fletcher and Camilla Rockwood for their strenuous copy-edits. I'd be lost without you all.

My editor, Wayne Brookes, is a joy to work with, and is always there to answer my lengthy queries with his joyous responses.

To Caroline Sheldon, my lovely agent, whose caring attention to my writing career is second to none.

I cannot forget my dear readers, whose messages about their memories and working lives at Woolworths remind me how important the store was to us all.

Finally, to my husband, Michael, for keeping me sane when I'm up against it with deadlines, edits and endless promotions, however enjoyable. The promise of a weekend away, a meal out, or a nice cake for afternoon tea always hits the spot. Oh, and Henry for helping with the cake!

A Letter from Elaine

~

Dear Reader,

It feels like five minutes since I was writing my last letter to you when *The Patchwork Girls* was published, and here we are again. How time flies!

It was a joy to write about the younger members of the Woolworths Girls' families now that we've reached 1950. To have Clemmie, Dorothy, Bessie and Claudette working at Woolies alongside family members was interesting to write. Of course, the working age was fourteen at that time even though it is hard to believe now. My own mother, born in 1931, also started working at that age, and I have recollections of her telling me about that time when she was working in a factory and bringing home her first pay packet and becoming an adult at such an early age.

I have fond memories of my Saturday job at the Dartford branch of Woolworths in Kent. I was allowed to start work at the age of fifteen and three months in 1969, and earning the princely sum of one pound, with thruppence (old money) being deduction for my National Insurance stamp. Along with friends from school I attended an interview and sat an arithmetic test, just as Sarah, Maisie and Freda did before they were offered their jobs in 1938. Thirty years later nothing much had changed apart from our uniform being a sludgy green colour. We still had to tally up sales with the pencil and notebook attached to our belt by a length of string. If a customer paid with a note (ten shillings was often the amount), we would have to hold the note on high and call out 'ten shillings!', hoping a supervisor heard us. I dreaded being offered a note as payment as I was quite shy in those days. My other dread was being put on the electrical counter where we had to test lightbulbs before they could be sold. I dreaded receiving an electric shock or one exploding – to this day I shudder when I think about it.

Tea breaks, lunch and store closing time were ruled by bells which would echo through the store and again when we were due back at our counters. We weren't allowed to chatter and in spare time between serving customers we would have to dust the products on our counter. My counter was often the one displaying toilet rolls, and yes, I dusted them!

I do hope you enjoyed reading about the younger generation of Woolworths girls. Please do let me know.

Why not sign up for my newsletter where I keep readers up to date with news as well as run competitions? You will find it on my website: www.elaineeverest.com

My blog can be found there too.

You can also find me on my Facebook author page where there are details of all my books: www.facebook.com/Elaine EverestAuthor. Or you can find me on Twitter: @elaineeverest

Until next time!

Much love,

Elaine xx